Cover designer's note

Wishing to continue the notion of Bernard Samson spying through windows or doors, I took the author's very good suggestion of having the book's protagonist peering through a glass public house window. I found a perfect example among my collection of photographs that I had taken of windows, this one from a London pub. Combined with the title of this book, *Hope*, it conjures up the saying 'last chance saloon', in which there is always hope, even for an ageing spy who is on the ropes in both his career and his love life!

For the back cover, I placed a china souvenir of London's Tower Bridge on a map of divided Berlin and straddled it across the Berlin Wall, which I likened to the River Thames. As readers of this series will by now know, London has exported something – or rather some*one* – more precious than a souvenir to the Eastern side of the Berlin Wall, and our Bernard still lives in hope of returning them to the West.

At the heart of every one of the nine books in this triple trilogy is Bernard Samson, so I wanted to come up with a neat way of visually linking them all. When the reader has collected all nine books and displays them together in sequential order, the books' spines will spell out Samson's name in the form of a blackmail note made up of airline baggage tags. The tags were drawn from my personal collection, and are colourful testimony to thousands of air miles spent travelling the world.

Arnold Schwartzman OBE RDI

LEN DEIGHTON

Hope

HARPER

Harper
An imprint of HarperCollins*Publishers*
1 London Bridge Street,
London SE1 9GF

www.harpercollins.co.uk

This paperback edition 2016

First published in Great Britain by
HarperCollins*Publishers* 1995

A catalogue record for this book is
available from the British Library

ISBN: 978 0 00 812505 9

Set in Ehrhardt by Born Group using Atomik ePublisher from Easypress

Printed and bound by CPI Group (UK) Ltd, Croydon, CR0 4YY

Introduction

In 1945 Europe was devastated. Food was scarce and bitter hatred was in the air. Parts of France, Belgium, Holland and the western half of Germany was battered but the vast area of land over which the Red Army had advanced was now largely rubble, a barren wasteland where millions of 'displaced persons', undernourished, infirm and undocumented, wandered in confusion.

Stalin ordered his Red Army to cling tight to all their gains. His promises made to Prime Minister Churchill and President Roosevelt, that the people of Eastern Europe would be allowed free elections, were ignored. The nations of Eastern Europe became satellites of Russia, ruled by expatriates who had been tutored in Moscow. Red Army soldiers complete with tanks and artillery remained in evidence everywhere.

With American generosity, programs such as the 'Marshall Plan' slowly revived the countries of Western Europe. But American hopes for a revised and truly democratic Russian political system faded as Moscow exerted its brutal power at home and abroad. An Iron Curtain had come down between the nations of the West and those in the East, and there was no reconciliation. Russia's military occupation zone was the eastern half of Germany and its heartless rule was fuelled by memories of the barbaric German violation of the Russian Motherland.

In the summer of 1961 the communists built a wall to surround the Western Sector of Berlin. It was, said Nikita Khrushchev, the Russian Premier, 'a barrier to Western Imperialism'. Anyone in the East trying to take a closer look at Western Imperialism was likely to be shot. Hundreds were killed in attempts to get to the West and the East German border guards were given commendations and bonus payments for killing escapers.

Situated amid this ocean of repression called the Soviet Zone of Germany there was a small island of capitalism. This was the sector of Berlin that had been assigned to British, American and French control. These three sectors of Berlin covered about 185 square miles and about two million people lived there. Technically it remained a 'military occupation zone' where soldiers still made all the important decisions. To get from this British-American-French 'island' to 'West Germany' traffic was confined to three specific highways, all of them over 100 miles long. Wandering off the approved roads could lead to difficulties. On a journey from Prague to Berlin, I was detained in a Russian Army barrack complex until, in the small hours of morning and with a help of an amiable Russian colonel and my bottle of duty-free cognac, I was released to continue my journey.

Any writer who pins his story to fixed dates had better hold on to his hat for it is likely to be a rough and rocky ride. My whole Bernard Samson series was based upon the belief that the Berlin Wall would fall before the end of the century. There were many times when I went to bed convinced that this assumption had been a reckless gamble, and there were many people asking me where the plot was going. Sometimes I thought I heard a measure of Schadenfreude. More than one expert advised me to forget the Wall, tear my plan down, and radically change its direction. I didn't yield to my fears. I stuck to my lonely task and to the original scenario and eventually was vindicated.

It is unlikely that the true and complete story of the collapse of the Wall and the whole communist system will ever be told. But the overall pattern is now fairly clear and the signs were there long before the newspapers and the TV camera crews arrived for the finale. The election of Karol Wojtyla to be John Paul II, a Polish Pope, changed the world's history. Here was a fearless man not afraid to declare that communism was a vile and repressive tyranny that denied the freedom that everyone deserved. His outspoken challenge, unlike those of most politicians, did not vary from time to time and place to place, no matter how unwelcome it was to some of his audiences. His words frightened the dictators, disturbed the apparatchiks, and made Poland's Catholics into a network of frontline activists. The Polish-American Catholics of Chicago provided a great deal of the money; the CIA added more and worked with the Vatican to route it to Poland's anti-communist networks. George Kosinski personifies the muddled, almost schizophrenic, mindset of many Poles. His fears and double-dealing provide us with a glimpse of the struggle, and *Hope* depicts the vital days when the USSR was deciding whether to move with military force against its recalcitrant ally or hold still and hope for the best. Warsaw was deeply in debt to Western banks and Moscow was in no position to pick up the bill. Bernard Samson is in Poland and near the frontier when the Soviet Union was poised and ready to occupy its politically unreliable but strategically essential neighbour. The events depicted here reflect the tension as the Poles waited for the tanks to come rolling westwards.

As Poland's communist regime was being undermined by the bravery of the Polish Pope, the Lutheran Church in communist Germany became more and more important in the struggle against Moscow. In *Hope* Bernard's journeys to the East record the fierce repressive measures the German regime resorted to when it became the final outpost of the communist empire.

Tying a story to events is not something to be undertaken lightly. But having a timescale for the stories provided some benefits. *Hope* was bountiful: with the astonishing Hurricane that tore a path through London, minor asides such as the Swiss elections and the devastating collapse of the world's stock exchanges. At the end of the year the Pope and Gorbachev met in the Vatican. What more eventful background could any writer wish for?

I was lucky to find so much of my story in Poland where communism collapsed so suddenly. The attractions of Warsaw are there for anyone to inspect but I was lucky to find the hideous Rozyckiego market so perfect for my purpose. Explorations into the countryside brought me to the Kosinski's grand old family mansion, a place even more mysterious than I had envisioned. Both places are faithfully described here in the book; there was no need to change a thing. As with many of the research trips I have made for my books I found it very beneficial to return to the location at the season it was to be depicted in my story. The Polish countryside in winter is not to be found in the tourist brochures but despite the discomfort and inconvenience I liked this strange fairy-tale mix of dreams and nightmares.

Every writer has different priorities, which makes reading fiction so rewarding. After the basic idea, my own priority has always been dialogue. From dialogue characterization must follow and from characterization comes motivation and plot. For all of the above reasons I try to inform the reader by dialogue and, when I read and reread the drafts of my books prior to publication, I search for ways of transforming authorial comment and description into dialogue.

At a creative writing school in California the students read (and enjoyed) studying the Bernard Samson books in reverse order. They noted and analyzed the changing character of Bernard and were kind enough to show me some of the results. By assigning various specific fictional characters to student teams the class unravelled the complex weave of the plot. Even without such close examination most readers immediately see that Bernard – without telling outright lies – is inclined to bend the truth to his own advantage.

But dialogue and characterization is more important than truth and plot. The purpose of characterization is to demonstrate the changes that take place as the story proceeds. I consider this process vital. Whether the time span is short as it is in *Bomber* (when there is only 24 hours from cover to cover) or long as in *Winter* (a family story lasting half a century) the characters must be seen to change, and that means to change in response to the events of the story. The Bernard Samson books take the characters through several years and the man we join in the first chapter of this book, *Hope*, is older, wiser and more psychologically battered than the man in the first book, *Berlin Game*. But Bernard, whatever his shortcomings, is always a loyal friend to us.

Len Deighton, 2011

1

Mayfair, London. October 1987.
A caller who wakes you in the small dark silent hours is unlikely to be a bringer of good news.

When the buzzer sounded a second time I reluctantly climbed out of bed. I was at home alone. My wife was at her parents' with our children.

'Kosinski?'

'No,' I said.

The overhead light of the hallway shone down upon a thin, haggard man in a short waterproof flight-jacket and a navy-blue knitted hat. In one hand he was carrying a cheap briefcase of the sort that every office worker in Eastern Europe flaunts as a status symbol. The front of his denim shirt was bloody and so was his stubbly face, and the outstretched hand in which he held the key to my apartment. 'No,' I said again.

'Please help me,' he said. I guessed his command of English was limited. I couldn't place the accent but his voice was muffled and distorted by the loss of some teeth. That he'd been badly hurt was evident from his hunched posture and the expression on his face.

I opened the door. As he tottered in he rested his weight against me, as if he'd expended every last atom of energy in getting to the doorbell and pressing it.

He only got a few more steps before twisting round to slump on to the low hall table. There was blood everywhere now. He must have read my mind for he said: 'No. No blood on the stairs.'

He'd taken the stairs rather than the lift. It was the choice of experienced fugitives. Lifts in the small hours make the sort of sound that wakens janitors and arouses security men. 'Kosinski,' he said anxiously. 'Who are you? This is Kosinski's place.' If he had been a bit stronger he might have been angry.

'I'm just a friendly burglar,' I explained.

I got him back on his feet and dragged him to the bathroom and to the tub. He rolled over the edge of it until he was full length in the empty bath. It was better that he bled there. 'I'm Kosinski's partner,' he said.

'Sure,' I said. 'Sure.' It was a preposterous claim.

I got his jacket off and pushed him flat to open his shirt. I could see no arterial bleeding and most of the blood was in that tacky congealed state. There were a dozen or more deep cuts on his hands and arms where he had deflected the attack, but it was the small stab wounds on his body that were the life-threatening ones. Under his clothes he was wearing a money-belt. It had saved him from the initial attack. It wasn't the sort of belt worn by tourists and backpackers, but the heavy-duty type used by professional smugglers. Almost six inches wide, it was made of strong canvas that from many years of use was now frayed and stained and bleached to a light grey colour. The whole belt was constructed of pockets that would hold ingots of the size and shape of small chocolate bars. Now it was entirely empty. Loaded it would have weighed a ton, for which reason there were two straps that went over the shoulders. It was one of these shoulder straps that had no doubt saved this man's life, for there was a fresh and bloody cut in it. A knife-thrust had narrowly missed the place where a twisted blade floods the lungs with blood and brings death within sixty seconds.

2

'Just a scratch,' I said. He smiled. He knew how bad it was.

To my astonishment George Kosinski, my brother-in-law, arrived five minutes later. George who had left England never to return was back! I suppose he'd been trying to head off my visitor, for he showed little surprise to find him there. George was nearly forty years old, his wavy hair greying at the temples. He took off his glasses. 'I came by cab, Bernard. A car will arrive any minute and I'll take this fellow off your hands.' He said it as casually as if he were the owner of a limousine service. Then he took out a handkerchief and began rubbing the condensation from his thick-rimmed glasses.

'He loses consciousness and then comes back to life,' I said. 'He urgently needs attention. He's lost a lot of blood; he could die any time.'

'And you don't want him to die here,' said George, putting his glasses on and looking at the comatose man in the bathtub. His eyes were tightly closed and his breathing slow, and with the sort of snoring noise that sometimes denotes impending death. George looked at me and said: 'I'm taking him to a Polish doctor in Kensington. He's expected there. He'll relax and trust someone who can talk his language.' George moved into the drawing-room, as if he didn't want to think about the man expiring in my bathtub.

'It's internal bleeding, George. I think he's dying.'

This prognosis showed no effect on George. He went to the window and looked down at the street as if hoping to see the car arrive. I think it was done to reassure me rather than because he really thought he'd see the promised car. George was Polish by extraction and a Londoner by birth. He was not handsome or charming but he was direct in manner and unstinting in his generosity. Like most self-made men he was intuitive, and like most rich ones, cynical. Many of the men he did deals with, and the ones who sat alongside him on his charity committees, were

3

Poles, or considered themselves as such. George went out of his way to be sociable with Poles, but he was a man of many moods. Where his supporters found a cheerful self-confidence others encountered a stubborn ego. And when his mask slipped a little, his energetic impatience could become raging bad temper.

Now I watched him marching backwards and forwards and around the room, flapping the long vicuna overcoat, or cracking the bones of his knuckles, and displaying that kind of restless energy that some claim is part of the process of reasoning. His face was clenched in anger. You wouldn't have recognized him as a man grieving for his desperately loved wife. Neither would you have thought that this apartment had been until recently his own home, for he blundered against the chairs, kicked his polished brogues at the carpets and fumed like a teetotaller held on a drunk-driving charge.

'He had nowhere to go,' said George.

'You're wrong,' I said, waving the key at him. 'He had a key to this apartment. He tried the doorbell only to discover if it was clear.'

George scowled. 'I thought I'd called in all the keys. But perhaps you'd better have the locks changed, just to be on the safe side.' He lifted his eyes quickly, caught the full force of the annoyance on my face and added: 'They can't just walk the streets, Bernard.'

'Why not? Because they're illegals? Because they don't have papers or passports or visas? Is that what you mean?' I put the key in my pocket and resolved to change the locks just as soon as I could get someone along here to do it. 'Damn you, George, don't you have any consideration for me or Fiona? She'll be furious if she hears about this.'

'Must you tell her?'

'She'll see the blood on the mat in the hall.'

'I'll send someone round to clean up.'

4

'I'm the world's foremost expert on cleaning blood marks off the floor,' I said.

'Then get a new mat,' he said with exasperation, as if I was capriciously making problems for him.

'I can't think of anything more likely to excite Fiona's suspicions than me going out to buy a new mat.'

'So confide in her. Ask her to keep it to herself.'

'It wouldn't be fair to ask her. Fiona is big brass in the Department nowadays. And anyway she wouldn't agree. She'd report it. She prefers doing things by the book, that's how she got to the top.'

George stopped pacing and went to take a brief look at the man in the bath, who was even paler than before, although his breathing was marginally easier. 'Don't make problems for me, Bernard,' he said in an offhand manner that angered me.

'My employers ...' I stopped, counted to ten and started again. More calmly I said: 'The sort of people who run the Secret Service have old-fashioned ideas about East European escapers having the doorkey to their employees' homes.'

George put on his conciliatory hat. 'I can see that. It was a terrible mistake. I'm truly sorry, Bernard.' He patted my shoulder. 'That means you will have to report it, eh?'

'You're playing with fire, George.' I wondered if perhaps the death of his wife, Tessa, had turned his brain.

'It's simply that I'm not supposed to be in this jurisdiction: tax-wise. I'm in the process of losing residence. Just putting it around that I've been in England could cause me a lot of trouble, Bernard.'

I noted the words – jurisdiction, tax-wise. Only men like George had a call on words like that. 'I know what you're doing, George. You're asking some of these roughnecks to investigate the death of your wife. That could lead to trouble.'

'They are Poles – my people. I have to do what I can for them.' His claim sounded hollow when pitched in that unmistakable East London accent.

5

'These people can't bring her back, George. No one can.'

'Stop preaching at me, Bernard, please.'

'Listen, George,' I said, 'your friend next door isn't just a run-of-the-mill victim of a street mugging or a fracas in a pub. He was attacked by a professional killer. Whoever came after him was aiming his blade for an artery and knew exactly where to find the place he wanted. Only the canvas moneybelt saved him, and that was probably because it was twisted across his body at the time. I think he's dying. He should be in an intensive-care ward, not on his way to a cosy old family doctor in Kensington. Believe me, these are rough playmates. Next time it could be you.'

I had rather hoped that this revelation might bring George to his senses, but he seemed quite unperturbed. 'Many of these poor wretches are on the run, Bernard,' he said cheerfully. 'Nothing in the belt, was there? And yes, you're right. It's inevitable that the regime infiltrates their own spies. Black-market gangsters and other violent riffraff use our escape line. We screen them all but it takes time. This one was doubly unlucky; a really nice youngster, he wanted to help. If you could see some of the deserving cases. The youngsters ... It's heart-breaking.'

'I can't tell you how to run your life, George. I know you've always contributed generously to Polish funds and good causes for these dissidents and political refugees. But the communist government in Warsaw sees such overseas organizations as subversive. You must know that. And there is a big chance that you are being exploited by political elements without understanding what you're doing.'

George rubbed his face. 'He's hurt bad, you think?' He stroked the telephone.

'Yes, George, bad.'

His face stiffened and he picked up the phone and called some unknown person, presumably to hurry things along. When there was no answer to his call he looked at me and said: 'This won't happen again, Bernard. I promise you that.' He waited only a few minutes before trying his number again and got the busy signal. He crashed the phone down with such force that it broke. I had been crashing phones down into their cradles for years but I'd never broken one. Was it a measure of his anger, his grief, his embarrassment, or something else? He held up his hands in supplication, looked at me and smiled.

I sighed. No man chooses his brother-in-law. They are strangers society thrusts upon us to test the limits of our compassion and forbearance. I was lucky, I liked my brother-in-law; more perhaps than he liked me. That was the trouble; I liked George.

'Look, George,' I said in one final attempt to make him see sense. 'To you it's obvious that you're not an enemy agent – just a well-meaning philanthropist – but don't rely upon others being so perceptive. The sort of people I work for think that there is no smoke without fire. Cool it. Or you are likely to find a fire-extinguisher up your arse.'

'I live in Switzerland,' said George.

'So a Swiss fire-extinguisher.'

'I told you I'm sorry, Bernard. You know I wouldn't have had this happen for the world. I can't blame you for being angry. In your place I would be angry too.' Both his arms were clasped round the cheap briefcase as if it was a baby. I suddenly guessed that it was stuffed with money; money that had come from the exchange of the gold.

At that I gave up. There are some people who won't learn by good advice, only by experience. George Kosinski was that sort of person.

Soon after that a man I recognized as George's driver and handyman arrived. He brought a car rug to wrap around the injured man and lifted him with effortless ease. George watched as if it was his own sick child. Perhaps it was pain that caused the injured man's eyes to flicker. His lips moved but he didn't speak. Then he was carried down to the car.

'I'm sorry, Bernard,' said George, standing at the door as if trying to be contrite. 'If you have to report it, you have to. I understand. You can't risk your job.'

I cleaned the mat as well as possible, got rid of the worst marks in the bathroom and soaked a bloody towel in cold water before sending it to the laundry. In my usual infantile fashion, I decided to wait and see if Fiona noticed any of the marks. As a way of making an important decision it was about as good as spinning a coin in the air, but Fiona had eyes for little beyond the mountains of work she brought home every evening, so I didn't mention my uninvited visitors to anyone. But my hopes that George and his antics were finished and forgotten did not last beyond the following week, when I returned from a meeting and found a message on my desk summoning me to the presence of my boss Dicky Cruyer, newly appointed European Controller.

I opened the office door. Dicky was standing behind his desk, twisting a white starched handkerchief tight around his wounded fingers, while half a dozen tiny drips of blood patterned the report he had brought back from his meeting.

There was no need for him to explain. I'd been on the top floor and heard the sudden snarling and baritone growls. The only beast permitted through the guarded front entrance of London Central was the Director-General's venerable black Labrador, and it only came when accompanied by its master.

'Berne,' said Dicky, indicating the papers freshly arrived in his tray. 'The Berne office again.'

I put on a blank expression. 'Berne?' I said. 'Berne, Switzerland?'

'Don't act the bloody innocent, Bernard. Your brother-in-law lives in Switzerland, doesn't he?' Dicky was trembling. His sanguinary encounter with the Director-General and his canine companion had left him wounded in both body and spirit. It made me wonder what condition the other two were in.

'I've never denied it,' I said.

The door to the adjoining office opened. Jennifer, the youngest, most devoted and attentive of Dicky's female assistants, put her head round the door and said: 'Shall I get antiseptic from the first-aid box, Mr Cruyer?'

'No,' said Dicky in a stagy whisper over his shoulder, vexed that word of his misfortune had spread so quickly. 'Well?' he said, turning to me again.

I shrugged. 'We all have to live somewhere.'

'Four Stasi agents pass through in seven days? Are you telling me that's just a coincidence?' A pensive pause. 'They went to see your brother-in-law in Zurich.'

'How do you know where they went?'

'They all went to Zurich. It's obvious, isn't it?'

'I don't know what you're implying,' I said. 'If the Stasi want to talk to George Kosinski they don't have to send four men to Zurich; roughnecks that even our pen-pushers in Berne can recognize. I mean, it's a bit high-profile, isn't it?'

Dicky looked round to see if Jennifer was still standing in the doorway looking worried. She was. 'Very well, then,' he said, sitting down suddenly as if surrendering to his pain. 'Get the antiseptic.' The door closed and, as he tightened the hand-kerchief round his fingers, he noticed the bloodstains on his papers.

'You should have an anti-tetanus shot,' I advised. 'That dog is full of fleas and mange.'

Dicky said: 'Never mind the dog. Let's keep to the business in hand. Your brother-in-law is in contact with East German intelligence, and I'm going over there to face him with it.'

'When?'

'This weekend. And you are coming with me.'

'I have to finish all that material you gave me yesterday. You said the D-G wanted the report on his desk on Monday.'

Dicky eyed me suspiciously. We both knew that he recklessly used the name of the Director-General when he wanted work done hurriedly or late at night. 'He's changed his mind about the report. He told me to take you to Switzerland with me.'

Now it was possible to see a little deeper into Dicky's state of mind. The questions he had just put to me were questions he'd failed to answer to the D-G's satisfaction. The Director had then told Dicky to take me along with him, and it was that that had dented Dicky's ego. The nip from the dog was extra-curricular. 'Because it's your brother-in-law,' he added, lest I began to think myself indispensable.

Using his uninjured hand Dicky picked up his phone and called Fiona, who worked in the next office. 'Fiona, darling,' he said in his jokey drawl. 'Hubby is with me. Could you join us for a moment?'

I went and looked out of the window and tried to forget I had a crackpot brother-in-law in whom Dicky was taking a sudden and unsympathetic interest. Summer had passed; we had winter to endure before it came again but this was a glorious golden day, and from this top-floor room I could see across the London basin to the high ground at Hampstead. The clouds, gauzy and grey like a bundle of discarded bandages, were fixed to the ground by shiny brass pins pretending to be sunbeams.

My wife came in, her face darkened with the stern expression that I'd learned to recognize as one she wore when wrenched away from something that needed uninterrupted concentration. Fiona's work load had become the talk of the top floor. And she handled the political decisions with consummate skill. But I saw in her eyes that bright gleam a light bulb provides just before going ping.

'Yes, Dicky?' she said.

'I'm enticing your hubby away for a brief fling in Zurich, Fiona my dearest. We must leave Sunday morning. Can you endure a weekend without him?'

Fiona looked at me sternly. I winked at her but she didn't react. 'Must he go?' she said.

'Duty calls,' said Dicky.

'What did you do to your hand, Dicky?'

As if in response, Jennifer arrived with antiseptic, cotton wool and a packet of Band-Aids. Dicky held his hand out like some potentate accepting a vow of fidelity. Jennifer crouched and began work on his wound.

'The children were coming home on Sunday,' Fiona told Dicky. 'But if Bernard is going to be on a trip, I'll lock myself away and work on those wretched figures you need for the Minister.'

'Splendid,' said Dicky. 'Ouch, that hurts,' he told Jennifer.

'I'm sorry, Mr Cruyer.'

To me Fiona said: 'Daddy suggests keeping the children with him a little longer.' Perhaps she saw the quizzical look in my face for, in explanation, she added: 'I phoned them this morning. It's their wedding anniversary.'

'We'll talk about it,' I said.

'I've told Daddy to reserve places for them at the school next term, just in case.' She clasped her hands together as if praying that I would not explode. 'If we lose the deposit, so be it.'

For a moment I was speechless. Her father was doing everything he could to keep my children with him, and I wanted them home with us.

Dicky, feeling left out of this conversation, said: 'Has Daphne been in touch, by any chance?'

This question about his wife was addressed to Fiona, who looked at him and said: 'Not since I called and thanked her for that divine dinner party.'

'I just wondered,' said Dicky lamely. With Fiona looking at him and waiting for more, he added: 'Daph's been a bit low lately; and there are no friends like old friends. I told her that.'

'Shall I call her?'

'No,' said Dicky hurriedly. 'She'll be all right. I think she's going through the change of life.'

Fiona grinned. 'You say that every time you have a tiff with her, Dicky.'

'No, I don't,' said Dicky crossly. 'Daphne needs counselling. She's making life damned difficult right now. And with all the work piled up here I don't need any distractions.'

'No,' said Fiona, backing down and becoming the loyal assistant. Now that Dicky had manoeuvred himself into being the European Controller, while still holding on to the German Desk, no one in the Department was safe from his whims and fancies.

Dicky said: 'Work is the best medicine. I've always been a workaholic; it's too late to change now.'

Fiona nodded and I looked out of the window. There was really no way to respond to this amazing claim by the Rip Van Winkle of London Central, and if I'd caught her eye we might both have rolled around on the floor with merriment.

We stayed at home that evening, eating dinner I'd fetched from a Chinese take-away. Fulham was too far to go for shrivelled duck and plastic pancakes but Fiona had read about it in a magazine at the hairdresser's. That restaurant critic must have led the dullest of lives to have found the black bean spare-ribs 'memorable'. The bill might have proved even more memorable for him, had restaurant critics been given bills.

'You don't like it?' Fiona said.

'I'm full.'

'You've eaten hardly anything.'

'I'm thinking about my trip to Zurich.'

12

'It won't be so bad.'

'With Dicky?'

'Dicky depends upon you, he really does,' she said, her feminine reasoning making her think that this dependence would encourage me to overlook his faults for the sake of the Department.

'No more rice, no more fish and no more pancakes,' I said as she pushed the serving plates towards me. 'And certainly no more spare-ribs.'

Fiona switched on the TV to catch the evening news. There was a discussion between four people best known for their availability to appear on TV discussion programmes. A college professor was holding forth on the latest news from Poland. '... Historically the Poles lack a consciousness of their own position in the European dimension. For hundreds of years they have acted out a totemic role that they lack the capacity to sustain. Now I think the Poles are about to get a rude awakening.' The professor touched his beard reflectively. 'They have pushed and provoked the Soviet Union ... The Warsaw Pact autumn exercises are taking place along the border. Any time now the Russian tanks will roll across it.'

'Literally?' asked the TV anchor man.

'It is time the West acted,' said a woman with a Polish Solidarity badge pinned to her Chanel suit.

'Yes, literally,' said the professor with that determined solemnity with which those past military age discuss war. 'The Soviets will use it as a way of cautioning the hotheads in the Baltic States. We must make it absolutely clear to Chairman Gorbachev that any action, I do mean any action, he takes against the Poles will not be permitted to provoke a major East–West conflict.'

'Who will rid me of these troublesome Poles? Is that how the Americans see it?' the Solidarity woman asked bitterly. 'Best abandon the Poles to their fate?'

13

'When?' said the TV anchor man. Already the camera was tracking back to show that the programme was ending. A gigantic Polish eagle of polystyrene on a red and white flag formed the backdrop to the studio.

'When the winter hardens the ground enough for their modern heavy armour to go in,' answered the professor, who clearly knew that a note of terror heard on the box in the evening was a newspaper headline by morning. 'They'll crush the Poles in forty-eight hours. The Russian army has one or two special Spetsnaz brigades that have been trained to suppress unruly satellites. One of them, stationed at Maryinagorko in the Byelorussian Military District, was put on alert two days ago. Yes, Polish blood will flow. But quite frankly, if a few thousand Polish casualties are the price we pay to avoid World War Three, we must thank our lucky stars and pay up.'

Loud stirring music increased in volume to eventually drown his voice and, while the panel sat in silhouette, a roller provided details of about one hundred and fifty people who had worked on this thirty-minute unscripted discussion programme.

The end roller was still going when the phone rang. It was my son Billy calling from my father-in-law's home where he was staying. 'Dad? Is that you, Dad? Did Mum tell you about the weekend?'

'What about the weekend?' I saw Fiona frowning as she watched me.

'It's going to be super. Grandad is taking us to France,' said Billy, almost bursting with excitement. 'To France! Just for one night. A private plane to Dinard. Can we go, Dad? Say yes, Dad. Please.'

'Of course you can, Billy. Is Sally keen to go?'

'Of course she is,' said Billy, as if the question was absurd. 'We are going to stay in a château.'

'I'll see you the following weekend then,' I said as cheerfully as I could manage. 'And you can tell me all about it.'

'Grandad's bought a video camera. He's going to take pictures of us. You'll be able to see us. On the TV!'

'That's wonderful,' I said.

'He's already taken videos of his best horses. Of course I'd rather be with you, Dad,' said Billy, desperately trying to mend his fences. Perhaps he heard the disappointment.

'All the world's a video,' I improvised. 'And all the men and women merely directors. They have their zooms and their pans, and one man in his time plays back the results too many times. Is Sally there?'

'That's a good joke,' said Billy with measured reserve. 'Sally's in bed. Grandad is letting me stay up to see the TV news.' Fiona had quietened our TV, but over the phone from Grandad's I could hear the orchestrated fanfares and drumrolls that introduce the TV news bulletins; a presentational style that Dr Goebbels created for the Nazis. I visualized Grandad fingering the volume control and urging our conversation to a close.

'Sleep well, Billy. Give my love to Sally. And to Grandad and Grandma.' I held up the phone, offering it, but Fiona shook her head. 'And love from Mummy too,' I said. Then I hung up.

'It's not my doing,' said Fiona defensively.

'Who said it was?'

'I can see it on your face.'

'Why can't your father ask me?'

'It will be lovely for them,' said Fiona. 'And anyway you couldn't have gone on Sunday.'

'I could have gone on Saturday.' The silent TV pictures changed rapidly as the news flashed quickly from one calamity to another.

'It wasn't my idea,' she snapped.

'I don't see why I should be the focus of your anger,' I said mildly. 'I'm the victim.'

'Yes,' she said. 'You're always the victim, Bernard. That's what makes you so hard to live with.'

'What then?'

She got up and said: 'Let's not argue, darling. I love the children just as much as you do. Don't keep putting me in the middle.'

'But why didn't you tell me?' I said.

'Daddy is so worried. The stock-market has become unpredictable, he says. He doesn't know what he'll be worth next week.'

'For him that's new? For me it's always been like that.'

This aggravated her. 'With you on one side and my father on the other, sometimes I just want to scream.'

'Scream away,' I said.

'I'm tired. I'll clean my teeth.' She rose to her feet and put everything she had into a smile. 'Tomorrow we'll have lunch, and fight all you want.'

'Lovely! And I'll arm-wrestle the waiter to settle the bill,' I said. 'Switch off that bloody TV, will you?'

She switched it off and went to bed leaving the desolation of our meal still on the table. Sitting there staring at the blank screen of the TV I found myself simmering with anger at the way my father-in-law was holding on to my children. But was Fiona fit and well enough to be a proper mother to them? Perhaps Fiona would remain incapable of looking after them. Perhaps she knew that. And perhaps my awful father-in-law knew it. Perhaps I was the only one who couldn't see the tragic situation for what it really was.

I woke up in the middle of the night. The windows shook and the wind was howling and screaming as I'd never heard it shriek before in England. It was like a nightmare from which there was no escape, and I was an expert in nightmares. From somewhere down below in the street I heard a loud crash of glass and then another and another, resounding like surf upon a rocky shore.

16

'My God!' said Fiona sleepily. 'What on earth …?'

I switched on the bedside light but there was no electricity. I heard clicking as Fiona tried her light-switch too. The electric bedside clock was dark. I threw back the bedclothes and, stepping carefully in the darkness, went to the window. The street lighting had failed and everything was gloomy. Two police cars were stopped close together behind a fire engine, and a group of men were conferring outside the smashed windows of the bank on the corner. They ducked their heads as a great roar of wind brought the sound of more breaking glass, and debris – newspapers and the lids of rubbish bins – came bowling along the street. I heard the distant sirens of police cars and fire engines going down Park Lane at high speed.

'Phone the office,' I told Fiona, handing her the flashlight that I keep in the first-aid box. 'Use the Night Duty Officer's direct line. Ask them what the hell's going on. I'll try to see what's happening in the street.'

With the window open I could lean out and look along the street. The garbage bins had been blown over, shop-windows broken, and merchandise of all kinds was distributed everywhere: high-fashion shoes mixed with groceries and rubbish, with fragments of paper and packets being whirled high into the air by the wind. There were tree branches too: thousands of twigs as well as huge boughs of leafy timber that must have flown over the rooftops from the park. Some of them were heaving convulsively in the continuing windstorm, like exhausted birds resting after a long flight. Fragmented glass was dashed across the road, glittering like diamonds in the beams of the policemen's flashlights.

I could hear Fiona moving around in the kitchen, then the gush of running water and the plop of igniting gas as she boiled a kettle for tea.

When she came back into the room she came to the window, putting a hand on my arm as she peered over my shoulder.

17

She said: 'The office says there are freak windstorms gusting over 100 miles an hour. It's a disaster. The whole Continent is affected. The forecasters in France and Holland gave out warnings but our weather people said it wasn't going to happen. Heavens, look at the broken shop-windows.'

'This might be your big chance for a new Chanel suit.'

'Will there be looting?' she asked, as if I was some all-knowing prophet.

'Not too much at this time of night. Black up your face and put on your gloves.'

'It's not funny, darling. Shall I phone Daddy?'

'It will only alarm them more. Let's hope they sleep through it.'

She poured tea for us both and we sat there, with only a glimmer of light from the window, drinking strong Assam tea and listening to the noise of the storm. Fiona was very English. The English met every kind of disaster, from sudden death to threatened invasions, by making tea. Growing up in Berlin I had never acquired the habit. Perhaps that was at the root of our differences. Fiona had a devout faith in England, a legacy of her middle-class upbringing. Its rulers and administration, its history and even its cooking was accepted without question. No matter how much I tried to share such deeply held allegiances I was always an outsider looking in.

'I've got a long day tomorrow, so I'm going right back to bed.' She lifted her cup and drained the last of her tea. I noticed the cup she was using was from a set I'd bought when I set up house with Gloria. I'd tried to dispose of everything that would bring back memories of those days, but I'd forgotten about the big floral-pattern cups.

Gloria's name was never mentioned but her presence was permanent and all-pervading. Would Fiona ever forgive me for falling in love with that glamorous child? And would I ever be able to forgive Fiona for deserting me without warning or trust?

Our marriage had survived by postponing such questions, but eventually it must be tested by them.

'Me too,' I said.

Fiona put her empty cup on the tray and reached for mine. 'You haven't touched your tea,' she said. She knew about the cups of course. Women instinctively know everything about other women.

'It keeps me awake.' Not that there was much of the night remaining to us.

'You're not easy to live with, Bernard,' she said, with a formality that revealed that this was something she'd told herself many times.

'I was thinking about something else,' I confessed. 'I'm sorry.'

'You can't wait to get away,' she said, as if taking note of something beyond her control, like the storm outside the window.

'It's Dicky's idea.'

'I didn't say it wasn't.' She stood up and gathered the sugar and milk jug, and put them on the tray.

'I'd rather stay with you,' I said.

She smiled a lonely distant smile. Her sadness almost broke my heart. I was going to stand up and embrace her, but while I was still thinking about it she had picked up the tray and walked away. In such instants are our lives changed; or not changed.

With characteristic gravity the news men made the high winds of October 1987 into a hurricane. But it was a newsworthy event nevertheless. Homes were wrecked and ships sank. Cameras turned. The insured sweated; underwriters faltered; glaziers rejoiced. Hundreds and thousands of trees were ripped out of the English earth. So widespread was the devastation that even the meteorological gurus were moved to admit that they had perhaps erred in their predictions for a calm night.

I contrive, as far as is possible considering our relative ranking in the Department, to make my travel arrangements so that they

19

exclude Dicky Cruyer. Several times during our trip to Mexico City a few years ago, I had vowed to resign rather than share another expedition with him. It was not that he made a boring travelling companion, or that he was incapable, cowardly, taciturn or shy. At this moment, he was practising his boyish charm on the Swiss Air stewardess in a demonstration of social skill far beyond anything that I might accomplish. But Dicky's intrepid behaviour and reckless assumptions brought dangers of a sort I was not trained to endure. And I was tired of his ongoing joke that he was the brains and I was the brawn of the combination.

It was a Monday morning in October in Switzerland. Birds sang to keep warm, and the leaves were turning to rust on dry and brittle branches. The undeclared reason for my part in this excursion was that I knew the location of George Kosinski's lakeside hideaway near Zurich. It was a secluded spot, and George had an obsession about keeping his name out of phone books and directories.

It was a severely modern house. Designed with obvious deference to the work of Corbusier, it exploited a dozen different woods to emphasize a panelled mahogany front door and carved surround. There was no reply to repeated ringing, and Dicky said flippantly: 'Well, let's see how you knock down the door, Bernard ... Or do you pick the lock with your hairpin?'

Across the road a man in coveralls was painstakingly removing election posters from a wall. The national elections had taken place the previous day but already the Swiss were clearing away the untidy-looking posters. I smiled at Dicky. I wasn't going to smash down a door in full view of a local municipal employee, and certainly not the sort of local municipal employee found in law-abiding Switzerland. 'George might be having an afternoon nap,' I said. 'He's retired; he takes life slowly these days. Give him another minute.' I pressed the bell push again.

'Yes,' said Dicky knowingly. 'There are few worse beginnings to an interview than smashing down someone's front door.'

'That's it, Dicky,' I said in my usual obsequious way, although I knew many worse beginnings to interviews, and I had the scars and stiff joints to prove it. But this wasn't the time to burden Dicky with the adversities of being a field agent.

'Our powwow might be more private if we all take a short voyage around the lake in his power boat,' said Dicky.

I nodded. I'd noted that Dicky was nautically attired with a navy pea-jacket and a soft-topped yachtsman's cap. I wondered what other aspects of George's lifestyle had come to his attention.

'And before we start, Bernard,' he said, putting a hand on my arm, 'leave the questioning to me. We've not come here for a cosy family gathering, and the sooner he knows that the better.' Dicky stood with both hands thrust deep into the slash pockets of his pea-jacket and his feet well apart, the way sailors do in rough seas.

'Whatever you say, Dicky,' I told him, but I felt sure that if Dicky went roaring in with bayonets fixed and sirens screaming, George would display a terrible anger. His Polish parents had provided him with that prickly pride that is a national characteristic and I knew from personal experience how obstinate he could be. George had started as a dealer in unreliable motor cars and derelict property. Having contended with the ferocious dissatisfied customers found in run-down neighbourhoods of London, he was unlikely to yield to Dicky's refined style of Whitehall bullying.

Again I pressed the bell push.

'I can hear it ringing,' said Dicky. There was a brass horse-shoe door-knocker. Dicky gave it a quick rat-a-tat.

When there was still no response I strolled around the back of the house, its shiny tiles and heavy glass well suited to the unpredictable winds and weather that came from the lake. From the house well-kept grounds stretched down to the lakeside and the pier where George's powerful cabin cruiser was tied up. Summer had ended, but today the sun was bright as it darted in and out of granite-coloured clouds that stooped earthward and became the Alps. The air was whirling with dead leaves that settled on the grass to make a scaly bronze carpet. There was a young woman standing on the lawn, ankle-deep in dead leaves. She was hanging out clothes to dry in the cold blustery wind off the lake.

'Ursi!' I called. I recognized her as my brother-in-law's housekeeper. Her hair was straw-coloured and drawn back into a tight bun; her face, reddened by the wind, was that of a child. Standing there, arms upstretched with the laundry, she looked like the sort of fresh peasant girl you see only in pre-Raphaelite paintings and light opera. She looked at me solemnly for a moment before smiling and saying: 'Mr Samson. How good to see you.' She was dressed in a plain dark blue bib-front dress, with white blouse and floppy collar. Her frumpy low-heel shoes completed the sort of ensemble in which Switzerland's wealthy immigrants dress their domestic servants.

'I'm looking for Mr Kosinski,' I said. 'Is he at home?'

'Do you know, I have no idea where he has gone,' she said in her beguiling accent. Her English was uncertain and she picked her words with a slow deliberate pace that deprived them of accent and emotion.

'When did he leave?'

'Again, I cannot tell you for sure. The morning of the day before yesterday – Saturday – I drove the car for him; to take him on visits in town.' Self-consciously she tucked an errant strand of hair back into place.

'You drove the car?' I said. 'The Rolls?' I had seen Ursi drive a car. She was either very short-sighted or reckless or both.

'The Rolls-Royce. Yes. Twice I was stopped by the police; they could not believe I was allowed to drive it.'

22

'I see,' I said, although I didn't see any too clearly. George had always been very strict about allowing people to drive his precious Rolls-Royce.

'In downtown Zurich, Mr Kosinski asks me to drive him round. It is very difficult to park the cars.'

'Yes,' I said. I hadn't realized how difficult.

'Finally I left him at the airport. He was meeting friends there. Mr Kosinski told me to take ... to bring ...' She gave a quick breathless smile. '... the car back here, lock it in the garage, and then go home.'

'The airport?' said Dicky. He whisked off his sun-glasses to see Ursi better.

'Yes, the airport,' she said, looking at Dicky as if noticing him for the first time. 'He said he was meeting friends and taking them to lunch. He would be drinking wine and didn't want to drive.'

'What errands?' I said.

'What time did you arrive at the airport?' Dicky asked her.

'This is Mr Cruyer,' I said. 'I work for him.'

She looked at Dicky and then back at me. Without changing her blank expression she said: 'Then I arrived here at the house this morning at my usual hour; eight-thirty.'

'Yes, yes, yes. And bingo – he was gone,' added Dicky.

'And bingo – he was gone,' she repeated in that way that students of foreign languages pounce upon such phrases and make them their own. 'And he was gone. Yes. His bed not slept upon.'

'Did he say when he was coming back?' I asked her.

A look of disquiet crossed her face: 'Do you think he goes back to his wife?'

Do I think he goes back to his wife! Wait a minute! My respect for George Kosinski's ability to keep a secret went sky-high at that moment. George was in mourning for his wife. George had come here, to live full-time in this luxurious holiday home of his, only because his wife had been murdered in a shoot-out in East Germany. And his pretty housekeeper doesn't know that?

I looked at her. On my previous visit here the nasty suspicions to which every investigative agent is heir had persuaded me that the relationship between George and his attractive young 'housekeeper' had gone a steamy step or two beyond pressing his pants before he took them off. Now I was no longer so sure. This girl was either too artless, or a wonderful actress. And surely any close relationship between them would have been built upon George being a sorrowing widower?

While I was letting the girl have a moment to rethink the situation, Dicky stepped in, believing perhaps that I was at a loss for words. 'I'd better tell you,' he said, in a voice airline captains assume when confiding to their passengers that the last remaining engine has fallen off, 'that this is an official inquiry. Withholding information could result in serious consequences for you.'

'What has happened?' said the girl. 'Mr Kosinski? Has he been injured?'

'Where did you take him downtown on Saturday?' said Dicky harshly.

'Only to the bank – for money; to the jeweller – they cleaned and repaired his wristwatch; to church – to say a prayer. And then to the airport to meet his friends,' she ended defiantly.

'It's all right, Ursi,' I said pleasantly, as if we were playing bad cop, good cop. 'Mr Kosinski was supposed to meet us here,' I improvised. 'So of course we are a little surprised to hear he's gone away.'

'I want to know everyone who's visited him here during the last four weeks,' said Dicky. 'A complete list. Understand?'

The girl looked at me and said: 'No one visits him. Only you. He is so lonely. I told my mother and we pray for him.' She confessed this softly, as if such prayers would humiliate George if he ever learned of them.

24

'We haven't got time for all this claptrap,' Dicky told her. 'I'm getting cold out here. I'll take a quick look round inside the house, and I want you to tell me the exact time you left him at the airport.'

'Twelve noon,' she said promptly. 'I remember it. I looked at the clock there to know the time. I arranged to visit my neighbour for her to fix my hair in the afternoon. Three o'clock. I didn't want to be late.'

While Dicky was writing about this in his notebook, she started to pick up the big plastic basket, still half-filled with damp laundry that she had not put on the line. I took it from her: 'Maybe you could leave the laundry for a moment and make us some coffee, Ursi,' I said. 'Have you got that big espresso machine working?'

'Yes, Mr Samson.' She gave a big smile.

'I'll look round the house and find a recent photo of him. And I'll take the car,' Dicky told me. 'I haven't got time to sit round guzzling coffee. I'm going to grill all those airport security people. Someone must have seen him go through the security checks. I need the car; you get a taxi. I'll see you back at the hotel for dinner. Or I'll leave a message.'

'Whatever you say, master.'

Dicky smiled dutifully and marched off across the lawn and disappeared inside the house through the back door Ursi had used.

I was glad to get rid of Dicky, if only for the afternoon. Being away from home seemed to generate in him a restless disquiet, and his displays of nervous energy sometimes brought me close to screaming. Also his departure gave me a chance to talk to the girl in Schweitzerdeutsch. I spoke it only marginally better than she spoke English, but she was more responsive in her own language.

'There's a beauty shop in town that Mrs Kosinski used to say did the best facials in the whole world,' I told her. 'You help me

25

look round the house and we'll still have time for me to take you there, fix an appointment for you, and pay for it. I'll charge it to Mr Cruyer.'

She looked at me, smiled artfully, and said: 'Thank you, Mr Samson.'

After looking out of the window to be quite certain Dicky had departed, I went through the house methodically. She showed me into the master bedroom. There was a photograph of Tessa in a silver frame at his bedside and another photo of her on the chest of drawers. I went into an adjacent room which seemed to have started as a dressing-room but which now had become an office and den. It revealed a secret side of George. Here, in a glass case, there was an exquisite model of a Spanish galleon in full sail. A brightly coloured lithograph of the Virgin Mary stared down from the wall.

'What are those hooks on the wall for?' I asked Ursi while I continued my search: riffling through the closets to discover packets of socks, shirts and underclothes still in their original wrappings, and a drawer in which a dozen valuable watches and some gold pens and pencils were carelessly scattered among the silk handkerchiefs.

'He has taken the rosary with him,' she said, looking at the hooks on the wall. 'It was his mother's. He always took it to church.'

'Yes,' I said. I noticed that he'd left *Nice Guys Finish Dead* beside his bed with a marker in the last chapter. It looked like he planned to return. On the large dressing-room table there were half a dozen leather-bound photograph albums. I flipped through them to see various pictures of George and Tessa. I'd not before realized that George was an obsessional, if often inexpert, photographer who'd kept a record of their travels and all sorts of events, such as Tessa blowing out the candles on her birthday cake, and countless flashlight pictures of their party guests. Many of the photos had been captioned in George's neat handwriting, and there were empty spaces on some pages showing where photos had been removed.

I opened the door of a big closet beside his cedar-lined wardrobe, and half a dozen expensive items of luggage tumbled out. 'These cases. Do they all belong to Mr Kosinski?'

'No. His cases are not there,' she said, determined to practise her English. 'But he took no baggage with him to the airport. I know this for sure. I always pack for him when he goes tripping.'

'These are not his?' I looked at the collection of expensive baggage. Many of the bags were matching ones embroidered with flower patterns, but there was nothing there to fit with George's taste.

'No. I think those all belong to Mrs Kosinski. Mr Kosinski always uses big metal cases and a brown leather shoulder-bag.'

'Have you ever met Mrs Kosinski?' I held up a photo of Tessa just in case George had brought some woman here and pretended she was his wife.

'I have only worked here eight weeks. No, I have not met her.' She watched me as I looked at the large framed photo hanging over George's dressing-table. It was a formal group taken at his wedding. 'Is that you?' She pointed a finger. It was no use denying that the tall man with glasses looming over the bridegroom's shoulder, and looking absurd in his rented morning suit and top-hat, was me. 'And that is your wife?'

'Yes,' I said.

'She is beautiful,' said Ursi in an awed voice.

'Yes,' I said. Fiona was at her most lovely that day when her sister was married in the little country church and the sun shone and even my father-in-law was on his best behaviour. It seemed a long time ago. In the frame with the colour photo, a horseshoe decoration from the wedding cake had been preserved, and so had a carefully arranged handful of confetti.

27

George was a Roman Catholic. No matter that Tessa was the most unfaithful of wives, he would never divorce or marry again. He had told me that more than once. 'For better or worse,' he'd repeated a dozen times since, and I was never quite sure whether it was to confirm his own vows or remind me of mine. But George was a man of contradictions: of impoverished parents but from a noble family, honest by nature but Jesuitical in method. He drove around a lake in a motor boat while dreaming of Spanish galleons, he prayed to God but supplicated to Mammon; carried his rosary to church, while adorning his house with lucky horseshoes. George was a man ready to risk everything on the movements of the market, but hanging inside his wardrobe there were as many belts as there were braces.

Downstairs again, sitting with Ursi on the imitation zebra-skin sofas in George's drawing-room, with bands of sunlight across the floor, I was reminded of my previous visit. This large room had modern furniture and rugs that suited the architecture. Its huge glass window today gave a view of the grey water of the lake and of George's boat swaying with the wake of a passing ferry.

The room reminded me that, despite my protestations to Dicky, George had been in a highly excited state when I was last in this room with him. He'd threatened all kinds of revenge upon the unknown people who might have killed his wife, and even admitted to engaging someone to go into communist East Germany to ferret out the truth about that night when Tessa was shot.

'We'll take a taxi,' I promised Ursi. 'And we'll visit every place you went on the afternoon you took him to the airport. Perhaps when we're driving you'll remember something else, something that might help us find him.'

'He's in danger, isn't he?'

'It's too early to say. Tell me about the bank. Did he get foreign currency? German marks? French francs?'

'No. I heard him phoning the bank. He asked them to prepare one thousand dollars in twenty-dollar bills – American money.'

'Traveller's cheques?'

'Cash.'

'Mr Kosinski is my brother-in-law; you know that?'

'He hasn't gone back to his wife then?' she said. She obviously thought that George's wife was my sister. Perhaps it was better to leave it that way. It was a natural mistake; no one could have mistaken me for George Kosinski's kin. I was tall, overweight and untidy. George was a small, neat, grey-haired man who had grown used to enjoying the best of everything, except perhaps of wives, for Tessa had found her marriage vows intolerable.

'He's in mourning for his wife,' I said.

She crossed herself. 'I did not know.'

'She was killed in Germany. When I was last here he talked about finding his wife's killer. That could be very dangerous for him.'

She looked at me and nodded like a child being warned about speaking to strangers.

'What did you think this morning, Ursi?' I asked her. 'What did you think when you arrived and found he had gone?'

'I was worried.'

'You weren't so worried that you called the police,' I pointed out. 'You went on working; doing the laundry as if nothing was amiss.'

'Yes,' she said, and looked over her shoulder as if she thought Dicky might be about to climb through the window and pounce on her. Then she smiled, and in an entirely new and relaxed voice said: 'I think perhaps he has gone skiing.'

'Skiing? In October?'

'On the glacier.' She was anxious to persuade me. 'Last week he spent a lot of money on winter sport clothes. He bought silk

29

underwear, silk socks, some cashmere roll-necks and a dark brown fur-lined ski jacket.'

I said: 'I need to use the phone for long distance.' She nodded. I called London and told them to dig out George's passport application and leave a full account of its entries on the hotel fax.

'Let's get a cab and go to town, Ursi,' I said.

We went to the jeweller's first. Not even Forest Lawn can equal the atmosphere of silent foreboding that you find in those grand jewellery shops on Zurich's Bahnhofstrasse. The glass show-cases were ablaze with diamonds and pearls. Necklaces and brooches; chokers and tiaras; gold wristwatches and rings glittered under carefully placed spotlights. The manager wore a dark suit and stiff collar, gold cuff-links and a diamond stud in his sober striped tie. His face was politely blank as I walked with Ursi to the counter upon which three black velvet pads were arranged at precisely equal intervals.

'Yes, sir?' said the manager in English. He had categorized us already; middle-aged foreigner accompanied by young girl. What could they be here for, except to exchange those vows of carnal sin at which only a jeweller can officiate?

'Mr George Kosinski is a customer of yours?'

'I cannot say, sir.'

'This is Miss Maurer. She works for Mr Kosinski. I am Mr Kosinski's brother-in-law.'

'Indeed.'

'He came to your shop the day before yesterday. He disappeared immediately afterwards. I mean he didn't come home. We don't want to go to the police – not yet, at any rate – but we are concerned about him.'

'Of course, sir,' he said sympathetically and adjusted the velvet pad on the counter, pulling it a fraction of an inch towards him as if lining it up more precisely with the other velvet pads.

'We thought he might have said something to you that would help us find him. He has a medical record of memory loss, and he has been under a severe domestic strain.'

The man took a deep breath, as if coming to an important decision. 'I know Mr Kosinski. And your sister, too. Mrs Kosinski is an old and valued customer.'

Here was another one who didn't know that Tessa was dead. So that was how George preferred it. Perhaps he felt he could keep out of trouble more easily if everyone thought there was a Mrs Kosinski who might descend upon them any minute. I let the jeweller think Tessa was my sister; it was better that way. 'Did he purchase something here?'

'No, sir.' For one terrible moment I thought he'd changed his mind about helping me. He looked as if he was having second thoughts about revealing details of his customers. But then he continued: 'No, he brought something to me, an item of jewellery for cleaning. He said nothing that would help you find him. He seemed very relaxed and in good health.'

'That's encouraging,' I said. 'Was it a wristwatch?'

'For cleaning? No, we don't service watches; they have to go back to the factory. No, it was a ring he brought for cleaning.'

'May we see it?'

'I'll enquire if it is on the premises. Some items have to go to specialists.'

He went through a door in the back of the shop and came back after a few minutes using a smooth white cloth to hold an elaborate diamond ring. 'It's a lovely piece; not at all the modern fashion, but I like it. A heart-shaped diamond mounted in platinum with four smaller baguette diamonds. Quite old. You can see how worn it is.' He held it up, gripping it by means of the towel. The ring was dripping wet with some sort of cleaning fluid which had an acrid smell. 'It was encrusted with mud and dirt when he brought it in. In twenty years I have never seen a

31

piece of jewellery treated in such fashion. A ring like this has to be cleaned very carefully.'

'He didn't say he was going abroad? His next call was the airport.'

He shook his head sadly. 'I'm afraid he gave no indication … it seemed as if he was on a shopping trip, doing everyday chores.'

We exchanged business cards. I gave him one of Dicky's, an anonymous one with one of our London-based outside phone lines on it. I scribbled my name on the back of it. 'If you remember anything else at all I'd be obliged.'

He took the card and read it carefully before putting it into his waistcoat pocket. 'I will, sir.'

'While you've been wasting your time, talking to the maid and looking at wristwatches, I have been thinking,' said Dicky after I told him what I had been doing that afternoon, omitting the bit about paying for Ursi's alarmingly expensive facial and manicure.

'That's good, Dicky,' I said.

'I suppose that analytical thinking has always been my strong point,' Dicky mused. 'Sometimes I think I'm wasting my time at London Central.'

'Perhaps you are,' I said.

'Reports and statistics. Those Tuesday morning conferences … trying to brief the old man.' As if remembering the last time he briefed the old man, he looked at red marks on his fingers which had not completely healed over. 'He's here,' said Dicky like a conjuror.

'The old man?'

'The old man!' said Dicky scornfully. 'Will you wake up, Bernard. George Kosinski. George Kosinski is here.'

'In the hotel? You've seen him?'

'No, I haven't seen him,' said Dicky irritably. 'But it's obvious when you sit and concentrate on the facts as I have been doing. Think it over, Bernard. Kosinski left home without even packing a bag. No one came to visit him; he just up and left the house. No cash, no clothes. How would he manage?'

'What's your theory then?' I asked with genuine interest.

'It's obvious.' He chuckled. 'Obvious. That bastard Kosinski is right here in Zurich, laughing at us. He's checked into one of these big luxury hotels, and he's biding his time until we depart again.' I said nothing; I knew what was coming; I could read Dicky's mind when his eyes glittered that way. 'Our visit here was leaked, Bernard old son.'

'Not by me, Dicky.' The reality behind Dicky's new theory was that his experimental dalliance with investigative enquiries at the airport had been met by airport security men as boorish, obstinate and status-conscious as Dicky could be. Having failed at the airport he'd come back to the hotel to evolve a more convenient theory.

'By someone. We won't argue,' he said generously. 'Who knows? It could have been some careless remark by one of the secretaries. The Berne office knew we were coming here. They have local staff.'

I nodded. Of course, local staff. No one British must be suspected of such a thing.

'Tomorrow you can start checking the hotels. Big and small; near and far; cheap and flashy. You can take this photo of him – I pinched it from the drawing-room – and go round and show it to them. We'll soon find him if we're systematic.'

'And which hotels will you be doing?'

'I will have to go to Berne. It's tiresome but I must keep the ambassador in the picture or the embassy people will feel neglected.'

'Dicky, I'm not a field agent any longer.'

'London staff.'

'No, I'm not London staff either. I'm on a five-year contract that can be terminated any time that someone on the top floor

33

sends me for a medical check-up having told their tame quack to give me a thumbs-down.'

'That's a bloody disloyal thing to say,' said Dicky, always ready to speak on behalf of the top-floor staff. 'No one gets treated like that. No one! We are a family. It doesn't serve your cause to become paranoid.'

I'd heard all that before. 'If I'm to go schlepping around these hotels for you, I must go back on to my proper field agent per diem, with expenses and allowances.'

'Don't moan, Bernard. You are an awfully nice chap until you start moaning.'

'What I'm saying …'

He waved his injured hand airily above his head. 'I'll see to it, I'll see to it. If you'd rather be a field agent than wait for a proper senior staff position in London.' I never knew how to deal with Dicky's bland reassurances. I felt unable to pursue my argument, despite knowing that he had no intention of doing anything about it.

'You want me to go chasing rainbows,' I said. 'This is Switzerland, it will cost a fortune. I must have an advance. Otherwise I'll be spending my own money and waiting six months while London processes the expenses.'

'Chasing rainbows?'

'Look, Dicky. George Kosinski isn't skulking around in some local hotel here; he's gone.'

'The girl told you?'

'She thinks he's gone skiing on the glacier.'

'Why?' Dicky chewed on his fingernail, anxious that he'd missed an opportunity. 'Did Kosinski tell her that?'

'He bought silk underwear and a ski jacket last week.'

'That settles it then.'

'George hates skiing,' I explained. 'He's hopeless on skis and hates ski resorts.'

34

'What then?' said Dicky.

'For one thing his bags have gone. It looks like he went to the airport in secret, and left them there ahead of time. He obviously wanted to get away without attracting attention; but who was he trying to avoid? And why?'

'And where?' added Dicky. 'Where has he gone?'

'Somewhere that gets damned cold; hence the silk underwear. My guess is Poland. He has a lot of relatives there: brothers, uncles, aunts and maybe a still-living grandfather. If he was in trouble, that's where he might well go.'

'We can't depend on a few odds and ends of guesswork, Bernard.'

'George has been raiding his old photo albums for snapshots to take along. He also took the rosary his mother gave him. It's a trip to his family. Perhaps that's all it is. Maybe someone is sick.'

'That's not all it is. Someone came here and talked to him. We know the Stasi people came through here.'

'The girl said no one came to visit,' I countered. I didn't want Dicky to condemn George and then start collecting evidence.

Even Dicky could answer that one: 'So Kosinski went out and met them somewhere else.'

'It's possible,' I said. 'But that doesn't prove that there is anything sinister about his disappearance.'

'I don't like it,' said Dicky. 'It smells like trouble … with all that Tessa business, we can't afford to just shrug it off. We must know for certain where he's gone.'

'He's gone home to Poland,' I said again. 'It's only a guess, but I know him well enough to make that kind of guess.'

'No zlotys from the bank?'

It was a joke but I answered anyway. 'They are not legally sold; he'd be better off with US dollar bills.'

A long silence. 'You're not just a pretty face, Bernard,' he said, as if it was a joke I'd never heard before.

'I may be wrong.'

'Where in Poland?'

'I got the office to sort out his passport application. His parents were from a village in Masuria, in the north-east. His brother Stefan lives in that same neighbourhood.'

'What are you holding back, old bean?' Dicky asked.

'The Poles in London are a small community. I made a couple of calls from my room … a chap who runs a little chess club knows George well. He says George goes back sometimes and sends his family money on a regular basis.'

'And?' he persisted.

'I can't think of anything else,' I said.

'You're holding back something.'

'No, Dicky. Not this time.'

'Very well then. But if this is simply your devious way of avoiding schlepping round these bloody hotels I'll kill you, Bernard.' He looked at me, his brow furrowed with suspicion at the thought I was withholding something. Then with that remarkable intuition that had so often come to his aid, he had it. 'The wristwatch,' said Dicky. 'Why did he take the wrist-watch for cleaning? And why would you bother to follow it up by going to the jeweller?'

'A man like George has dozens of flashy watches. He doesn't take them for cleaning, not when he has other things on his mind.'

'So why follow it up? Why go to the jeweller then?'

I rubbed my face. I would have to tell him. I said: 'It was his wife's engagement ring.'

'Tessa Kosinski's engagement ring? Jesus Christ! She's dead. In the East. You bastard, Bernard. Why didn't you tell me right away?'

'It was dirty, muddy, the jeweller said.'

He shook his head, and heaved a sigh that combined anger and content. 'Never mind whether it was dirty or not. My God,

Bernard, you do spring them. You mean some Stasi bastards came here with his wife's engagement ring? They're talking to him? Pushing him? Leading him on? Is it something about the burial?'

'My guess is they are saying she's still alive.'

'Alive? Why? What would they want in exchange?'

'I wish I knew, Dicky.' Dicky's phone rang. I looked at my watch, got to my feet and waved goodnight. 'Shall I see you at breakfast downstairs?'

Dicky, bending low over the phone, twisted his head to scowl at me and held up a warning finger. I waited. 'Hold it, Bernard,' he said. 'It's London on the line. This is something you might want to stay awake thinking about.'

I waited while Dicky took his call, nodding and grunting as if someone at the other end was reading something out to him. It took a long time, with Dicky doing little but register pained surprise. Then he hung up and turned to me and gave me a canny smile.

'What is it?' I asked when it looked as if he would go on smiling all night.

'The whole bloody stock-market collapsed today. In New York the Dow crashed 508 points, the biggest slump on record. By the time the New York market closed it was 22.6 per cent down. Twenty-two point bloody six! The first day of the '29 crash only went down 12.8 per cent. This is it, Bernard.'

'London too?'

'Tokyo opened first, of course. Selling began with the opening bell. When London opened, everyone began unloading dollar stocks. By the end of the day, London was down more than 10 per cent, the 100-share index dropped 249.6 points.'

'I don't follow all that financial mumbo-jumbo,' I said.

'It dropped 249.6 to 2,053.3! You don't have to be a mathematical genius to see what manner of fall that is,' said Dicky, who was a well-known mathematical genius.

'No,' I said.

'Here in Zurich it fell too. Milan, Stockholm, Amsterdam, Brussels, Frankfurt ... it's a massacre. When New York opened the blood was already running over the floor.'

'Did they suspend trading?' I asked in a desperate attempt to sound astute and knowledgeable.

'The Hong Kong market ceased trading,' said Dicky, who now seemed to be in his element. 'There's panic everywhere tonight. The City is getting ready for another onslaught tomorrow. Last Thursday's hurricane buggered up the computer and prevented some people getting to work. An upset of this magnitude will spill over into politics, Bernard. It's impossible to guess the implications. Mrs Thatcher has made a pacifying statement about the strength of the economy, and so has Reagan. Bret Rensselaer is sleeping in the Night Duty Officer's room. The lights are on in every office in Whitehall they tell me. They are on a war footing. My pal Henry, in the embassy here, says the Americans will declare martial law tomorrow, in case of widespread rioting and runs on the banks.'

'Did he really?' I said, knowing that Henry Tiptree, an employee of the Department, a man with whom I'd crossed swords more than once, was even more excitable and unreliable than Dicky. 'But what's this got to do with George Kosinski? He left on Saturday.'

'Yes, Kosinski saw it coming. He sold out everything before coming to live here.'

'He said he had to do that. It was a necessary part of his changing his tax residence.'

'He cleared out and gave you his London apartment.'

'That was in Tessa's Will; a gift to Fiona,' I protested. I didn't like the way that Dicky was implicating me in his theories about George. 'But why would he run away? These money men like George have all their assets in companies. And George has

38

companies that are registered all over the world. What would he run away from? No one is going to knock on the door and arrest him.'

'It's a well-known fact that severe psychological stress often provokes people into physical action. Spontaneous physical action.'

'Not George,' I said.

'He's a dark horse,' said Dicky with cautious admiration. 'And you thought he came here as a reaction to his wife's death? But he started to sell off his companies two months back. He must have seen this crash coming for ages. Didn't he warn you about it?'

'He doesn't confide in me,' I said. 'George is his own man.'

'I'd love to know what he's up to,' said Dicky, and stared at the phone. 'I'm running a credit check on him but this stock-market thrashing is going to delay things like that.'

'What about his lovely house on the lake?'

'Rented on a monthly basis. I checked that before we came. He never owned it. Not even the furniture.'

'And you think he ran because he's deep in debt?' It seemed more likely that George had found some artful advantage in having corporations own his house and contents.

'Now you see it, do you?' said Dicky, treating my question like an endorsement. 'It fits together doesn't it? You've got to know how these financial wizards think. He's bust. Now you see why he would clear off without notice and leave no forwarding address.'

'Poor George.'

'Yes, poor George,' said Dicky in a voice not entirely devoid of satisfaction. Dicky loved dramas, especially tragedies: and especially ones that brought disaster to people he envied. He relished reciting it all, and now his tone reproved me for not mirroring his delight. 'Are you listening, Bernard?'

39

'I'm listening.'

'Well, don't sit there with your head in your hands, as if you're about to break down and weep.'

'No, Dicky.' But the truth was that I did feel concerned about George. It wasn't just a matter of money – George would probably find money from somewhere, he always had done. But George had enough worries already. The news of Tessa's death had made him talk of revenge, and disturbed him in a way I would never have thought possible. All that, and a financial crisis too, might be more than he could handle.

'So you want to go to Warsaw?' said Dicky.

'Not particularly. But if you want me to go and find him, that's where I would start.'

'You have contacts there?'

'Yes, but I'm not much good with the language.' I didn't want Dicky expecting miracles. If George had fled to Poland it was because Poland's state of chaos provided a promising place in which to hide. Finding him would not be easy.

'Who is good with the language?' said Dicky blithely.

'It makes it difficult to work on an investigation if you can't understand what anyone is saying,' I said. 'Polish is not like Italian or Portuguese, where you grab at the root of a couple of words and guess the rest. Polish is impenetrable.'

'We'll manage,' said Dicky. 'I know you; you can always manage in any language. You've got a knack for languages.'

'We?'

'I'd better come with you. Two can always do better than one … on a job like this.'

'Yes,' I said. He was right: unless of course the other one is Dicky. He looked at me and then, after catching my eyes, looked away again. I said: 'Is this something to do with Daphne?'

'No. Well, yes. In a way. She has a very nervous disposition,' said Dicky, his eyes narrowing as if suspecting me of being in league with his wife. 'Edgy. Bitter. Full of wild talk. She keeps digging up silly things that are ancient history. It's better if she's on her own for a week or so.'

So that was it. We weren't going to Warsaw to hunt down George Kosinski, we were going there to provide a divertissement that might smooth over some domestic rift between Dicky and his long-suffering wife. I had other worries too. Ursi's facial was going to cost ten times as much as I'd anticipated; I wondered if I could persuade the hotel cashier to pay it, and charge it somewhere deep in Dicky's room-service bills.

2

Warsaw.

September is the time many visitors choose to visit Poland. It was during September half a century ago that German visitors, with Stukas, Panzers and artillery, came. So devoted were they to this ancient kingdom that they wanted to own it. They chose September because the heavy summer rains had passed by then and the land was firm; the skies were clear enough for the bombers, and the working days were long enough for them to fight their way deep into Poland's heartland.

But once September is gone, the days shorten suddenly and the temperature drops. This year, like an omen, the first snow had come unusually early. As the thermometers hovered at zero, the moist air produced the heavy wet snowstorms that come only at the very beginning of the bad weather. The snow and sleet would eventually disappear, of course, as snow, visitors and invaders had always eventually done, but that did not make such chronic afflictions easier to suffer.

Warsaw is not an old city, it only looks like one. In beauty it is eclipsed by its rival Cracow; its lop-sided high position on the west bank of the Vistula exposes it to the harsh east winds, and it has no backdrop of hills or mountains or attractive coastline. But for Poles, Warsaw has a significance that is not explained in either political or cultural terms but is inextricably linked to

Polish nationalism. Perhaps the Germans knew this, for when the German army retreated from Warsaw they destroyed it in a way they did no other capital city. They razed it not by haphazard bombings or shellings but stone by stone, as an act of deliberate and vindictive devastation. The steel street-car tracks, the drains and even the sewers were ripped from the cobbled streets like the guts from a plucked chicken.

But with the same sort of determination, the Poles built it up again stone by stone. With the fastidious zeal that only hatred can feed, they scoured the museums and the archives to look at old paintings and drawings, and they copied the nineteenth-century plans of Corazzi. And using the skills of architects and historians, carpenters and artists and masons and labourers, and the contributions and good will of Polish men and women throughout the world, they built Warsaw again the way they remembered it.

It was October when we arrived. Generals loyal to communism had appointed themselves to government, the nation was deeply in debt, virtually everything was in short supply, and Warsaw's streets were grizzled by snow that, despite being unseasonably early, fell without respite. Dimly lit windows of shops on the Nowy Swiat were displaying a final few miserable heirlooms, and there were people huddled on every corner accosting any well-dressed passers-by and trying to swap their last treasures for anything edible or combustible.

In the gloomy entrance hall of the Europejski Hotel there was less evidence of such deprivation. Crowding around the bar at the side of the lobby – their waist-belts straining, and faces flushed – black-marketeers were mingling in noisy accord with army officers and surviving elders of the Party faithful. Behind the bar at busy times like this there was the regular barman. He'd been there for years: a jovial retired member of the ZOMO, the widely feared anti-riot police. Stuffed behind the vodka bottles, and in plain view, he always kept a copy of *Trybuna Ludu*, Warsaw's Communist Party daily paper; it was in effect a proclamation warning one and all of the political climate to be found there. But that didn't preclude jokes, and this evening he was getting anticipatory grins while telling a long involved story about how scientists in the government laboratories were working hard to transform the nation's vodka supplies back into potatoes. The same joke was being repeated everywhere, but outside in the streets it was received with laughter less hearty.

It was late that evening, and the crowd at the bar were at their noisiest, as I pushed my way through the crowded lobby of the Europejski Hotel for a second time. Dicky was sitting on a leather sofa facing the reception counter. I had been back to the airport on a mission to find Dicky's extra suitcase, which had lost its label and gone astray in the baggage room. As Dicky explained, it was better that I went because I could speak the language. Now it was almost midnight and I wiped the wet snow crystals from my face and polished them from my glasses with a handkerchief. One of the two solemn-faced young women behind the hotel desk reached behind her for my room key without looking to see where it was. It was the sort of practised gesture that made Western visitors to Poland uneasy. 'Well?' said Dicky.

'I found your suitcase. But those bastards in customs took their time. It was all those fragile labels you stuck on it that had them worried. They probably thought you were smuggling bombs for Solidarity.'

'They didn't hold on to it?'

'It's here, and it's gone up to your room.' We both turned our heads to watch six tall girls in bright green tartan skirts and tam-o'-shanter hats walk across the lobby. They stopped at the door of the restaurant and blew softly into the bagpipes they carried before proceeding inside. After a moment of silence there was the sudden explosion of massed drums, soon joined by the skirl of the pipes. Then the sound of the music was muffled by the closing doors.

'There's only cold food,' said Dicky. 'I argued, but you know how they are; they stare at you blankly and pretend they don't understand.'

'What was all that about?' I asked him.

'It's a girls' pipe band from Chicago. All from Polish neighbourhoods. They're here for three nights. They go to Cracow tomorrow. I was talking to one of them; a blonde eighteen-year-old drum majorette. She's never been away from home before.'

'I'd watch your step, Dicky,' I advised. 'Her father is likely to be a 200-pound butcher in a canning plant, and very protective.'

'I'm going to bed,' said Dicky, chewing a fingernail. 'I'm getting a cheese sandwich from room service and hitting the sack. You'll do the same if you've got any sense.'

'I've got phone calls to make, but first I must have a drink at the bar.'

'I'm bushed,' said Dicky. 'I thought you were never coming back. I would have gone to bed but my pyjamas are in that case.' He thought about what I'd said. 'Telephoning? Your contacts must be insomniacs. I'd leave it until the morning.' He yawned.

'Goodnight, Dicky.' It was useless trying to explain to him that my sort of contacts are working people who get out of bed at five in the morning, and slave all day.

I watched Dicky walking across the lobby to the main staircase. He cut a slim long-legged elegant figure in a way that I would never again become. One hand was in the pocket of his tight-fitting jeans, the other brought a chunky gold Rolex into view as he flicked his long bony fingers through his curly hair. He was studied with anthropological detachment by the two girls behind the reception desk. When his decorative cowboy boots had disappeared up the stairs, they looked at each other and sniggered.

I crossed the lobby and edged my way through the noisy drinkers at the bar. Here was the essence of Poland in 1987, a nation commandeered by its army. I recognized the pale faces of an army captain I'd met in Berlin, and a pimply lieutenant who was an aide to a general in the Ministry of the Interior. The young officers, both dressed in mufti, watched the Party officials with superior and impartial amusement. As part of the settlement with the army, the Party had promised to reform Poland's system of government while the most active Solidarity protesters were locked away. But socialist theoreticians are not noted for their zeal in self-reform, and debt-ridden Poland was sinking deeper and deeper into economic ruin. Rumours said the Russians would take control of the country within a week or so, and that the Polish army had already agreed to let them do it unopposed. But tonight the nation's misery was temporarily forgotten as the revellers celebrated the end of capitalism that they proclaimed the West's stock-market crash heralded.

Among the celebrants there were university lecturers, a diplomat, some journalists, and assorted writers and film-makers. These were the intellectuals, the *nomenklatura*, the establishment. These were the people who knew how to read the signs that pointed to shifts of power. To them it was obvious that Lech Walesa, and his fellow workers in the Lenin shipyard, had failed in their bid for power. This was a time for the establishment to close its ranks, to find a modus vivendi with the nation's military rulers; and with the Russians too if that was what Moscow demanded. Meanwhile they would indulge in long, jargon-loaded discussions with the Party's reformers, watch the Polish generals for danger signals, and down another double-vodka before going back to their warm apartments.

From the restaurant the girls' pipe band started playing 'My Wild Irish Rose'. The music was greeted with heady applause and shouts of appreciation from an audience fired by enthusiasm for things American, or Polish, or Irish. Or perhaps just overcome with vodka.

I alternated mouthfuls of strong Tatra Pils with sips of Zubrowka bison-grass vodka. With both drinks in my hands I moved around, keeping my eyes and ears open. The UB men were here too. The ears of the Urzad Bezpieczenstwa were everywhere. I counted six of them but there were undoubtedly more. These security policemen were another sort of élite, their services needed by the Party and by the military rulers too. The UB thugs enjoyed their own private shops and housing and schools, and their own prisons into which their enemies disappeared without the formalities of arrest and charge. Such secret policemen were not new to Poland. Dzierzynski, the founder of Russia's secret police, was a Pole. His statue stood outside KGB headquarters in a square named after him in Moscow. While here in Warsaw another Dzierzynski Square celebrated his widespread fame and power.

I saw no one I both knew and trusted. Eventually I grew tired of listening to the chatter and watching the deals, and went up to my room on the first floor where, after making my phone calls, I stretched out on the bed and waited. It was two-thirty in the morning when a knock came. A woman pushed at the door and came in without waiting for an invitation. 'Zimmer hundert-elf?' she said in heavy and precise German.

'Ja. Herein!' She was wearing too much make-up. At her throat an expensive Hermes silk scarf looked incongruous with the cheap fur-trimmed overcoat and well-worn white leather high-boots. Snow crystals sparkled on her face, in her dark hair, and on her fur-trimmed hat. She snatched the hat off and, as she shook it, beads of icy water flashed in the light. Noticing that the curtains weren't closed, she went and tugged them

47

together. She moved across the room with that haughty tottering step that is the mark of the young whore, but she must have been all of thirty-five, perhaps forty, and no longer thin.

For a long time she stood there – her back to the window – peering around the dingy hotel-room as if imprinting it on her memory. Or as if trying to manage without her glasses. She was no longer the Sarah I remembered: one of a crowd of exuberant young students bursting out through the gates of Humboldt University into the Linden after morning lectures. Now all the mischievous joy had disappeared, and it was hard to find the fragile bright-eyed girl I'd known. That was twelve, maybe fifteen years, ago; a hot dusty day of a sweltering Berlin summer. She was wearing a home-made pink dress with large white polka dots, I was a few yards behind her and she'd turned and called to me, asking me something in Polish, mistaking me for a student from some village near her home.

Now she put her tote-bag on the floor and stood there looking at me again: 'Room one one one?' she repeated in English.

'It's me, Sarah.'

'Bernd. I didn't recognize you.' She said it without much excitement, as if recognition would only encumber an already burdensome life.

'Do you want a drink?' I got a glass from the bathroom.

'My God I do.' She pulled off her coat, threw it across the bed, and sat down. As the light of the bedside lamp fell upon her I could see that her hair was greying, and one side of her face was yellow and blue and mauve with bruises that paint and powder could not quite conceal. She poured herself a large measure from the bottle of Johnny Walker I'd picked up at Zurich airport, and drank it swiftly. Poor Sarah. I'd seen a great deal of her after that first meeting. She was studying plant biology and when she went off with her friends, tracking down specimens of rare weeds and wild flowers, I'd sometimes tag along with them.

It gave me a chance to get into parts of the East Zone that were forbidden to foreigners. 'Give me a minute,' she said, and slipped off her heavy boots to massage her feet. 'It's been a long time, Bernd.'

'Take your time, Sarah.' She was from the south; a Silesian village in a frontier region that had been under Austro-Hungarian, Czech, Polish, German and Russian army jurisdiction in such rapid succession that none of her family knew what they were, except that they were Jews.

'Boris couldn't come. He's on the early flight to Paris tomorrow.' She was married to a bastard named Boris Zagan who was a flight attendant for LOT, the Polish government airline. He wasn't exactly a British agent but he worked for Frank Harrington, the Berlin Rezident, delivering packets to our Berlin office and sometimes doing jobs for London too. I'd heard from several people that he regularly attacked Sarah during his bouts of drunkenness.

'It's good to see you,' I said. 'Really good.' There had never been any kind of romance between us; I'd liked her too much to want the sort of on-again off-again affairs that were a necessary part of my life in those roughneck days.

She rummaged through the contents of her patent-leather handbag, found a slip of paper and passed it to me. Pencilled on it there were three lines of writing that I guessed to be an address. I studied it and laboriously deciphered the Polish alphabet. 'Can you read it?' she asked. 'I remember you speaking good Polish in the old days.'

'Never,' I said. 'Just a few clichés. And what I learned from you.' Poles liked to encourage with such warm words any foreigner who attempted their language. 'I never was good at the writing; it's the accents.'

'Accent on the penultimate syllable,' she said. 'It's always the same.' She'd told me that rule ten years ago.

'I mean the writing: the "dark L" that sounds like w; the vowels that have the n sound, and the c that sounds like cher.' I looked at the address again.

'It's a big house in the lake country,' she said. 'Stefan, George Kosinski's brother, lives there. It's miles from civilization: even the nearest village is ten miles away. You'll need a good car. The roads are terrible and I don't recommend the bus ride.'

'Or the ten-mile hike from the village,' I said, putting the paper in my pocket. 'I'll find it. Tell me about Stefan.'

'The family are minor aristocracy, but Stefan prospers because Poles are all snobs at heart. He makes money and travels in the West. He even went to America once. He displays great skill at expressing his intellectual pretensions, but not much talent. He writes plays, and all of them conclude with deserving people finding happiness through labouring together. Poems too; long poems. They are even worse.'

'Big house?'

'He married the ugly only daughter of a Party official from Bialystok. Boris said the house is vast and like a museum. I've never been there but Boris has stayed with them many times. They live well. Boris says it's Chekhov's house.'

'Chekhov's house?'

'It's a joke. Boris says Stefan stole all Chekhov's best ideas, and his best jokes and best lines and aphorisms, and then stole his house as well. He's jealous. You know Boris.'

'Yes, I know Boris.'

She finished her whisky with that determined gulp with which Poles down their vodka, and then studied her glass regretfully. 'Would you like another?' I asked.

She looked at her watch, a tiny gold lady's watch with an ornate gold and platinum band. The sort they sell in the West's airport shops. 'Yes, please,' she said.

50

I poured another drink for her. If she wanted to sit there and recover, there was little I could do about it, but I wondered why she hadn't just handed me the address and departed. As if reading my mind, she said: 'Another few minutes, Bernard, then I'll leave you in peace.' She fingered her cheek, as if wondering whether the bruises were noticeable.

Of course! She had bribed the desk who let her in as if she was one of the whores who serviced the foreign tourists. It was a cover, and she would have to be with me for long enough to make it convincing. Something to be hidden is always a good cover for something worse, as one of the training manuals deftly explained. She said: 'It's George Kosinski isn't it?'

'What?' I must have looked startled.

'Don't worry about microphones,' she said. 'There are none installed on this floor. The Bezpieca know better than to bug these rooms. These are where the committee big-shots bring their fancy women.'

'I still don't know,' I said.

'Don't go cool on me, Bernd. Do you think I can't guess why you are here?'

'Have you seen him?'

'Everyone's seen him. As soon as he arrives he shouts and yells and spends his money and gets drunk in downtown bars where there are too many ears. Boris is worried.'

'Worried?'

'Has George Kosinski gone mad? He's swearing vengeance on someone who killed his wife but he doesn't know who it is. He's violent. He knocked down a man in an argument in a bar in the Old Town and started kicking him. It was only after he convinced them that he was a tourist that the cops let him go. What's it all about, Bernd? I didn't know funny little George had it in him to do such things.'

51

I shrugged. 'His wife died. That's what did it. It happened in the DDR. On the Autobahn, the Brandenburg Exit.'

'A collision? A traffic accident?'

'There are a thousand different stories about it,' I said. 'We'll never know what happened.'

'Not political?'

I went and got another tumbler and poured myself a shot of whisky. At the bar I'd been abstemious but I could smell the whisky on her and it made me yearn for a taste of it.

'Don't turn your back on me, Bernd. I'll start to think you have something to hide.'

I'd forgotten what she was like: as sharp as a tack. I turned to see her. 'There are political traffic accidents, Sarah. We both know that.'

She stared at me as if her narrowed eyes would find the truth somewhere deep inside my heart. What she finally decided, I don't know, but she swigged her drink, got to her feet and went to the mirror to put her hat on.

'Where is George now?' I asked her. Her back was towards me while she looked in the mirror. She turned her head both ways but spent a fraction of a moment longer when looking at the bruised side of her face.

'I don't know,' she said calmly. 'Neither does Boris. We don't want to know. We've got enough trouble without George Kosinski bringing more upon us.'

'I was hoping Stefan or the family might know.'

'The last I heard, he was scouring through the Rozyckiego Bazaar trying to buy a gun.' She looked at me, but I looked down as I drank my whisky and didn't react. 'You know where I mean? Targowa in the Praga?'

I nodded. I knew where she meant: a rough neighbourhood on the far side of the river. Byelorussians, Ukrainians and Jews lived there in clannish communities where strangers were not welcome. Even the anti-riot cops didn't go there after dark without flak jackets and back-up.

'Boris said this is what you wanted,' she said, bringing a brown paper parcel from her tote-bag and putting it on the table.

'Have you got far to go?' I asked.

'I'm being met,' she said to the mirror in a voice that didn't encourage further questions.

I let her out and watched her walk down the long cream-painted corridor. The communist management showed the usual obsession with fire-fighting equipment: buckets of sand and tall extinguishers were arranged along the corridor like sentinels. When she reached the ornate circular staircase she turned and said 'Wiedersehen', and gave a wan smile, as if saying a final cheerless farewell to those two young kids we'd been long ago.

After she had gone I thought about her and her bruised face. I thought about the way they had allowed her into the hotel, and let her come up to my room. That wasn't the way it used to work in Warsaw; they checked and double-checked, and the only kind of girl you could get into your room was a genuine registered whore who was working with the secret police.

And eventually I even began wondering if perhaps Sarah had got past the desk so easily because she was just such a person.

I opened the brown paper parcel. Inside it Boris had put two tyre levers and a looped throttling wire. So he hadn't been able to get a gun for me; or maybe it was too much trouble. Boris was not the most energetic of our contacts.

'What did she say?' It was eleven o'clock in the morning. I'd been out and about. I'd avoided Dicky by missing breakfast, and I could see he was not pleased to be abandoned.

For a moment I didn't answer him. Just to be back in the heated hotel lobby, where the warmth might get my blood circulating again, was a luxury beyond compare after tramping the streets of the city looking for George and his bloody relatives.

The old place didn't look so forbidding in daytime. It had been a fine old hotel in its day. A *fin-de-siècle* pleasure palace built at a time when every grand hotel wanted to look like a railway terminal. Crudely modernized from the empty shell that remained after the war, it wasn't the sort of hotel that Dicky sought. Dicky was unprepared for the austerity of Poland, no doubt expecting that the best hotels in Warsaw would resemble those plush modern luxury blocks that the East Germans had got the Swedes to build, and Western firms to manage for them. But the Poles were different to the Germans; they did everything their own way.

'Come along, Bernard. What did she say?'

'What did who say?'

'The woman who went up to your room last night.'

I'd avoided him at breakfast, guessing that he wanted me to be his interpreter to interrogate the hotel management. It was not a confrontation I relished, for the interpreters are always the ones left covered in excrement, but what I hadn't anticipated was that he'd be able to prise from the staff the secret of my nocturnal visitor.

'It was one of those things, Dicky,' I said, hoping he would drop it but knowing that he wouldn't.

'You think I'm a bloody fool, don't you? You don't send out for whores in the middle of the night; that's not your style. But you are so devious that you'd let me believe you did, rather than confide in me. That's what makes me so bloody angry. You work for me but you think you can twist me around your finger. Well, you listen to me, Bernard, you devious bastard: I know she was here to talk with you. Now who was she?'

'A contact. I got the address of George Kosinski's brother,' I said. 'It's in the north-west and it's a lousy journey on terrible

54

roads. I thought I'd double-check that George was there before dragging you out into the sticks.'

Dicky evidently decided not to press me about the identity of my lady visitor. He must have guessed it was one of my contacts, and it was definitely out of line to ask an agent's identity. 'That's a natty little umbrella you're wielding, Bernard.'

'Yes,' I said. 'I bought it this morning.'

'A folding umbrella: telescopic. Wow! Is this a power bid for Whitehall? I mean, it's not really you, an umbrella. Too sissie for you, Bernard. It's just desk wallahs who come into town on a commuter train from the suburbs who flourish umbrellas.'

'It keeps the snow off,' I said. Dicky was of course merely showing me that he didn't like being deserted without permission, but that didn't make being the butt of his tiresome sense of humour any more tolerable.

'An umbrella like that is not something I'd recommend to the uninitiated, Bernard. A fierce gust of wind will snatch you away like Mary Poppins, and carry you all the way to the Urals.'

'But the desk didn't tell you anything about our pal Kosinski?' I asked, to bring him back to earth.

'I left that to you,' said Dicky.

'George knows his way around this town. He speaks Polish. He might lead us a dance before we get a definite fix on him.'

'And by that time he could be on a plane and in Moscow.'

'No, no, no. He won't leave until he's done what he has to do. With luck we'll get to him before that.'

'Very philosophical, Bernard. Abstract reasoning of the finest sort, but can you tell me what the hell it means?'

'It means we can't find him, Dicky. And there are no short cuts except miraculous good luck. It means that you have to be patient while we plod along doing the things that a village policeman does when looking for a lost poodle.'

This wasn't what Dicky wanted to hear. As if in reproach he said: 'Last night, when we first arrived, the reception people admitted that George Kosinski had been here in this hotel. So why won't they tell us where he's gone?'

'No, they didn't say he had been in this hotel, Dicky. They suggested that we try to find him in another hotel with a similar name. It's on the other side of the airport. It's a sleazy dump for overnight stays. He won't be there. It was just a polite way of telling us to drop dead.'

'I'll never get the hang of this bloody language,' said Dicky. He smiled and slapped his hands together in the forceful way he started his Tuesday morning 'get-together meetings' when he had something unpleasant to announce. 'Well, let's go there. Anything is better than sitting round in this mausoleum.' He produced his room key from his pocket and shook it so it jangled.

I was tired after doing the rounds of the city. The official line was that the last of the political prisoners had been released the previous year, but for some unexplained reason all the people given to airing political views the government didn't like were still serving indefinite detention in a labour camp near Gdansk which had been doubled in size to accommodate a couple of hundred extra detainees. Most of my other old contacts had moved away after the big crack-down, leaving no forwarding address, and my enquiries about them had not been met by neighbourly smiles or friendly enthusiasm.

Now I wanted to have a drink and then sit down to a leisurely lunch, but Dicky was a restless personality, ill-suited to the slow-paced austerity of communist society. I followed his gaze as he looked around with pent-up hostility at everything in the hotel lobby. Its institutional atmosphere was like that of a hundred other lobbies in such gloomy communist-run hotels. The same typography on the signs, and the same graceless furniture, the dim bulbs in the same dusty chandeliers reflecting in the polished stone floor, the same musty smell and the same surly staff.

The skittish way in which Dicky nagged his Department into doing his will was less effective when pitted against the ponderous systems of socialist omnipotence. And so Dicky had found that morning, as he tried to press the hotel manager – and individual members of the staff – into providing him with a chance to search the hotel register for George Kosinski's name. I knew all this because a full description of Dicky's activities had been provided to me by a querulous German-speaking assistant manager who was placated only after I gave him a carton of Benson and Hedges cigarettes.

'I'll have a quick drink, Dicky, and I'll be with you,' I said.

'Good grief, Bernard, it's eleven o'clock in the morning. What do you need a drink for at this hour?'

'I've been outside in sub-zero weather, Dicky. When you've been outside for an hour or two you might find out why.'

'Thank God I'm not dependent upon alcohol. Last night I saw you heading for the bar and now, next morning, you are heading that way again. It's a disease.'

'I know.'

'And the stuff they call brandy here is rot-gut.'

'I can't buy you one then? The barman is called "Mouse". Pay him in hard currency and you'll get any fancy Western tipple you name.'

He disregarded my flippant invitation. 'Make it snappy. I'll go and get my coat. I didn't bring an umbrella but perhaps I can shelter under yours.'

When we emerged on to the street Dicky seemed prepared to yield to my judgement in the matter of avoiding a senseless trek to the hotel's inferior namesake on the other side of town. 'Where shall we go first?' he offered tentatively.

'I heard George was trying to buy a gun,' I said.

'Are you serious?'

'In the Rozyckiego Bazaar in the Praga. It's a black-market paradise; the clearing house for stolen goods and furs and contraband from Russia.'

'And guns?'

'Gangs of deserters from all the Eastern European armies run things over there and fight for territory. It may look law-abiding but so did Al Capone's Chicago. Keep your hands in your pockets and watch out for pickpockets and muggers.'

'Why don't the authorities clear it out?'

'It's not so easy,' I said. 'It's the oldest flea-market in Poland. The currency dealers and black-marketeers all know each other very well. Infiltrating a plain-clothes cop is tricky, but they try from time to time. They might think that's what we are, so watch your step.'

'I can handle myself,' said Dicky. 'I don't scare easily.'

'I know,' I said. It was true and it was what made Dicky such a liability. Werner and me, we both scared very easily, and we were proud of it.

The Praga is the run-down mainly residential section of Warsaw that sprawls along the eastern side of the river. Most of its old buildings survived the war but few visitors venture here. Running parallel with the river, Targowa is the Praga's wide main street, the widest street in all the city. Long ago, as its name records, it had been Warsaw's horse market. Now dented motors and mud-encrusted street-cars rattled along its median, past solid old houses that, in the 1920s, had been luxury apartments occupied by Warsaw's merchants and professional classes.

Now the wide Targowa was patched with drifting snow and, behind it – its entrance in a narrow sidestreet – we suddenly came to the Rozyckiego market. Overlooked on every side by tenements, there was something medieval about the open space filled with all shapes and sizes of rickety stalls and huts, piled high with merchandise, and jammed with people. This notorious Bazaar had been unchanged ever since I could remember. It had drawn traders and their customers from far and wide. Gypsies and deserters, thieves and gangsters, farmers and legitimate traders had made it a vital part of the city's black economy, so that the open space was never rebuilt.

'And are you going to buy a gun too, Bernard?'

'No, Dicky,' I said as we went through the gates of the market. 'I'm just going to find George.'

The ponderous sobriety that descends upon Eastern European towns in winter was shattered as we stepped into the active confusion of the market. Women wept, men argued to the point of violence, whole families conferred, children bickered. And scurrying to and fro there were men and women – many bent under heavy loads – shouting loudly to call their wares.

'Those communist old clothes smell worse than capitalist ones,' said Dicky as we made our way through the crowds. Noisy bargainers alleviated the bizarre variety of deprivation that communism, with its corruption, caprices and chronic shortages, endemically inflicts. Here, on display, there were such coveted items as toilet paper and powdered coffee, used jeans in varying stages of wear, plastic hair-clips and Western brands of cigarettes (both genuine and fake). Women's shoes from neighbouring Czechoslovakia were hung above our heads like bright-coloured garlands, while exotic sable, fox and mink furs from far-off regions of Asia were guarded behind a strong wire fence. Elderly farmers and their womenfolk, enjoying a measure of private enterprise, offered their piles of potatoes, beets and cabbages. A solemn young man sat on the ground before a prayer-rug, as if about to bow his forehead upon the rows of used spark plugs that were arrayed before him.

A tall man in a green trenchcoat stopped me, waved a cigarette, and asked for a light. I tucked my umbrella under my arm, held up my lighter, and he cupped his hands and bent his head to it. 'I thought you were on the flight to Paris,' I said.

'They've killed George Kosinski,' he said hoarsely. 'They lured him out to his brother's house, slit his throat like a slaughtered hog and buried him in the forest. You'll be next. I'd scram if I was you.'

'You are not me, Boris,' I said. Tiny sparks hit my hand as he inhaled on his cigarette. He threw his head back, his eyes searching my face, and blew smoke at me. Then with an appreciative smile he tipped his grey felt hat in mocking salute and went on his way.

'Come along!' said Dicky when I had caught up with him again. 'They just want to talk to foreigners. We can't be delayed by every bum who wants a light.'

'Sorry, Dicky,' I said.

By this time Dicky had eased his way into a small group of men who were passing booklets from hand to hand. Two of the men were dressed in Russian army greatcoats and boots; the civilian caps they wore did not disguise them. One was about forty, with a face like polished red ebony. The other man was younger, with a lop-sided face, half-dosed eyes and the frazzled expression that afflicts prematurely aged pugilists.

'Look at this,' said Dicky, showing me the book that had been passed to him. It had a brown cover, its text was in Russian with illustrations depicting various parts of an internal combustion engine. Another similar book was passed to him. He looked at me quizzically. 'You can read this stuff. What's it all about?'

I translated the title for him: 'BG-15 40mm grenade-launcher – Tishina. It's an instruction manual. They all are.' The booklets were each devoted to military equipment of wide appeal: portable field kitchens, rocket projectors, sniperscopes, nightsights, radio transmitters and chemical protection suits. 'They're Russian soldiers. They're selling in advance equipment they are prepared to steal.'

Dicky passed the booklets to the man standing next to him. The man took them and, seeing Dicky's dismay, he looked around the group and snickered, exposing many gold teeth. He liked gold: he was wearing an assortment of rings and two gold watches on each wrist, their straps loosened enough for them to clatter and dangle like bracelets.

The hands of the two soldiers were callused and scarred, and covered from wrist to fingertip in a meticulous pattern of tattoos like blue lace gloves. I recognized the dragon designs that distinguished criminal soldiers who'd served time in a 'disbat' punishment battalion. Until very recently, to suffer such a sentence had been universally regarded as shameful, and kept secret from family and even comrades. But now men like these preferred to identify themselves as military misfits, defiant of authority. Such men liked to use their tattoos to parade their violent nature, to exploit frightened young conscripts and sometimes their officers too.

'Let's move on,' I said.

'What were they saying?'

'Gold-teeth seems to be the black-market king. You heard the soldiers say *tak tochno* – exactly so – to him instead of "yes". It's the way Soviet soldiers have to answer their officers.'

My whispered aside to Dicky attracted the attention of the soldiers. The limited linguistic skills of all concerned were clearly hampering the transaction, and I didn't want to wind up as the interpreter for these Russian hoodlums and their Polish customers. 'Move on,' I said.

Dicky got the idea. He moved away and the black-marketeers closed in upon the soldiers again. At the next stall Dicky hunkered down to feign interest in piles of old brass and copper oddments piled up for sale. I took the opportunity to look around. There was no sign of George anywhere.

'Look – umbrellas!' said Dicky, standing up and rubbing his knees, and then pointing to an old woman carrying dozens of them, of all shapes and sizes and colours. 'What did you pay for yours?' When I didn't reply, he said: 'Can you imagine those bloody soldiers selling their weapons! That's what comes of having all those races and nations mixed together. Thank God the British army could never sink to that.'

'The elder of them had four small kids, and his unit hasn't been paid for three months,' I said.

'I knew you'd find some excuse for them,' said Dicky in a voice that mixed jokiness with sincerity. 'Where do you draw the line, Bernard? If you hadn't been paid for three months, would you simply sell off anything you could lay your hands on?'

Knowing that a flippant answer would be stored up in Dicky's memory and used when I least expected it, I found something to occupy his mind: 'I think I see one of George's relatives,' I said.

'Where? Where?'

'Take it easy, Dicky. Or we'll start a stampede.'

'Selling the beads?'

'It's amber,' I said, 'and that can be expensive. But the leather bag round his neck almost certainly contains diamonds. He's a well-known dealer.'

'You know him?' Dicky slowed, as if intending to stride across the aisle to confront the old man, but I took his arm and kept him going.

'I saw him in London at one of George's cocktail parties. But I didn't speak with him; he arrived as I was leaving. He's rich; leave him for another time. Appearances are deceptive in Poland; there are probably quite a few rich people in this market today.'

'And are George Kosinski's family all rich?' Dicky stopped at a stall piled high with sports shoes: Nike, Reebok and all the famous brands in cardboard boxes. It was hard to know whether they were counterfeit or imports. Dicky picked up a pair of running shoes and fiddled with the laces while trying to decide.

'I don't know, but names ending in ski denote the old Polish gentry. It's especially so in the country areas, where everyone knows everyone and you can't get away with adding a ski ending to your name, the way so many of the townspeople have.'

'I like the padded ankle collar ... What have you seen?' He started to replace the shoes he was inspecting.

'Keep hold of that pair of shoes, Dicky. Bring them up before your face and admire them.' I was moving round to the other side of the market stall to see better.

'Look, Bernard ...'

'Do as I say, Dicky. Just keep talking and holding up the shoes.' He held them up for me and provided an excuse for a good look at the far side of the market.

'What's happening?'

'Three of them; at least three. With maybe two or three more watching from other top-storey windows. They've marked us, and two of them are coming this way.'

'Who?'

'Hoodlums. Just take it easy. Stay stumm; let me talk to them.'

'Where?'

'The fat fellow in the fur coat signalled to someone at an upstairs window. Bodyguards. Minders. Stay cool.'

'Your papers?' demanded the first of the men to arrive, and announced himself: 'Inspector Was of the UB.' He spoke in English while showing me a card with his photo on it. He snapped the card closed and put it away. His eyes were jet-black, his face thin and drawn. He wore a woollen hat and a short leather jacket. I held out to him the West German passport that carried the business visa permitting repeated entries into Poland. He passed it to a fat man in a dark fur coat who had by this time arrived slightly flushed and out of breath. The fat one pushed his steel-rimmed glasses tighter on to his ears before reading it. He was red-faced and sweating. I guessed he had impetuously descended too many flights of steps after watching our arrival from his vantage-point in the nearby tenements.

'Him?' said the wiry Inspector Was, pointing at Dicky.

'Him?' I echoed, pointing a finger at the fat man and gently prising from his fingers my bogus passport.

'Search them,' Was told the fat man. I held up my arms and he frisked me, and then Dicky, to see if we were carrying guns.

'Come with me,' said Was when the fat man gave him the okay. 'Both of you.' He unbuttoned his jacket as if he might be making ready to reach for a pistol.

'We have to go with them, Dicky,' I said.

The somewhat Laurel-and-Hardyish pair pushed us ahead of them through the crowds, which parted readily to allow us to pass. As we got into Targowa, our two guards closed in tightly upon us. The streets were crowded with beggars and pedlars and people going about their business. At the kerb, two men were changing the wheel of a truck heavily laden with beets, while a man with a shotgun sat atop them balanced on a bundle of sacks. No one gave us more than a glance. It was too cold to enquire too deeply into the misfortunes of others, and too dangerous. There were no cops in sight and no one showed concern as we were escorted along the street. We had gone no more than fifty yards before the thin one signalled to an entrance that led into one of the open courtyards that were a feature of these buildings.

The cobbled yard, littered with rusty junk and rubbish that could not be burned for fuel, held a couple of cars and a line of large garbage bins. It was difficult to decide if the cars were in use or had been dumped here, for many of the trucks and cars on the street were even more rusty and dented than these ancient vehicles.

'Here,' said Was and prodded me with his finger. The fabric of the building was in a startling state of neglect, with gaping holes and broken brickwork and windows that were held in position by improvised patchworks of timber and tin. The only fitments in good order were the bars and grilles that fitted over half a dozen of the lower windows, and the ancient steel door through which we were ushered.

There were more grilles inside. They were made from steel and fitted from floor to ceiling. Along this 'wall' there was a long table, like the lunch counter of a roadside cafe. Behind the counter there was a heavy safe and some filing cabinets. The other half of the room – the part where we were standing – was windowless and empty of furnishings except for a calendar advertising canned milk.

The man who called himself Was closed the steel door that led to the yard. With only a couple of fluorescent tubes to illuminate the room it became stark and shadowless. 'Through here and upstairs,' said Was. He opened a door and pushed us into a smaller room. 'Upstairs,' said Was again, and we went through a narrow door that opened on to the lobby of a grand old apartment house. I led the way up the wide marble staircase. On the landing wall hung two grey racks of dented mail-boxes. Some of the flaps were hanging open; it would need a great deal of confidence to put mail into them. Perhaps the whole building was owned by these men. At the top of the second flight of steps we came upon a silent tableau. Two flashy young women were propping a plump well-dressed man against the wall. He was white-faced and very drunk, his tie loosened and wine stains down his crisp white shirt. The trio watched us as we passed, as curious about us as we were about them, but the three of them remained very still at the sight of our escorts and no one spoke.

'In here.' There were two doors on the top landing. They were freshly painted light brown. They'd been repainted so many times that the decorations in the woodwork, the peephole and the bell push were all clogged with paint. There was a surfeit of wiring too: phone and electricity wires had been added and none ever removed, so that there were dozens of wires twisted and drooping and sometimes hanging to show where a section of them had been chopped away to make room for more. He unlocked one of the doors. 'In here,' he said again and pushed Dicky, who fell against me. And we stumbled into the darkness.

'Stand against the wall,' said Was. He switched on the light. It was a low-wattage bulb but it gave enough light to see that one side of the room had sandbags piled up to a height of six feet or more. Was slipped out of his pea-jacket and hung it on the door. This revealed him to be wearing a dark blue sweater and a military-style leather belt with a pistol in a leather holster. It was a Colt 'Official Police .38', something of a museum piece but no less lethal for that. 'Hand over your wallets, both of you bastards,' he said. The fat one stood by and grinned.

'I don't think you are police,' said Dicky. 'And you can go to hell.'

'What you think doesn't concern me, shitface,' said Was, leaning forward and putting his face close to Dicky. 'Get out your wallet before I break you in two.'

It was now or never, I decided.

Hampered by my back-against-the-wall position, I put both hands high in the air and, so that the men were not frightened by this sudden movement, I said: 'Please don't hurt us. You can have all my money but please don't hurt us.'

Was began to reply as I brought my umbrella down to hit him on the side of the head. It landed with a terrible crunch and he slid to the floor with no more than a short choking sound and a guttural groan that ended as he lost consciousness.

I swung round but the fat man already had his fur coat open wide and was tugging at an automatic pistol that was tucked into his waistband. I watched the gun coming up to point at me as I brought my umbrella round to hit him. It was like one of those agonizingly slow nightmares from which you awaken in a body-drenching sweat. Inch by inch our arms moved in balletic slow motion until his gun fired, making a deafening cannon's roar in the tiny room. As the flash of the gun came, my arm brought the umbrella up under the fat man's jaw. His jawbone snapped and his glasses jumped off his face and flew across the room, spinning and flashing with reflected light.

The fat man dropped his gun and slumped back against the wall. Both his hands clasped his face as he supported his jaw, and I could see him screaming soundlessly as my ears still rang with the sound of the gun. I hit him a second blow, and this time he toppled to the floor with his eyes closed. His cheeks bulged and a tiny drip of blood came from the corner of his tightly closed mouth.

'Jesus Christ,' said Dicky from behind me, but then I saw that Fatty was not out of play. He was scrabbling around on the floor reaching for his gun. I kicked him and then kicked him again, but my kicking had little effect on him through his thick fur coat, so that I had to use the umbrella to hit him again. I was only just in time. His fingers were touching the gun as my blow landed. Perhaps I hit him too hard: his head slumped sideways, his mouth opened and a torrent of bright red blood spilled over the rag-strewn floor.

For a moment Dicky was frozen. He had his hands clasped tightly together as if holding something that might escape. Or praying. He was looking down at the two unconscious men. 'My God. Are they cops?' he said.

'Who cares?' I said. 'They were going to kill us, or didn't you follow the conversation? This is a killing room. The sandbags make sure the rounds don't end up next door, and the rags on the floor mop up the blood.'

I bent down and started to search the bodies. It was a hasty job. After comparing the two pistols that the men had been using, I took the thin one's Colt revolver, rather than Fatty's Model 35 Browning. The Colt fitted my pocket better.

'This isn't a police station?'

'Are you with me?' I said. 'The room downstairs is a money exchange. Hard currency for local cash. That's what the bars and shutters are for: to protect the money.' Having second thoughts, I picked up the Browning Hi-Power and took that too. It was a pity to leave it behind. He might come after us and shoot me with it. It was then that my fingers encountered a small .22 Ruger pistol in Fatty's inside overcoat pocket. With it, loose in his pocket, there was a screw-on silencer and half a dozen mini-magnum rounds. 'Know what these are, Dicky?' I asked, holding up the gun, the silencer and one of the rounds for him to see.

'Yes,' he said.

'There's only one thing you do with a silenced Ruger twenty-two and a mini-mag round. One shot into the back of the neck is all you need. It's a gun these people keep for executions, and for nothing else.' I had no doubt now about why they'd brought us here.

'What shall we do?' said Dicky plaintively as he looked out of the barred window and down at the empty courtyard. He didn't look round the room or look at me. He didn't want to see the gun and the inert men. He didn't want to even think about it.

'I'll finish searching these bastards and we'll get out of here.' I was bending over them and taking their money and stuffing into my pocket their various identity documents. I got to my feet and sighed. Having Dicky along to help was like being accompanied by a pet goldfish: I had to sprinkle food over him regularly, and check his fins for fungus.

'Are they dead?' He wasn't frightened or sorrowful; he just wanted to know what to write in his report. I would have to find some way of preventing Dicky writing a report. London hated to hear about the grim realities of the job; they believed that firm words and two choruses of 'Rule Britannia' should be enough to bring any recalcitrant foreigner to his knees.

'I don't give a shit, Dicky.' Reluctantly I decided that life in Warsaw was safer without a gun. I pushed all three pistols into the rubbish bin. I could tackle freelance heavies like these, but the resources of the boys from the UB were rather more sophisticated, and I didn't fancy trying to explain away a pocket full of hardware if I was stopped in the street.

'That's not an umbrella,' said Dicky suddenly as he watched me rewrapping tyre levers into the umbrella's fabric from which I'd removed the wires and stays.

'No,' I said. 'It's a good thing it didn't rain.'

3

Masuria, Poland.

Dicky was silent for much of the time we were driving north through the wintry Polish countryside to find Stefan Kosinski's country mansion. I could tell he was thinking about the encounter with the two men in the market. It had not been pretty, and Dicky had seldom glimpsed the rotten end of the business. All field agents soon learn that the pen-pushers in London don't want to be told about the spilled blood and the nasty treacherous ways that their will is done. With undeniable logic Dicky said: 'We can't be *absolutely* certain they intended to kill us.'

'To be *absolutely* certain they were going to kill us,' I said, 'we would have to be dead.'

Three times – in various ways – Dicky had asked me if the two men were dead. I told him that it was a special sort of glancing blow I'd given them, and assured him they would have woken thirty minutes later with no more than a slight headache and a dry feeling in the mouth. Offended by this attempt to comfort him, Dicky went back to staring out of the car window. The dirt road was too bumpy for him to chew on his fingernails.

The roads were bad, pot-holes and ridges jolting the car to the point of damage whenever we were tempted to put on speed. Most of the villages we passed seemed empty and deserted but here and there peasants were to be seen scavenging for over-looked remains of bygone crops. As if in sentry boxes, roadside Holy Virgins stood guard in their wooden shrines, and often rows of dented tins held floral tribute to them.

We headed north-east to the region of the Masurian Lakes. It is a bleak province that nostalgic Germans like to call East Prussia. This low-lying corner of Poland would border on the Baltic Sea, except that the Russians had seized a slice of coast surrounding what once was called Königsberg, to create for themselves a curious little enclave with no other purpose than giving the Baltic Fleet a headquarters, a shipyard and a base for two Soviet air divisions.

The Masurian district, 'the land of a thousand lakes', is a photographer's paradise. Its lakes, forests and primitive villages are charming, the sunrises idyllic, the sunsets sublime. But the camera does not adequately record the hordes of flies, the bites of the mosquitoes, the fetid marshland and dark decaying forests, the smelly squalor of the villages or the icy cold that whitened the land.

For his war against Russia, Hitler built an extensive military headquarters in huts and bunkers here near Ketrzyn in Masuria. Ketrzyn was called Rastenburg in those days, but Hitler preferred to call it 'the Wolf's Lair' and decreed that a monument should be created there to mark the place where he'd created a New World Order. Hitler departed, the monument created itself and real wolves came to live in it. The eight-metre-thick walls are now just chunks of broken masonry, the wooden huts are rotting firewood, the barbed wire has rusted to red powder and a few still-active minefields lurk along the perimeter.

'What a place to be in the middle of winter,' said Dicky suddenly, as if he'd been thinking about it.

'In summer it's worse,' I said.

'Not another road check.'

71

We were halted on the road, not once but three times. The first time it was cops. Six bored policemen occupying a road-block, checking everyone's identity and giving special attention to car papers. They inspected our rented Fiat as if they'd never seen one before. I suppose there wasn't a great deal of traffic on that road.

Twenty-five miles onwards we were stopped by three soldiers in combat dress. They were Polish military police standing in the snow outside a large property that in long-ago capitalist days had been a roadside inn. One of them, a senior NCO, was armed with an AK-47, its butt and metal parts shiny with wear. It remained slung over his shoulder while he questioned us. Our foreign passports seemed to satisfy him, although they made us get out of the car and held us for half an hour while the NCO made telephone calls and a procession of horse-drawn carts trundled past, their occupants staring at us with polite curiosity.

A short distance further on we came to the beginning of miles of tall chain-link fencing. Our road ran alongside the fence past a dozen doleful-looking Soviet soldiers guarding six large signs that said 'no photography' in Polish, German and Russian. It was a Soviet army base extending five miles along the road. The wooden barrack huts were unheated, judging by the patches of snow that had collected on the roofs and the men going in and out of them, all of whom were bundled into overcoats and scarfs. Behind the huts I could see long rows of armoured personnel carriers, some fitted with bulldozer blades and others with 'barricade remover' grilles on the front. There were two tracked missile-launchers and sixteen elderly tanks, some of which were being repaired and maintained by soldiers in greasy black coveralls.

Perhaps, further back in the tank hangars, and out of sight, there were air-launched tactical missiles, attack helicopters or other vehicles and equipment suited for a combat-ready brigade charged to dash westwards through Germany and engage the NATO forces in battle. But I couldn't see any sign of it. And the way in which this amount of anti-riot equipment was parked, and arranged so that it could be seen from the road, made me think that these Russian occupiers were troops relegated to internal security operations, and that their presence served no other purpose than being a tacit reminder to the Poles that the brotherly patience of the Soviet Union and its fraternal Leninist rulers should not be tested too hard.

We followed the road and passed the grandiose main entrance of the compound. There was a cinder-block guard-hut with sentry boxes and sentries in ill-fitting uniforms and moth-eaten fur caps. The main gate was surmounted by an elaborate cere-monial arch, topped with a golden hammer and sickle. Lovingly emblazoned on the arch there were the badges of two Guards and three Pioneer regiments, and lists of their battle honours. But the red paint had faded to a dull pink, and the gold had tar-nished to brown. The hammer's paint had cracked and chipped to reveal a green undercoat, the sickle had lost its sharp tip and the crack regiments were no longer living here. Instead the youthful sentries lolling against the fencing were unmistakably draftees, stocky little village boys with spotty faces and wide eyes, with elderly senior NCOs to breathe vodka fumes over them, and not an officer in sight anywhere. I waved at them and they stared back at me with not a flicker of recognition or emotion of any kind.

'It will be dark soon,' said Dicky. 'Perhaps we should look for somewhere to spend the night.'

'Marriott or Hyatt or Holiday Inn?' I asked.

'There must be somewhere.'

'There's that place where we saw the men selling sugar-beet.'

Dicky bit his lip and looked worried.

'We'll find the Kosinski place before dark,' I said, more in order to relieve Dicky's evident anxiety than because there was any reason to believe it.

We reached a T-junction devoid of any direction signs. Rather than consult with Dicky, a process which would have made him even more despondent, I swung to the left as if I knew where I was going. Very low on the flat horizon I suddenly saw a blood-red splinter of the dying sun. Then, from below the horizon, it spread blood and gore across the clouds, and the trees veined an ever darkening overcast. The road deteriorated until there was little sign of anything more than a few deep-rutted cart-tracks frozen hard enough to jolt us from side to side. It was darker now that the sun had gone and the shadowy spruce and beech joined to become a murky wall.

It was at this time that Dicky broke a long pensive silence. 'I have a feeling,' said Dicky. 'I have a feeling we're very near to the Kosinski place.'

My heart sank. 'That's good, Dicky,' I said.

'They said there was a forest,' said Dicky.

'That's good,' I said again, rather than point out that half the Polish hinterland was forest. As sundown brought a lowering of temperature, icy rain began, speeding up so that it was hitting the windscreen where the wipers whisked it into slush and threw it from one side to the other.

Twice that afternoon we had taken a wrong turning to follow roads that became trails, and then tracks and finally petered out altogether. This path promised to be leading to another such fiasco, with all the worry of turning the car round without getting bogged down and ensnared in tree roots, pot-holes or ditches.

'Careful. There are men in the road,' said Dicky. In Warsaw we'd been warned that after dark sentries opened fire on vehicles that were slow to respond to halt commands. 'Another road-block.'

This time it was half a dozen civilians who blocked the narrow road in front of our car. There was no avoiding them, the forest was too dense to drive round them. A Volkswagen van was parked under the trees, and more men stood there.

These armed civilians provided a sign of the confusion, bordering on anarchy, that Poland suffered that winter. Out in the rural areas it was clear that men were reverting to some primitive form of post-feudal mercantilism. Goods and services were exchanged in small transactions that did nothing beyond providing for a few days of subsistence at a time. Such societies seldom welcome strangers. I stopped the car.

'Where are you going?' He spoke Polish, his accent so thick that it took me a moment to understand.

'To the castle,' I said. It was a tourist spot that would account for our foreign passports. I didn't want to say we were looking for the Kosinski house.

'The road is blocked.' He was the leader, a big red-faced man with an unruly black beard, a lumpy overcoat and fur hat; an angry peasant from a Brueghel painting. He carried a shotgun in his hands, a bandolier of cartridges slung across his shoulder. The others held spades and pickaxes.

The clouds were scurrying away to reveal some stars and a moon but the sleet was still falling. It dribbled down his face like snot, but in his fur hat the same icy driblets sparkled like diamonds.

'We're looking for Stefan Kosinski,' said Dicky in English. I'd told him to leave the talking to me, but Dicky was incapable of remaining silent in any kind of confrontation.

Blackbeard replied in German, good fluent German: 'Who are you? What do you want here? Show me on the map where you are headed.'

Dicky pointed a long bony finger at me. 'George Kosinski's brother-in-law,' he explained slowly in his schoolboy German, uttering one word at a time.

'Switch off the engine,' said Blackbeard. I did so. With the headlights extinguished the scene was lit by hazy blue moonlight. He pulled a whistle from his pocket and gave two short blasts on it then turned to watch one of his comrades leaning through the open side-door of the VW van. There were faded bouquets painted on its panels, and the name and address of a Hamburg florist shop just discernible. I could see the butts of rifles and assault guns piled inside the van. With our engine switched off all was silent: the forest soaking up every sound of movement. We sat there like that for two or three minutes. Dicky availed himself of the opportunity to chew his fingernail. A man in a short plaid coat and patched jeans appeared from the forest, obviously in response to the signal. He was carrying a pickaxe over his shoulder and now, in a show of anger, he swung it so that its point was buried in the frozen ground. He glowered at everyone, then turned on his heel and was gone again. Suddenly there was the ear-wrenching noise of a two-stroke engine and he reappeared out of the gloomy forest riding a lightweight motor cycle. 'Follow him,' Blackbeard ordered.

The motor-cyclist leaned over dangerously as he swung round in front of the car, leaving a trail of black smoke. He roared up the track ahead of us. I started the car engine, the main beams picked him out and I followed him, driving cautiously over the pot-holed road. Behind us, two youths of indeterminate age followed on bicycles. Perhaps they had never seen a vehicle with lights before; an accessory not deemed indispensable in rural Poland.

The narrow road led over a rise and passed close to a small lake; grey crusts of ice along its rim. A rowing boat had been pulled out of the water on to a pier, and left inverted to drain. Our appearance, and the noise of the motor cycle, sent dozens of birds into the air with a thunderous clattering of wings and shrill cries. They circled low over the water and then came back to earth in a circuit that seemed more like a practised gesture of protest than a sign of fear.

Immediately beyond the tiny lake there was the Kosinski property. I had seen it in George's family photos. Behind the house, framing it against the dark sky, there was a line of beech-trees, giant growths reaching about a hundred feet into the sky. Nicely spaced, their massive boughs stretched out like giants linking hands. The rambling property had once been a grand mansion; a typical dwelling of the minor nobility, the class that the Poles called *szlachta*. When George's parents had fled penniless to England, other relatives had tenaciously held on to this mansion and preserved it as a family dwelling while other such houses were seized by socialist reformers. The main building was big and, despite its run-down condition, it retained a certain grandeur. Only a few of the windows were lit. Through the fuzzy glass I saw a shadowy interior and the mellow glow of oil-lamps.

Light from the windows made patterns and revealed a path describing a circle round an ornamental stone fountain. The fountain was drained, and the stone maidens standing between two slumbering lions were wrapped in newspapers, and neatly tied with heavy string, to protect them against frost. Two more stone lions stood guard each side of the steps that led up to the front door, while above the entrance a pediment was supported by four columns. The overall mood of dereliction was endorsed by the tattered remains of several storks' nests, abandoned by those free to seek warmer sojourn.

'I was right,' said Dicky triumphantly. 'It's the Kosinski place isn't it?'

'Yes, Dicky. You were right.'

'People are always telling me I have a sixth sense: *Fingerspitzge-fühl* – intuition, eh?'

'Yes,' I said. 'Fingertip sensitivity. It's what safe-crackers and pickpockets have too.'

'Very bloody funny,' said Dicky, his usual sense of humour failing him.

We parked our rented Fiat at the side of the house where a long wooden veranda would in summer provide a shelter against the sun. Behind the house there were various coach-houses and stables and other outbuildings arranged around a wide cobbled courtyard. By the dim light of the moon a couple of youthful servants could be seen there pumping water from a well and clearing up, having finished washing a horse-drawn carriage that was obviously still in regular use. Horses poked their heads out of stable doors to watch them. Which aspect of this rural scene could have stirred Boris's literary memories – of Chekhovian stage-sets lit by golden spotlights – was not easily recognized in this harsh moonlit winter setting. As a literary reference, Solzhenit-syn's gulag came more readily to mind.

Alerted by the approach of our noisy cavalcade, two women in aprons emerged from a side-door and stood on the covered wooden deck that formed one side of the house. The front door also opened. We parked the car, went up the steps and were greeted politely and ushered inside by a seemingly unsurprised man in a dark suit, stiff collar and plain tie, who used accentless German to announce his name as Karol, and his position as Stefan Kosinski's secretary.

A maid closed the door behind us and the hallway was darkened. I looked around. Glinting in the moonlight that came from an upstairs window, there were on every wall trophies of the hunt; so many furry, feathered, horned and melancholy heads that there was little space between them. A wide staircase gave access to a balcony over the front door and then continued to the upper floor where more inanimate beasts were displayed.

From somewhere far away came the sound of a piano playing a simple melody, and the high reedy voice of a young girl singing.

'Herr Samson and Herr Cruyer?' said the secretary, as a maidservant hurried forward with an oil-lamp. Now that we were more closely illuminated, the man looked quizzically from one to the other of us. I must have looked just as quizzically at him, for Dicky and I were both travelling on false passports, and had not used our real names anywhere since arriving in Poland.

'I'm Cruyer,' announced Dicky. 'How did you know?' The piano and the singing ended suddenly. Footsteps ran lightly across the upstairs floorboards and a child's head appeared and gazed solemnly down at us for a minute before disappearing again.

'You were expected, sir,' said the secretary, switching to English. 'You both were. Mr Stefan has been called away – a domestic problem. Madame is with him. They will join you tomorrow evening.'

'We are looking for Mr George Kosinski,' said Dicky.

'Perhaps Mr George too. Shall I show you your rooms? May I have your car keys? I will have your bags brought in.' Karol was a thin stiff-backed fellow, with an unnaturally pale face and bloodless lips. His hair was cut short and he wore very functional glasses with gun-metal rims. Adding this Teutonic appearance to his somewhat unconvincing deferential manner left the effect of a German general pretending to be a waiter.

Karol went to the front door, opened it and made a signal with his hand. After spasmodic bursts of engine noise, the motor-cyclist lurched forward and made a tight circle around a patch of land that in summer might become a front lawn. Then he roared away in a cloud of foul-smelling exhaust fumes. The two youths on bicycles followed him and were soon swallowed by the gloomy forest.

He closed the door and picked up an oil-lamp. We followed him slowly, Karol, and the wooden stairs, both creaky and arthritic. We stepped carefully around a large collection of potted plants which had been brought in from the front balcony for winter, and now occupied most of the staircase. Upstairs he took us to the far end of the corridor and held the light while we looked inside a bathroom. It echoed with the sound of a dripping tap and there were long rust stains patterning its tub. The faint smell of mildew that pervaded the house was at its strongest here, where the warm air from the boiler no doubt promoted its growth. Each side of the bathroom – and with access to it – there were our bedrooms. My window overlooked the forest that came close to the rear of the house. Immediately under this window there was the wooden roof that sheltered the long veranda along the side of the house. Cloud was draped across the vague shape of the moon but there was still enough light to see the veranda steps, and a well-used path led to a woodshed and a fenced space where half a dozen garbage bins were imprisoned. They were tall containers with stout metal clips to hold the lids on tight, the sort of bins needed in regions where wild animals come foraging for food after dark.

Under the supervision of Karol a young manservant came struggling under the weight of our cases. We watched him as he lit all the oil-lamps and then arranged our baggage. A long-case clock in the hallway downstairs struck nine. The secretary announced gravely that we should gather in the drawing-room in time to go in to dinner at ten o'clock. He looked at me. I looked at Dicky. Dicky said we'd be there.

Once we were alone Dicky said softly: 'So he is here! George Kosinski. You were right, Bernard, you bastard! You were right.' He groaned and sat down on his cotton crochet bedcover, pulled off his cowboy boots and tossed them into the corner.

'We'll see,' I told him. 'We'll see what happens.'

'What a place! Where's Baron Frankenstein, what? There must be fifty rooms in this heap.' The house was big, but fifty rooms was the sort of exaggeration that expressed Dicky's pleasure or excitement; or merely relief at not having to spend the night on the road.

'At least fifty,' I said. It was better not to correct him; Dicky called it nit-picking.

'I wonder if the whole house is as cold as this. I need a hot shower,' said Dicky, rubbing his hair and looking at the dirt on his hand. He went and inspected the bathroom and grabbed the only large towel. Then, with the towel over his arm, he bolted the door that led to my bedroom. 'Driving on those cart-track roads leaves you coated in filth.' He said it as if adding to the world's scientific knowledge; as if I might have arrived at the house aboard a cruise ship.

I went to my room and unpacked. Having taken possession of the bathroom Dicky could be heard whistling and singing above the sounds of fast-running water. I opened the doors of the wardrobe and looked in all the more obvious places in which a microphone might be concealed. As part of this exploratory round I tried the door to the bathroom, and it opened to reveal a second door. In this space, the thickness of the wall, someone had left cleaning things: a mop and a broom, a packet of detergent and tins of floor polish. It was I suppose an obvious place to store such things. Scented steam came from the bathroom and Dicky's voice was louder. I closed the door quietly. The provision of hot water was encouraging, for this seemed to be a mansion without many of those utilities taken for granted in the West. No electricity supply was in evidence. The elaborate brass electric-light fittings and parchment shades were dusty and tarnished, and had clearly not worked for many years. The equally ancient paraffin lamps, one each side of my bed, were clean and bright, their carefully trimmed wicks giving a mellow light without smoke.

I looked around my room. There was only one window, the upper part of which consisted of leaded panels of stained-glass, artistically depicting some of the more savage episodes of the Old Testament. The room was made more gloomy by the panelling, the heavy carved furniture and an embroidered rug with folk-art designs, that hung against the wall alongside the bed. Arranged facing towards the bed – as if for visitors in a sickroom – were two large armchairs with upholstery from which horsehair stuffing emerged in tufts, like unwanted hair in depilatory advertisements. Upon a glass-fronted bookcase there was an antique clock – silent and still – and an ashtray from the Waldorf in Paris. There was a case of dusty unread travel books dating from the long-ago days when Poles were free to travel, and a threadbare oriental carpet; the sort of once-cherished objects that were relegated to the guest-rooms of grand houses. The only picture on the wall was a lithograph, an idealized profile portrait of Lenin, his bearded chin jutting out in what might be construed as a gesture of foolhardy provocation. Directly under the picture, on the chest of drawers, there was a tray covered with a linen cloth. Under the cloth I discovered a china teapot, a tin of Earl Grey tea from Twinings in London and a cup and saucer. Stefan Kosinski was seemingly a man who didn't encourage his guests to join him for breakfast. The large wood-fired white porcelain stove in the corner was warm to the touch. Everything was ready. Who, I wondered, had foreseen our imminent arrival? And what other preparations awaited us?

There was something contrived about the formality with which dinner was served in this remote country house. Poland's *szlachta* had always been the bulwark against social changes, both good and bad. No doubt such meals served by maidservants were a way for the Kosinski family to distinguish themselves from villagers, some of whom might in these days of black-market boom be making more money than their betters. It was an appropriately formal gathering. Karol presided as if a delegate of his master. Stefan's elderly Uncle Nico and Aunt Mary took their seats either side of him. Aunt Mary was a cheery granny of the sort that the Poles called *Babcas*. When we first entered the drawing-room it was she who got up from the sofa to greet me. Having tucked her needlework into a basket that she carried with her almost everywhere, she smoothed her skirt with both hands and smiled. Karol the secretary introduced me. Aunt Mary said: 'How do you do?' in perfectly accented English. Those were the only perfectly accented English words I ever heard her use.

Her husband Uncle Nico was frail; a thin white-faced man with yellow teeth and a cane to support himself as he walked. He was wearing a hand-knitted shawl over a dark, well-tailored suit that was shiny with wear. 'You've come to visit Stefan?' Uncle Nico asked in good English. He inhaled on a cigarette, having first flicked ash into an ashtray which he carried with him. It was already loaded with ash and butts. His face was chalky white and his eyes large with the stare that comes with old age. I remembered the stories George had told me, and I knew that this was the man who had adopted Stefan when George's parents escaped; his father just a few steps away from arrest and charges of being an agitator and class enemy.

'And to visit Mr George,' I reminded him. The room was cold, the ceiling too high for the elaborate tiled stove to make much difference, and I looked at Uncle Nico's shawl with ever-increasing envy.

'Oh, dear!' said Uncle Nico. '*Ach Weh!*' and from then onwards spoke in German.

Dicky's entrance was more considered than mine. He kissed Aunt Mary's hand in the approved Polish style. He smiled and, using a low resonant voice, did the warm-and-delightful-shy-young-man act that he used on anyone influential, infirm and over fifty. Dicky went to the stove and laid both hands on its top hopefully. Disappointed, he patted the sides of the stove and then felt its chimney. Finally he turned to us, smiled again and slapped his hands together, rubbing his arms to encourage circulation.

Through the partly open folding doors I caught sight of the dining-room and the polished mahogany table where cut glass, silver and starched linen had been arranged as if for a banquet. It looked promising; I was cold and hungry and the water hadn't warmed enough to provide a hot bath. Karol offered us a drink. It was potato vodka from Danzig or tap water. I decided upon vodka.

'Dinner,' announced Karol suddenly as if to a roomful of strangers.

As we went into the dining-room half a dozen more people – mostly young – quietly appeared and sat down at the table with us. Dicky's hot bath and a change of clothes had worked wonders upon him. Even before I had my napkin tucked into my collar, Dicky had found out that Uncle Nico was writing a book. He'd been working on it for more than twenty years, thirty years perhaps. It was a biography of Bishop Stanislaus, the Bishop of Cracow, who had been canonized in 1253 and became the patron saint of Poland.

With vivid movements of the hand and head, Uncle Nico related the story of the saint's death. According to Uncle Nico, King Boleslaw the Bold personally beheaded the bishop upon a tree-trunk, before having him chopped into pieces and dumped into a nearby pond. That was in 1079, since when pond, tree-trunk and saint have become unrivalled objects of pilgrimages.

Dicky nodded and told us that the mortal remains of Saint Stanislaus are to be found in the Wawel Royal Cathedral in

Cracow. Dicky had discovered this in a guidebook he'd been reading in the car. Showered with praise for displaying this knowledge he smiled modestly, as if keeping some succulent morsels about the doings of Saint Stanislaus to himself. My vodka finished, I picked up the cut-glass tumbler and its contents: water. There was no wine in evidence; just tumblers of water, one at each place setting.

'When will the book be published?' Dicky asked.

Perhaps the book would never be finished said Aunt Mary. But it did not matter. The writing of the book was essential to the household, and indeed to the nearby village. She spoke of the book, as everyone was to do, in a hushed and respectful voice. Each night Uncle Nico told his family assembled round the dinnertable some aspect of the book that he felt they should know. Often this was something they had all heard many times, but that did not matter. All that mattered was that a long and seemingly important book about Poland's medieval history was being written in this house, and they were all sharing the glory of it.

A young servant girl in a black dress and starched frilly apron served vegetable soup from a large chinaware tureen, measuring each ladleful with care. It took a long time.

The dining-room was memorable for the large stuffed, and somewhat moulted, bird of prey that, cantilevered from the wall, seemed about to swoop upon the table. It was a huge creature, about six feet from tattered wing-tip to wing-tip, with realistic glass eyes and open beak. The flickering candles encouraged the illusion that it was alive. Residents no doubt soon grew accustomed to dining under the sharp talons of this menacing creature, but I noticed Dicky glancing up at it apprehensively while the soup was being served, as I admit I did too.

'Did you read the Premier's speech?' Uncle Nico asked the assembled diners, tapping the weekly newspaper that was jutting from his coat pocket. When no one replied he repeated his question, holding his head to one side and fixing us, one after the other, with his glassy stare.

Still no one replied until I told him, no, I hadn't.

'More reforms,' he said. 'Capitalism mixed with socialism.'

'Is that good?' Dicky asked, smiling.

'Is champagne good when mixed with prussic acid?' the old man asked sarcastically. Dicky didn't answer. Uncle Nico drank some water. Someone at the other end of the table picked up a basket of roughly sliced bread and passed it around.

Karol tore up his thick slice of dark bread and dropped pieces of it into the fruity vinegar-flavoured vegetable soup. While doing this he said: 'There will be no reforms; the Soviet Union will prevent Poland making reforms.'

'By invading us?' said Aunt Mary.

'Why invade us? The Kremlin have already made sure that apparatchiks have the key positions in Poland. Their job is to block or sabotage all meaningful reforms here. They will say yes and do nothing. In that way the men in the Kremlin can sleep soundly.'

It seemed to be the accepted view, for no one argued; they just drank their soup. In the Soviet Union, Mikhail Gorbachev had come to power. The optimists in Warsaw were saying that the men in the Kremlin were too concerned with their own troubles to wield Soviet military power against their neighbours as belligerently as once they had done. But Mikhail Gorbachev, for all his posturing, was a dedicated Marxist, and, as we had seen on the road from Warsaw, he had his soldiers discreetly positioned should he decide the Poles were changing things too quickly. So the going was slow. Uncle Nico sighed deeply, and in that way that families communicate without speech, a sudden mood of resignation followed the exchange. Or was it a reluctance to speak frankly in front of the servants?

'Art is long,' proclaimed Dicky encouragingly. 'Life is short, opportunity ...'

Before Dicky could continue with this provocative display of classical learning, Uncle Nico interjected: 'The Premier? The communists? These are the people who suppressed Dostoevsky!'

As if heading off a diatribe, Aunt Mary picked up a small porcelain bell and jingled it loudly as a signal for the soup dishes to be cleared. From upstairs there came the sudden sound of the piano. The technique was the same as the afternoon performance: Chopin played with precision. But again it was given a slow deliberate tempo that marred its graceful melodies.

The main course was stewed cabbage with flecks of bacon hiding in it. Even the privileged, with all the countryside to forage, did not eat meat on a regular basis.

'It's getting better,' said Dicky, investigating the cabbage suspiciously with his fork. 'The generals are becoming more tolerant towards Solidarity aren't they?'

Uncle Nico snorted. 'Because in some parts of the country *Solidarnosc* branch leaders advertise their meetings and hold them, and no one gets arrested? Is that what you've been told? Don't believe the newspapers. Only the ineffective groups are tolerated. Hardnosed *Solidarnosc* activists remain in prison. Anyone talking of strikes or demonstrations is likely to disappear forever.'

Karol the secretary asked for the salt to be passed to him. He did it in such a manner that Uncle Nico began eating and said no more. The plates were soon emptied and the maidservant brought the next course: crepes with stewed apple.

'The generals and the Party leaders are paralysed by indecision,' said Karol, adding to the conversation for the first time. 'But the army has a tricky course to steer between Moscow's tanks and the Solidarity hotheads.' His voice was moderate, as if hoping to calm Uncle Nico's temper. 'Do you know how much cash Poland owes to the Western banks? It's alarming. And rising higher and higher every minute. Who will lend us more?'

87

'We'll manage,' said Uncle Nico defensively.

'No one,' said the secretary in answer to his own question. 'Finally we shall invite the Russians to occupy us. We will need their oil and grain. It will be our only way out of this economic mess. That, or we will starve to death.'

'I say we'll manage,' repeated Uncle Nico.

'You don't buy the food and run the house,' said the secretary earnestly. 'This week again the dairy men from the village went to Warsaw, selling their soft cheeses from the back of a truck. They won't sell to local people any more; in Warsaw people will pay in American dollars or pounds or German marks. All the hard cheeses disappeared months ago. Our pickled vegetables are already almost eaten. Our apples have all been stolen. These are almost the last of them.' He mashed the stewed apple with his fork as if angry with it.

'You shouldn't have traded those apples,' said Uncle Nico.

'For paraffin oil? What would we do without light?'

'When they saw the apples, they knew where to come and help themselves,' said Uncle Nico.

The secretary would not be distracted from his woe. 'This winter will see starvation and ruin right across the land. Disease will follow. It could destroy the whole of Europe, and perhaps the world.'

We all looked at him. The candlelight flickered across his face. The Poles have a style of melancholy that is entirely their own. Russian melancholy breathes vodka fumes; Scandinavian melancholy is masochistic. Austrian melancholy is entirely operatic, while German melancholy is disguised self-pity. But Polish melancholy is a world-embracing philosophy impervious to cheer.

Beyond him, and through the window, I could see the dark forest. Now flickering lights amongst the trees revealed the approach of men with a handcart. They were carrying flashlights. Karol turned his head to see what had caught my attention. By this time the two callers had approached close enough to the windows to be lit by the lamps in the drawing-room.

'Men from the village. They are delivering meat,' explained the secretary, as if this was the normal time for meat deliveries in this part of the world. I nodded.

Aunt Mary got to her feet and rang her bell and ordered that coffee should be taken to the drawing-room. The young people who had joined us for the meal slipped away without a word. In the drawing-room I tried to secure a seat near the stove but I was too late, Aunt Mary got it. A servant set the coffee tray before her and she poured it from a huge silver pot. The maid-servant took the cups, one by one, to each of us and offered us canned milk and sugar. Uncle Nico put two level teaspoons of sugar into his tiny cup of black coffee, measuring them with the exaggerated care a pharmacist might devote to mixing a dangerous sleeping draught for a valued customer. Then he stirred furiously and watched the whirlpool slow before sipping some and burning his lip.

'It is made with boiling water, you old fool,' said Aunt Mary in low and rapid Polish, an admonition clearly not intended for our ears.

He nodded without looking at her and turning to me said: 'They've found a body.' Absent-mindedly he spoke in Polish.

'I beg your pardon?' I said.

'The body. Didn't they tell you?' He tutted as if at some inexcusable lapse of good manners. 'Didn't they tell you they are digging up a corpse? It's why they are out there.'

I looked at Karol the secretary. He had declined coffee and had moved his chair closer to the stove. With one arm resting on the back of the sofa he could actually walk his fingertips along the warm white porcelain, and this he did. As if totally occupied with warming his fingers he made no reaction to the old man's startling revelation.

89

'No,' I said, 'I didn't know.' I drank some coffee. Speaking Polish is difficult for me; understanding it brings on a headache.

'What did he say?' Dicky asked me.

'Nothing,' I said. 'I'll tell you in a moment.'

'A body,' said Karol to Dicky in English. 'They are talking about a dead body. A copse ...' he corrected himself: 'A corpse.' Then he covered his mouth with his hand and burped.

'Oh,' said Dicky and smiled to hide his confusion.

'He might have stayed there for years,' said Uncle Nico. 'But the dog found him. About twenty metres off the forest path ... buried. But the dog found it. An arm. It's fresh.'

'That's Bazyliszek,' said Aunt Mary. 'That's the dog they take when they are looking for truffles.' She reached for my empty cup and poured me a second cup of coffee. It was very good coffee; very strong.

'A body?' I said without putting too much emotion into it.

'The ground is hard,' said Uncle Nico. 'Didn't you see the men at work when you arrived? When you asked the way.'

'Yes,' I said.

'They are always finding bodies,' said Aunt Mary calmly. She discovered a ball of wool on the floor. She picked it up and looked at it as if suspecting that it might belong to someone else, but eventually she put it in her work-basket. Everyone was watching her and waiting upon her words: 'Those woods are full of secrets,' she said. 'The Germans buried people there during the war. Mass graves. Jews, soldiers, villagers, gypsies ...'

'You silly old woman. This is nothing to do with the war,' said Uncle Nico.

Undeterred Aunt Mary continued: 'The partisans fought here. Thousands died. The remains of the old wartime encampments and bunkers and hideaways run right through our land.'

'I say it's not the war,' said Uncle Nico, puffing angrily at his cigarette.

'No,' agreed Aunt Mary, suddenly changing tack. 'It will be that girl Anna from the pig farm. She was pregnant. I could see it when she was in church the Sunday before she disappeared.'

'Be quiet, you foolish woman,' said Uncle Nico. 'She went to her cousin in Gdynia to have the baby. She writes letters home.'

'Letters! Rubbish! I say it's her. She's dead. Her father went to the next village and said prayers for her.'

'It's not the pig girl; it's a man,' said Uncle Nico. He looked at the secretary but Karol was staring at the floor.

'We will see tonight when they dig it up. They'll put it in the barn and the police will come,' Aunt Mary said. She opened her needlework basket, looked down to be sure everything was inside, and closed it again.

'Not tonight. The ground is as hard as rock,' said Uncle Nico. 'It will take a lot of digging.' He got to his feet and Aunt Mary got up too. They wished us goodnight and departed.

'Vodka?' the secretary asked.

'Not for me,' said Dicky. I shook my head. I was shivering with the cold. All I wanted was to get into bed and pull the blankets over me.

'I shall have one,' said Karol the secretary, getting to his feet very slowly. I suddenly realized he was very drunk. Some of the glasses at the dining-table had not contained water. He poured himself a large vodka. Standing propped against the sideboard, with the drink in hand, he said: 'Uncle Nicolaus is a fine old fellow: a fighter. Each year, on the anniversary of the uprising, he goes, together with a few old comrades, to stand in front of the Palace of the Republic at the place where he, and the rest of the patriots, descended into the sewers for the final act of the battle against the German beasts.' He sipped his drink. 'The police don't like that sort of celebration. One year they arrested all the survivors; they said they were a threat to public order.'

From upstairs the piano started again. This time it seemed to be a nocturne. 'Let me pour you a vodka? Perhaps you don't like the potato vodka. Pertsovka with the red and black pepper makes a good nightcap.'

'No, thanks,' I said. 'I have to keep a clear head for dreaming.' Karol shrugged and topped up his own drink. He had downed two more of them by the time I was half-way up the stairs. As I got to the door of my room I heard him trip over the walking-stick rack in the hall and get up cursing.

That night I took a long time getting off to sleep. Drinking strong black coffee keeps me awake at night nowadays. It's a sign of getting old, at least that's what Dicky says. He's two years younger than I am. He drinks a great deal of coffee and sleeps even during the daytime. As I was nursing my headache, and thinking about the family conversation, I heard soft deliberate footsteps along the corridor outside my room. It was someone in padded shoes, walking in a fashion that would minimize the sound. The steps halted outside my bedroom door. I reached for the flashlight, switched it on and looked at my wristwatch. It was ten past two in the morning. Instinctively I looked for something to use as a weapon but I had nothing except the metal flashlight. The footsteps went away, but in no more than three minutes they were back again. I visualized someone standing in the corridor and not moving, and tried to guess what they might be doing. Next there came a rumbling noise very close to my head. I sat up in bed and put my feet on the floor. There was a muted clang of metal and I jumped up in alarm only to hear the padded footsteps slowly moving off along the corridor again. I realized it was one of the servants putting a log into my stove. All the stoves were built so as to be fuelled from outside the rooms.

I remained awake for a long time after that. From the forest there were the cries of animals: foxes or wild dogs perhaps.

Once I fancied I heard the barking of wolves. Dogs locked in their kennels in the courtyard joined in the howling. Perhaps tomorrow George would come. Unless it was George they were digging up in the forest in the dark.

4

The Kosinski Mansion, Masuria, Poland.
The following day brought no further news of either George or Stefan Kosinski. I got up early and, having abandoned the effort of making a palatable pot of tea with the warm water delivered to my room, I went to the kitchen and ate porridge and drank coffee with the servants. Dicky didn't like porridge. He slept late and then went out to examine the vehicles in the coach-house. There were six of them. They included a sleigh – with hand-painted edelweiss and functioning jingle bells – a coach, a carriage and a pony trap, the last two in good condition and evidently in regular use. Apart from the car in which we had arrived, there were no motor vehicles to be seen except for the remains of a tractor which had been stripped bare for tyres and spare parts.

Dicky had heard a story about a young Dutch banker finding two vintage Bugattis in a barn not far from where we were. This Dutchman was said to have persuaded the farmer to exchange the priceless old cars for two modern Opels. I didn't believe the story but Dicky insisted that it was true, and the thought of it was never far from his mind. Several times on our journey from Warsaw I'd had to dissuade him from going to search likely-looking farm buildings for such treasures.

'Do you think the Russians will come?' Dicky asked me as I found him opening the door of a carriage and looking inside to see the amazing muddle of cobwebs.

'Invade? I don't know.'

Dicky closed the door, but the lock didn't engage until he tried three times, finally slamming the door of the carriage with enough force to shake the dust out of the springs. 'I don't want to find myself explaining my presence to some damned Russian army intelligence officer,' he said. 'And I don't want you here explaining yourself either.'

There was little I could say to that. It established Dicky's superiority in a way that required no elaboration. I reasoned that the danger was not imminent. My own guess was that the Soviets would order the Polish security forces to stage a mass round-up of every possible Polish odd-ball, opponent and dissident, before risking their infantry in the Warsaw streets, or even the open countryside. But it was better to let Dicky worry; he was a worrier by nature, and it kept him occupied and off my back.

I followed him as he walked to the far end of the coach-house where a trestle bench had been cleared. It was covered with clean newspaper, and there were three shiny black rubbish bags, empty, folded and ready, at one end.

'A body,' mused Dicky, picking up one of the plastic bags and putting it down again. 'That's all we needed.' He sneezed. 'I've picked up some sort of virus,' he said after wiping his nose on a large handkerchief.

'It's the dust,' I said.

'How I wish it was dust,' said Dicky with a brave smile. 'You're lucky; you don't get these damned allergies and suffer the way I do.'

'Yes,' I said. I could recognize the symptoms; Dicky had had enough of Polish austerity – hard beds, potato soup and chilly bedrooms – and now he was preparing to make his excuses and depart.

Dicky looked at his watch. 'Shall we go down to look at the digging? Everyone seems to have disappeared. Except that secretary fellow, he left the house at six-thirty this morning. It was scarcely light.' Dicky went out into the courtyard and stamped around on the cobbles. The sky had cleared in the night, and the temperature had dropped enough for the cold to sting my face and give Dicky a glittering pink complexion.

'You saw the secretary leaving?'

'On a horse. A beautiful hunter. Dressed up to the nines in riding breeches, polished boots and a hacking jacket, like some English country squire. He's a shifty sod, we must watch him.'

'And he hasn't returned yet?'

'I was checking the stables. The horse is not here. I wonder where the bastard's gone. He was very quiet last night, wasn't he? He was watching you like a hawk, did you notice that?'

'No, I didn't.'

'All the time. You should be more observant, Bernard. These people are not to be trusted. They tell us only what they want us to hear.'

'You're right, Dicky.'

'You probably didn't notice that there is no telephone in that house.'

'That's probably why the secretary went off somewhere on his horse.'

'Damned odd, isn't it? No phone?'

'Maybe. Stefan's a writer; perhaps he doesn't want a telephone in his house.'

'Writer, huh. I'm going to see what those people are digging up in the forest, just in case it is a body. I'll jog there, it's not far. Better we both go.'

Today Dicky had delved into his wardrobe for a three-quarter-length military jacket. It was an olive-green waterproof garment with huge pockets, a long-sleeve version of the sort of garment General Westmoreland modelled in Nam. The name-patch had been carefully unpicked from it, leaving the impression that it was an item of kit retained after Dicky's military service. This was an interpretation that he liked to encourage, but Daphne once confided that all Dicky's military wardrobe came from a charity shop in Hampstead.

It did not matter that Dicky had brought his oddments of demode military uniform; half the population of Poland seemed to be outfitted by the US army. But other men wore stained and patched ones, and wore them in a sloppy and informal way. Dicky's well-fitting jacket was clean and pressed. With the jacket fully buttoned, and a red para-troop beret worn pulled down tight on his skull, Dicky was conspicuous in this country governed by soldiers. Only his trendy blue-and-white running shoes saved him from looking like a general about to inspect an honour guard of the riot police.

'It's a long hike,' I warned.

'Come along, Bernard. A brisk canter would do you good. Ye gods, I jog across Hampstead Heath every morning before breakfast.'

'Daphne said you'd given up the daily jogging,' I said.

My remark had the calculated effect. 'Daphne!' Dicky exploded. 'What the hell does Daphne know about what I do? She's in bed when I get home, and in bed when I get up in the morning.'

'I must have got it wrong,' I said. 'I noticed you'd put on weight, and thought it must be because you'd cut out the jogging.'

'You're a bloody shit-stirrer,' said Dicky. 'Do you enjoy making mischief? Is that it?'

'There's no need to get upset, Dicky,' I said, trying to look pained.

'I'll show you who is out of condition. I'll show you who is puffing and collapsing. Come on, Bernard, it's no more than three miles.'

'You start. I'll go upstairs and put on my other shoes,' I said. My accusations about his lack of exercise had aroused something in Dicky's metabolism, for he began running on the spot, and punching the air around him to fell imaginary assailants.

'You'd better hurry,' he called and, with no further prompting, went jogging across the cobbled courtyard through the gate and along the path that led through the woods. I watched him slow as he entered the meadow that was now knee-high with dead ferns and weeds. They produced a crisp puffing sound as Dicky jogged through them. The impression of a choo-choo train was completed by the white vapour his breath left on the cold air.

I went inside the house to the kitchen. There was no one in evidence. I helped myself to a cup of warm coffee and toasted a slice of dark bread before following Dicky down the forest path at a leisurely pace. There were starlings, blackbirds and sparrows foraging for food. I understood their shrill cries; being without food in Poland was a grim plight. I was moved enough to toss a few bite-sized fragments of my breakfast bread to them, and decided that if I started to believe in reincarnation I'd go for something migratory.

'My God, where have you been?' Dicky said when I got to him. He had joined some men standing around looking at a shallow ditch. It was where they had been digging when we passed them the previous day. Accompanying the men there was a brown shaggy-haired mongrel dog; presumably it was Basilisk, the noted truffle-hound. It was sniffing at Dicky's running shoes that were now caked in mud.

'I took it easy; it was icy,' I explained.

'I know, I know,' agreed Dicky, gently kicking the dog's nose aside. 'I slipped on a patch of it near the stream. I went full-length and hurt my back. But still I was here half an hour before you.'

'It's just as well that one of us remains uninjured,' I said.

'Very droll,' said Dicky. Then, turning his dissatisfaction upon the labourers, he said: 'They say they got a part of a leg yesterday – not an arm, the old man got it wrong – but it's gone off to the police station.'

'What kind of leg?' I kicked at the ground. Here under the trees where no sunlight ever came, it was hard, very hard.

'What kind of leg?' Dicky scoffed. 'How many kinds are there? Left and right?' He coughed. His exertions seemed to have exhausted him and now he stood arms akimbo and breathed in and out slowly and deliberately, smiling fixedly while he did it, like those girls who sell exercise machines on television.

'Young? Old? Decomposing? Tall? Short? Hairy? Smooth?'

'How do I know?' said Dicky, abandoning his breathing exercises. 'It's gone to the police.'

I turned to the men and tried my inadequate Polish on them but got only vague answers. Their attitude to the dismembered corpse was not unlike Dicky's; a leg was a leg.

'You didn't change your shoes,' said Dicky accusingly.

'No,' I admitted. 'I only brought the pair I'm wearing.'

'You said you were going to change.'

'I forgot I'd not brought spares.'

'You're a bloody scrimshanker,' said Dicky.

I didn't deny it. I singled out the German-speaking Blackbeard and said: 'Show me the leg.' Before he could start his excuses I added: 'These are human remains. I'll bring the priest. If you try to prevent me arranging proper Christian burial I'll see you damned in hell.'

He stared at me angrily. After a moment in which we stood motionless he pointed to a battered old wooden box. I pulled the top off it to see a shoe, a wrinkled sock and a grotesque hunk of chewed flesh that was undoubtedly a leg.

99

'The dogs got it,' explained Blackbeard. I glanced at the sleepy Basilisk. 'Not this one ... dogs from the village. They run wild in packs at night.'

I leaned over to see the well-chewed piece of flesh the men had discovered. It was chafed and grazed as if it had been scraped with a wire brush. Chunks of flesh were bitten away deeply enough to reveal the tibia bone. The big toe had been entirely torn off, leaving some of the small neighbouring grey bones visible. The four other toes were intact, and complete with toenails. I reached into the box and turned the remains over to see where it had been detached from the upper leg. Surrounding the rounded stump of the bone there was a mop-like mess of ligaments, cartilage and tendon. 'It's a human leg all right,' I said, carefully replacing it in the box. 'And it looks like the dogs made a good meal of it.'

'Uggh!' said Dicky. 'How repulsive.'

I picked up the shoe. Despite being damaged it was an Oxford brogue of unmistakably English origin. It was the expensive handmade sort of shoe that George Kosinski liked, and the leather had a patina that comes when shoes are carefully preserved by servants, as George's shoes were. Such shoes, in such condition, were not commonly to be found in Poland even on the feet of the most affluent. The sock was silk, and although I couldn't decipher all the markings, there was enough to establish that it was English too.

'George Kosinski?' said Dicky.

'It looks like it,' I said as I leaned over to estimate the size of the shoe against the foot.

'You don't seem very surprised.'

'What do you want me to do ...? No. In fact, someone in Warsaw told me he had been killed.'

'In Warsaw? Why don't you bloody well confide in me?' said Dicky in exasperation.

'You don't want me to repeat every last stupid unlikely rumour I hear, do you?'

'How did you know?' Dicky turned to glance at the men. 'That these buggers still had it, I mean. They told me the police had collected it.'

'The police?' I said. 'You think the police would have come out here, parcelled up a bloodstained section of cadaver, said thank-you, and then gone quietly back to the barracks to think about it? In this part of the world, Dicky, the cops come complete with armoured cars and assault weapons. Fresh human remains dug up out here in the sticks would have had them interrogating everyone in the house. We would have been paraded in our night-clothes in the courtyard, while search and arrest teams tore up the floorboards and kicked shit out of the servants.'

'Yes, yes, yes, you're right.'

'That's why no one sends for the bastards. That's why I knew they were still thinking about what to do with this.' I tossed the shoe and the sock into the box with the severed leg, and then put the lid on it. I looked round and found the diggers looking at me.

'Where did you dig it from?' I asked them.

'That's the problem,' said Blackbeard. 'The dogs had it here, under the beech-tree. It could have come from anywhere. It could have come from miles away.'

'So why are you digging here?'

'The ground was disturbed. Shall we stop digging?'

I wasn't going to fall for that one. 'No, keep digging. We'll keep it to ourselves,' I suggested. 'Tell no one. When Mr Stefan returns he'll know what to do.'

This wait-and-see solution appealed to the men. They nodded and Blackbeard picked up the wooden box and placed it further back in the darkness of the forest.

'Are you jogging back for lunch?' I asked Dicky.

'Can't you see I've hurt my back?'

'We'll walk then,' I said. 'I'll show you the ruins of the generator house and traces of what must be the German fortified lines from the Tannenberg battle in 1914.'

'Tannenberg?' said Dicky doubtfully.

I said: 'Every German schoolboy knows about Tannenberg, just as every English boy is taught about Trafalgar. Fifty miles of Masurian lakes split the Tsar's attacking army. The invincible General Hindenburg walloped one half and then the other, to win a classic victory.' I stopped abruptly as I realized to what extent my upbringing at a Berlin school had caused me to forget that the Tsar and his army were fighting on the Allied side. In 1914 Hindenburg had been Britain's deadly enemy.

'Do you know why you've never got on?' said Dicky in a friendly tone, while putting a hand on my shoulder. 'You can't distinguish the important things in life from self-indulgent trifles.'

'Yes,' I said. 'And anyway, it was General Ludendorff who did the work while Hindenburg snatched all the credit.' Dicky smiled to show he knew which general he was.

Karol arrived back at the house just after two o'clock. Everyone was fretting for their lunch but it was delayed until he arrived. Dicky had somewhat overstated Karol's riding attire. He came into the drawing-room dressed in stained slacks, scuffed high-boots and a baggy tweed jacket. He sat down after no more than a gruff greeting and we were served more soup made from unidentifiable vegetables followed by a plate of peppery mashed swede with onion in it.

'Father Ratajczyk said he would come,' Karol said suddenly. This seemed to be directed to Uncle Nico, but he turned to take in the whole family. 'He had a christening and then he is coming directly here.'

'There is no need for him to go into the East Wing,' said Uncle Nico.

102

'Every room,' said Karol. 'He said he would go into every room and that is what I want.' Uncle Nico said nothing. 'It's what Stefan wanted,' Karol added defiantly.

After the swede plates were cleared away, we were served a heavy pudding with a few raisins in it, and a sweet white sauce over it. There were murmurs of satisfaction from everyone and the pudding was devoured to the last drip of sauce and the final crumb.

'I have saved some food for Father,' said Aunt Mary.

'Yes,' said Karol. 'He will be hungry. They never serve food at christenings.'

The priest arrived about an hour after lunch was eaten. He came striding through the house, a small scrawny figure who gestured extravagantly with hands high in the air. 'I'll start here,' he said, looking into the dining-room and sparing no more than a glance at the big stuffed eagle. 'We'll bring the box.' He said it as if to himself and then turned abruptly on his heel, so that the skirt of his ankle-length cassock swirled around him. He sped back to the hallway and shouted through the front door to the sweaty old chap he'd brought with him: 'Bring the box, Tadeusz.'

It was a large wooden box and weighed heavily, judging by the panting, flush-faced old man who carried it into the house and put it down in the dining-room with a deep sigh.

'I'll need the second box too,' said the priest. 'It's a big job.'

The priest looked around. As if seeing for the first time the crowd of spectators who'd gathered round him he said: 'You must leave the house. All of you. Right away.' He again made a fidgety gesture with his hands high in the air, as a child might shoo away worrisome hens.

'What's it all about?' said Dicky.

I didn't know. 'What's it all about, Uncle Nico?' I asked.

It was Karol who answered. 'Everyone must leave the house,' he said. 'There is a little cottage near the lake. I ordered that it should be swept and a fire lit to warm it. You will be comfortable there for as long as this takes.'

'How long is that likely to be?' I asked.

'We'll be finished by the time Stefan arrives,' he replied. 'Two hours ... three at the most.'

'I see.' I looked at Dicky. We both knew that three hours in Poland could take you into the following week.

'Why?' said Dicky.

'We mustn't talk about it,' Karol said. 'Something happened ... something bad. Each room must be restored to us.'

'Restored how?' said Dicky.

Karol looked to see if the priest was listening, but he wasn't, he was opening his boxes and counting the contents. 'There is an evil spirit in the house. He must be expelled ... exorcized. You know this word?'

'Yes, I know this word,' said Dicky. 'Bell, book, and candle. So that's it?'

'You'll be comfortable in the little house,' said Karol. 'I must stay here to help.'

'My God,' said Dicky bursting with suppressed excitement by the time we were along the path on the way to the cottage near the lake. 'Bell, book, and candle, eh?'

'Not exactly,' I said. 'Bell, book, and candle is the ceremony of excommunication. This is exorcism. Expelling evil spirits by ringing a passing bell.'

'Passing bell?'

'A consecrated bell. Rung for people at death's door who might have their soul snatched away as it passed from the body.'

'Are you making this up, Bernard?'

'Of course not.'

'Yes, well you know all this foreign religious mumbo-jumbo,' said Dicky. 'Perhaps it doesn't seem so suspicious to someone like you. But you've got to admit it, this is a damned weird set-up. Bells. Dismembered bodies. Priests exorcizing the rooms. He'll start in the dining-room: it didn't take him long to decide that, eh? So it's obvious that George Kosinski was murdered in that dining-room. My God! Think of it. Why a dining-room? Because there are sharp knives to hand, right?'

'They are doing all the rooms,' I pointed out.

'Maybe the Church figures it's a sin that has spilled over and stained the whole house. In this part of the world, what the Church says goes.'

'Maybe that's it,' I said.

'Maybe that's it.' Dicky mimicked my words angrily. 'Yes, maybe that's it, and maybe you are holding out on me again. You've got your own theory, haven't you? So why don't you bloody well say so?'

'I think it's all a lot of bullshit. It's just a way of getting everyone out of the house.'

'Why? Why, why, why?'

'I don't know, Dicky. That's why I didn't say anything.'

'What can that bugger Karol do when we aren't in the house that he can't do when we are in it?'

'Listen, Dicky,' I said. 'I was looking around this morning, and there's a room at the top on this side with a locked door. The windows are clean – I can see that from the outside – and the handle is well used. They are keeping the stove going there. Warming an extra room doesn't come cheap. So why?'

'Wait a minute! Wait a minute. What do you mean – when you were looking around this morning?'

'I got up early. I couldn't sleep.'

'And searched the house? Bloody hell, Bernard. What if they had caught you?'

'What could they do?'

'They could chop you into pieces like they've chopped up poor old George Kosinski. That's what they can do. Take it easy, Bernard. I don't want to arouse their suspicions.'

105

What Dicky meant by not wanting to arouse their suspicions was not clear to me. I would have thought their suspicions were already sufficiently aroused by the unannounced arrival of two nosy foreigners. But I didn't want to get sidetracked. 'I think this is a good chance to take a look at that room,' I said.

'At the room you found?'

'They won't be expecting us to defy them and go through the house while they are going through it too. We know there are only the three of them and they're bound to make a noise carting all that ecclesiastical paraphernalia from room to room and doing their phoney routine. The servants are all in the barn. We can get in and go up the back stairs, take a look, and be back in the cottage, twiddling our thumbs, within half an hour.'

'No, Bernard. I don't think so.'

'Okay, I'll do it alone. If you would keep a look-out for me downstairs there's not much chance I'd be caught.' Dicky came to a halt on the path and started kicking the toe of his cowboy boot into the dead vegetation. 'We'd be in and out in a jiffy,' I urged.

'You're a bloody maniac, Bernard. I must be mad, but okay. How do you want to do it?'

'All the servants are in the barn. We won't use the front door in case they hear us. If we go along the wooden veranda, and climb through one of the windows there, we can go up the back stairs that only the servants use. I know how to find the room.'

'But it's locked.'

'I've got something with me that should do it. It's not a real lock.' I'd had a good look round the kitchen while eating with the servants. In my pocket I now had a fruit knife with a thin pliable blade, and a couple of long skewers.

Once Dicky had agreed, he became quite keenly involved in our caper. Warily we skirted the barn, where a crowd of pitiable servants were grouped around an inadequate open fire. We then returned to the big house and went up the steps to the veranda, where we soon found a conveniently loose window. I slid it open and let Dicky climb through first, in case something went wrong. Then I followed him and pushed the window closed. Once inside the house we could hear the voices of the three men. They were in the drawing-room now. The priest was talking very quietly in Polish and the man he'd brought with him was answering in monosyllabic grunts. I could neither hear clearly nor understand their words but it didn't sound like any sort of religious ceremony.

Dicky and I climbed the back stairs very slowly. We both kept to the side where the staircase supporting beams fitted into the outside wall, for the stairs were at their most secure there, and least likely to creak. Once up on the top floor we stayed away from the windows in case one of the men in the garden looked up and spotted us. Then we were at the door of the room I wanted to investigate.

The lock was easily prised back with the thin knife-blade. Once we were inside, even Dicky could see that it was worth looking into. It was a double room separated by a folding screen which was at this time open. These two rooms were obviously the best-maintained ones in the house. Together they formed a self-contained unit with a private bathroom and a fine bed with a mattress so new it still had its transparent wrapping intact. There was new wallpaper too, and some of the household's better antique furniture.

One room was furnished as a study, with extensive bookcases, a large gilt-framed mirror reflecting the whole room and a couple of landscape paintings. A lovely inlaid desk was placed diagonally so that someone seated at it, in the corner of the room, would get the light from two windows. A side-table was entirely occupied by family photographs of all shapes and sizes, some of them in elaborate silver frames. A series of deep shelves held dusty cardboard models of theatre sets with cut-out figures to show the effect of the costumes against the scenery.

I followed Dicky into the bedroom side of the unit.

'Look,' said Dicky, having opened a closet door. Inside there were men's clothes. One glance was enough for me to recognize George Kosinski's expensive attire. There were suits and sports jackets that I'd seen him wearing. There were new ski clothes and a sheepskin waistcoat. Some of the garments were in zipper covers and everything was arranged in that neat way that suggested a servant's hand; shoes on trees and in shoe-bags bearing exalted Italian names.

'It doesn't mean they've killed him,' Dicky said hastily.

This *non sequitur* seemed to be generated by the expression on my face. I said nothing. From downstairs I heard the litany of the old priest, and curious little sounds, like shrieks of pleasure, that I could not identify. I picked up a single shoe from the row of pairs, a brogue exactly like the chewed-up one we'd seen in the forest. 'Where's the other one?' I said.

'They're getting closer, Bernard. Did the priest and his man arrive in separate cars?' He was looking out of the window. 'There's another car there.'

'Calm down, Dicky. We can't cut and run now. There's too much at stake.'

'Yes, our lives,' said Dicky. 'This is becoming a personal vendetta for you, Bernard. I warned you about taking things personally, didn't I?'

'Shirts, underclothes ...' I was pulling out each of the drawers, starting with the bottom drawer so that I didn't have to push them back. 'Socks.' It was a burglar's way of searching, and burglars didn't put anything back afterwards. It was this reckless procedure that alarmed Dicky. He followed me as I searched, trying to restore the room to its former tidy state. 'No wires, no transmitters as far as I can see ...' I said.

'Let's go, Bernard. Please!'

I opened the door to the bathroom. 'Jesus!' I was startled almost out of my skin. I jumped back. There was a man there. He was jammed into the shallow space between the double doors. He was tall and thin, with long wavy grey hair. His face had skin so drawn and tight that all the muscles could be counted.

For a moment I thought it was a dead body propped there. Then he moved forward. 'I was listening,' he said in good clear English. 'My brother wasn't killed in this house.' Now I could see him more clearly I recognized him as George Kosinski's brother; I'd seen photos of him. But while George was short and active this man Stefan was tall, thin and deliberate in his movements. His clothes were Western and expensive: a thigh-length jacket of soft brown leather, a red silk roll-neck and drainpipe trousers of the sort the fashionable man was wearing in the Sixties.

'You are Stefan Kosinski?' said Dicky. There was no hint of discomfort or apology in his voice, and I admired him for the way he could control his feelings when he really wanted to.

'You abuse my hospitality,' said Stefan. He took his time putting a cigarette into a long ivory cigarette-holder and lighting it with a gold lighter. 'I return home early and what do I find? I find you have invaded my home to ransack it.'

'We're looking for your brother,' said Dicky. 'If you've nothing to hide you'll let us talk to him.'

'Are you an insensitive fool?' asked Stefan in a strangled voice. 'Do you have no human feelings? My brother is dead. I have been to complete the formalities. The authorities have seen enough evidence, a death certificate has been signed. What more do you want of me?' Stefan sank down into the armchair and sighed deeply. 'I am totally desolated and I'm tired. I'm very tired.'

From along the corridor the little procession of the priest, his helper and Karol the secretary could be heard. The men were talking softly as they progressed methodically from room to room accompanied by occasional shrill musical notes.

Stefan said: 'We Kosinskis like to keep our family together. You English don't care about your dead, but for us it's different.'

'What happened here?' said Dicky. 'Why this exorcizing? Why the priest?'

Stefan, one hand under his chin, looked up at him from under lowered eyelids. Stefan was an actor; every movement, every stance was a contrived pose. No wonder the regime was so happy to have him go abroad to represent the Polish theatre, he was the sort of handsome romantic Pole every foreigner might envisage. The thin body, the tragic expression, the soulful look, the burning eyes: everything about him contributed to this casting-director's dream. 'They are sweeping for hidden microphones,' said Stefan wearily. 'The apparatus sends a signal when the wand is held near to an active transmitter. The Church sent their own apparatus from Lublin. They have to have such devices: the secret police target the churches and their meetings.' Now I understood. Stefan had been examining each room for new wiring or fresh paintwork, keeping ahead of the detector team. He must have heard us talking when looking around the bathroom.

'I still don't understand,' said Dicky. 'Who killed your brother?'

Stefan smiled. Along with all the other attributes of the actor, he had a charm that he could switch off and on at will. He looked at Dicky and gave him both barrels. Bringing his hand from his pocket he opened his fist and dropped a wristwatch and a man's gold signet ring on to the table with a calculated clatter. 'Look at them,' he said. I didn't need to look at them. I could see from where I was standing that they were George's.

'I killed him,' Stefan said, gesturing with his long ivory cigarette-holder. He let this alarming statement linger to extract from it the fullest dramatic effect. 'Poor George. I killed him when I let him go out in the forest on his own. He was depressed about the death of his wife. I thought perhaps some time to think the situation through would do him good.'

The door opened and Karol poked his head round it and raised his eyebrows. He seemed startled to see me and Dicky

110

there, but he recovered immediately. Stefan said: 'Yes, you can come in here now, but I can see no sign of anything.'

The three men came into the room dragging the two boxes with them. The priest's helper was carrying a detector. It was a heavy black plastic machine resembling a transistor radio. There were red and green indicator lights on it, a volume control and a small meter. He directed the antenna up and down the wall, systematically covering every inch of it.

Stefan watched them and absent-mindedly picked up George's shoe; the one I had put on a side-table. To Dicky he said: 'And my brother knew that you two were chasing him. It didn't help.'

Tadeusz, the man with the detector, ran its antenna around the window-frame, always a favourite place for concealed microphones.

Dicky said: 'You are talking in riddles.'

Stefan looked at him and said: 'The police are interrogating the killers. Two Russian army deserters. Middle-aged *praporshchiks* – warrant officers – not tough conscript kids. They picked them up last night. They were trying to sell poor George's gold Rolex watch in a bar.'

'How did it happen?' said Dicky.

'The Nazis built fortified bunkers through these woods in the summer of 1944. They held up the Russian army for weeks and weeks. The line runs for eighty miles and right through the forest: tunnels and ventilation shafts, trenches and tank-traps. When the timber supports rotted, the tunnels collapsed, but the deep bunkers were made with concrete and steel. They'll last for ever and now gangs of deserters use them. There are not enough policemen to clear them out of there.'

Suddenly the detector's hum changed to a shriek. 'There's one here,' said the priest.

'I knew there was. I knew it,' said Karol.

'Is it active?' said Stefan.

Karol said: 'It's active.'

'Is this your doing?' Stefan asked Dicky, while the priest climbed up on a chair to look more closely at the hidden microphone that was concealed in the curtain rail over the window.

'No,' said Dicky.

'You haven't got some British comrade out there in the forest with headphones clamped round his skull?'

'Listening to your foolishness?' said Dicky. 'The answer is no.'

The priest ripped the microphone down and there was a tearing sound and a little puff of white dust as a long wire emerged from the paint under which it had been hidden. He pulled the battery from the transmitter and put it in his pocket.

'They arrested the killers?' asked Dicky.

'Do you want to talk with the bastards? I can perhaps arrange it.'

'Will the authorities issue a death certificate?' said Dicky.

'It will take a few days. Getting official paperwork takes a long time here in Poland. But yes, the police are satisfied that it is murder. Now they have two men they'll find their hideout and round up the rest of that gang. They'll beat a confession out of one of them. They live by robbing the farms. Local people will be pleased to hear there are a few less of those bandits.'

'Can you get me a certified copy of the certificate?' Dicky asked. 'I'll need it for my records.'

'Of course,' said Stefan with studied politeness. 'You'll need it for your records.'

Without knocking at the door, Uncle Nico came into the room. He seemed not to notice the tension and bad feeling. He looked first at Dicky and then at me: 'I've made tea,' he announced. 'Real English tea with boiling water the way I used to drink it in England. It's all made. I took it to your room. Come downstairs and have some. It will spoil if it's left too long.'

112

Glad of a chance to escape, we followed the old man to where he'd set out the tea things on a tray on a low table in my bedroom. He'd set cups for three tea-drinkers and he sat down with us.

'Just like being in England,' said Dicky.

'Well, it's not like Poland, if that's what you mean,' said the old man sarcastically. 'This house is a museum ...' He restated this. 'Or a theatre. And we're all playing roles devised by Stefan.'

Dicky had been eyeing the teapot anxiously – he hated strongly brewed tea – and now he leaned forward and poured some for us. The old man seemed not to notice. But he went to the door, looked down the corridor to be sure no one was listening, and then closed the door.

'How can you understand all this?' asked the old man, taking from Dicky the offered cup of tea and sipping some. 'Stefan has us all in his power. He likes to play with us. He knows we can't fight back.'

'Why are you in his power?' Dicky asked him.

'He's rich and famous.'

'I've never heard of him,' persisted Dicky.

'No,' the old man agreed. 'Stefan is not famous outside Poland – he is not translated. But his plays are sometimes performed by Poles living abroad, and they help to form the opinions of those exiles. His plays are sometimes made into Polish films which, in video form, are distributed to Poles living abroad.'

'Is he a communist? Is he a supporter of the generals?' said Dicky.

'Tolerant. Stefan's tolerant views of the communist and military rulers are valuable to them. So is the way he equates "evil Russia" with "evil USA". Many people in his unsophisticated audiences are happy to accept this simplistic view of world politics. Many American liberals will tell you that Reagan's America and its CIA is no better than Stalin and his KGB. But if you live here you know that racist policemen in Alabama and the U2. spy planes are not to be compared to extermination camps, or to our secret police with thousands of informers and the regular use of torture.'

'He wrote one called *Let's Murder Stalin*,' said Dicky.

'Oh yes, Stefan's plays are outspoken in a superficial kind of way, but Stefan is a clever man. He knows that it is better to appear to be a protester. But always his plots and their conclusions do the work that the government here needs done.'

'And yet his study is bugged?'

'The microphone? Ha, ha. Did you see the look on the face of Father Ratajczyk?'

'No,' admitted Dicky.

The old man smiled and drank some tea. 'No matter who comes to sweep the house, they always find a bug. Stefan plants them himself. Always it is placed somewhere that suggests that Stefan is the man they are after.'

'Plants them himself? Are you serious?' said Dicky.

'You may as well ask Stefan if he is serious, for by now everyone in the house knows his tricks.'

'But why?'

'It's all part of his role: this character he plays of a martyr and patriot, ever fighting against the regime. He will go to his authors' club and protest loudly about being persecuted and harassed by the secret police.'

'And will he be believed?'

'Yes. Yes. Yes. Writers are by their very nature paranoid. Every now and again they all put their signatures under letters published in the newspaper. Stefan adds his signature willingly.'

'And such protests don't anger the government?'

'It looks like free speech. The government worries most about Western banks. And Western banks are looking for signs of stability with just a trace of intellectual latitude. Also such

114

protests reassure Moscow that our regime is not giving way to liberal reformers.'

'And no one ever challenges Stefan and his beliefs?' Dicky asked.

'Is that your English way of asking whether I confront Stefan with my views? Yes, of course it is. Well, let me tell you that I am not mad. It is Stefan, and his elastic relationship with the regime, that ensures that I live in this magnificent house. How many lovely estates like this have been preserved from one generation to the next? Stefan burns a candle for the devil – is that the expression? He prevaricates and compromises in order to keep his family in comfort, and I am a part of that family. I enjoy all the material comforts: heating, hot water, a sound roof, something to eat every day. In Poland today these are not benefits to be taken lightly. I'm not complaining.'

'I thought you *were*,' said Dicky.

'I'm explaining,' said Uncle Nico, becoming slightly flustered at Dicky's deadpan accusation. 'I thought you should take back to England the truth … the true state of affairs, rather than believe a lot of play-acting.'

'Ah, that's different,' said Dicky.

'You will see,' promised Uncle Nico. And he rang the bell so that a servant would come and collect the tea-tray.

That evening Stefan took his rightful place at the head of the table. He was casually dressed in a pale yellow cashmere sweater, tailored linen pants and white buckskin shoes. His long wavy hair was perfect and his freshly shaved face dusted with talc. Next to him sat his wife, Lena, a plumpish woman with long fair hair that was plaited and coiled in a 1940s style. Her high-neck grey dress had a similar old-fashioned look. So this was the daughter of the Party official. Marriage to her had no doubt furthered Stefan's career. She spoke little apart from giving monosyllabic orders to the servants.

That evening the long dining-table was differently con-stituted. The younger people had now been banished to the kitchen, from where I could hear their youthful and far less inhibited exchanges whenever the door was opened. There were two extra people at dinner. Muscular men in their early twenties, they sat at the very end of the table. It was difficult to decide whether they were employees or members of the family. At dinner Stefan dominated the conversation with stories about his adventures abroad. Despite his obvious vanity he had a dis-arming way of telling stories of his folly and naive misunder-standings of how things worked in the West.

He told of throwing away the royalties on his finest play by betting on the horses in Paris and the English races too. 'With horses I am always unlucky,' said Stefan. 'Every horse I bet on lets me down.' He reached out to caress his wife's hand. 'But with women I am lucky beyond words.'

Lena smiled.

After dinner Stefan insisted that Dicky and I made up a four for bridge with Uncle Nico. It was a miserable game. I have never been able to play bridge with any skill, despite a lifetime of fierce instruction from Tante Lisl, the gloriously unpredict-able woman who'd so influenced my childhood in Berlin.

At ten minutes before midnight, Stefan brought the game abruptly to an end. He threw down his hand – it was a winning one of course – got up suddenly, sighed, consulted his thin gold wristwatch and poured brandy for himself from a large bottle that he took from the sideboard's cupboard. Only when he had done this and turned to meet everyone's eyes did he offer us all a drink. It wasn't meanness as much as a desire to be the centre of attention, at least that was my interpretation of his every move.

This feeling about Stefan was endorsed when he returned to the green felt-topped card-table, picked up the cards and, without a word, started performing card-tricks. He went on for half an hour. His hands were slim and elegant and this was a chance to display them. The ease with which he was able to manipulate the deck of cards – fanning them across the table or tossing them into the air so that his hand emerged holding the ace – held everyone's attention. His wife Lena watched him too, and Aunt Mary put down her knitting. Even Uncle Nico, who must have seen the tricks a thousand times, was as engrossed as any of us.

Watching his card-tricks was an opportunity to study Stefan. Nothing about his appearance, or the elegance of his movements, would have been remarkable had he been twenty years old. But Stefan was a mature man who'd left his youth far behind. And there were other contradictions apparent too. Who was this well-bred man in whom suppressed anger could be frequently glimpsed? Having guests obviously inconvenienced him and spoiled his household routine. He made sure we understood that, but his hospitality was always on tap. He was bored but he was passionate; he was intellectual but he was obsessed with his physical self. He supported the communist regime but lived in pampered luxury. Was it all these tensions inside him that provided him with his charm?

'One last little trick,' said Stefan. 'It's called find the knave.' He offered a fanned deck of cards from person to person. Each one took a card and then thrust it back into the pack. With that casual detached indifference that is a part of the magician's art he handed the pack to me to shuffle. Then he fanned the cards and chose a card for each of us. Turned over to reveal the faces, they were the cards we'd selected.

'Why is it called find the knave?' Dicky asked.

Stefan gave a slow smile and then leaned across to Dicky and, with a superb demonstration of palming, produced a knave of hearts from Dicky's pocket.

'Well …' said Dicky, somewhat flustered. 'How …?'

'Someone always asks why it's called find the knave,' explained Stefan. His wife Lena and Aunt Mary exchanged amused smiles. It was clearly a trick designed to dismay visitors and small children.

Soon after that Uncle Nico said goodnight and the gathering broke up and everyone went to bed.

'What's going on here?' said Dicky when we were upstairs, as he patted his stove to see how warm it was before deciding whether to wear his woollies in bed.

'What?'

'This Stefan, is he crazy or some sort of saint? I mean, they all watch him all the time. Even his wife. Are they all shit-scared of him? Or are they all enslaved? Dependence. It's as if he is their analyst, and they are frightened of facing life without him. I don't get it. Can you understand?'

'He's the breadwinner.'

'He's more than that, old pal. He's the messiah. It's almost scary. I can feel his presence. I mean it: I can feel his presence in the house. Ever since he jumped out of that cupboard and put the fear of God into you …'

'He didn't put the fear of God into me,' I protested.

'Come on, Bernard. You went white.'

'I was surprised, that's all.'

'You were shit-scared. You nearly jumped out of the window.'

'Take it easy, Dicky.'

'Look out! Jesus!' Dicky suddenly yelled. 'Wow! He's coming through the door like a spirit.'

'Cut it out, Dicky. I'm tired.'

'You looked round, Bernard,' said Dicky gleefully. 'Stefan coming through the door: that made you look round.' Suddenly his face crumpled up and he held this grotesque expression for a moment before surrendering to a tremendous sneeze. He wiped

118

his nose on a clean handkerchief. Dicky had an inexhaustible supply of very large clean handkerchiefs. 'I've picked up some sort of bug,' he said. 'I'm sneezing and I have stomach cramps too. Have you been drinking the water?'

'No.'

'How do you clean your teeth?'

'In booze.'

'Red wine is a stain.'

'But Polish vodka is bleach.'

'Comics die younger than straight men. Have you noticed that, Bernard?' He wiped his nose again, and then folded his handkerchief and put it away. 'We'll have to get out of here very soon.'

'How soon is very soon?'

'Maybe tomorrow.'

'You don't want to check out his story about George being murdered?'

'What could we do?'

'Go and ask the cops if they are holding these Russkies. Give the cops some money to get lost, and then grill the Russkies.'

'Is that what you would do if I wasn't with you?'

'Shall I stay on?'

'Better we keep together,' said Dicky. 'You'd bribe the cops?'

'Possibly,' I admitted. I was exaggerating a little. Dicky brought out my desire to push it.

'We'll keep together, Bernard. As soon as Stefan gives me a proper certified copy of the death certificate we can get out of here.'

'I think we should check it out.'

'Do you know what that death certificate will empower me to do? George is a British subject. I'll get court authority to seize all his possessions. We'll go through him with a fine-tooth comb.'

'And is that what you really wanted all along?'

'That's part of what I wanted.'

119

'I see.'

'Why did Stefan stop playing cards tonight? Did I upset him earlier on when I asked if anyone around here owned an old Bugatti?'

'No. It was nothing to do with that, Dicky.'

'He jumped up suddenly and let the game end. And it was just as I hit a winning streak.'

'You didn't stand a chance, Dicky.'

'What puzzles me – he says he loses all his money on horses but tonight he won and won and won at cards.'

'They don't let him shuffle the horses,' I said.

He gave a pained smile. 'You don't think …?'

'A man who can pull an ace of spades out of your ear is likely to know what you're holding in your hand.'

'No, no, no. Stefan is from a fine old family … goes back two hundred years. That old man Nico told me Stefan is a duke, or the Polish equivalent.'

'It's not mutually exclusive, Dicky. Cheating at cards and being a duke.'

'You haven't answered my question. Why did Stefan stop playing cards on the stroke of midnight?'

'Because he's going to Mass in the morning. Playing cards after midnight would have prevented him taking communion.'

'You're a bloody fund of information, Bernard,' he said, as though annoyed at having his question answered. 'Mass. Yes, I suppose that would be it.' Dicky went to his suitcase and got out a heavy roll-neck to wear over his pyjamas. 'I'll say goodnight, Bernard.'

Thus I was dismissed. 'Goodnight, Dicky.'

It was three-thirty in the morning when I was awakened by a commotion from downstairs. I could hear men's voices shouting and a woman sobbing. I put on my trenchcoat over my pyjamas and went downstairs. In the front hall there were two strangers in heavy overcoats, red-faced and radiating cold air. There were servant girls too, standing on the stairs with overcoats buttoned tightly over frilly night-clothes that were evident at throat and legs. Stefan was there too, but he was fully dressed in a three-piece suit complete with collar and tie.

'What's going on?' I asked.

'The alarm. They say the Russians have crossed the border,' said Stefan calmly. 'These two villagers are insisting that I must go with them to a meeting in the village.'

'An invasion?'

At that moment Dicky came down the stairs behind me. 'An invasion?' scoffed Dicky. 'They wouldn't dare ...'

Stefan said: 'One of the young men has taken the short-wave radio upstairs. He'll connect it to the big antenna on the roof. He'll get the London overseas service. They will probably be the first to announce it if it's true.'

'Have these men seen anything?' Dicky asked.

'I will go with them. You may as well go back to bed and get some rest,' said Stefan. 'It's probably not true. These rumours spread very quickly when the vodka is flowing. Both these fellows stink of booze.' The two villagers smiled, not understanding what Stefan was saying about them in English.

A servant helped Stefan into a magnificent fur coat and he went out to where Karol the secretary was sitting at the wheel of a car, keeping the engine ticking over.

'Go to bed!' Uncle Nico told the servant girls, who had now grown in number, and he clapped his hands and raised his voice as he said it again.

'Could it be true?' Dicky asked Uncle Nico when the young women had hurried off to their beds.

'I doubt it,' said Uncle Nico. He lowered his voice. 'But what he didn't tell you is that two more bodies have been found. That's what the two farm-hands came here for. Some drunks coming home through the forest stumbled over two dead bodies late last night. Two full-grown men thrown into the bottom of a ditch. God knows who they can be. It could be something to do with the rumours. In the village they are saying they must be Russian parachute spies.'

'Stefan should have waited for the radio,' said Dicky.

'He'll want to go to Mass,' confided Uncle Nico. 'There is a Mass at 5.50. Stefan likes to go early; he doesn't meet anyone he knows.'

Still not fully awake, I returned to my room, climbed back into bed and went into a deep sleep peopled with marching men and barking dogs, arguments with Dicky and a disinterred corpse. I woke up with a headache as I tried to distinguish dream from reality.

Dicky was already up and dressed. He was standing over me shaking me. 'The Russians are coming. You'd better get up and shave.' I could tell from his jokey voice that it was not true.

I got out of bed very slowly and became aware of the howling wind. When I went to the window I saw that the invasion from Russia *had* come, but it was in the shape of ice and snow. The blue sky had gone: snow was whipping past, the streaks of it almost horizontal in the fierce wind that was blowing all the way from the Steppes.

'We've got to get out of here right away,' said Dicky. 'The snow is falling heavily. We must get to the main road or we'll be snowed in until they dig us out, and that could take weeks.'

'It's not cold enough for snow to build up. It has to be colder than two degrees centigrade for it to survive and build up on the ground ...'

'I'm not in the mood for another of your science lectures,' said Dicky with unaccountable fury and stomped out of the room.

'And the ground is still too soft for heavy tanks and artillery,' I called after him.

There was no hot water by the time I got into the bath. The hot tap of the shower produced a blizzard of cold rusty water and then spluttered and stopped altogether. I'd given up on the bath and was starting to shave in cold water when Stefan appeared at the door of the bathroom.

'Did you sleep?'

'Yes, I did,' I said.

'There is no truth in the invasion rumours. We get these crazy panics frequently and we are used to them. One day it will be true, of course, but by that time we will have grown accustomed to the notion and be ready to submit.' He said it with a bitterness that I'd not seen in him before.

Dicky came bearing three cups of hot sweet coffee from the kitchen. I interrupted my shaving to drink a mouthful and used the rest for shaving.

Stefan watched me without commenting. 'Everyone in Warsaw was complaining about the sudden shortage of black-market booze,' he confided. 'There's not a drop of the really good stuff to be had anywhere. You can name your own price for a case of Scotch whisky or real French cognac. Foreign gangsters are moving in to take over from our own people. Two brothers from Cracow had the monopoly until now, but they have stopped trading. I heard they were enticed up into an apartment in Praga and nearly killed by American gangsters sent here specially to murder them. One of the brothers is in hospital with multiple fractures and the other is back home on crutches, and with his jaw in wires. Meanwhile all the tourist bars and illegal dives in the Old Town are desperate for supplies.'

'Umm,' said Dicky.

'Any guesses who they are?' Stefan asked me. 'They must have arrived about the time you did. Did you see anyone suspicious in the Europejski Hotel?'

'Me?' I said. 'No.' I dipped the razor in my coffee and continued dragging it through my beard.

'The underworld has put a price on their heads: fifty thousand zlotys for delivering either of these American killers to the black-market people. At least that's what I heard.'

'That's only about fifteen hundred dollars apiece,' said Dicky. 'I'd have thought two top-notch hit men were worth more than that.'

'I'm sorry you are departing so soon,' said Stefan. 'But winter is not the best time to show you Polish hospitality. And we Poles enjoy providing a show for visitors.'

We were back on the road by noon, our bellies filled with hot potato soup and our gas-tank with precious fuel. But we were still on the estate – and only three miles from the house – when we found the road ahead blocked by two army trucks and a bulldozer. There was a huddle of men: some soldiers were talking to two men hefting a 16mm film camera and recording equipment. Father Ratajczyk, the priest who had exorcized the rooms, was there too, together with Tadeusz, the technician who had assisted him.

A young officer of the Polish army, in sheepskin overcoat and military-style fur hat, detached himself from the group and walked towards us through the fast-falling sleet. He saluted and then leaned in to the car window.

'You're the two Englishmen from the Kosinski house?'

'Yes,' said Dicky. There was little point in denying it.

'I'm sorry to delay you. You can't get through. It will take about half an hour.' He spoke good English. 'We have to bring a big earth-moving machine up the road and there is only just enough clearance to get it between the trees.'

'What's happening?' said Dicky.

'We have to work quickly. By tomorrow the snow could be making it very difficult.'

'What's happening?'

'You don't know? Another mass grave. Trees have grown over a part of it and we can't estimate the size of it yet.'

'My God,' said Dicky. 'A mass grave?'

'At least five hundred bodies. My own guess is that there might be anything up to a thousand poor souls buried here.' He made the sign of a cross.

'They said they found two bodies last night,' said Dicky. 'Are they a part of it? When do they date from?'

'Yes, it's from the war,' said the young officer.

'Murdered by the Russians or by the Nazis?'

'Who knows?' said the officer, and wiped the wet snow from his face. 'They are Polish and they are dead, that's probably all we'll ever be sure about.'

5

'You haven't told me what it's like in Warsaw these days,' said Harry Strang, newly retired and relaxed in his baggy roll-neck sweater and worn corduroy trousers. I was used to him in suits and stiff collars, and with his hair combed to conceal the bald patch that I now noticed for the first time.

'I haven't told you that I've been to Warsaw.'

'You can't keep a secret from an old agent. Isn't that what they say?' Harry Strang was one of the few pen-pushers who could legitimately claim to have been an agent. I'd first met Harry in Berlin. I was very young, and too insensitive to see how miserable and out of place he felt in that city. It was my father who persuaded him not to resign from the service altogether. Harry was posted to Spain and made his reputation infiltrating Catalonian communist networks at a time when the Franco government had made communism a hazardous faith. Despite his remarkable Spanish, Harry couldn't look anything but what he is: a middle-class English gent, but he moved easily amongst an assortment of Spanish reds: terrorists, apparatchiks, opportunists, theorists and politicians. Then with Franco on his death-bed, Harry went to Argentina and worked for a shipping company, and was there working for us right through the Falklands war. Apart from the fingernails that never grew

126

straight after being torn off, malfunctioning kidneys damaged during a series of beatings in Franco's police stations, and a liver that was the casualty of cheap Rioja and inferior sherry, he had survived intact. Eventually he had been given a position in Operations in London and stayed there long enough to collect his pension. Not many field agents managed that.

'The kids are climbing around your Peugeot,' I warned him.

'It's an old wreck. Come away from the window. Let them alone, they can't hurt it, Bernard.'

'You haven't left the keys in?'

'Why kidnap your kids if you're going to spend every minute worrying about them?'

'I didn't kidnap them; I told my father-in-law I was collecting them from school.'

'You said you left a message on his telephone recording machine,' he corrected me. 'You didn't actually tell him.'

'What's the difference?'

'If he doesn't monitor his messages before he collects the kids from school himself, you'll find out what the difference is,' he said grimly. 'He'll tell the cops, and the TV news will say they are hunting for a tall child-molester with wavy hair and glasses.'

'Very funny.'

'It wasn't a joke, Bernard.'

'My father-in-law monitors his bloody messages every five minutes. He was born with a telephone in his ear and right now he's frantically picking up the pieces after the stock-market crash.'

Without moving from his chair, Harry looked out of the window at the full extent of his property. No doubt he saw five acres of root vegetables, soft fruit and a dozen plump pigs, but winter had all but eliminated the vegetation, and left only a ramshackle shed in a sea of shiny mud. With only a scrawny youngster to help him it was too much work, but Harry seemed to be content.

'They are nice kids, Bernard. The boy is the image of you.'
We had eaten lunch, squelched through the mud in borrowed
boots, been shown round the pigsties by a soft-spoken amiable
farm-hand, and come back inside to drink tea and inspect every
last one of Harry's collection of Japanese swords.

'I hear Dicky is very active lately,' said Harry, keeping his
tone neutral.

'Very active,' I said. 'He's fighting with Daphne so he tries to
get away every weekend. And he drags me with him. Then he
gives me odd days off. But what good is that when Fiona is at
work and my kids at school?'

Harry ran his hands together, pushing the fingers of his
white cotton gloves tighter on his fingers. 'The children should
be living at home with you,' he said. He rescued a sword which
was precariously balanced on the sofa, and held it up to admire
the engraving on its blade. There were swords everywhere; on
the floor, on the sofa and on the dining-table. Glittering blades
and shiny scabbards were exploding out of the little box-room
where he stored his collection, protruding through the door as
if some huge metallic hedgehog was trying to break out from
hibernation there.

'I know,' I said.

'But Fiona is keeping busy at work eh?' He slashed the air
with the sword and then slid it into its scabbard. He found a
place for it on the sideboard which had been until then the only
place free of edged weaponry.

'She's Dicky's Deputy,' I said.

'I heard. And he's hanging on to the German Desk and
running the Europe Desk too?'

'Only because Fiona is there to do the real work – trying to
keep the networks running on less and less money.'

'Any familiar faces in Warsaw?'

'Only Boris.'

'Boris Zagan?'

'Who else.'

'Was that girl with him? … the German one?'

'Sarah. Yes, she was there. She's married to Boris.'

'Is that so? The way I heard it she was whoring for him.'

'I don't think so,' I said.

He opened a simple but beautifully made wooden box. From it he took a sword and held it up to me. 'Personally inscribed as a presentation sword for General Hoyotaro Kimura.'

I looked at it and nodded my appreciation. But swords all look very alike to pacifists like me.

Perhaps sensing that, he added: 'Burma: the commander of the Japanese 15th Army.'

'Yes,' I said as he put the sword away in its box again.

'You were always sweet on her. In Berlin … when you were a teenager doing little jobs for your dad. I remember you were mad about her then.'

'No,' I said. Harry looked at me with raised eyebrow. 'We were just kids,' I said. 'Silly teenagers.'

'Not her. She'd grown up in a hurry. Women had to grow up fast in Berlin in those funny old times. She was jumping into bed with everyone who beckoned. Five cigarettes a time is the way I heard it. American cigarettes.'

'You always were a romantic,' I said.

'And you always were a pragmatist, weren't you, Bernard?'

'I don't know; I've never pragmarred.'

'You didn't come down here so that your kids could play hide-and-seek among my dead cabbages. And to get a bellyful of canned lager and that lousy rubber quiche, which I notice even you didn't finish.'

'Why did I come?' I said.

He stared at me and furrowed his brow as if thinking about it for the first time. 'Perhaps because I spent nearly five years

129

sitting in the Deputy Director-General's office filling in his appointment books and keeping the riffraff at bay. That's usually why Department people want to see me out of office hours.'

So there were others? He'd only been retired five minutes. Or did he mean before retirement? 'Never a social call?'

'Sometimes. But not from you, Bernard. You are not a starry-eyed teenager any longer. You haven't been starry-eyed for a long time. You've changed a lot.' I wanted to explain but he waved me silent. He'd warmed to the idea of guessing what I had come to discuss with him. 'Which year would it be ...' he said, as if thinking aloud. 'It won't be anything about your dad. I wasn't there at the right time to have ever dealt with your dad's personal files. No, it will be something about that time when the German Desk fell vacant, and you and Dicky Cruyer were the contenders for it.' He looked at me and smiled. 'You had a lot of ardent supporters, Bernard. Let me say it – you were the best man for the job. Is that what you wanted to know about? The arguments and the meetings and how the old man finally turned you down for it?'

The pained smile was back on his leathery face. His eyes moved as if he was daring me to say yes. As if he could provide me with some remarkable and scandalous facts if I wanted to hear them.

'It wasn't about that,' I said.

'No?' His face was set in that jovial but omnipotent grimace that you see in cheap bronze Buddhas. After his field work he'd come to the office and ended up as a not-unusual example of the Eton Oxbridge Buddha class: sadistic, self-sufficient apparatchiks who controlled Whitehall by stealth, wealth and consanguinity and – no matter how friendly – inevitably closed ranks against intruders like me. Could I have become a Harry Strang? A close friend of my father, Silas Gaunt, had put my name down for Eton and offered to pay the fees, but my self-made father

130

was strongly opposed to having his son made into a janissary who would fight the battles of the ruling class. Better, said my father, that I remained with my family, went to the local school with the Berlin boys I played with in the street. My father told his friends (although he never told me) that I would grow up with such an intimacy with Germany and Germans that I would inevitably rise to become Director-General.

Well, Dad proved wrong. A Berlin school – even if you were the top scholar there – was no preparation for Whitehall. Or for boys like Harry Strang and Dicky Cruyer, who had grown up learning how to survive the loves, tears and terrors of expensive English boys' boarding schools; learning how to conceal all human feelings until they faded and stopped coming back.

'No,' I said. 'I want to know about the night we brought my wife out of the East.'

'What can I tell you about that, Bernard? You were there. You shot the bastards who trapped her. You brought her to Helmstedt and safety.'

'I need some background,' I said. 'Who gave the order? Who chose that night for it?'

'You remember. There was that fancy-dress party … Half Berlin was celebrating at Tante Lisl's hotel. It was perfect timing.'

'There must have been a written order?'

'No. It would have been left to the people on the spot.'

'I don't think so, Harry,' I said. 'Frank Harrington, the Berlin Rezident, was technically the senior man. He certainly didn't know it was happening until the Sunday morning. Dicky Cruyer, from London, was at the party. He came out to find me and ask what was happening. Who gave the order, Harry? It would require at least twenty-four hours to fix up all the preparations. There was a chopper waiting at Helmstedt, and the RAF positioned a big transport plane for us. We were flown directly to America that same night. There was a hell of a lot of planning. Inter-service planning; you know how long that takes.'

'Yes, you're right. There were a lot of people on standby: soldiers, field agents and our own liaison people at the border posts. It's coming back to me now. The RAF were phoning and complaining about the delay. They'd been told to supply a doctor, and after six hours waiting in the transit barracks the quack buggered off to a local bar and got paralytic drunk.'

'So who arranged it all?'

'You did, in effect. You were briefed by Frank weren't you? You went to the rendezvous and blew away two Stasi men, or KGB or whatever they were.'

'Why do you say that?'

'It was in the report you wrote.'

'I never wrote any report.'

'Then you must have told Bret Rensselaer when he debriefed you in California.'

'And he told you?' Harry smiled one of his inscrutable smiles. Artfully he had led the conversation away from my question. 'But I am still curious about who gave the order. When was the decision made? There must have been meetings with someone at top level.'

'There was no time.'

'Even a phone call would have gone into the log, Harry.'

'Not this one.'

'Planting my wife in the DDR was the greatest hit the Department ever scored. It was vital to bring her out happy, healthy and intact. It had to be a story to be told to the politicians, and that means one with a happy ending. The decision about when and how to bring her out was going to be decisive. The D-G would have to be kept informed, even if he didn't give the order.'

'I was the personal assistant to the Deputy, not to the D-G himself. The D-D-G was not always a party to the day-today operational doings. Especially tricky ones.'

'That famous Strang total recall is letting you down, Harry,' I said. 'You weren't with the Deputy at that time. The D-G's PA was in hospital; you worked for the D-G while the Deputy's secretary filled in for you with the Deputy.'

'What a memory you've got, Bernard,' he said, without demonstrating unbridled admiration or delight. 'Yes, of course, young Morgan was in hospital with gunshot wounds.' He smiled. Morgan – the old man's personal assistant – had suffered multiple minor wounds to his leg when a fellow guest at a weekend shooting party discharged a shotgun by accident. By the time the story got to the office, it was inevitably Morgan's arse that was the target, and in some embellishments it was an irate husband who fired the gun. Harry Strang allowed himself a chuckle; Morgan was not the most popular man in London Central. I waited. I could see that Harry was putting something together in his mind. 'Yes, there were meetings. But I don't know who he was with, or where they took place.'

'Away from the office, you mean?'

'You know what the old man is like. He's getting old and eccentric. He pops up here and there, like a jack-in-the-box. That's why he's always had two duty drivers. There were days when he was not in the office at all. The Thursday and Friday before the weekend that Fiona came out. On those days the D-G didn't come in to the office at all as I remember it.'

'It's been great, Harry. But I must be getting along,' I said, getting to my feet.

'I wish I could give you more details.'

'It was just idle curiosity,' I said. 'But I suppose we'll never know the whole story.'

'Not many people know the whole story about anything,' said Harry.

'Can I help with the washing-up?'

'I have a machine,' said Harry.

'I'll see if the kids want to use the bathroom.'

As I got to the back door Harry touched my arm. 'You should have been given the German Desk, Bernard. Everyone said so. But the old man was against it.'

I opened the back door and shouted: 'Sally! Billy! We're leaving now. Come and say thank you to Uncle Harry.' The clouds had become a cauldron of molten lead, silvery-grey cumulus boiling and swirling around the red blobby parts. And yet the sky behind the clouds remained clear blue, as if from some other day and some other season.

'They treated your dad badly,' Harry said softly as we watched the children slowly and reluctantly getting out of his old car. 'The D-G was afraid that giving you the German Desk would seem as if the Department was trying to make amends for that past wrong they did your dad, and for God knows what else.'

'We couldn't have that,' I said sarcastically.

'No, that would never do. You won't stay for tea?'

'I must get back on the road,' I said.

The children arrived breathless, having run from the end of the garden. 'Do you want to use the bathroom?' I asked.

'What does a Frenchman eat for breakfast?' Billy asked Harry Strang. He'd already used his joke on me.

'I don't know,' said Harry, playing along with him.

'*Huit heures* bix,' said Billy and laughed. Sally laughed politely too. 'Weetabix,' Billy repeated, in case we had missed the joke. Harry produced a fine baritone laugh.

'It's a long drive to Grandma,' I said.

'It will seem even longer if he tells us all his corny jokes,' Sally said.

'Dad said he likes corny jokes,' said Billy. 'I save them for him. Isn't that right, Dad?'

'There's no joke like an old joke,' I said.

'That's right,' said Harry. 'It's like friends.' He looked at me as if trying to decide whether our friendship had anything going for it.

Billy went upstairs to the bathroom while Sally cleared away the dishes on the table. Harry began putting his swords back into the cupboard where they belonged.

'Lovely kids, Bernard. They are a credit to you. I thought your boy would have been keen on the swords.'

'He is,' I said, 'but he hates white gloves.'

'You can't handle them with your bare hands,' said Harry, who was not renowned for joke recognition. 'The acid perspiration would destroy the blades.' Harry looked at each sword lovingly as he put it away. 'Yes, nice kids. Count your blessings, Bernard.' Harry's voice was different now; warmer and more trusting. 'I wish my marriage had lasted, but you can't have everything. It took me a long time to realize that, but it's true.'

'When did the heavy-glove men come here, Harry?' I said. 'Am I a lot too late?'

'Don't be silly, Bernard.' The shutters came down with a clang and his face was blank.

'Yesterday? Last week? What did they say they would do? They can't touch your pension can they?'

'Careful how you drive, Bernard. Those Frenchmen, in the big trucks coming from the ferry, drive like maniacs. Sometimes I wonder if it's all that vin rouge.'

'How do they do it? I've often wondered. High-level, low-level, or anonymous? Do they send one of those bastards from Internal Security?'

He smiled another of those mirthless smiles. It completely prevented one reading anything into his expression; maybe

135

that's why he did it. 'I miss the old man,' he said. 'I enjoyed my time working on the top floor. And Sir Henry is a gentleman of the old school. Even during the hectic days when your wife was coming out, he went down to pay his respects to Uncle Silas. He kept in touch to make him feel he was still a part of things.' Harry looked at me. 'Uncle Silas was sick. He'd fallen off a horse, they said.'

'He was too old for horses.'

'That's what I thought,' said Harry sharply, as if I had suddenly solved a mystery that had puzzled him.

I knew it was as far as Harry would go. In reversed circumstances – with a pig-farm and pension in the balance – it was perhaps more than I would have risked for him.

As we were departing, Harry's young farm-hand came up the path carrying a bucket of newly dug potatoes. He was very muddy and looked perished with the cold, but he wore the same gentle bemused smile that he'd worn when showing us his favourite porkers.

'Come along, Tommy!' Harry shouted to him. 'Come in and get warm. I'm brewing up some tea.'

6

Mayfair, London.

'What a lovely idea – to take the children to see your mother. How is she?'

'She's fine,' I said.

It was typical of the polite exchanges that enabled our happy marriage to continue so smoothly. Fiona didn't really think it was a lovely idea that prompted me to take our children to visit my mother. She thought it a stupid, inconsiderate exploit that was done to worry my mother-in-law and annoy my father-in-law while leaving her to soak up their dismay, anger and resentment. And my mother was not fine. She was anything but fine. She was in a nursing home that she didn't like, and the only time I saw flashes of the mother I remembered was when she was showing her annoyance about being incarcerated far from her friends and the home she loved. But despite everything my mother said, she was seriously infirm and incapable of living on her own. I'd taken the children to visit her only because I thought she would be dead before another year was past.

'Good,' said Fiona, and smiled to show me that she could read my mind. She was wearing her magnificent fur coat. She became almost animal in that soft glistening sable. It made her remote and exotic; so that I found it difficult to remember that this lovely creature was my wife.

'Shall we go out for dinner?' she said. She'd been with the D-G almost all day, and I could see she'd had her hair done and put on her extra-special make-up for him. She was standing by the stove-top reading an almost indecipherable note left there by Mrs Dias. The indomitable Mrs Dias had cooked our meals, minded our children, washed, swept and cleaned for us – and piled up astounding hours of labour – back when we lived in Duke Street, before Fiona had pulled her defection stunt. Now Fiona had tracked her down and persuaded her to work for us again. I'm sure the smart Mayfair address, in an apartment block with lords and ladies and recording stars, was an enticement for Mrs Dias, who was, like most domestic workers throughout history, a resolute and uncompromising snob.

'We said we'd economize this month,' I said.

Fiona was still reading the note. She'd let her nails grow longer and today they were painted, albeit in a natural pink colour. She looked up. 'I can never read her handwriting. Sometimes I think some of the words must be Portuguese.' Then: 'I'm sorry, I forgot about the economy drive. I had no time to shop, I'll dig something out of the freezer.'

'Do you want a drink?' I said.

With no more than a glance at the opened bottle of Bell's on the kitchen table in front of me, she had noted its level. 'Not whisky,' she said, 'but I'll have a tonic water, and sit with you for a moment. I'm absolutely exhausted.' She took a chilled can of tonic from the refrigerator, a cut-glass tumbler from the shelf and then ice from the dispenser.

This apartment, a legacy from Fiona's wealthy sister, was extraordinary. The kitchen had been cleverly designed to conceal its function. It had fake-antique cupboards in which to hide away the saucepans and crockery so that I could never find anything. The refrigerator was disguised as wall, and the twin ovens concealed behind decorative tiles. Every working surface was stark

138

and bare, and lingering in the air there were the scented sprays with which Mrs Dias staked out her territory. As usual she'd been through the whole apartment mercilessly eliminating all traces of human presence. Flower arrangements past their prime were protruding bent and broken from shiny black trash-bags. No trace now of food or drink; of bowls of peanuts, half-read books, carpet slippers, newspapers or magazines, or any other evidence that human beings had ever passed this way. What this morning had been a comfortable apartment now looked like a set erected for a photographer from *House and Garden*.

'Everything all right with Mrs Dias?' I asked cheerfully.

'It's about her money,' said Fiona, still examining the note. Indecipherable writing or not, this was a safe bet.

'Sit down,' I told her. She looked uncomfortable standing there in her fur coat, hands resting on the back of the Windsor chair.

'I'm better standing. It's my back again.' As if in demonstration she arched her back and grimaced. 'I'll be fine if I stand for a minute.' There came an impatient fanfare of assorted car horns from the street below. This was the penalty for living in the most exclusive part of London's West End. Here were the nightclubs, fancy restaurants and top hotels and the never-ending noise of traffic, car doors slamming and the high-pitched exchanges of the rich and famous. Fiona gave up reading and dropped the note on the table.

'Is there something wrong?' I said.

'They've made it official. George. We've notified the Warsaw embassy to request a copy of the death certificate. The D-G just nodded it through; there was no argument or discussion.'

'Was Dicky there?'

'For the morning meeting, yes.'

'Dicky is obsessed about proving George Kosinski's contacts with the Stasi. He'll chalk it up as a success story. I suspect he'll use the Polish death certificate to turn over everything George owned or had contact with.'

'How?'

'It's in the new Police and Criminal Evidence Act. He'll use the certified death to support a claim that an arrestable offence has been committed. On that basis he could claim that all George's property is "of substantial value to the investigation". His one-time property too. Nothing could stop Dicky seizing, searching and entering anywhere he fancies, and grabbing what he wants to look at.'

'Does it matter?'

'Are you forgetting that this apartment would be included in that description?'

'He wouldn't dare.' She paused. 'Would he?'

'I don't like it, Fi.'

'Because you don't like Dicky,' she declared categorically.

'No, not because I don't like Dicky. I don't like it because I don't believe this is Dicky. I think Dicky is acting on instructions.'

'From above? Who?'

'I don't know. Who has he been with recently?'

'No one. He came in for the first meeting and then said he was too ill to work and went home.' She was still standing. Remembering her tonic water, she sipped some as if it was medicine, and then put the glass on the table, sliding the note from Mrs Dias under it to prevent ring-marks on the polished table-top.

'I thought that he was suddenly taken ill because the Polish beds were too hard and there was no central heating.'

'No, it was genuine,' she said.

'Genuine hypochondria. Well, that's a step in the right direction. Should you see a doctor about that back of yours?'

'Dicky says George is dead. He wants to put a notice in the newspapers. What do you think?'

140

'About Dicky or about George?'

'Dicky wants them to repatriate George's body. But I said George is a Swiss resident. What would be the legal position? Is there any member of George's family who might be persuaded to request the return of the body you saw?'

'We saw no body. Just a lower leg and foot.'

'What's the difference?' said Fiona. 'It's the burial I'm thinking of.'

'You sound like Dicky,' I said. 'Examining a leg is inconclusive. No one files away records of toe-prints. And most hospitals amputate far more legs than arms, so it's often possible to buy a leg from some unscrupulous incinerator man or theatre orderly.'

'How disgusting. Why do they amputate more legs than arms? And why couldn't anyone see it had been surgically amputated?' This was Fiona as she used to be; argumentative and challenging.

'It hadn't been surgically amputated; it had been crudely hacked away from the upper leg.'

'Doesn't that rather overturn your theory that it came from a hospital?'

'On the contrary; it strengthens it. The reason hospitals amputate more legs than arms is due to the way that circulatory problems more commonly affect the legs when patients become unable to walk or exercise. Such limbs are dead and blackened, but these jokers needed a good-looking leg – that means one amputated because of physical damage … in a traffic accident or whatever. But such a limb would have come complete with the trauma, the damage. To make it convincing they would have to cut it off at the knee, and that's what they undoubtedly did. Anyway it wasn't George, rest your mind on that. The foot wouldn't have fitted into George's shoe.'

She was still standing, resting her hands on the back of the chair. She stared at me for a moment: 'No one else noticed that?'

141

'That's why they'd hacked off the big toe. And anyway it was all too phoney: the flesh obviously hadn't suffered that kind of damage while the shoe was still on it. The shoe was in relatively good condition. Obviously they got one of George's shoes afterwards, then they saw it was too small for the foot, so they hacked the big toe off the foot. That meant they had to make the injury look as if it had been chewed by an animal. So then they had to make the shoe look like some animal had bitten into it while the foot was still inside it. It would be a difficult piece of fakery even if it was done in a laboratory. Far beyond those jokers.'

'Is that conclusive? Perhaps the leg you saw wasn't George's leg, but that doesn't prove that George isn't dead.'

'I know I'm right,' I said in a way that perhaps I wouldn't have chosen except for the last drink or two. 'And no killer would have had time enough to dig a grave into that icy rockhard ground. Then he'd have to dispose of the spade. How? Worry about fingerprints and other traces? No way. You'd be crazy to think about burying a corpse when you could simply toss it into the river and let it be carried away for miles. Or hide it somewhere it would never be found. That whole forest is a tangle of old bunkers, trenches and decaying fortifications.'

'Did you discuss all this with Dicky? He seems certain that George is dead.'

'He didn't ask me. He didn't ask because it suits him to believe it.'

'I didn't ask you either.' She was still standing behind the chair, gripping the back of it so tightly that her knuckles were white.

'No, you didn't, but I'm telling you anyway. I'm telling you because I think your ownership of this apartment might be in jeopardy.'

'Why should you care? You hate this apartment. I can see it in every move you make.'

'You are my wife and I love you: that's why. And I don't hate this apartment.'

'Of course you don't. How could you? You're hardly ever here.'

'I'm trying to help you.'

'This belief that Dicky is about to barge in here and ransack the apartment ... Is that anything to do with the suitcase you removed and took with you yesterday?'

'There were personal things of mine that I've now stored elsewhere. Things I wouldn't want Dicky rummaging through.'

'Things the Department might not approve of?'

'About a thousand quid in foreign currency, plus fifty gold sovereigns my father left me. My father's moth-eaten army tunic. Some forged identity papers, some documents that could incriminate old friends, or get them into bad odour. My parents' wedding photos and a leather-bound copy of *Die schöne Müllerin* that was a present from the von Munte library. A couple of hand-guns – one of them Dad's army-issue Webley – and some ancient ammunition.'

Her face softened. 'I didn't mean to pry, Bernard. I'm sorry. I get upset.' She pulled out the chair, sat down and sipped more of her tonic water. Then she gave me her attention in a softer and more friendly way. 'What's it all about, Bernard? Why would they want to sequester George's possessions? What do you think might be behind it?'

'I don't know, Fi, and that's the truth. But it's probably something to do with Tessa's death. That's the only connection that could link George to the Stasi.'

'You were there when Tessa was killed,' said Fiona.

'We were both there,' I pointed out gently. 'But why was Tessa there?'

'You brought her with you in the van.'

'I know, but she was meant to be there, Fi. Soon after I left the party at Tante Lisl's there was a man looking for her. He had

143

a motor bike and he turned up at the Brandenburg exit. I think he'd arranged to take Tessa there.'

'But why was she there?'

'She had some strange friends, Fi, you know she did. And she was taking some kind of dope. I think it was coming to her through one of the Stasi people. Someone wanted her there and arranged for her to be there, but whether the man on the motor bike was one of our people I still don't know. He might have been one of Tessa's casual affairs. You know how batty she could be.'

'I let the family down,' said Fiona. 'If I'd been here with her, it might have all turned out differently. Yes, she probably was on some kind of dope. I've been reluctant to face it, but it goes back a long time ...'

'Stasi agents talked to George in Zurich. Polish Bezpieca too, I suspect.'

'That's what Dicky said.'

'George was moved so smoothly from Zurich to Warsaw. Really professional job. No trace of tickets or paper or witnesses.'

'Dicky has our people in Berne still looking.'

'Don't hold your breath: Berne will find nothing. It was beautifully done; not in their league.'

'Not so beautifully done, if you tracked him down to his brother's house.'

Clever, logical Fiona; I wondered if she was going to bring that up. 'A lucky guess. I picked up the trail. Suddenly I hear about him getting drunk in Warsaw bars and making a nuisance of himself. He must have broken away from his minders.'

'Wouldn't his minders have grabbed him back?'

'Not if they were Germans. Germans, even Stasi, tread warily in Poland. And George's brother Stefan is still influential there. I think George escaped from his Stasi minders, and made such a nuisance of himself that they backed off to watch what happened.'

'And killed him?'

'There's nothing conclusive to say that George is dead. Everything we saw in Poland points to a lot of phoney clues to make us think he's dead. Or make someone else think that.'

'Clues left by his Stasi minders? But you were not fooled.'

'Pros who can spirit George out of Zurich to Warsaw without leaving a trace are not the sort of dudes who leave a wristwatch, a laced and tied brogue shoe and a decomposing foot as evidence of death.'

'So who arranged it?'

'It could be George himself.'

'How could George arrange for the death certificate?'

'Oh, Stefan is in on it, of course. Stefan has a lot of clout and Stefan's wife is the daughter of some top-brass Party official. And this is Poland we're talking about. Germans are not popular there, German communists are heartily despised. If a big-shot like Stefan wants a death certificate so that his brother can escape the clutches of the Stasi, what Pole is going to say no?'

'Dicky will riot when he hears all this,' she said sadly. Despite all her experience, Fiona was reluctant to believe that death certificates could be fixed; even in Poland. Sometimes I wondered whether it was university education that produced that kind of unquestioning belief in signed pieces of paper.

'So don't tell him,' I suggested.

'But darling ...'

'This is Tessa's husband we are talking about. If George wants to be written off as dead, he must have a good reason for it. He's family.'

'It's not right to mislead Dicky,' she said.

'No one's misleading him, he's chock-full of theories. If you persuade Dicky that George is alive, Dicky will rush out a long and elaborate report saying so. Dozens of people will have access to it. One word in the wrong place could put George in jeopardy.'

'From what you've told me, the faked death won't fool any experienced Polish police investigator for longer than two minutes.'

'That depends on whether the Polish investigator wants the truth to be known. Stefan is a fixer. He no doubt fixed the cops at the same time as he fixed the death certificate.'

She sighed. 'I suppose you could be right. But I feel very uneasy keeping this from the Department. We're supposed to be loyal employees. We've signed the Official Secrets Act, and our contracts … I mean, darling!'

'I went to see Harry Strang.'

'With the children?'

'Yes, with the children.'

'I wondered how it could have taken you so long to get to your mother. How was he?'

'Up to his eyebrows in pig-shit, but he seems to like it.'

'Some people do. And let's face it, would that make much of a change for any of us?' Wow – this was Fiona showing her feelings; something that didn't happen often. 'And his son was with him?'

'Son?'

'The retarded one. Tommy. He must be grown up by now.'

'I didn't know Harry had a son.'

'How can you be so thick, Bernard? Harry's wife had a nervous breakdown after the baby's condition was diagnosed. That's why they split up. It's every mother's nightmare. There wasn't any kind of a row between the two of them; his wife just couldn't take it. Little Tommy. It was a tragedy. After that, Harry gave every spare minute of his life to looking after the child.'

'I didn't know,' I said.

'So why did you go down there? He obviously isn't your closest old pal.'

'Over that period … That time when they brought you out of the DDR, Harry Strang was filling in as the personal assistant to the D-G.'

'Yes, of course. Morgan was sick.'

'He had an arse filled with lead shot. Harry says the old man had no meetings about you, or your escape.'

'But would Harry tell you?'

'He'd been warned off, I think. Top-floor alarm bells have been ringing. Recently.'

'If you've been roaring around making enquiries about how they brought me out ... Of course they are alarmed. I'm not surprised at that.'

'No meetings, Fi! Are you listening? The D-G had no meetings. I've already had one of the Night Duty people go to his office and take a look at the old man's appointments and desk diary, and that confirmed it.'

There came a sharp intake of breath to let me know that getting a pal to sneak a look at Sir Henry's personal appointment book and diary was not playing the game, so I didn't tell her that I'd also phoned Mrs Porter, Uncle Silas's housekeeper, and discovered that there were indeed meetings – one particularly long meeting – between Silas and the D-G immediately before they spirited Fiona out of the East.

Fiona asked: 'So what am I supposed to say now?'

'Don't you see, Fi, it means the D-G was keeping everything outside the office.'

'It's a bit of a leap in the dark, isn't it, darling?'

'Meetings with Uncle Silas, for instance.'

'You can't be sure.'

'Of course I can't be sure, but Harry hinted. Uncle Silas and the D-G hatched it up together. I'd love to hear what they said about Tessa.'

'I wish you'd drop it all, Bernard. Tessa's dead. You know how much I'd like to see her given a decent burial, but that doesn't mean I want to turn the Department upside-down. I'm worn down with it. Perhaps it would be better to let her rest.'

Well, well. This was quite a change of heart from the woman who conspired to send Timmermann to investigate her sister's death on a freelance basis. I said: 'Suppose that the plan was to kill Tessa? Would you still prefer to let it go?'

Fiona was good at controlling her feelings. Perhaps our marriage would have benefited from her being less good at it. 'You always go off at a tangent, darling. How does this connect up? What has it got to do with George going to Poland?'

'It's a part of the same business, it's got to be.'

'George went willingly, didn't he? You're not going to tell me they drugged him and rolled him in a carpet or something?' Since working in the East, Fiona had become less condemnatory about our enemies, or perhaps more realistic would be a fairer way of describing it.

'I don't know. Yes, he went willingly. George employed that fellow Timmermann. Timmermann was killed and then George goes away, covering his sudden disappearance by making sure Ursi his housekeeper girl wasn't too alarmed.'

Fiona stroked the arm of her fur coat while she thought about it.

I said: 'Those Stasi hoodlums took Tessa's engagement ring to Switzerland to show it to George.'

'What?' She almost jumped out of her skin. 'How do you know?'

'I went to the jeweller in Zurich. George took the ring there for cleaning. I saw it; a heart-shaped diamond with four small diamonds. It was Tessa's engagement ring all right.'

'Why would George take it to be cleaned?'

'You know how distrustful George can be. I think it was a way to find out whether it was a paste copy without actually asking them.'

'But it's real?'

'It's real.'

148

'I won't tell Dicky or anyone about your thinking George is alive. At least for the time being. After all, it's only your theory, it's not as if you're withholding evidence.'

'No,' I said. Fiona had now assuaged her middle-class anxieties of being disloyal to the Crown. 'There's no hard evidence; it is just my theory. If I persuaded Dicky to say George is alive, and then suddenly the body arrived, Dicky would have something to complain about.'

'Very well, darling. But I want you to be honest with me in future. You're awfully secretive, Bernard, and that's putting a terrible strain on your career, and on this marriage too.'

'Yes,' I said, and drank some whisky and smiled at her. This was not the time to remind her that she had plotted and planned her defection to the East for years, and never included me in the secret. But that if I wait forty-eight hours before telling her that Dicky's wide-eyed acceptance of George's fake death is just one more example of his stupidity, I get scolded for marital infidelity.

Perhaps Fiona guessed what I was thinking, for she avoided my eyes and turned away. 'I'll have a biscuit,' she said, and reached into the kitchen drawer for a packet of oatmeal cookies that are there for Mrs Dias's sole use, and are replenished faithfully. I didn't know Fiona was hooked on them too. 'Fancy one?'

'No.' We sat there for a long time, each thinking our own thoughts until I said: 'Remember Cindy Prettyman?'

'Of course. Was she in Warsaw?'

'Not her. Last I heard, she had a cushy job in Brussels with lots of money and lovely tax-free allowances and lots of good restaurants. Or perhaps it was Strasbourg; some kind of European Community pen-pusher's racket anyway.'

'Lucky her. She was the first person I showed my engagement ring to.'

'That's a long time ago.'

'I was so proud. I told her, Bernard sold his Ferrari to buy my ring.'

'You didn't tell her it was up on blocks and needed a new transmission?'

She smiled. It was a joke. That old Ferrari could make a little black smoke when it was in a bad mood. And it stalled to show how much it didn't like being slowed up in heavy traffic. But it could still do its stuff when I sold it. When I saw it drive off, with its new owner at the wheel, there were tears in my eyes.

I said: 'Cindy came to me with a story that Jim Prettyman was embezzling millions from the Department.'

'He was,' said Fiona. 'It was the funding for my operation in the East. Jim Prettyman was on the Special Operations Committee. He was named as the account holder along with Bret Rensselaer, who arranged the chain of payment from Central Funding through a few brokers to a West Berlin bank Bret's family are associated with.'

'Could Cindy's lovely job have been arranged just to stop her prying further into the money set-up?'

'I would imagine so,' said Fiona, clearly untroubled by the ethics of such a recourse. 'Having someone like Cindy trumpeting our fiscal secrets up and down Whitehall would have brought disaster.'

'She came to me ready to blow the whistle on what sounded like a big embezzlement. She thought it was some kind of KGB slush fund. She'd been notified that Jim had just been killed in a parking lot in Washington DC and the Department said she wasn't entitled to the pension because he'd married again.'

'Jim married again? I didn't know,' said Fiona.

'And it was a Mexican divorce. But Jim wasn't dead, he was put on the back-burner. Eventually the Department paid both widows rather than let Jim's bogus death come under scrutiny.' I looked at Fiona. She nodded. She knew all this already. How many more dark secrets were inside her head? 'So Cindy was right?' I said. 'There was an illegal transfer?'

'It was fundamental to placing me in the DDR. I had to get the Church people over there organized and motivated. They are not all selfless dedicated people with money of their own. You know that; you're the field agent.'

'You don't have to be defensive, Fi. You did a great job.'

'Five point seven million pounds sterling. It will work, Bernard. A bargain. They'll topple the regime eventually but they need time.'

'And then Jim suddenly came back to life and visited us in California,' I reminded her. 'I wonder if the Department asked Cindy for her money back.'

'It wouldn't be a lump sum,' said Fiona, as if she had already found out what happens to those widowed in the service of their country. 'Is there a connection? A connection with Tessa's death?'

'Cindy clammed up suddenly. The Europe job came through and she didn't want to continue the crusade she'd started. Crusade ... I mean she'd really built up a head of steam when I saw her. This is Tessa country. There must be more behind it.'

'Are you going to find her?'

'Cindy? No,' I said. 'I've other things to do right now. And if Dicky is going to be sick in bed, suffering from Polish plague or something, there will be all his work piling up on my desk.'

'The funny thing is that Daphne thought he'd be away in Poland at least another week. She arranged for the builders to come in and fix the damp in the attic and refurbish both bathrooms. It will be hell for Dicky. He won't even have a loo to himself.'

'I must drop in and say hello,' I said. 'I love hammering. I hope they all have transistor radios.'

'You *are* going to find Cindy aren't you? I can always tell when you are lying to me.' She said it in a genial way, as if my

151

lies pleased her; or perhaps it was always being able to catch me out in my lies that gave her that satisfied look.

'Lucinda Matthews,' I said. 'She prefers her maiden name nowadays. Have we got an up-to-date Michelin Guide that would cover it?'

'Dicky no doubt has one in his office.'

'We could both go. In the old days they were our closest friends, weren't they?'

'I might have to remind you of that, Bernard.'

'I wouldn't do anything to hurt Cindy.'

'You'd shop your own mother if she stood in the way of you finding out something you really wanted to know.' Fiona laughed in that sincere and friendly way that married couples do laugh when they have said something to their partner that they really mean. When her smile faded she said: 'This morning there was a "resources" meeting. There are going to be big cut-backs, Bernard.'

'They are always talking about cut-backs and it winds up with a memo asking everyone to save the paper clips on their incoming mail.'

'Not this time. Even people on permanent contract are not safe. Central Funding have set aside separate money for severance pay.'

'I'm not on a permanent contract,' I said flippantly.

'I can't argue with them on your behalf, darling. You understand that don't you?'

'No of course not. It would look bad if friends or family argued on behalf of someone it was expedient to get rid of. The only people who can legitimately argue on my behalf are my enemies.'

'Dicky isn't your enemy.'

'Who said anything about Dicky?'

'That shooting at the Campden Hill flat … VERDI was killed. The inquiry exonerated you and Werner, but losing such a

152

promising source leaves a bad impression.' She paused. 'You want it straight, don't you? You don't want me to baby you along?'

'No, don't baby me along, Fi.'

She ignored the bitter tone in my voice and said: 'Nothing is decided yet, but all senior staff will be asked to submit a list of people they ...'

'They want to get rid of.'

'Yes, and if that won't provide savings enough, they will start listing the necessary cuts ... so many grade threes, so many grade fives and so on. Bret says there may be constitutional implications. He said it might be beyond the government's lawful powers to demand big cuts in the nation's security services without consulting Parliament and getting all-party consent.'

'Good old Bret. He's a flag-waver, isn't he?' I got to my feet and patted the stopper on the whisky bottle to be sure it was tightly plugged. I wasn't enjoying this conversation.

'You'll be all right Bernard.'

'I've got no contract; no pension plan; no tenure; no severance pay, no rights at all. I'd be the cheapest employee to get rid of. Even the doorman has a trade union to back him if he appeals to a tribunal for unfair dismissal. They could push me out of the door at a minute's notice.'

'At least I will be able to tell you what's happening and when, darling. It won't just come out of the blue like that.'

'I'm not going to stay awake all night worrying,' I said. 'There's nothing I can do about keeping my job, so screw them.'

She came close to me and I held her. She was still wearing her big soft fur coat and my fingers disappeared. With uncharacteristic spontaneity, she put her hand to the back of my head and kissed me with unusual verve. Holding me tight she said: 'There is something you can do: stop fighting Dicky.' The soft mellowness of her voice was laced with wifely concern. This

153

was the voice she used to hint that I was drinking too much; the voice that had persuaded me to give up smoking.

'I'm not fighting him.'

She pulled away from me and modelled her coat in the mirror, as if there was no one there watching her. Then she looked up and said: 'Explain to Dicky your reasons for thinking that George is still alive. Get him to tell you what he's trying to achieve. Do whatever is needed to help him clear up the George Kosinski file. A neat success might see him confirmed as Controller Europe. Bret wants that ghastly Australian fellow back, I suppose he thinks Dicky is getting too powerful. The D-G is wavering.'

'So I heard.'

'And yet you are standing back to watch Dicky fall flat on his face? Your best bet is to stand behind Dicky and make sure he gets everything right. Let him take the credit.'

'Is that what you are doing?' She'd known him since they were at Oxford together and, no matter how clearly she saw what a fool he was, that gave them an intimacy which I could never share.

'For Dicky? Perhaps. I've never thought about it.' A grin. 'You're surely not jealous. You think Dicky has got his eye on me?' She laughed. 'I can't believe it.' She went and sat in a chair near her tonic water.

'No, I'm not jealous of him,' I said.

'Dicky will need someone reliable in Berlin. Frank Harrington has asked for a Deputy.'

'So that's official now? He's managed without one for a long time.'

'Deputy to the Berlin Rezident? Berlin Field Unit. You'd love that, darling, I know you would. Allowances and expenses! You would be upgraded to a senior staff pension. And it would make you virtually invulnerable to the cutback.' So this is what

154

she really wanted to tell me. I suppose she'd planned to explain it over a brandy in some fancy restaurant, rather than over a can of Schweppes tonic water in the kitchen, but this was the sponsor's message all right.

'Did Dicky mention my name?'

'It's in his gift and there's no one better suited,' she said. 'And if Dicky felt sure you were his man, he'd back you to the hilt.'

'Oh, I see.'

'What's the matter? What did I say?'

'As Dicky's snooper, you mean? I go to Berlin to keep an eye on Frank Harrington, and undermine him if he ever tries to go against Dicky's good advice.'

'Of course not, darling,' she said, but she wasn't standing on the table and shouting the denial.

'My children are here in London,' I said. 'You are here in London.'

'You're so loyal to us, Bernard. To your family, I mean. It's what I love about you. But careers count too. Loyalty to the job.'

'You don't mind that our children are living with your father, do you? It suits you to have them there in the country with your parents, and visit them when you can.'

'You'd be back and forth regularly, to consult with Dicky. How much more would we see of the children if they were living here in this apartment with us? You are always being sent off to the other side of the world at little or no notice. I leave early in the morning and work into the night. What kind of life would they have?'

'It sounds as if you don't want the children back home ever,' I said.

'That's not true, Bernard. It's a beastly thing to say.' She shifted in her chair and tugged at her coat to wrap it more closely around her legs.

'Fi, suppose I do help Dicky find George, and then coax from him whatever there is to know about his Stasi contacts ...? Can you live with that?'

'Whatever do you mean?'

'Have you asked yourself how it's going to look if George has been helping the Stasi, or the KGB, or some other enemy outfit? There'll be one hell of a rumpus. You'll be implicated. He's your brother-in-law.'

She pursed her mouth. She obviously hadn't considered that angle before, but she didn't take long to resolve it. 'We can't take that into account, darling. We can't ... it's national security, whatever the consequences to us personally.'

'You're right,' I said, but I was far from convinced. Fiona's middle-class schooling and upbringing had made her rigidly patriotic, so that serving the Crown – and the nation – was life's highest ambition. I didn't yield to her on high motives but I had come from different stock. The rough and tumble of my work as a field agent had made me hard and distrustful, so that one small part of my psyche – and of all my other resources – was reserved for me and mine. 'This job that's waiting for me in Berlin,' I said. 'That wouldn't be something you and Dicky have cooked up to get me away from Gloria, would it?'

Fiona was holding her tonic aloft and trying again to interpret the note from Mrs Dias. She looked up. 'So that's it? No one is conspiring against you, darling. But suppose it was a scheme that Dicky and I had cooked up, would that make a difference?'

'No, it wouldn't make any difference,' I said without getting angry. 'There is no way I am taking any job in Berlin. I know what it entails and I'm too old for all that tough-guy stuff. And too cynical to believe in it.'

Her head was bent as she studied the note and she gave no sign that she had heard my response. 'Do let's eat out,' she said, and put her glass back on to the note. 'Somewhere lovely: Annabel's. I'll pay. Daddy's raised my allowance this month.'

She raised her eyes to mine. Her lips smiled sweetly as if she adored me. She didn't answer my question of course. She didn't have to; her eyes said gotcha.

7

Fletcher House (SIS annexe), London.
'Your wife loathes me,' said Gloria. 'She won't be happy until I am fired.'

'No,' I said. I'd had no warning that she was going to track me down to the other side of Oxford Street and burst into this miserable little office, hugging a parcel, her face filled with indignation and despair.

'And I say yes,' she said.

I remembered the way Gloria always said 'your wife' as if Fiona existed only by means of the status our marriage conferred upon her. 'You're imagining it,' I said. In wishful and stupid desperation I added: 'I'm not sure she even knows about us.'

Gloria glared at me for a moment and then said: 'I'm not completely bonkers,' spitting out the words with anger that made me flinch. Of course I had gone too far. Gloria no doubt needed reassurance of some kind, but there was no way that her self-deception would extend to believing that Fiona didn't know that, after she'd gone away, I'd fallen foolishly and irretrievably in love with this beautiful girl, about the way we'd set up house, and the way in which Gloria had loved, cared for and enchanted the children.

'I'm sorry.' I worried what she would do next. She was cuddling a large white polystyrene box in her arms. I wondered

158

if she'd brought it to throw it at me, and if so what it might contain.

'You're a smooth talker, Bernard. Perhaps that's why I fell for you in the first place. You're a smooth talker and I'm the most gullible woman in the world.'

Some of the initial rage seemed to have gone out of her and she stood there looking at me, silent as if trying to think of the next thing she'd planned to say. She was dressed in a long suede coat and fur hat; an outfit that suited her so well that it was the image of her that returned to my mind when I thought of her. A great ball of fur like a clown's fright-wig. She'd never taken off that hat during the entire night that we spent together waiting in the hospital, worrying about little Billy's bronchitis. It was a long time ago but I remembered it vividly. Brown roll-neck sweater, brown wool skirt, pale leather ankle-boots and that crazy hat. No one could have taken Billy's plight more to heart than she did. She paced up and down, I remember, disappearing into the toilet so that I wouldn't see her crying.

'What a spooky place to work. I've never been here before.' She'd tracked me to Fletcher House, a Departmental annexe building lost in the confusion of offices and cheap dress factories behind Tottenham Court Road. A neo-Georgian building of dull red brick with Portland stone, it dated from the early Thirties and followed the design that the government then favoured for Britain's telephone exchanges.

'I'm not working here permanently; just for a few days while Dicky talks to the surveyors and looks at the library and so on. They want the Department to vacate the building. The Treasury people say they need it.'

'Where will the library go?'

'It's not really a part of our main library. It's a leftover consignment of German-language books and documents brought over in 1945 – Nazi Party publications and reference books and even some ancient telephone directories – some of it still in its packing cases. I'd send it all back to Bonn and let the Germans sort it out.'

'Is that what Dicky will do?'

'I shouldn't think so. The books provide our only legitimate excuse for hanging on to the building; we're using less than half the office space, and there's no way of hiding that.'

'I don't get it.'

'There are sixteen parking spaces in the back yard here. The car pool uses them. Dicky would get hung, drawn and quartered if he gave way and the Department lost any of its Central London parking spaces.'

'I'm relieved to hear that they are not locking you away here for ever, Bernard.'

'Just while Dicky thinks up reasons for hanging on to it.'

'Couldn't you find a better room than this?'

'Not all the floors are heated,' I explained. 'And I had to have a phone that was working.' I'd made myself at home with a decrepit desk and a couple of chairs in a long narrow room. It was little better than a corridor really, situated between a seldom occupied 'police liaison office' and a room where three cheerful women clerks kept frantically active operating a dozen or so copying machines.

'No one seemed to know where you'd gone to.' Gloria put her parcel down on my desk and then went rummaging in her handbag for a handkerchief. The white foam box was sealed with sticky tape, and adorned with labels and writings that indicated that it had been on a roller-coaster ride through every last nook and cranny of the Foreign Office, a place with a surfeit of nooks and crannies. She wiped her nose on her handkerchief and put it away before saying: 'They asked me to bring this parcel over to you. It's fragile.'

'Thanks,' I said.

160

It had the big red international signs for fragile contents – a drinking glass in jagged pieces – and Via Air Bag markings, and the elaborate Courier Service rubber stamp, with date and clock-face to record receipt. There were also the instantly recognizable Foreign Office Inward Bag Room marks crossed through with decisive strokes of blue pencil, as if in angry denial that it had even arrived there. 'Try Cruyer – SIS' was written in neat penmanship underneath it. My name was not in evidence anywhere.

'It came last night … in the bag from Warsaw,' she said, stroking the top of it. 'I know you both went to Poland last week.'

'I'll see Dicky gets it.'

'I shouldn't have come in and yelled at you, but I've just lost my job.'

'What do you mean?'

'Your wife has got what she wanted.' Gloria's face was bright red, or at least bright pink. Whether this flushed countenance was due to exertion, embarrassment or anger I was not sure. Despite the intimacy that living with her had provided, she still had me guessing. Perhaps it was her Hungarian background, perhaps it was the generation gap, perhaps it was my chronic failure to understand women, perhaps it was all those things and perhaps that was what made her so alluring. 'I'm going to work in Budapest. I'm there as from the beginning of next month. I'm taking time off to straighten things out before I leave. I won't be in the office any more.' She gave a smile that lasted only a split second before adding breathlessly: 'So it's goodbye.'

'Goodbye? I'd heard that you were going to be working for Bret Rensselaer. I heard you were going to be promoted to be some kind of big-shot trouble-shooter on the top floor.'

'Haven't you heard? We're all going before a Review Board. They're going to decimate the Department: twenty-five per cent staff reductions. Going to the Budapest embassy is my chance to escape.'

'Sit down, Gloria. Who told you that?'

'They will make a position for me there. No diplomatic status, of course, but I'll be near my dad.'

'I see.'

'I'll be living in Budapest as a private citizen. My office job in the embassy will be just a nine-to-five arrangement. So I won't need diplomatic protection.'

'Your father's still there?'

'I worry about him,' she said.

'But he's okay?'

'He was a field agent for years, Bernard. He should never have gone back to live in Hungary. No matter how badly the Russians treated us, there will always be some Hungarians who see what Daddy did as treachery.'

'Your father can look after himself.'

'He's getting old, Bernard.'

'We all are. Except you, of course,' I added hurriedly. 'So you turned down the job with Bret?'

'Bret couldn't believe I didn't want to work with him.' She gave another tight-lipped grin. 'He insists that I think it over. But I've thought it over.'

'Don't be a fool, Gloria. Forget Budapest and all those embassy buggers. If you are working here, as a personal assistant to Bret, you can stop worrying about the Review Board.' When she didn't respond I persisted: 'No timeserving zombie on a Review Board is going to risk firing anyone's personal staff, and certainly not bouncing someone recently appointed to the personal staff of the Deputy D-G.'

She looked at me, thought about it, and then said: 'Too late now.' She shrugged. 'Anyway I've begun to fancy the idea of living in Budapest.'

'Stay here in London Central, Gloria. You'll be no better than a supernumerary over there. You'll have no job security whatsoever. These embassy pen-pushers have all got PhDs in self-preservation: they'll dump you the moment they are told to cut back. And if you get into any sort of problems with Hungarian officialdom, you'll find yourself all on your own. I know how it works. It's not unlike what happened to me.'

'I don't want to stay in London.'

'Sometimes you have to do things you don't like,' I said, and immediately heard echoes of my father's voice.

She looked at me. She was so very young and she brimmed over with life and energy. Like so many animated people she subjected the world around her to a constant examination. I knew every mood and every signal. That zany tight-lipped grin, when fleeting, was a harbinger of delight. But the same grin held for a few extra seconds was a reproof. And when accompanied by a flicker of the eyelids was imminent trouble. So it was now. 'You're not human, Bernard. You're just a bloody machine.'

'Don't cry, Gloria. For God's sake … What's wrong?'

'It doesn't affect you, does it? You say hello Gloria, and you give me your advice about my job and say you like my new hair-do. But that's all you care about.'

'Your hair-do? What else should I care about?'

'I hate you, Bernard. I really do. I can't take it any longer.' She got out her handkerchief and blew her nose. 'It's tearing me apart, seeing you every day and trying not to care that you go home to your wife each night. But I do care. I can't just stop loving you, the way you evidently can stop loving me.' She got up and turned away so that I would not see the tears in her eyes. From next door there came the relentless noise of the copying machines groaning, sighing and clanking.

'Wait a minute, Gloria. You've got it wrong …' But then I stopped. I felt the water grow deeper as I waded onwards.

163

'Or didn't you ever love me?' she said, without turning round to look at me. 'Was it all just an act? Another of your highly skilled cover stories?'

'No, it wasn't an act.'

'We have a saying in Hungary: When you dine with the rich man, you wind up paying the bill.'

'How could I know she was coming back?' I said, only just managing to conceal the exasperation I felt.

She turned to face me. 'You are the rich man, Bernard. And now I am left paying the bill.'

In other circumstances I might have thought it was some roundabout way of telling me she was pregnant, but I knew it wasn't that. It was all too long ago for that. 'Please, Gloria,' I said. Her eyes were blobby with tears and she looked pitiful. Every cell in my body was telling me to embrace her, dry her tears and comfort her, but my brain said that it would only make matters a thousand times worse. And my brain was right.

'I've got to get away from you,' she said. 'I'll do something desperate if I stay here, working in places where I meet you and hear you.' She sniffed, in a childlike way that brought back a thousand memories.

'I was going to Berlin anyway,' I said in a desperate attempt to stop her crying. I might have been able to cope with an all-out screaming exchange of insults and recriminations but this surrender to grief affected me. 'Frank has suddenly decided that he can't manage over there without some kind of helper.'

She said nothing but I could see she was making a big effort to pull herself together. She bent her head over her handbag, fiddled with a mirror and dabbed at her eyes carefully enough to avoid smudging her make-up. It was because she was facing that way that she noticed the man walking along the corridor. 'Who is that man?' she said.

My so-called office was little more than a corridor. In a desperate attempt to allow some daylight to penetrate into it, some unknown architect had built the upper part of its interior wall with small panes of glass. At one time they had been frosted glass, but over the years, due to careless slamming of doors, many of the glass panes had been shattered and replaced with clear ones.

'A messenger I suppose,' I answered.

'Yes. Did you hear about Jennifer phoning Dicky last Saturday morning, trying to find out where he'd left the keys to the filing cabinet?' Gloria smiled, trying to show me how cheerful she could be. 'When she got through to him on his mobile phone Dicky didn't recognize Jennifer's voice. He said: "I'm over here by the fish, darling. Do hurry." He was shopping in Safeways with Daphne. They both have mobile phones.'

'I hope that wretched girl Jennifer hasn't gone round telling everyone that story. It doesn't help to have Dicky made into a figure of fun.'

Gloria held up her hand in a gesture of submission. 'My mistake.' Then in a different voice she said: 'There he goes again. He's walked past three times now. I saw him in the street when I came out of the FO. He's following me.'

'That bearded freak? Are you sure?'

'Call Security. Yes, I'm sure.'

'Let me tackle him,' I said. I was sure it was just some new messenger.

As I was saying it, the door opened and Dicky came in. Dicky's attire had changed since his trip to Poland. Still the trendy Wunderkind, he'd forsaken his cashmere and silk for a more proletarian image. He was wearing a scarred leather jacket with a coarse grey roll-neck and battered corduroy trousers.

Dicky said: 'Do you know anything about architectural structures, Bernard?'

'Not a great deal,' I admitted.

'I think I've hit upon a perfect solution for us,' he said. 'I knew I'd crack it. It was just a matter of sitting down and thinking seriously about what we're trying to do.' He said this as if it was likely to be a recourse as entirely new to me as it was to him. I nodded.

'I mean, look at this place –' As he turned to indicate the peeling paintwork, and the widening cracks in the ceiling, he caught sight of Gloria. 'Gloria! Darling! What are you hiding from behind the door?'

'You, Mr Cruyer,' said Gloria.

Dicky laughed. 'My God, but you are looking fabulous these days. What are you doing? New hair-do. New coat.'

'It's an old coat,' said Gloria, and smiled. She knew as well as I did that Dicky's outburst was his standard greeting for nubile female staff, but that didn't seem to lessen the boost it gave her.

'It looks wonderful on you,' said Dicky. 'And I love those boots. Sexy!' She gazed at him adoringly as he turned back to me and studied the ceiling again and said: 'We'll get the whole building condemned.' He turned to Gloria and said 'condemned' again. To me he said: 'You get it, don't you?'

'I believe I do,' I said. I'd spent long enough with Dicky and his devious schemes to guess how his mind was working.

'We'll get some friendly surveyor to write a long and fearsome report … We'll say it's about to collapse on to the swimwear factory next door.'

'Is next door a swimwear factory?' I said.

'Bernard, Bernard. Are you the spy or am I?' said Dicky, and turned to Gloria and winked. Gloria nodded. Dicky said: 'Yes, I checked out the whole street. I know which occupiers are leaseholders and which are the freeholders. And I know the "use and purpose" as defined by the owners and permitted by local by-laws. You never know when you might want to jump on your neighbours for misuse. I always do that when property is involved. Yes, a swimwear factory.'

'You'll ask for another building?' I said.

'Yes, and if Treasury want this place, let them come in and get it back into shape. There's a lovely little building the Education Ministry have in Mayfair that would suit us perfectly.' Dicky looked at Gloria and at me; I heard the ratchets grinding in his brain. 'Is this a tryst?'

'No,' I said hurriedly, too hurriedly.

Dicky gave us his Cheshire-cat smile: 'You both can rely on my discretion. Bernard knows that already,' he told Gloria. 'Your secret is safe with me.'

'Gloria was looking for you,' I said.

'Well, as long as I'm not intruding.' He gave another smile to show that he now considered himself a party to our conspiracy. Then saw the polystyrene box.

I said: 'Gloria brought this package. She was looking for you. It came in the pouch from Warsaw.'

Dicky lifted it briefly to estimate its weight. Then he picked up my Swiss army folding knife, which, when Gloria arrived, I'd been using to prise open a catering-sized tin of powdered coffee. He used my knife to slash the sticky paper which sealed the two halves of the polystyrene box and the pieces fell apart to reveal a large jar. It was a preserving jar, the sort of heavy glass container used in kitchens back when wives stayed at home and cooked things, sealed at the top with a heavy wire clip and a red rubber washer. Its contents were completely hidden by a large label wrapped around the jar. 'It's in Polish,' complained Dicky as he tried to read the typewritten label. Having given up on it he ripped the label off to see for himself what he'd been sent from Warsaw. 'What's that say?' he asked, pushing the label at me.

Dicky said afterwards that he fully expected it to be a kilo of caviar, which he'd discovered to be relatively cheap and relatively plentiful in Warsaw. If so, the shock must have been all the greater as he impatiently ripped away the remaining parts of the label and held the jar aloft. It was filled to the top with liquid, almost clear liquid, apart from a few large specks of organic matter disturbed by the sudden movement. Held so close to the overhead light the jar shone brightly. The thickness of the glass distorted and elongated the shape of the contents but the clarity of the liquid provided a good view of the severed human hand that was suspended in it, with shreds of skin and tendon swinging and swaying in the glittering preservative.

'Ahhh!' said Dicky. His face contorted in disgust and he almost dropped it. Gloria took a step back. I was the last to look up and react because I'd been trying to decipher the typewritten label. 'George Kosinski, it says,' I told Dicky. 'It's an excerpt from a post-mortem report dated last week.'

'With gold rings still on his fingers?' said Dicky, as if refusing to believe it was a human hand at all. He'd put the jar on the table by now, and was keeping his distance from it.

'Fingers too swollen to get the rings off,' I said. 'They must have decided not to amputate the fingers if it was going back to the relatives.'

'This will be definitive,' said Dicky, plucking a succession of paper tissues from the box on the table and wiping and rewiping his fingers with them. 'Now we'll stamp out all this argument about Kosinski not being dead.' He dropped the tissues into a waste-bin and looked at me.

It was while we were looking at the jar – our backs turned towards the door – that it opened and the bearded man stepped in. 'I'll take that,' he said, and reaching forward took the jar from the desktop and backed out through the door.

With the glass jar tucked under his arm, he put his other hand into the pocket of his jacket and pointed it at Dicky. 'I don't want anyone to get hurt,' he said. 'You just stay there and stay quiet.' Then he backed out into the corridor, closed the door, and moved away still watching us through the glass panes.

As soon as the intruder was beyond our vision, Dicky was pulling the door open and racing after him along the corridor and out of sight. There came the sound of a shot.

'I've got the bastard!' shouted Dicky. When I got to the corridor I was amazed to see Dicky posed in that legs apart, knees bent posture that they started teaching at the training school when they replaced the traditional circular targets with ugly drawings of pugnacious humans. Clasping both hands together, Dicky was holding a revolver, another one of those old 'Official Police' models, and aiming along the corridor at the fleeing man. 'Come on!' said Dicky and fired, although by the time the shot rang out the bearded man had disappeared down the stairs.

Dicky raced along the corridor and I followed him. By the time I reached the far end of the corridor the bearded man had made the most of his good start. He was a small lightweight fellow, and in an excellent state of physical fitness, judging by the sound of his feet echoing in the narrow space of the stairwell.

I glimpsed Dicky as he raced down the flights of stairs but I couldn't see the man he was chasing. As I got to the next level a shot rang out, and two flights lower I passed a long smear of blood on the wall and spots of it on the stairs. Then there was the sound of another shot. The sound of the footsteps continued uninterrupted, which made me guess that Dicky was firing as he ran and his quarry was simply running. There were more blood smears at the next level; one of them was a smudged handprint dribbling with shiny-wet blood.

As I got to the ground floor Dicky was flattened with his back against the corridor wall holding his .38 Colt at arm's length. His face was flushed and glistening with sweat, his chest was heaving and his hand trembling.

But whatever shape Dicky was in, one glance along that long corridor, which led past three rubbish-bins and the double back doors, made every fibre in my body go out to the poor devil who was trying to escape through the exit door alive.

'Stop shooting, Dicky!' I called loudly. 'Let him go.' But Dicky was past reasoning or listening or thinking. The adrenalin was pumping, his sinews stiffened, blood summoned up, and his eyes opened wide. He couldn't stop. I know what it's like, I'd been there.

Before I could claw at Dicky's arm the crack of his gun deafened me. There was a whine followed by a doleful clank as the spent round ricocheted and hit a metal bin. It was the subsequent shot that brought the fleeing man down. It hit him somewhere about the middle of the back and threw him full-length, as effectively as a footballer grabbed by his ankles in a flying tackle. He crashed to the wooden floor with a sickening thud that would have hospitalized most men.

The jar flew from his clasp, went tumbling through the air and smashed against the wall, so that a sudden smell of ether and formaldehyde was added to the faint smell of the burned powder. But the little man got up from the spreading puddle of blood and chemicals. He staggered forwards a couple of steps and with a superhuman effort of will threw all his weight against the doors. His weight on the crush-bar was enough to activate the fastenings, and the door banged open as he fell through it into what must have been someone's waiting arms, for there came the almost immediate roar of a revving car engine. Before Dicky or I could reach the back yard they were burning rubber on the far side of the car park. The parked cars were in the line of fire and there was only a blurred glimpse of the speeding car as, with horn blasting, it accelerated through the open gates and recklessly forced its way into the London traffic.

'Did you get the licence number?' said Dicky, standing in the yard looking at the gates through which the car had gone.

'I saw it.' It was Gloria coming out of the back doors to find us. 'I saw it all from the window. There were three men and a black Ford Fiesta. No licence plates. I looked for the number but there were no plates.'

'He must have been wearing armour,' said Dicky. 'Did you hear the clank as I hit him?'

'No I didn't,' I said.

'Well, thanks for all your help, Bernard,' said Dicky with biting sarcasm. He was standing arms akimbo: panting, excited and angry. And frustrated that his quarry had escaped.

'I wasn't sure what it was you were going to do,' I explained.

'I would have thought your training and know-how would have taken care of that. I thought the instincts of an experienced field agent would show him what to do in an emergency.'

'The developed professional instincts of all the field agents who survive tell them to get quickly out of the line of fire when the bullets are flying.'

Gloria looked at me. I'd disappointed her too, I could see it in her face. After all she'd heard about my exploits, the first time she sees me in action I demonstrate a remarkable capacity for self-preservation while Dicky does the tough-guy stuff.

'Jesus, Dicky,' I said in exasperation. 'He didn't shoot. He probably wasn't armed. Can you imagine what sort of clamour there would have been if you'd killed him? Or even if we had him here now, badly hurt and unable to move?'

Dicky wasn't listening. 'I hit him on the run. My skeet-shooting days were not wasted. No, sir!' Dicky was still glowing with the heat of battle and there was nothing for it but to give him time to cool off.

I went back into the building and looked at the broken pieces of glass jar, the puddle of chemicals, and the severed hand

171

– unnaturally white and puffy – that was sitting on the floor like some large and venomous species of spider.

Dicky came and looked too. 'I suppose you are right,' he said. Now it was dawning on him what he'd done. And what he'd have to say in his report.

'Where did you get that Colt revolver?' I asked him. It looked familiar.

'I've had it since you took it from those gorillas in Warsaw.'

My God, Dicky. On the plane? Going through customs and everything? I would have died of fright if I'd known what that idiot had got concealed under his duty-free gin and Viyella pyjamas. But I didn't tell him that. I just said: 'Better get rid of that piece right away. It might be ballistically identifiable – all kinds of crimes may already be attached to it.'

Dicky didn't respond. 'We must get this place cleaned up,' he said. 'The staircase and the walls. Get on to the Works people, Gloria. I want it all done by this evening. Reliable people. We don't want word to get out.'

Dicky put away his gun and nibbled at his fingernail. He was beginning to worry.

Gloria joined us to stare down at the severed hand and the pool of smelly liquid.

Dicky said: 'This will prove wrong all those dotty ideas about George being alive, Bernard. This is George's hand. It will be conclusive evidence.'

I said: 'You won't easily get a print from flesh that's been marinating in that brew. That skin tissue is like wet Kleenex.'

'Could you pick it up, Bernard?'

I balanced it upon the largest remaining piece of the broken jar, its thick saucer-like base.

'What shall we do with it?' Dicky asked.

'Take it to the mail-room,' I said. 'Tell them to put it in a plastic bag and send it to forensic by motor-cycle messenger.'

172

'That's right,' said Dicky, then: 'He had a beard. That's what baffles me. How could he hope to be inconspicuous with all that face fungus?'

'He'll shave it off, Dicky. Men like him don't disguise themselves by growing beards when they can disguise themselves by shaving them off.'

'Maybe,' he conceded.

'Can I use your phone, Dicky?'

He reached into his pocket and gave me his mobile phone. I punched in the number of a friend of mine in the Berne embassy. 'Who are you calling?' said Dicky, who'd watched what I was doing and recognized the Berne prefix.

'Masterson at the embassy.'

'I don't know him.'

'No, probably not,' I said. Masterson was a lowly toiler in the embassy ant-hill. He didn't have the right school ties, the right accent nor – most decisively of all – the right wife, to win any decent position in the embassy rat-race. Mrs Masterson was a French socialist intellectual who used social functions to lecture her husband's superiors on Britain's failings. The fact that his wife's criticisms were well-founded and well-argued was the final fatal blow to his career.

When the phone was answered, a girl came on the line. She'd come fresh from one of those training courses where telephone staff learn how to rudely deter callers from making contact with their employers. 'He's not here. He's at a meeting. Call later,' she told me.

'Get him out of the meeting,' I said. 'This is urgent.'

'Is it personal?' she asked.

'In a way,' I said. 'I'm his live-in lover and I've just been checked positive.'

She made a noise and went away for a long time, but eventually Masterson came on the phone. 'Hello?'

'Batty? It's Bernie.'

'Of course it is. Who else would phone up to offend my secretary and make trouble for me by pulling me out of a staff meeting with the First Secretary presiding?'

'Those tourists who went to see my brother-in-law. Any of them feature a pigtail haircut, and beard?'

'Yes, Bernard.'

'Short, dark. About one hundred and forty pounds?'

'That's him. A Stasi major. We've got a smudgy Photo-fit picture somewhere if I can find it.'

'Put it on the fax for me, Batty. You have Dicky Cruyer's fax number on file.'

'I'll do that for you, Bernie.'

'Thanks, Batty. I'll do the same for you some day.'

'You're always saying that, Bernard.'

I rang off. 'Stasi?' said Dicky excitedly.

'Sounds like it,' I said.

Dicky emerged from his melancholy mood. He could put aside his thoughts on how he would explain shooting an innocent passer-by in Central London. 'I knew it. I knew it,' he said, and rubbed his hands together in satisfaction. 'Incidentally, Bernard. A propos telephone procedure: in future I counsel you to simply inform Berne – and such people – that you are calling from London Central, and give them your priority code, so you won't have to go through all that jokey rigmarole.'

Dicky looked at Gloria and smiled broadly to make sure she enjoyed this crushing directive. Gloria, whose feminine instinct for the right timing seldom let her down, returned this intimacy with a confidence. 'I'm going to work for Mr Rensselaer,' she told Dicky. When Dicky seemed not to hear her, she reached out and touched him on the arm to get his attention. I had no claim to her of course, but seeing her make that most ordinary of physical contacts with another man was enough to make me want to shout

174

my protest aloud. Despite whatever look of horror was written across my face, Gloria gave me her most beguiling smile and said: 'And Bernard's decided to go and work in Berlin.' I suppose she wanted to be quite certain I couldn't wriggle out of it.

'Brilliant,' said Dicky. He studied my face for a moment and said: 'You're fond of Frank, and Lisl Hennig is a mother to you. Berlin's your home, Bernard. Admit it.'

'It sometimes seems that way,' I said.

'And lovely Gloria stays in London,' said Dicky, and looked at her and chuckled in a tone that sounded predatory.

Gloria laughed too, as if Dicky had made a very good joke that only she shared. It was a lovely laugh and came bubbling up like milk boiling over. I didn't join in.

'I'll take the hand to the mail-room,' I said. 'They may be a bit squeamish about touching it.'

Something in what I'd said or done – or failed to say or do – seemed to outrage Dicky. Perhaps he was expecting that his one demonstration of manly daring should bring expressions of admiration and respect. He seemed to forget Gloria's presence. 'You won't be told, will you?' he said, pushing his face very close to mine but keeping his voice soft and low in a studied demonstration of restraint. 'I suppose you expect me to believe that George Kosinski bolting at exactly the same time that the stock-market crashed is pure coincidence?'

'Tell me, Dicky,' I said, 'do you think that London getting hit by a hurricane, at exactly the same time that the stock-market crashed, is something more than just coincidence?'

'You're determined to believe that George Kosinski is still alive; not because you want to spare the feelings of his friends or relatives but just to prove that you are the clever one. You just have to show us that you remain sceptical, while all of us dullards are sucked in to some conspiracy ... or whatever it is you think is going on.'

175

'I just said I'd take the hand –'

'I know what you bloody said,' said Dicky. 'It's your whole superior attitude that gets up my nose. Now will you look at that hand?' He pointed at it as if without his help my attention might be drawn elsewhere. I looked at it. 'Do you see the signet ring? Look at the Kosinski family crest. It belongs to George Kosinski, and we both know that. Didn't I hear you say it's there because the fingers are too swollen to get it off? Now will you see sense?'

'I hear what you're saying, Dicky.' I spoke slowly and soberly in the hope that it would cool him down. 'But the trouble I have with that is that the last time we saw George Kosinski's signet ring it was in the palm of Stefan Kosinski's hand, and he was telling us that he'd just brought it back from the police station where the cops were holding the murderers.'

'But it's the same ring,' said Dicky, and all the wind went out of him.

'The same crest, yes. I'm not so sure about the ring. Gold signet rings are usually pretty much the same for everyone in the family.'

'Oh yes, of course.'

'I'll ask the lab to remove it,' I said. 'We can get a closer look at it then. Perhaps the size will show whether it belongs to some other member of the family. There may even be an engraved inscription on the inner side.'

8

'Hold on, Bernard, hold on. I'm just a simple old desk wallah. You'll have to explain this one to me. You say this chap was a Stasi man?'

'Looks like it, Frank,' I said.

Frank raised an eyebrow. 'Dashed in, and grabbed this amputated fist or whatever it was?'

'Yes, a hand.'

'Well, why?' He leaned back in his chair. Frank Harrington never seemed to grow older. His countenance, pale, stern and bony, and the stubble moustache he'd cultivated to make himself look more military, had given him this same appearance decades ago, when I was a child and he was an indulgent 'uncle'.

'I don't exactly know, Frank.'

'You don't exactly know, Bernard? I won't write that down, because when you say you don't exactly know in that tone of voice, I am quite confident that you have a clever theory of some kind.'

'I can only think that someone was keen to prevent the severed hand going to the forensic lab.'

'Because?'

'Perhaps they didn't want us to establish for certain that the hand wasn't that of George Kosinski.'

'But they didn't stop us,' argued Frank. 'The hand went to the lab, and we didn't find out that it wasn't George Kosinski's, did we?'

'The lab said they couldn't make an identification. The flesh was too soft.'

'Well then. How does your theory hold together?'

'I assume that someone was afraid the lab would say categorically that it wasn't the hand of George Kosinski.'

'That's quite a long leap, Bernard. I mean: we still don't know for certain that it's not.'

'That's right,' I said.

'You mean perhaps it was a double bluff? They give us the hand, then pretend to want it back, because that will make us think it belongs to George Kosinski?'

'Perhaps,' I said.

'Perhaps ...' Frank reached for a wooden pencil, one of a dozen or so he liked to keep in a decorative drinking mug emblazoned with a talking doughnut proclaiming itself *lecker locker leicht* — tasty, spongy and light. He used the pencil to tap a closed dossier on his desk and give emphasis to his words. 'But I am tempted to believe that this Stasi agent ... I visualize him as a sharp and devious fellow, always ready with a bit of double bluff or treble bluff, if that suits him. A Stasi hoodlum ... but otherwise a bit like you, Bernard, I suspect. I am tempted to believe that his superior is a blunt old fool like me, incapable of working out in advance the sort of intricate games you youngsters like to play.'

'Yes, Frank.' This was one of Frank's favoured poses: the blunt, no-nonsense, pipe-smoking Englishman who had no time for knavish foreign tricks. But I knew Frank better than to fall for that. I might have been heard more than once saying that the esteemed prizes he won at university as a Classics scholar did not make him the ideal man to run the Berlin Field Unit, but I had no doubts about Frank's agile mind. And this was

Berlin: this was Frank's kingdom, and this was Frank assuming that humble manner that comes naturally to men with extensive and absolute powers.

'It's just as well you are here in Berlin, and away from it all, Bernard. Of course you'd rather be with your lovely wife … and your children. But in many ways it's better that you are here with me. George Kosinski being your family … It's not fair, not appropriate, that you should be closely involved with this rumpus about him. I'm surprised Dicky didn't see that.'

'Is that why you asked for me?'

'I didn't ask for you, Bernard,' said Frank, holding the pencil to his face, scowling as he studied it carefully, as if he'd never encountered one before.

'You said that feelingly, Frank.'

'I didn't ask for you, because I thought London would never let you go. I set my sights rather lower.' Frank dropped the pencil back amongst its fellows in the doughnut mug, and opened the brown folder he'd been tapping. 'So you've read this?'

'DELIUS? Yes, it kept me up all night.'

'Yes, it would,' said Frank. 'It's not pleasant to think that any of our people are in trouble over there. What should we do?'

'There's nothing we can do for the time being, Frank. The Stasi are waiting for our reaction. You know their methods far better than I do.'

'Perhaps.' He fingered his telephone. 'But your instincts are often good ones. I want to bring Robin into this.' He picked up the telephone handset and waved it in the air while he called the extension. 'The young man who went with you to Magdeburg. I want you to go through your thoughts while he's here with us.'

'I hope I've not come here to be the resident nursemaid, Frank.'

'Don't be a curmudgeon, Bernard. Think of all the people who played nursemaid to you when you were a youngster. We've got to mould the people who are coming up.'

179

'Very well, Frank. If that's what you want.'

The lanky kid came in almost immediately; he must have been waiting for Frank's call. He gave me a smile that revealed his crooked teeth, but his deep polished voice was one hundred per cent English upper-class. After we'd shaken hands and confirmed each other's well-being, he sat down and I went through what little we knew about the sudden and ominous silence that had descended upon the normally very active DELIUS network operating for us in Allenstein, a small town – or more accurately a sprawling village – a few miles east of Magdeburg.

'The very last we heard was on the Friday,' I said, flicking the folder. 'And that could have been a garbled routine from some other network. So there has been enough time for the contact string.'

Frank raised a schoolmaster's eyebrow at Robin.

'The roll-call for survivors,' said Robin patiently. 'But we don't do that from this end any more. These cells are virtually self-contained nowadays.'

'Out-of-contact signals?' I said. 'I suppose that's none of our business either?'

Frank said: 'There have been no out-of-contact signals. None at all. They have closed down. My best radio man will vouch for that.'

The kid said: 'We just have them send us the reports nowadays. The Stasi interception people are very efficient. The less time spent on the air the better, even with these modern high-speed sets.'

I said: 'Are we still monitoring the Stasi signals?'

'Not the Berlin teleprinter any more, alas,' said Frank. 'We lost Berlin in the big Stasi shake-up last summer, and so far we've made no breakthrough on the new codes.'

'But nothing on the police radio?' I said. 'No general alarm? Not even a suspicious activity alert for the local cops?'

'Nothing at all,' said the kid. 'It may all be a non-starter. You know how these amateur nets blow apart and then come together again. There have been domestic flare-ups before with this group. Two years ago: November.'

'Amateurs have a role to play,' said Frank, enduringly paternal and preparing his response to the reprimand from London that almost invariably followed the collapse of a network. 'Don't underestimate their skills and effectiveness. Amateurs built the Ark, remember; professionals built the *Titanic*.'

'Are they all Church people?' I asked, after we'd all smiled at Frank's joke. I knew they weren't all Church people – at least one of them was a declared atheist – but I wanted to see what they'd say.

'No. And two of them are chronically difficult. It's a small community. The wives don't all get along and there are the usual feuds and vendettas. It's only the pastor who holds them together.'

Frank said: 'You met the pastor.'

'Yes,' I said. He'd sheltered me and the kid when we were leaving Magdeburg in a hurry.

'The funny old man,' said the kid. 'The turbulent priest.'

Frank said: 'Allenstein is critical. If it was BARTOK or one of the networks in the Dresden area, or those troublemakers in Rostock, I might say thank goodness, and let them stew in their own juice. But we pass too many people through Magdeburg. It's our most reliable line for people coming and going. We need an active setup in Allenstein to nurse them and pass them back if they get into trouble.'

'Isn't this a problem London Central should deal with, Frank?' I said. 'Any failure in Operations should have the Coordination people watching it to see if it's part of some bigger pattern.'

'London won't wear that, Bernard. I tried that on Monday morning. I went through it all with Operations. But we're not

181

dealing with Harry Strang any more. Operations are more cautious since Bret Rensselaer has been Deputy D-G. London Ops don't want to hear: they spend their time trying to dump their problems on us. I tried hard.'

'I'm sure you did, Frank,' I said, although I wondered to what extent Frank wanted to let London take control, or whether he only wanted London to know how hard he worked. Berlin's power and influence had been eroded over the last year or more. I suspected that he needed to ring all the bells about an occasional crisis out there in the DDR sticks if he was to make a convincing case for Berlin Field Unit's finances next year.

After I'd taken rather too long in offering any comment, Frank said: 'You know how things work over there at ground level. What's the prognosis, Bernard?'

'I went right back through the three years of DELIUS files.'

'Did you? When?'

'This morning.'

'Oh,' said Frank, as if I'd taken unfair advantage of him. Frank never checked back through old files. The file clerks in the Berlin Registry wouldn't have recognized Frank had he ever knocked on their door.

'Yes,' I said, 'DELIUS has had a lot of arguments and splits and reassembling. I don't like that. Every time a network regroups, more and more people get to see each other. It's the sort of risk the Stasi are good at provoking and exploiting.'

'They are amateurs,' said the kid. 'We can't treat them as if they were trained and experienced professionals.'

'Well that's how the Stasi treat them,' I said.

'Someone will have to go and sort it out,' said the kid, obviously seeing himself as the right one to do it.

'Not necessarily,' said Frank hurriedly. Then added: 'Unless that's what Bernard thinks.'

'Let's leave it for a few more days,' I said.

182

'I thought you would want to get in there immediately, Mr Samson,' said the kid.

'Why?'

He looked at Frank before saying to me: 'The Romeo Effect.'

'Oh, Jesus,' I said. 'I don't think so.' Trust the kid to pluck that old joker out of the deck.

'What is the Romeo Effect?' Frank asked.

The kid said: 'Mr Samson once said that when a network is penetrated, there is a danger that it will simply destroy itself without outside action. Romeo effect. Kill itself in despair, the way that Juliet did when she awoke from drugged sleep to find that Romeo was dead.'

'Too poetic for me,' said Frank.

'Destroy the network in a panic,' explained the kid, giving me a self-conscious glance. 'Eliminate the codes and all traces. Split and destroy the network so that not a trace of any evidence remains.'

'Oh,' said Frank, touching the end of his nose with a pencil. 'I thought it was Juliet who killed herself first.'

'It wasn't my theory,' I said. 'It's a KGB theory and they named it. The Soviets lost two important networks in Washington in the Fifties. The Moscow inquiry afterwards lasted six months, and finally produced a report that said that neither network had been truly penetrated.'

'And had they?' Frank asked.

'Sort of. One net had been under observation for a long time. A new man arrived in town. The FBI banged on his door and found a list of contacts. He claimed diplomatic immunity and they gave him his list back and apologized. But the other one might have gone on for ever. Husband and wife, both working in the Pentagon, feeding torn but not shredded photocopies out through a clerk who had the job of disposing of top-secret waste paper. The wife had her handbag stolen; the thief found

183

papers marked secret inside and told the cops. Nothing much more than that would have happened, but once inside the police station the husband panicked and confessed the whole works.'

'The Romeo Effect,' said Frank reflectively. 'What a name to give it. I'll never fathom the Russians.'

'I mentioned it in a lecture at the training school,' I explained. 'Years ago. The real lecturer hadn't turned up. I filled in at short notice.'

'Six more working days before we act,' said Frank, closing the cardboard folder and pressing upon it with his flattened hand like a man testifying on oath.

'All days are working days in the field,' I said.

Frank gave me the sort of smug and distant smile used by VIPs inspecting guards of honour. 'We'll probably hear from them tomorrow,' he announced in a cheerful clubby voice. 'I remember this time two years back. Christmas. Those people in Zwickau went off the air for ten days, and then blandly explained that they had had trouble with their batteries.' He gave an avuncular chuckle to show that he bore them no ill will.

'But they were wiped out the following year,' I reminded him. 'Six months later the Stasi went in and picked them off one by one, like ripe cherries. I've always wondered if that six-month period was the Stasi waiting a decent interval while their own inside man got clear.'

'No,' said Frank, who preferred not to give the enemy the benefit of the doubt. 'We looked into it. A review board spent six weeks on it. There was no penetration of that network. The batteries fiasco wasn't a cause, but it should have been a warning to us at this end. It should have reminded us that ill-disciplined networks are vulnerable. It's always been that way. Look at France in nineteen forty-four.'

Keen to avoid Frank's account of what intricacies of ill-discipline afflicted the French networks in 1944, I said: 'Don't

184

let's say six days; or specify any period of time, Frank. Let me keep my ear to the ground and report back to you.'

'I'm away for a few days in London,' said Frank. 'I'm catching the seven o'clock flight. Another of those Estimates Committees. I have to be there, or the others will gang up to persuade the old man to give Hong Kong, or some other god-forsaken outpost, the money Berlin needs.'

'Yes,' I said. 'Do you want a record of this meeting?'

'We'd better have something on the file,' said Frank. 'Something that will make it clear that we earn our pay,' he added, in case his reference to the Estimates Committee hadn't alerted us to the fact that all our jobs were in constant jeopardy unless we not only did our work but recorded it in triplicate.

I stood up, but the kid remained sitting in his chair and flipping through thick files of paperwork he'd brought with him. It was not until Frank said 'Look at the time' to politely indicate that his presence was no longer required that he suddenly slammed his papers together and remembered unfinished work downstairs and departed.

'Robin is a good lad,' said Frank.

'Yes,' I said.

'You heard that Dicky Cruyer is giving a dinner at Claridge's? To celebrate the official commendation he got for the shooting ... the severed hand and all that.' Frank looked at me quizzically. 'The old man is attending, so is Bret. I'm surprised that you're not going too, Bernard.'

'I thought it was better to get here and report to you,' I said. In fact, joining the fawning admirers at Dicky's celebration had not appealed to me greatly.

Perhaps Frank read my thoughts. 'Give Dicky credit for fast thinking, Bernard. He recognized the Stasi man, retrieved the severed hand and shot the fellow carrying it. Mind you, he admits to feeling nervous until he'd phoned Berne and confirmed his identification.'

'Dicky has always been very fast-thinking,' I said. 'I've never denied it.'

'A commendation will do wonders for Dicky,' said Frank. 'It will probably be enough to get him confirmed as Europe supremo. And the word is that this Stasi fellow Dicky shot is the sniper they used to kill that defector in the safe house.'

'That's the first I've heard of it,' I said.

'VERDI, the ruffian you and Werner Volkmann took to the Notting Hill safe house.'

'Who says so?'

'Special Branch appointed an investigation team for it. They're now saying it was the same man; but no solid evidence as yet. I can't think why you and Werner took that VERDI chap to Notting Hill. Isn't that safe house known to every Stasi and KGB man in Europe?'

'It is now,' I said.

'And the Fletcher House annexe job was very nearly successful for them wasn't it? Nothing to suggest to you that that was a Stasi operation? You're the one who wrote the book.'

'They used a black getaway car,' I said blandly.

Frank laughed. 'They used a black car, did they?' There was a long-standing belief in the Berlin office that the hoodlums we faced would always choose a black car. The official cars used by the Eastern Bloc Party officials, the top cops and the security generals were invariably black. The lesser lights – the heavies and the hit men – let loose in the West could seldom resist adopting this status symbol. 'And you are feeling well?' he asked.

'Do I look ill?'

'I would have thought you'd have been raring to go and sort out the DELIUS problem. In the old days you never passed up a chance to chase around over there.'

186

'I was younger then. And even more foolish.'

Frank looked at me and nodded. 'You'll be in charge here for the next few days, but I'm not far away. Don't do anything without we discuss it.'

'On the matter of the DELIUS net?'

'In the matter of anything.' He got to his feet and looked at his appointment book. The page was blank, as the pages of Frank's appointment book so often were.

'No, sure.'

He fixed me with his clear and piercing grey eyes and said: 'The last thing I need is a débâcle here now. I'm too old for it.' I knew what he meant. Berlin was to the Department what Las Vegas was to the glittering stars of show-biz: a perfect showcase for a brilliant youngster, but a burial ground for has-beens. But where did that leave me? I was too old to be a promising youngster but still too young to be a has-been. Too old to seek employment elsewhere, and that was the bitter truth of it. I could see that verdict in Frank's eyes too as he looked at me and added: 'But we both have to make the best of things, Bernard.'

'Yes, Frank.'

He took my arm: '"'Tis not hard, I think, for men so old as we to keep the peace." *Romeo and Juliet*, Act One, Scene Two. We did it at my prep school for half-term; I played the apothecary.'

'The apothecary,' I said. 'What perfect casting, Frank.'

As soon as Frank had departed for his plane, I exercised my new-found authority as Deputy Director of the Berlin Field Unit. I took a set of false identity papers from the safe and went across to the car pool and signed out a big BMW motor cycle. Once through the checkpoint – as a West German national – I left the motor cycle in the East, in a lock-up garage in Prenzlauerberg. From there I took instead a noisy little Trabant motor car that was kept fuelled and ready for such purposes. From a hiding place in the garage I picked up a suitcase containing a new lot of identity papers and I changed into a baggy suit of the cut that made citizens of the DDR instantly recognizable.

Skirting the city I drove westwards, the Trabant's two-stroke engine running smoothly, as such engines did in the cold weather. There was very little traffic on the road. At one time the East German army and the Soviet garrison forces had always made their military redeployments after dark, but nowadays there were far fewer tactical military movements. Soviet troops, and East German units too, were being kept out of sight. There were few signs of individual soldiers either. Their pay constantly in arrears, they found it cheaper to get drunk in their camps and barracks. The only military vehicles I passed were three eight-wheel armoured personnel carriers, their hatches closed down, and bearing the markings of some northern factory militia. They were rattling along at high speed, manned by workers ordered away from their benches for their regular two weeks of winter exercises.

The streets of Allenstein bei Magdeburg were dark and silent. I left the Trabbie out of sight in the alley behind the primary school rather than park it where it would be noticed by passers-by. As I got out of the car I saw all round me a landscape etched with frost, and heard the crackle of ice under my feet. My nose and ears were stung painfully by the chilly wind that moaned through the overhead wires. Perhaps some member of the Forster family had heard the clatter of my Trabbie's two-stroke engine, for a woman came down and opened the main door of the apartment block before I rang the bell.

Once inside, the biting cold with its ever-present odour of brown coal was exchanged for warm stale air upon which rested the faint smells of recently cooked food. I took off my trilby hat and unbuttoned my coat. One of the few compensations of living in the DDR was having a warm home. It was a part

of the tacit compact that the self-serving communist masters
had struck with the inhabitants of this sad and deprived police-
state; warm rooms and crime-free streets were offered as com-
pensation for everything inflicted upon them.

'Hello, Bernd,' said the woman. 'I knew you'd come.'

'Good,' I said. She hadn't known I was coming of course;
it was a way of saying that she only saw me when trouble was
in the offing. At first I thought it was Theo's mother-in-law
who had answered the door, but she'd died two years before.
It was Theo's wife; poor little Bettina, she'd aged so much and
was wearing her mother-in-law's red spotted dress. I hadn't
recognized her. Now I leaned forward and kissed her on both
cheeks.

'I thought they'd send you, Bernd,' she said without enthusiasm.

'Yes,' I said, and followed her into the gloomy living-room
where two children were sprawled on a threadbare oriental carpet, constructing angel's wings from coloured paper.
It was the sort of gesture to religion that the regime discour-
aged, but Theo Forster had never been an ardent believer; his
churchgoing was only done to please his wife. There were many
such lukewarm worshippers in the networks that London had
formed and coordinated, but streetwise cynics like Theo were
needed in the mix.

'Theo,' she announced. 'It's Bernd come to see you.'

Theo was propped up in a bed in the corner in the living-
room. It was not a good sign, for he had never been strong. The
walls of the apartment were thin and from the next room there
came the sounds of conversation and Bing Crosby singing.
There must have been a dozen people in that tiny apartment;
talking without being overheard was difficult.

'I knew you'd come, Bernd. I told Betti you would. This is
Uncle Bernd,' Theo called out to the children, who looked up,
nodded at me politely and went back to their wings.

189

Theo Forster, number four of the DELIUS group, had been at school with me. He'd been a boisterous young teenager in those days, the classroom clown with a pointed nose, a gnomish face and remarkable facility for advanced mathematics. Theo's father had been good at mathematics too. He'd been an artillery sergeant who'd served under an artful old war hero named Rolf Mauser, and was with him at Vinnitsa on the Bug that fateful day in 1944 when Mauser earned his Knight's Cross. In postwar Berlin, Rolf Mauser did secret tasks for my father. Inevitably young Theo came to know what I did for a living. We'd kept in touch from time to time. Now so many years later, when the DELIUS network went on the blink, he was the most obvious person for me to contact. I loved him dearly, but Theo would never make a good field agent; he was too principled, too honest, too sensitive.

'How are you feeling, Theo?'

'I'll be all right by Christmas, Bernd.'

It was disconcerting to deal with any of these Church groups. They'd been organized, and encouraged, during my wife's pretended defection to the DDR. Such people weren't at all like field agents or trained spies. Such well-meaning amateurs were armed and equipped to fight the good fight against sin and the devil, rather than against a pitiless communist regime. Many of them were brave beyond measure, but it was difficult to make them see the dangers they faced. They were in every respect a *Volkssturm* – a 'Dad's Army' – and had to be treated like those well-meaning civilian soldiers.

'Take off your coat, Bernd.' The room was dimly lit, but as my eyes became accustomed to it I could see Theo's waxy face beaming at me. His pale complexion and sparse eyebrows gave emphasis to those dark staring sorrowful eyes. Looking around I recognized the heavy Biedermeier wardrobe and armchair that had come from his parents' Berlin apartment. They looked

190

out of place here amid the cheap unpainted wooden chairs and table that were the standard products of DDR factories.

'The doctor says I'll be out of bed in time for Christmas Eve,' he said as briskly as he could manage. 'I get these attacks from time to time. I might look like death but I will soon be back at the factory.' He grinned, his face impish, looking very like the teenager I remembered.

'That's great, Theo,' I said. I'd often passed the Stern bicycle factory where Theo worked as an electrician. The blackened brick buildings on the railway siding dated back to the Kaiser's days. But the newer prefabricated sheds where Theo worked were cold and draughty, so that in winter the workers wrapped up in coats and sweaters. There was a constant haze of dirt in the air for miles around, while into the nearby river the factory poured a filthy torrent of brown pollution. It was no place for a sick man.

'Is this official?' he asked anxiously.

'No, not official. I was passing. I brought you a packet of coffee,' I said. 'Are you allowed coffee?'

'Now and again. Betti loves it. She's a wonderful woman, Bernd.' He looked at his watch, looked at me and then at his watch again.

'I know she is,' I said.

'I do a good deal of thinking when I'm dozing here and Betti is at work. I was remembering you the other day. What was the name of that teacher who always gave you such a rough time?'

'I forget.' It seemed as if whenever I met someone I'd been at school with, they wanted to commiserate with me about that bad-tempered bastard.

'He never gave you a minute's peace, Bernd.'

'His brother, or his best buddy or someone, had been killed in Normandy,' I said.

'His son,' supplied Theo. 'Shot dead while trying to surrender; that's what someone told me. Do you think it was true?'

'Maybe. I don't know. He was a Nazi. Remember when he looked in your desk and found your collection of Nazi badges and medals? He took them away to look at them, then he gave them back and never reported you.'

'You hated him.'

'At the time I did,' I conceded. 'But when I thought about it afterwards I saw that it was his endless bullying that made me do so well at lessons. Being top of the class was the only way I could get back at him.'

'And he was the reason why you were so popular,' said Theo.

'He was? How do you make that out?'

'Didn't you ever see that, Bernd? The more he bullied you, the more the rest of us kids wanted to be decent to you.'

'And I thought it was my English charm.'

'And your charm, yes.' He managed to produce a laugh.

'Why are you looking at your watch? Are you expecting a visitor?'

'No,' said Theo.

I moved a tray containing a soup bowl and a plate with some dry biscuits, so that I could sit down at the little chair at his bedside.

Theo said: 'Remember that morning he came into the classroom with the wooden pencils?'

'No.'

'One by one he snapped them in half and gave the pieces out to us. Pencils are like earthworms, he said. Break one in half and it becomes two pencils.'

'There weren't enough pencils for us to have one each.'

'I know, but it was a good joke,' said Theo.

'Tell me about the DELIUS net,' I said.

He looked at the children and said: 'Go and have your supper. Opa is in the other room waiting for you.' As the kids departed, a skinny cat went slinking after them. Theo said: 'You say this visit's not official?' I shook my head. 'Better if your people stay

192

out of this,' he said. 'It's a local matter for us to solve our own way. That damned pastor is "an unofficial collaborator".'

An unofficial collaborator was the Stasi description for people the rest of the world called secret informants or snitches. 'Surely not,' I said.

'It's the only explanation.'

'I was with him after a job I did in Magdeburg. The pastor sheltered me after a shooting fiasco in the KGB compound. He knew Fiona when she was in Berlin; he knew she was working for London.'

'Did he tell you that?' said Theo mildly.

'Yes, when I was here before he told me that.'

'He's clever isn't he?'

'It was some sort of trap for me?'

'He never knew Fiona was working for London. It's what he's been told since she escaped. I doubt if he ever met her.'

'He knew I was working for London.'

'But the Stasi are not going to blow the cover of a wonderful source like him in order to collar a minnow like you, Bernard.'

'Ouch, that hurt, Theo.'

I was sitting at his bedside, and now he reached out and clutched my sleeve. 'It's true, Bernd, he's one of them, believe me. Maybe I can't prove it, but we all know it. We know it in our bones.'

'You've got to do better than bones, Theo. It's a serious accusation.'

'He snoops around everywhere. The Church has given him some sort of roving commission – standing in for clergy who are sick or on leave. He goes to Berlin. He goes to Dresden. He goes to Zwickau ...'

'Zwickau? He was never a part of the Zwickau network.'

'On Sundays. He was conducting services in the church and assisting the pastor there.'

'When?'

'Two years ago. Over the busy Christmas period.'

'You saw him there?'

'Of course I did. It was his idea to put the antenna in the spire. The network had had radio trouble but getting the antenna really high solved it overnight.'

'I see.'

Theo persisted: 'The following year the whole Zwickau group went into the bag didn't they?'

'Not as far as I know,' I said, not wanting to break security. 'The last I heard they were still going strong.'

'I must have got it wrong,' said Theo in a voice that clearly told me that he knew he had it right. 'I suppose a rumour like that would be bad for morale, wouldn't it?'

'It's need-to-know, Theo,' I said. 'We shouldn't be discussing other groups.'

'You're a cold fish, Bernd. Did anyone ever tell you that?'

'Only my very close friends.'

'My oldest brother – Willi – was one of the Zwickau net. They took him away in the middle of the night, and that was the last we heard of him. His wife has written to everyone she can think of – First Secretary Honecker even – and all she gets back is a printed form. They can't even be bothered to type a letter for her.'

'He may be all right,' I said. 'They hold people longer nowadays … Yes, I remember Willi. I forgot that he was your brother; but don't jump to conclusions about the pastor. We can't move against him just because you feel it in your bones, Theo. Carry on with everything as normal. As you say, if he's reporting to the Stasi they will keep your network safe and intact indefinitely. Maybe the only reason you've been safe so long is because they don't want to reveal that he is an informer for them.'

'If London sent you to give us the pep-talk, forget it. I know the old bastard betrayed my brother. He's a rattlesnake. We will settle it ourselves.'

'That's stupid talk, Theo. We don't do it like that. No one does.'

'And you swear this is not official? Why tonight, Bernd?'

'I just arrived. No one knows I'm here. I wanted to come and see for myself.'

'Get out of here, Bernd. Go now. See no one else. Leave it to us to sort out.'

'Don't be a fool,' I said. 'If the network breaks up now – and he is an informer – they'll take you all into custody and toss you into a Stasi prison. They will have nothing to lose. The Stasi have independent powers of arrest and detention. They don't have to provide evidence to an examining magistrate or anything like that.'

He gave me a weary smile. It was like explaining the Christmas menu to a fattened turkey. To him such facts of life were obvious, but sometimes people like Theo have to be reminded of them. 'I know you mean well, Bernd. And I'm grateful.'

'Then do as I say.'

'Will you promise to go away and not contact him?'

'What difference does it make?'

'Please, Bernd. Please leave us alone. Give us a week. After that if we've failed we'll do it your way.'

'I doubt if your network could manage to operate without him.'

'Don't be stupid, Bernd. Of course we could. We've discussed it.'

I wondered how to reassure Theo. 'I'll vet him personally and if necessary London will neutralize him.'

'What does that mean?'

'We'll get rid of him. But it has to be done in some way that won't make all the alarm bells ring. London will probably arrange that he is sent to some other job in some other place by the Church authorities. Somewhere he can't do any mischief.'

'Pass me that glass of water and the red pills. I have to take two of them every four hours.'

'It's the only way, believe me,' I said, passing him his medicine. 'I hate him.' He gulped his pills and drank some water.

'You may have got it wrong, Theo. Keep it all going until we know what's really happening.'

'Are you going to talk to him?'

'I wanted to see you, Theo, to see how you were. Now I'll go back to Berlin. Forget I came here. Tell Betti the same.'

'She won't say anything, Bernd. Her family were high-ranking Nazis – her uncle was the *Politische Kreisleiter*. She grew up keeping her mouth shut.'

'Good.'

'When will I see you again?'

'Get your network people together,' I said without answering his question. 'Make sure they visit you here while you're sick. It's a perfect cover. Don't tell the pastor what you are doing.'

'No.' In his worried face I could see a thousand questions trying to get out, but he didn't ask me anything more. On his bedside table there were photographs of his wife and a portrait photo of their married son Bruno, who worked for the *Schnell-Bahn*, the elevated railway that was owned by the East and went through both parts of Berlin.

'Is Bruno well?' I asked politely.

'We haven't seen him for a long time,' said Theo. 'It's just as well; we don't see eye to eye about the regime.'

'He's trusted,' I said. 'He has to be careful what he says.'

'Yes, he's trusted,' said Theo, for his son was one of the carefully selected railway personnel whose daily duties took them into the West.

I got up and reached for my hat. 'Good luck, Bernd,' said Theo. 'Thanks for coming, and for the packet of coffee. I think a lot about the old days. I must have been crazy to stay here in the East. That damned Wall. I could see what was coming.'

'How could you be certain?' I said. 'Half the kids in the class had homes or family connections in the East.'

'But most of them knew when to get out. It didn't seem so important then, did it?'

'No,' I said. 'It didn't seem so important.'

I didn't keep my promise to Theo. He was sick and I didn't want to alarm him, but coming all this way without talking to the turbulent priest would have been absurd. So I went to his 'church' and waited until the last of the worshippers had left. The service had been held in a meeting hall that was a part of the crypt, all that remained of a church destroyed by wartime bombing. At the bottom of the steps, when I stepped into the light, the pastor looked up and smiled. He recognized me. It was only a few weeks before that I'd sheltered here with him. I was with the kid, Robin, and on the run from a grim half-hour in nearby Magdeburg. Now the pastor came forward and shook hands, gripping my arm with his free hand, like they do in Hollywood. He beamed. His rosy face was that of an elderly cherub.

'Good evening, young man,' he said. 'Have you come specially to see me?'

'Yes,' I said.

He indicated that I should follow him into a small side-room where the smell of incense failed to cloak the stronger one of tobacco smoke. He closed the door and pulled out a chair for me, one of three hard little chairs arranged around a rickety table upon which I put my hat. Adorning the wall there were half a dozen hand-coloured photos of previous pastors and an engraving of the church as it had been a hundred years ago.

The pastor opened a metal locker in which he kept his street clothes and took his time as he divested himself of his clerical garments and put on an old grey suit. He then removed his steel-rimmed glasses and polished them with that dedication that is sometimes the sign of thoroughness, and sometimes a device for delay.

'You know what I do for a living?' I said, more to confirm that his memory was functioning than because I had doubt of it.

'Yes, I do. I know your name, your wife and your job.'

'I've come to tell you that it's all over: *kaputtgemacht*,' I said. 'You've come to a standstill.' I was being provocative of course, I wanted to see how he would react. He looked at me, used a forefinger to push his glasses a fraction up on his nose, but gave no sign of having heard or understood. 'This network is blown,' I said. 'DELIUS is coughing blood. The network can't be salvaged.'

'We looked for peace, but no good came; and for a time of health, and behold trouble.' He paused and looked at me. 'Jeremiah.'

'Yes, I know,' I said. 'I'm talking about the network. It's blown and you blew it. You know my name and my job. Well I don't know your name – not your real name – but I do know your part-time job. You report to the Stasi.'

'You've been listening to gossip. Village gossip is the worst kind,' he told me with an indulgent smile.

'I came over here to pick up the pieces, but I don't see how it can be put together again.'

'Like Humpty-Dumpty?'

'Yes, like Humpty-Dumpty. You've had a long run, but nothing lasts for ever.' I waited for him to respond but he stood very still, his eyes staring at me, his expression calm. He showed no sign of wanting to argue or explain. For 'an unofficial collaborator' I found his coldness disconcerting. Informers usually lived on their nerves and were easy to jolt. 'I've been authorized to offer you a deal,' I said after a long pause.

'Oh? What kind of a deal would that be?'

'Everyone goes into the bag eventually,' I said. 'For every agent who is good at what he does ... who pushes opportunities to extremes and consistently takes chances, being exposed is the inevitable career climax.'

'Being a pastor is not a career; it is a vocation,' he said, as if determined to bluff his way out of it.

I continued my spiel: 'But a career's climax doesn't have to be a career's end.'

'I can't believe you are serious. Are you saying what you seem to be saying?'

'Think what we could do. London would put the network together again. We'd reassemble it to be even better – more productive – than before. You'd go on reporting to Normannenstrasse as usual. And drawing your pay from them.'

The pastor scratched his cheek with a fingernail and said: 'The Gospel of St Matthew tells us that no man can serve two masters without coming to hate the one, and love the other.'

'I thought that was putting the finger on materialism and spirituality,' I said. 'Isn't that the passage that Matthew continues: "Ye cannot serve God and mammon"?'

'You have an enviable memory.'

'It's a part of the job,' I said. 'So what's your answer? London or Berlin?'

'I thought I'd given you my answer.'

'Not quite. You haven't told me which is God, and which is mammon.'

'You come here to my country, and you threaten me as if I was in your country.' His voice was still calm but he was hardening and that was good. This was the nearest he'd come to bluster, but I could see now that I'd had it all wrong. He wasn't an unofficial collaborator; this man had the resilience of a trained and experienced Stasi man.

I said: 'You understand what I'm offering, don't you? You see the alternatives?'

'Why don't you make them clearer?'

'I can't make it much clearer,' I said. 'You know as well as I do that if you don't cooperate, London will have to eliminate you. They can't permit you to walk away.'

'Eliminate me,' he said, repeating my word '*ausschalten*', and making a movement with his fingers as if operating a light-switch. 'Is this your idea? To give me a chance to join you in spying against my own people?'

'No,' I said. 'They wouldn't listen to me. I wanted to waste you, without the option.'

He responded with a grim smile. He was annoyed with himself for being stampeded into discussing a deal. The face remained as calm as ever, but there was suppressed anger to be seen around his mouth. 'You shit-head!' he said softly. 'I'll show you how we do the switching off – of filth like you.'

We had both started off this conversation with the wrong idea. It was nothing but good luck that had made my error of judgement work, while his misfired. Now, from his back pocket, he took a pigskin wallet. From a compartment in it he produced a sheet of paper and placed it on the table in front of me. I recognized what it was before he flattened it out for me to read. It was crudely printed on coarse yellowing paper. Constant folding had worn the paper so that it had almost separated into four quarters. It was a Stasi warrant. In the bottom corner there was a solemn man holding a numbered board up to the camera's lens. The text identified him as a captain employed by the Ministry of Security and enjoined all comers to help and assist him.

'I've seen one before,' I said, pushing the paper back towards him.

'I'm sure you have.'

'Think it over,' I said, getting to my feet. This was the dangerous moment; the time when he was deciding whether to arrest me, kill me, or keep me warm as some kind of insurance policy for his old age.

He smirked. It was a stand-off; the knowing smile was his acknowledgement of that fact, just as my telling him to think it over was my way of admitting as much. 'How would we make contact?' he said. 'Is there a code? ... I mean in the event that I thought it over, and wanted to do a deal?'

'Usual network procedure. Ask for a dozen gold sovereigns in any context, and I'll come and see you.'

'Not thirty?' He looked at his watch. Everyone I talked to kept looking at their watches; it was beginning to give me a complex.

I buttoned up my coat and picked up my battered felt hat. I wondered if he would phone to have me stopped at the checkpoint. I was pleased that I had taken the extra precaution of changing transport and identity in Berlin.

'I have sick parishioners to comfort,' said the pastor as he struggled into a heavy overcoat and put on a woollen hat. 'I do my rounds every night, like a shepherd.'

'Or maybe like a jailer?' I said.

'I used to ask myself that question sometimes.'

'And?'

'In the end I decided there is no difference.' His voice was firmer now. He had called my bluff and ended up master. For the next few hours – while I was in the DDR – I was a card in his hand and he could play me any way he liked. I opened the door. 'Good-night, Herr Samson,' he said. 'May the Lord protect you.'

I grunted a goodnight.

I'd parked in the school alley across the road but the pastor's car – a Trabant even older than mine – was sheltered in the nearby barn. It took me a few minutes to scrape the frost from my glass but the pastor had had the foresight to protect his windscreen with newspaper. Now he removed it and jumped into his car to watch me as I made repeated attempts to start up. He was going to see me off before he left; he didn't want me following him.

Finally the loud rattle of my engine came, provoking a clatter of wings from the nearby trees as alarmed birds climbed sleepily into the night sky. I let in the clutch and moved forward cautiously, glancing in the mirror as I carefully negotiated the narrow stone entrance that bridged the ditch.

Reflected in the driving mirror I saw the pastor's Trabant. As I watched, it lit up inside, as if he was testing a powerful flashlight. In its bright interior I could see his scowling face, his spectacle lenses flashing like silver dollars. Later I realized that this preliminary glow was some kind of misfire. Immediately the first blaze of light was overcome by a brighter one that transformed the car's glasswork into sheets of polished silver. Fragments of flying glass caught the light of the explosion and enclosed the car in what was, for one brief instant, a great globe of glittering mirrors. Then it all fell to the ground and disappeared like snowflakes. By the time the force of the explosion came, I was through the entrance gate and on to the road. The blast almost rolled my car into the ditch, and the sound hit my eardrums like a thunderclap. The echoes of the explosion rolled across the yard and were replaced by a low hoarse roaring sound as the pastor's Trabbie became a sizzling furnace.

Theo, you stupid bastard! They'll come in and tear you all to pieces now. In my younger days I might have turned around, briefed them about reassembling and started them all running for cover. But I was no longer young. I stabbed the gas pedal. The glow of the fire disappeared behind a hill and I rolled up my car window and kept going.

All the following day I sat behind my desk waiting for the next hammer blow to fall.

'A teleprinter intercept from Dresden,' said Lida, putting it on my desk together with a fiercely strong cup of coffee. I looked at her; she stared back without expression. Frank Harrington in a characteristic gesture of support had assigned to me the brightest and best secretary in the building. Lida was a fifty-year-old widow with diamante-studded bifocals, a remarkable supply of brightly coloured woollens, an encyclopaedic memory and adequate command of most Western European languages.

'How many of them is that?' I asked her.

'Five.'

'But not Theo Forster?'

'Not yet.' Lida was a realist.

'No,' I said grimly. 'Not yet. They'll leave him to last.'

Lida had left my door unguarded and now the kid poked his head around it. 'Can I see you, boss?' His arms loaded, he pushed the door with a shoulder and entered crabwise.

'I suppose so.'

The kid put two box files on my desk and opened the top one. 'I'd better show you what I found,' he said.

'I know what you found,' I said. 'You found that there is no way to immediately replace the DELIUS network as a means of putting people into place.'

'Yes.'

'No matter,' I said. 'With DELIUS compromised, all the Church networks are suspect. We'll have to think of something drastic.'

He stood by my desk stroking his files. 'Why do they pick them up one at a time?' he said. 'Why not a swoop that brings them all in together? Keep the prisoners apart and interrogate them separately.'

'It's their system,' I said. 'Always one by one. They tap all the phones and watch all the houses and try to stampede the other suspects into doing something foolish. They hope to get leads to people they don't know about.'

'They have more or less got the lot now.'

'More or less,' I agreed.

'Are you all right?'

'I'm one hundred per cent,' I told him.

'You look done in. I hope you didn't catch that Chinese 'flu that's been going around the girls in the cashier's department. It starts with a rough furry tongue. Have you got the same?'

'I don't think so, but I haven't had time to match tongues with the girls in the cashier's office.'

'And stomach pains,' explained the kid earnestly.

'I've got a lot of work to do.' He meant well, I could see that, but I needed time on my own. I needed to think.

'They didn't arrest the pastor,' said the kid, waving some more papers at me.

'Give them time,' I said. 'We'll look at all the intercepts tomorrow. And we'll see what Frank has to say. He might want to come back here and take charge.'

'You haven't told him yet?'

'I'll phone him in London. He'll probably want to warn the D-G what's happening.'

'That should spoil his evening,' said the kid.

'Frank's been around a long time. He's seen the networks come and go.'

'I suppose you get used to it. Is that what you mean?'

'No, you never get used to it,' I said. 'You don't break down and weep, but you don't get used to it.'

'I'll see if there's anything on the Magdeburg criminal police sheets,' said the kid, balancing the contents of my out-tray on the top of his box files and making for the door. Then he stopped and said: 'My father wrote to me the other day and asked me what I thought I would be doing when I was fifty years old. He said that if a man thinks about where and what he's going to be when he's fifty all the preceding years fall into place. Do you agree, boss?'

'I'll let you know,' I said. Sometimes I wondered if he said these things to wind me up.

When he had gone, Lida said: 'Shall I stay on tonight?'

'No. Go home. Tell the night-duty man to switch his internal line through to me and give me two outside lines. I'll sleep on the sofa.'

'I sent your bags over to the Hotel Hennig but I didn't ask for a room for you.'

'It's okay,' I said. 'There's a little attic room. Frau Hennig lets me use it when I'm in Berlin.'

'And what about a meal?'

'I'm all right,' I said. I didn't want her to mother me. She nodded and said goodnight, but about thirty minutes later she returned waving a flimsy sheet from the monitoring service. 'I thought you'd want to see this immediately,' she said. 'Magdeburg area. A pastor severely burned in a vehicle fire. With it the news services are putting out a government warning about illegal storage of gasoline.'

'Thanks,' I said.

'I think it's our man. They are trying to play it down by means of the warning.'

'Can I smell burning?' I said. She looked at me and shrugged. 'There is a burning smell,' I said.

'I was making toast. Is it forbidden?'

'No, Lida,' I said.

'There is an electric toast machine for the office staff … If it is forbidden …'

'No. No. Get along home, Lida. I'll see you in the morning.'

'Goodnight, Herr Samson.' As she went out through the door the smell of burning was stronger and far more pungent.

Any last hope I was nursing, about Theo being eliminated from the list of suspects, was gone by midnight when it was confirmed that he'd been arrested. Theo was the last one to go into the bag. I read the message twice and then closed my eyes to think about everything that had happened. The next thing I knew it was six in the morning and I was waking up with a headache and dry mouth, just like the girls with the Chinese influenza. I had just keeled over and gone to sleep at my desk. It wasn't 'flu, it was nerves. Never mind all that stuff about the adrenalin flowing; real petrifying fear and despair brings only an overwhelming weariness.

Yawning and dishevelled I went and sniffed at early-morning Berlin – with all the sounds and smells I remembered as a child going to school. I had a stubbly face, bleary eyes and an urgent need for a cup of coffee. A car-pool driver took me to one of my old haunts, an all-night bar tucked away between the bus terminal and Witzleben S-Bahn. Its neon sign looked pale in the watery pink dawn. I went in and looked around at the people in there – truck drivers, railway men, pimps and night-shift workers – but the only face I recognized belonged to the proprietor.

'Bernd. Long time, no see,' called Sammy the owner without removing the cigar from his mouth. He was a plump, pink-faced Hungarian who used to earn a comfortable living from Berlin clubs and restaurants to which he sold alcohol, cigarettes and cigars stolen from the big trucks. Now he'd become almost completely respectable, providing food and drink to long-distance truck drivers at the end of the Autobahn that led through the DDR to West Germany. He was still selling alcohol and tobacco but his days of thieving were gone; he had a wholesale business and two large warehouses from which he could make just as much money without breaking the law.

I sat down and waited. The air was laden with smoke and coffee and the sweet smell of doughnuts. I drank a strong espresso coffee with a schnapps chaser and read a newspaper that some customer had left behind. There was no real news in it, just stories about TV stars and sports. Bruno Forster arrived eventually as I felt sure he would. He stood in the doorway looking around the room to find me. He was bareheaded and wearing mechanic's coveralls with a railway uniform jacket. He was obviously on duty. When he spotted me he did not smile or wave, he came over to the table holding a packet as if he was about to deliver a warrant.

'There it is, Herr Samson. Dad said you always wanted it.' He dropped a heavy white envelope on to the plastic table-top.

'Hello, Bruno,' I said, looking up at him. Apart from a small wispy moustache he looked very much like Theo had looked in the old days. I didn't touch the envelope.

'He told me to give it to you. It's the *Blutorden*.' He spat it out – Blood Order – with all the contempt he could muster. It was a medal – one of the rarest of the Nazi decorations – and Theo had had one in his collection since he was a school-kid. I'd desperately wanted to add it to my modest little collection.

'Thanks, Bruno. Will you have coffee? Or a drink?'

'He'll never survive prison. You know that don't you?' He stood over me and ignored the invitation.

'Did you see him?' I said.

'You bastard. Are you satisfied now?'

'Did you see him?'

'Yes, they let me see him. He was crying.' Bruno let me absorb that one. 'He was sitting hunched up, with his arms round his knees. Sitting in the visitor's room sobbing his heart out … like a child.'

'Had they hurt him?'

'What do you care? No, they hadn't hurt him. They hadn't tortured him the way your rotten Western newspapers say our detectives torture their prisoners. And if you'd left him alone he would be free and happy.'

'He's sick,' I said. 'They'll probably let him out soon.'

'You come into people's lives and interfere, and make them miserable and stir up the shit. And where does it get you?'

'It wasn't like that, Bruno,' I said. 'Your father wanted to help.'

Bruno Forster looked around to be sure we weren't being overheard. He had come through to the West on his S-Bahn train and I suppose they would ask him to account for every minute of his time. The S-Bahn management made sure their staff weren't wandering around in the Western Sector of the city, for the managers were also vetted and kept under the strict scrutiny of the Stasi. That's how the system worked.

'Open your present,' he said.

'How is your mother?' I could feel the medal through its wrapping but I didn't open the envelope. It was as if by accepting the legacy I would be hastening poor Theo's demise.

'My mother won't talk to me. I talk to her but she looks at me and doesn't reply.'

'She loves your dad.'

'She blames me.' He gave a short angry laugh. 'They both do.' His indignation came out with a rush. 'You come along, and you tear the family apart. You tell them about the West. You tell them freedom is everything. You encourage the old man to help these maniacs who want to overthrow the State. I warned him over and over again. My mother takes him along to the Church and involves him and then, when he's in trouble, who do they blame? Not themselves or you. They blame me!'

I fingered the envelope and I could feel the ribbon to which the medal was attached. Alone of all the Nazi medals it was worn on the right breast pocket, its ribbon threaded through the buttonhole.

'I'm a socialist,' said Bruno. 'I'm loyal to my country. The DDR is a good place to live. They try. We have proper medical care and jobs for life. No crime, none of the perversion and hell

208

you've made in the West. I tell my DDR friends that if they came over here and saw it for themselves they'd see the filth and the misery. They'd see how brainwashed your wretched workers are. They'd see the people living on the streets, the drugs and the horrors ...'

'But they can't,' I said. 'They can't come over here and see anything. You built the Wall.'

'I've got to go back to work. I haven't got time to argue.'

'No, well maybe I've been brainwashed into thinking freedom is everything,' I said. I restrained the desire to tell him that it was the filthy pollution – and the appalling working conditions at the government-owned cycle factory – that had brought his father prematurely to the point of death.

'Open it up.' He tapped the envelope. 'Dad made me promise to give it to you. He told me over and over. I don't know why you'd want it.' As he looked around another thought struck him: 'How did he know you'd be here? And how did you know I'd come?'

'I guessed you might look in here. A lot of the S-Bahn workers look in here for a schnapps or a coffee.'

But he wasn't to be fooled. 'This place is a drop, isn't it? Your bloody spy system! Is this how Dad's network communicated with you? Is that how you told them you were coming? The S-Bahn?'

'Don't even start thinking about it, Bruno. You live in a place where even thoughts can be severely punished.'

Perhaps he was persuaded by that argument, for as he got to his feet he repeated his Party line about the West's exploited workers and about me in particular. 'You are a hyena, Samson,' he said softly, so that his voice was almost a hiss. 'You live on the corpses of good people who believe your damned fairy tales.'

'Perhaps you are right, Bruno,' I said. I'd known him since he was an infant in knitted hats and waving a rattle. I remember crossing Checkpoint Charlie bringing him a push-chair from the Ka-De-We department store. It only just fitted into the back of my car, and the frontier police were about to seize it from me until I gave them four cartons of American cigarettes. It was a foolish risk, for in those days the guards would sometimes react fiercely to any sort of attempted bribery.

'You couldn't leave him in peace could you? Not even when he was sick.' He took a handkerchief and blew his nose loudly. 'You call yourself his friend?'

I recognized his ranting for what it was: grief at the prospect of losing his dad, and regret that his ill will had meant missing so many precious years with his parents. I didn't answer.

'A Nazi medal,' said Bruno. 'It's an appropriate gift. I'm glad I gave it to you in person.'

I knew he wouldn't stay more than a few minutes; his masters became suspicious of prolonged delays in the West.

9

Hennig Hotel, West Berlin.
After my bruising encounter with Theo's son I went to Tante Lisl's hotel. The room I used was under the roof, reached by a steep flight of narrow wooden stairs originally intended only for the use of servants. It was midday. I closed the curtains against the daylight, undressed and went to bed. I needed sleep but sleep did not come easily; the cramped little room held vivid memories for me, not only of my school-days with Theo but of my father and of the day he died. Exhaustion finally claimed me and I did not wake up until late afternoon. I remained in bed for another half hour or so, hoping that someone would appear with comforts like broth and Bratwurst, but no one came. When I phoned the office to be sure no new emergency had developed Lida told me that her attempts to reach me had been met with someone telling her that I needed rest. Fortunately she had handled the office routine without my assistance.

Lida showed a disconcerting insight into everything that went on in the office. She told me that a query had arisen concerning someone who had checked out a BMW motor cycle the previous evening without entering into the book the required details of the driving licence and authorization code. In a voice devoid of any emotion she reported having told the motor pool to mark it 'special arrangement for Mr Harrington'. That meant

211

that she could just nod it through without it attracting further attention. Lida was a treasure.

My head ached, my eyes were difficult to open fully, and my mouth was dry. I pulled on an old roll-neck sweater and corduroy pants and picked my way down the creaking little staircase, along the landing, and downstairs to find something to eat. There was no one about; this was not the time of year for tourists, and businessmen found reasons to stay home when the Christmas season approached. From now onwards there was a slack period until the Berlin Film Festival in February. Lisl prospered in the Festival: her hotel had a reputation for being lucky. Directors, producers and even well-known actors and actresses thronged here because over the years so many of her guests had won the Silver Bear and all sorts of other awards. The two big expensive suites on the first floor were particularly lucky ones, so she said, although I'd noticed that when anyone asked which winners had slept in them, and won which prize at which Festival, Lisl always became somewhat vague.

At the bottom of the lovely old marble staircase, with the polished wooden rail that I liked to slide down when a child, I found Lisl Hennig in her room. Its door was wide open, for Lisl liked to be able to see what was going on in her domain, but now her eyes were closed and she appeared to be sound asleep. A plate was on the floor beside her, its contents – a half-eaten apple, a segment of cheese and two water biscuits – scattered across the carpet. I stood there for a moment, looking into her darkened study. The way the overhead reading-light made a marble-like shine on her dress, the lock of hair falling forward on her forehead, the way her arms rested along the thronelike seat, the newspapers and abandoned lunch around her, made a scene that suggested a litter-strewn Lincoln Memorial.

This was her den, into which only the privileged were invited and where only her intimates were permitted to sit

212

down. The big ornate clock stood at three-thirty and Wilhelm II waved his sword and scowled menacingly at me. The only incongruity came from a newly installed desktop computer on the side-table. Like some sort of contrived comparison the dark screen and keyboard stood alongside the old mechanical adding machine with which Lisl had always calculated the guests' bills. Pinned on the wall behind the table there was a page carelessly torn from a newspaper; a six-column-wide coloured reproduction of the Van Gogh *Irises* that had been recently auctioned at Sotheby's for a record bid of fifty-three million dollars. This news item had commanded worldwide interest; proving, by quantifying the priceless, that everything was possible.

Suddenly Lisl gave a snort and came awake: 'Bernd, darling! Come and give your poor old Lisl a big kiss.' As usual she was instantly awake, and unwilling to admit to having dozed off.

Her name was Liese-Lotte, but as a girl she'd adopted the more gemütlich Viennese form of Lisl, and that touch of kitsch suited her. I went and kissed her carefully so as not to disturb the lipstick and the carefully rouged and powdered face. She twisted her head to accept a kiss on each cheek.

'Let me look at you, darling.' She twisted the table light so that it floodlit me and I stood obediently, feeling an absolute fool, while she scrutinized me from head to toe. She was not admiring me. 'You are ill. You must see a doctor.'

'I'm just hungry,' I said.

'You need proper food. Berlin food. Tonight: *Schlacht-platte!*'

'That sounds wonderful,' I said and meant it. The huge plate of mixed boiled meats and sausages was something for which I had yearned for a long time.

'I still say you should see a doctor, Bernd. I know when you are ill; I've known you all my life haven't I?'

'I'm okay.'

'It's only you I'm thinking of.' She phoned the kitchen and ordered a snack for me. When she'd done that she picked up a newspaper that was folded into a small bundle to expose the crossword puzzle. 'You have come just at the right moment. I've started doing the crosswords in the English newspapers every day. It is good for my English.' She said this in German, which made me believe that her desire to master English was not a top priority. 'A Christian kingdom ruled by a General? Seven letters ending THO.'

'Lesotho,' I said.

'There is such a country?'

'In Africa.'

'You have saved my life, darling. You are a wonderful darling, a genius. I was driven almost insane. Lesotho. Ah! That makes sixteen down STOIC. The rest are easy. I will complete it later. Good.' With a sigh of relief she put the newspaper aside and turned to me: 'Now, Bernd. What have you done to poor Werner?'

'Done to him? I haven't seen him for ages. Is he here?'

'You haven't argued again with that wife of his?'

'Zena do you mean?' Zena was Werner's diminutive and combative first wife, to whom he'd recently returned for no reason that I could fathom.

'Yes, Zena,' said Lisl. 'You don't like her. She is …' List's arthritic fingers played a remarkably nimble trill in the air as she searched for a word that was both appropriate to Zena's nature and repeatable to Werner. '… touchy. Yes, touchy sometimes, I know.'

'Werner's private life is nothing to do with me,' I said.

Perhaps I put a little too much feeling into this reply, for Lisl said: 'Is this to say I am an interfering old woman?'

'No, Lisl darling,' I said hastily. 'Of course you aren't.'

She looked at me under lowered eyelids while deciding to accept my cowardly assurance. 'It's a pity you didn't find some

214

nice German girl, I've often thought that.' She had often said it too. Werner's marriage and mine were topics she could discuss at length, and about which she could become very emotional. Lisl had been an aunt to me, but for Werner – after his Jewish parents died – she had been a mother. And yet Werner's marriage to the pugnacious Zena had not troubled Lisl as much as my marriage to Fiona. Of course Lisl never criticized Fiona. Her old-fashioned respect for the institution of marriage ruled out destructive criticism. But I knew Lisl very well indeed, and I knew she secretly saw Fiona as a cold and remote foreign woman who had intruded into our cosy family circle.

Lisl was as different to Fiona as anyone could possibly be. Born into a wealthy Berlin family, her girlhood spent in a formal and exclusive world, Lisl had nevertheless inherited the fearless vulgarity and tenacious sense of humour that is the hallmark of the Berliner. Her innate toughness had made her unhesitatingly offer shelter to Werner's parents at a time when hiding Jews usually brought a one-way ticket to a concentration camp. Lisl was generous to a fault, but she was also narrow-minded, chauvinistic and selfish. 'A nice German girl,' she mused. 'And you could have lived here in the city, and got a proper job.' Lisl was fishing for news of my domestic life. I could tell by the look on her face.

'I have a job,' I reminded her. 'And now I'm living in the city too.'

'You always have an answer, don't you, Bernd? A still tongue makes a wise head. Have you heard that saying, Bernd?'

I didn't answer; I just smiled.

But you couldn't win with Lisl. 'It struck home did it, my little remark? A nice German girl. Someone who kept your shirts nice, looked after the children and cooked you proper meals.'

'I was working all night,' I said. 'I haven't shaved yet. I put on this old sweater and came down because I was hungry.'

'Don't complain, Bernd. The girl in the kitchen is working as fast as she can.'

'I know, Tante Lisl.' I looked around. 'The hotel is very quiet.'

'We'll be full for the Festival,' she said. 'The best suite is already booked. We'll be turning people away, you just see. Will you be here for Christmas?'

'It seems likely.'

She looked at me, sniffed loudly and reverted to the subject of wives: 'A warm-blooded German girl would have been better for you. A German girl knows how to keep her man.'

'I'm happily married,' I protested.

'Uggh!' She challenged my claim with a rude sound. 'I know all about that,' she said, pressing a forefinger against the side of her nose in a promise of confidentiality. 'I know all about your *ungarische Hure* … Do you think I have not heard about your adventures living with the Gloria woman?'

It was of course a shot in the dark; an artful ploy calculated to make me protest, and in protesting provide her with more information about both Fiona and Gloria, and my relations with them. I suppose she was puzzled that I'd come to Berlin without my wife. I didn't reply, except to yawn and rub my face wearily.

She didn't leave it at that: 'Your Gloria is staying here in town with her new friend Mr Rensselaer. Together. Did you know that?'

'I don't think so, Lisl,' I said patiently.

'And I say yes. At that flashy new American hotel in Wilmersdorfer Strasse. Red shutters and flower boxes,' she said disparagingly, as if such trappings were self-evident signs that it would encourage the illicit sharing of bedrooms.

I smiled.

'This hotel isn't good enough for them, I suppose.'

So that was the affront. It wasn't Gloria or Bret, or the rumour of them sharing a bed, that had annoyed Lisl; it was the idea that they might have preferred another hotel to hers. I didn't dwell upon it; Lisl loved rumours and she always got them wrong. Soon a tray arrived with broth and Bratwurst and warm potato salad, with a slice of the sort of Roggenbrot that I remembered from my childhood snacks – when I came home from school and helped myself to such good dark bread from the hotel kitchen.

'What have you done to Werner?' she said again.

'Nothing. Where is he?' I said between mouthfuls of soup.

'Eat! Eat! Don't talk to Werner until he's finished decorating my tree. He's gone to buy more coloured lights.'

'What did he say I'd done to him?'

'Good sausage? I have a new butcher. You should see the Eisbein he sends me. And the Bockwurst: real Berlin style.' She watched me while I ate some more. 'Whatever you did to Werner, you've upset him.' Despite her love for me she loved to jolt me with disturbing news. 'Two wasted lives – you and Werner. What prospects do either of you have?'

'Werner is making a fortune,' I said.

'What's wrong with your broth? Why haven't you finished it? I have a new cook; just to do the lunches. He's a Schwab, a nice boy. Can you taste the goose gravy in it? That's how he gives it that lovely colour.' She sniffed. 'Yes, Werner is always telling me he is doing well. But if he was really doing well would he still be working for you British?'

'He's not working for us,' I said.

'How do you know?'

'I'm Frank's Deputy.'

'Eat your bread. Is there too much garlic in the potato salad? Eat it then. Frank's Deputy? Ummm. That's not so bad then. Will you get allowances, car and driver, and all the trimmings?'

'I suppose so.' I finished the last morsel of potato salad. 'But the government in London is cutting back.'

217

'It's a family matter.' I looked up and she met my eyes. 'Whatever you've done to Werner … it's about your family; he said that it was. It's none of my business of course, so I don't expect him to confide in me about it. I told him that. I said, if it's something concerning only you and Bernd, it's private. It's better I don't know about it.'

'I can't imagine what it might be.'

'I've never interfered with you, Bernd. I've always let you live your own life in your own way. Even when I could see you were making that terrible mistake …' She fixed me with a stare and nodded to be sure I understood that this referred to my marriage to Fiona. 'I never interfered. I never commented. I never criticized. When your father died – God bless his soul – I told him that you would always have a home to come to here. But your life is your own, Bernd. Whatever you and Werner have to discuss, I don't want to know about it.'

'I respect that wish, Tante Lisl,' I said, not without a shade of *Schadenfreude*. 'And I'll see Werner keeps to it.'

Her eyes narrowed. She felt her parental role in my life entitled her to full and frank disclosure, the way all parents feel. 'He's back upstairs now, doing the tree. I heard the upstairs door bang. Keep where you are, I'll send for coffee. It's better Werner finishes doing the tree first. I'm determined to have the tree decorated and lit up early this Christmas. Trees are so expensive this year, and a Christmassy look brings in casual customers to drink at the bar.' As I kissed her goodbye she was still complaining that I wouldn't go and see a doctor. 'Dr Litzmann is a wonderful doctor; I wouldn't be here today without him.'

When finally permitted to depart and go upstairs I found extensive decorating under way. Bunches of holly and mistletoe, and golden foil decorations, were arranged on the floor upon sheets of brown wrapping paper. A ten-feet-tall Christmas tree had been erected near the bar at the far end of the saloon, the step-ladder alongside it repeating its shape in shiny alloy, like some futuristic tree by a trendy designer. Heightening this effect, there was a set of coloured fairy-lights, draped over the ladder and winking on and off.

This large *fin-de-siècle* room was the best-preserved part of Lisl's lovely old family home. The same panelling and the ceiling could be recognized in many of the old photos that she treasured. One photo in particular stayed in my memory, a photo so full of action that I could almost hear the orchestra. This sepia-tinted grand salon was depicted sometime during the 1920s, with mothers in voluminous gowns and girls in scanty Twenties dresses; elderly men in elegant evening dress and young veterans in carefully tailored uniforms, military and political. The ancient camera's roller-blind shutter that had made the flowing ball gowns blur had frozen the splayed coat-tails of the whirling men. Fittingly so, for this was the time, and Berlin the place, where old and new Europe began to split apart, and where the Second World War was born.

'Werner, old pal. Where have you been?' Only after the golden star was fixed atop the Christmas tree, and it was garlanded in twinkling lights, did Werner stop work, put aside the ladder and go through the formalities. His jet-black hair was long and wavy and he had the discreet tan that the rich folk wear in winter. He was slim and elegant in black pants, patent loafers and a mustard-coloured roll-neck. And when I grabbed his arm I knew I was holding several hundred D-marks' worth of silky cashmere. Such signs usually proclaimed that Zena was back on the flight-deck, and sitting in the left-hand seat.

'Bernie. I was trying to reach you in London. It was only when I got Fiona on the line that I found out you were right here in Berlin.' Werner sat down beside me on the sofa near the bar, plucking at the knees of his trousers to preserve the creases.

'Where did the tan come from?'

'Punta,' he said self-consciously.

'Oh, Punta,' I said, as if I was an habitué of Punta del Este in Uruguay, the secret southern hideaway where the jet-set went to get tanned, while *hoi polloi* pulled on their woollen underwear to face the northern winter.

'Zena loves it there.'

'Your tree looks good, Werner.'

He smiled nervously, not sure if I was joshing him. 'Lisl told you that I was looking for you?'

'She didn't say why,' I said.

'You didn't track down George Kosinski in Warsaw?'

'Not in Warsaw. Not in Switzerland. Not anywhere.'

'He's alive.'

'I think so,' I said.

'No, I mean I know he's alive. Someone I know saw him and recognized him. Very recently.'

I looked at Werner for a moment. It wasn't a joke; there were some things that Werner never joked about and my work was one of them. 'And did this someone know what George Kosinski looks like?'

'Definitely.'

'Where?'

'His brother's house.'

'I went there.'

'So I heard,' said Werner.

'The bastards. So they were hiding him. I thought they were.'

'But you didn't keep trying?'

'No,' I said. 'I figured that everyone has to draw the line somewhere, and man-hunting a fugitive brother-in-law might be the right spot for me to blow the whistle.'

'The Kosinskis outsmarted you, and you're sore?'

'Finding George is the easy part,' I told him. 'I'm still trying to figure out what he's doing there.'

'He's Polish,' said Werner.

'He's been Polish for a long time. But why should he suddenly up-sticks and rush off to rural Poland in time for winter?'

'He's been pestering the DDR people about his wife's remains, hasn't he?'

'If all they wanted to do is return Tessa's body to him, they could just push it across Potsdamerplatz on a mortuary trolley.'

'What's Dicky Cruyer's theory?'

'Dicky doesn't have theories; he just gives orders.'

'Yes, he's the Europe supremo in London nowadays isn't he?'

'There is a rumour to that effect,' I said.

'Will you go back?'

'To Poland? Not if I can avoid it. Not at this time of year.'

Werner smiled as if I'd amused him. 'They'll ask you, Bernie. You can bet a million dollars to an old shirt-button that they'll send you back there.'

'What makes you so sure?'

'George Kosinski's behaviour worries them. You worry them. Sending you there with a direct order to bring George back will put you both on the line.'

'Is that the way you see it?'

'It's the way London will see it.'

'For London read Dicky?'

'No, not Dicky. You have nothing to fear from Dicky; he's too lazy, too concerned with his ambitions to spend much time planning your downfall. It's the back-room boys and the D-G. It's Uncle Silas talking to Frank Harrington. It's Bret and … the others.'

'Were you going to say Fiona?'

'No, no, no,' said Werner, rather too emphatically to be convincing. 'She's one hundred per cent on your side. She loves you, Bernie.'

'You said that with wholehearted conviction, Werner.'

He rubbed his face reflectively. 'I shouldn't tell you this, Bernie, but I was Fiona's case officer while she was working for the Stasi.'

'You were?' I took a grip on the chair so as not to fall to the floor with surprise. 'I was told that Bret Rensselaer was Fiona's case officer.'

'It depends what you call being a case officer,' said Werner. 'Can you imagine Bret going across to the other side? Bret couldn't find his way to *Femsehturm* without a guide dog.' Since East Berlin's TV tower was 365 metres tall this verdict was quite a slur on Bret's sense of direction.

So Werner had been Fiona's contact all that time? The Department had painted Werner the deepest shade of black while using him as a key figure in one of the most risky, delicate and vital tasks they'd ever undertaken. 'Jesus Christ, Werner. You. Fiona's case officer?'

'I wasn't going to tell you. Not ever. You'll keep it to yourself, won't you? I thought perhaps Fiona would have confided in you, but I should have known better. She's amazing isn't she?'

'Amazing,' I agreed.

'I saw her in some of the worst times,' said Werner, his hand shielding his eyes as if he was seeing the past all over again. 'She was suicidal at times. More than once I thought we'd have to grab her and run with her.'

'Was there a contingency plan for that?'

'No. No contingency plan. London said any emergency preparations would mean telling more people ... and endangering her.'

'Oh, yes. Good old London Central. They wouldn't want to endanger her.'

'Endanger her more,' explained Werner, who could sometimes become surprisingly defensive about the callous antics of London Central. 'How is Fiona? How is she now?'

'Since we are exchanging confidences,' I said. 'I think she's slowly coming unglued.'

'Everyone says she's fit and well and fully recovered.'

'You asked me what I thought,' I said. 'I don't enjoy saying it. The others only see her when she is putting on a show; I see her at home when her defences are down. I see her as she really is.'

'Yes, I asked you,' said Werner.

'It's largely the fact that she's in such a vulnerable condition that gives me the strength to go on.'

'With the marriage?'

'Don't get me wrong; I love her. I love her to distraction but I no longer find it easy to live with her. Does that sound crazy?'

'How could I find that crazy? Do you think it's easy living with Zena? She's a spiteful egoistical nagger. And anyway I have always wanted to have a family. And Zena is determined not to have kids. But I love her; I can't bear the idea of someone else being with her. When I'm not with her I think of her all the time.'

Werner had never bared his heart like this to me. I didn't know how to react to his confession. I looked away. I looked at the cupboard behind the bar where the booze was locked.

'You're lucky,' said Werner. 'Fiona never goes out of her way to give you a bad time, does she?'

'No,' I admitted.

'You say she's not well. How can I doubt it? That night when we pulled Fiona out ... that night of the shooting on the Autobahn. She was ill then – she was ill a long time before that. Fiona should have been hospitalized.'

'That night – before we flew to California – she saw a doctor and the shrink too.'

'Department people; ordered to put an okay rubber stamp on her and send her off for debriefing.'

'I suppose so.'

'What about you, Bernie? Maybe you should have seen the shrink too.'

'Me? There's nothing wrong with me, Werner.' It came out too quickly and Werner noticed that.

'You shot two men that night, Bernie. What do you know about them?'

'Two hoodlums. One of them was Stinnes, the one we chased around Mexico; a hard-line Party man with a lot of deaths on his conscience if the file has got it right.'

'And the other man?'

'His side-kick?'

'His name was Harry Kennedy,' said Werner. 'Canadian, someone said, but that may have been a cover. He was a doctor of medicine working in London. Then he wangled some temporary job here at the Charité in Berlin. Ardent lefty. Party member from a long time back.'

I could tell from Werner's voice that more was coming and that it was not going to be something to celebrate. But Werner was not enjoying being the bearer of bad tidings; his face had become as hard as stone and almost as grey. He wet his lips. 'Go on, Werner,' I said.

'Kennedy was assigned to monitor Fiona.'

'For the Stasi?'

'And for Moscow. He made regular visits to East Berlin to see her. The Charité was just a cover. He met her in London first. They saw a lot of each other.'

'Were they …?'

'Yes, Bernie, they were.'

At that moment I saw Werner's face vividly. I saw the set of his mouth and that black moustache, the narrowed eyes and the bushy hair in which for the first time I saw strands of grey. But his words were not so clear: they rattled around in my head like loose marbles in an old tin can, and made as much sense. Yes, they were. Yes, they were. Yes, they were. What did Werner mean? I remembered shooting that man on the Autobahn. It was one of those few times when it's necessary to waste an unsuspecting sitting target. No one likes that kind of 'execution hit', but it was in the line of duty. Once done I had never brooded about it.

'I almost went along there unarmed,' I told Werner. He nodded. By a bizarre stroke of fate I was carrying that night a massive Webley revolver that I'd found amongst my dad's old possessions in a suitcase at Lisl's. My father's army-issue hand-gun! I had rested the gun when I fired it, and in my mind's eye I could recall my target. He was still and unsuspecting. This unknown man, this Dr Kennedy, this lover of my wife as I now know him to be, took my first shot in the chest. It must have punctured the heart. His heart: how well I had chosen my point of aim. That sort of slow heavy round, fired by an expert gunman, picks a man up, carries him along with its force and dumps him on the ground a lifeless bundle of rags. And I was an expert gunman.

'There was a lot of shooting,' I said. 'That fellow Teacher was there with a 9mm, and that American bastard brought along a pump-handle shotgun.'

'There was a lot of shooting. We'll never be sure exactly what happened,' said Werner. He got up, went to the bar and poured large measures of malt whisky into two of Lisl's best cut-glass tumblers. Lisl allowed him to have the key of the cupboard because he was so damned abstemious. I downed the whisky he gave me in one gulp. I felt it blazing a trail through my insides.

Werner sat down again. He scarcely sipped his whisky before putting it aside. 'I'm sorry, Bernie,' he whispered. 'I thought about it, and I decided I had to tell you.'

'Yes,' I said. I burped softly and tasted the garlic from the potato salad. It was revolting.

'I didn't want you to hear it from anyone else, Bernie.' He was the only German who called me Bernie. I wondered why. 'And I know you are big enough to see it from Fiona's side too.'

225

'It was serious then?'

'Yes, it was very serious. Both of them. He wasn't toying with her. It was the real thing.'

'The real thing,' I said, as I started to understand what I was hearing. 'Not just a quick piece of grab-arse then?'

'Don't do that to yourself, Bernie.'

'You did a great job on the Christmas tree, Werner.' I got to my feet. Werner watched me warily but remained seated. 'Did I tell you that?'

'Yes, you did, Bernie. Thanks.'

I reached for Werner's whisky and downed it; downed it too quickly. I wiped my mouth with the back of my hand. 'Thanks, Werner,' I said, putting the empty glass back on the table beside him.

'Any time, Bernie,' he said grimly.

I looked around the big room and it all looked different to the room I'd seen before. The women in their swirling dresses and the men in their flying coat-tails had departed, never to return. Ever since I was a child I had cherished this room, but now I knew I would never see it again without feeling the knife-thrust of my wife's betrayal.

10

Hennig Hotel, West Berlin.
I awoke in the middle of the night, bathed in sweat and with a headache that slowly sliced the top off my cranium if I remained still, and plunged red-hot pokers into my brain every time I moved. From the street below, there came the rumble of police and ambulance sirens, and the ceiling of my little attic room was frantic with the jagged shapes of their flashing lights. I looked around and suffered a moment or two of disorientation before remembering where I was. I'd lain in this bed when suffering so many childhood afflictions: colds, whooping cough, chicken pox and measles. It was like revisiting my past.

The phone started ringing. I grabbed it to stop the sound it made. 'Hello?'

'Bernard?'

'Yes, who is it?'

'Your wife, darling. How many women do you have calling you in the middle of the night?'

'What time is it?'

'I'm sorry, darling. I just arrived home and I didn't want to leave this until tomorrow.'

'Leave what?' The telephone was slippery in my sweaty hands.

'Daddy has to know.'

'Know what?'

227

'Now don't be upset, Bernard. Promise me you won't shout.'

'I won't shout,' I said grimly. 'Now will you please tell me what this is all about.' My mouth was dry. I looked for the glass of water I'd had last night, but when I found it the water was finished.

'I saw Frank tonight. He said you'd be in Berlin over Christmas. I didn't realize that.'

'I didn't realize it myself.'

'Frank has arranged to spend the Christmas holiday with his wife's family in Yorkshire.'

'He said he was just going to London for a couple of days,' I said.

'It's to be a family get-together; they arranged it on the spur of the moment. His wife's aunts from Australia were on holiday in Europe. It was an opportunity not likely to come again. Frank's wife has been awfully sick. He said he felt bad about letting you down.'

'And what does your daddy have to know?'

'Billy has got that awful cough again. The matron at school says a break in the sun would do wonders for him.'

'Is this anything to do with his safari park investment? The all-inclusive ten days in South Africa?' Her father had recently bought shares in a travel company and was determined to get a generous share of freebies.

'The Caribbean. They've given him a wonderful deal on a beach house in Jamaica for Christmas. A pool and cook and car and gardener and two maids are all included.' She rattled it off like a tour guide.

'Jamaica?'

'I don't have to go with them,' said Fiona. 'I could come to Berlin and be with you. It's just that the children are delirious at the prospect and the sun would be good for them.'

'Better you go with them,' I said grimly.

'Are you sure you don't mind?' she said in a voice unmistakably lightened. 'I feel bad at going there while you are working hard, and on your own.'

'I'll be all right. There's no point in your kicking your heels in the hotel while I'm in the office all day.'

'Will you work every day over Christmas?'

I was going to snap back some wisecrack about Christmas not being a big holiday for the communists, but she'd been there. So I swallowed it and told her I loved her and asked her to kiss the children for me.

'And I love you, Bernard,' she said. 'I adore you. And I miss you very much. You're always so understanding. I'll buy unsuitable presents for the children and say they are from you.'

'Can you find toys unsuitable enough?' I said. It was an ongoing joke that had originated with a plastic 'death-ray' gun I'd given Billy about five years ago. Daphne Cruyer had never stopped chiding me about giving my children 'totems of violence', and it had become part of Fiona's Christmas banter. Cleverly phrased to be a joke about Daphne, there was always enough reproach to spill over on to me.

I said goodnight, put the phone back on its rest, and sank back on to the pillow again. I'm not exactly certain of the order in which things happened next, but I know that Werner looked round the door and asked if I wanted anything. One of the maids brought me a tray with chicken broth and a toasted cheese sandwich. I couldn't face it. Lida swooped down in a camel-hair coat and large velvet hat. I told her that perhaps the kid – Robin what's his name – should monitor any developments arising from the DELIUS débâcle. Only then did Lida tell me that Robin had gone.

'Gone where?'

She hesitated and asked if I wanted anything from the tray of food at my bedside. She was hoping that I would not repeat the

229

question, but when I did she said Robin had gone 'over there'. *Drüben* meant only one thing, and Robin had no right to take off without my direct order. I was angry.

'Perhaps I should get the doctor,' said Lida, when I had finished telling her how much I disapproved of Robin's disappearance. 'Your face is very bad-looking.' Even allowing for Lida's English it was not reassuring.

'Did he get a vehicle?' I persisted.

'The motor cycle that was used the other day.'

'He signed for it?'

'I'm only guessing it was him,' Lida said. 'Someone had copied the scribbled signature of the previous user.'

'And said it was "a special arrangement for Mr Harrington" I suppose? Is this your doing, Lida?'

'No, Herr Samson. I swear it is not. I would not help him to flout your authority. And anyway he is not experienced enough to go alone. It is dangerous for him.'

'He'll try to find that damned pastor,' I told her.

'The pastor is perhaps dead,' she said.

'Let's hope so. Dead or in an intensive-care ward,' I agreed. 'But either way, anyone trying to locate him is going to walk straight into a bear trap.'

'Yes,' she said bleakly.

I could see that Lida felt protective about the kid, but she was too German to have helped him defy me. 'Okay, Lida,' I said. 'We'll have to manage without him. It's too late to bring someone else into this crisis. I'll come into the office and we'll sort it out.'

'You must stay in bed, Herr Samson. You are too sick …'

'You get back to the office, Lida. Someone must be there. I'll see you in about an hour.'

'You won't go after him?' she said.

'Of course not.'

I could see she was trying to think of some conclusive arguments that would persuade me not to try to extricate the kid from the mess he would undoubtedly get into over there in Allenstein. She knew the Stasi arrest teams were already in position, no doubt sitting patiently and twiddling their handcuffs. 'Herr Harrington will place the blame to me,' Lida said. 'He'll say I should have stopped you.'

'If you send for a doctor, Lida, your job is on the line.'

'I won't send for a doctor, Herr Samson.'

When Lida had gone, something Fiona had said on the phone came back to me. She'd said that Frank Harrington's family liked to get together. It suddenly brought to mind the moment when Stefan Kosinski had leapt out of the bathroom. He'd said the Kosinski family kept together, or liked to keep together, or something of that sort. I'd let it pass at the time, but looking back on it I could see what he meant. Was he perhaps referring to a Kosinski family tomb to which the mortal remains of George Kosinski would be consigned? I'd seen no family tomb, neither had it ever been mentioned. Was the family tomb the answer to why George Kosinski had gone back to Poland? Poles liked to be buried in their homeland; there was no doubt about that. Was he going to die there? Or was it about burying his wife Tessa in Polish soil?

With these fuzzy thoughts in my mind I dozed a few minutes more. Then I climbed out of bed and dressed myself very slowly. I felt dizzy and nauseated but I was sure that moving about and working would be rehabilitating. I steadied myself with one hand while getting my shoes on, and made sure my wallet and keys were in my pockets. When finally I was ready to face the world I went out through my little bedroom door, locked it and then turned round. The act of turning was all that was needed to bring on a sudden attack of dizziness, and I crumpled at the knees and fell down the short steep flight of stairs. I heard a blood-curdling scream which I belatedly recognized was my own, then I landed at the bottom with a crash. I couldn't move. I was upside-down on the narrow staircase with my legs twisted behind me. My face and arm hurt very much. I tried to reach out a hand, but that increased the pain and I blacked out.

When I came round again I was back in bed and some moon-faced fellow was rubbing alcohol on my bare arm. He then proceeded to take a sample of my blood.

'Hold still, Mr Samson. This won't take a moment.'

'Are you Dr Litzmann?' I asked him.

'Alas no. My name is Picard; I'm English. Major Picard; Royal Army Medical Corps.' I recognized him as one of Frank's drinking pals: Major 'Picky' Picard, the oldest surviving member of the British garrison. The plummy British accent, florid complexion, hair brushed tight against his head, loud and lumpy tweed suit with a battery of pens and pencils protruding from his waistcoat pocket, all contributed an element of the self-parodying Englishness to which the long-term exile sometimes resorts. Army, yes. The brisk manner of his professional attention was frequently found among doctors who had learned their trade tending battle casualties.

'Did Lisl send for you?' I said suspiciously.

'I'm the departmental medical man for Mr Harrington,' he said reassuringly, while devoting his attentions to the little red worm of blood that he'd just taken from my arm. 'I'm army: I'm vetted. I do all the medical checks for you people.'

'I'm not sick,' I said.

'You've got to rest, Mr Samson. No bones broken but you will be nothing but bruises by morning,' he said, not without a certain relish.

'I've got work that must be done.' I eased back the bed cover as if to jump out of bed. He didn't stop me; I suppose he knew that I hadn't enough strength to blow my own nose.

'Work to be done, but not by you,' he said, rummaging through his case where I could see a large selection of nasty shiny implements. 'You're a civvie,' he said as if I might have forgotten that. 'I can put you into the Steglitz Clinic or I can let you rest here. Take your choice but there must be no question of your getting out of bed ... not for three or four days. You've had a bad fall. As soon as you are fit enough I shall send you off for a couple of routine tests and a head scan. We mustn't take chances.'

'I'll stay in bed,' I said.

'That would be the best,' he said, and smiled as if accepting my word of honour. But really his smile was on account of the fact that he was filling his syringe. The next moment, with the merest prick of pain, he pumped enough dope into my arm to float me to the moon and have me doing my one-small-step-for-man routine, without a space-suit.

'Did Lida send for you?' I asked him while the room was going soft.

'No,' he said.

'Then who did?'

'Everyone has your best interests at heart, Mr Samson.'

'I know. I want to send my benefactor a box of chocolates COD.'

'Mr Volkmann might like that,' said the doctor, 'but his wife tells me he's on a strict diet at present.'

As my head sank back into the pillow I noticed that the sheets and bedding had all been changed. Looking around the room I could see in the corner of it my sheets and blankets, soiled by vomit, squashed into a black plastic rubbish-bag. 'That bloody Werner,' I said sleepily. 'I'll kill him.' I looked up at the doctor. He was watching me with that dispassionate expression with which zoo-keepers observe restless apes. I knew he'd given me a very generous dose of pain-killer; that too was a characteristic of the army medicos.

233

'Yes, kill him,' said the doctor calmly. He pretended to look at my hand while taking my pulse in that furtive way that doctors always do, knowing that pulse-taking is something that will make the pulse-rate quicken. 'When you are stronger perhaps. I'm going to prescribe some pills for you. They are just aspirin, vitamin C and glucose, but in winter they sometimes help.'

I looked at him suspecting that he was feeding me sleeping pills or some other sort of dope. 'What do you think is wrong with me, Doctor?'

'Apart from your fall down the stairs, nothing serious. Debilitating but not serious. I think you must have picked up the virus that has been affecting the young women in the cashier's office. The newspapers are calling it Chinese 'flu.'

11

West Berlin.

What Lisl called 'the flashy new American hotel' was really three Berlin town-houses tastefully converted into unobtrusive 'residential apartments'. It was the sort of place that rich American businessmen liked. The apartments were no larger than suites, but for men passing through, an apartment number and a street address looked better on the personal notepaper that was supplied to every guest. And each apartment had a study equipped with fax and a photocopier and multiple phone lines and modem plugs. Laptops for rent: call reception.

Gloria was booked into apartment number seven on the third floor. It came complete with antique German-style furniture, colourful drawings of somewhat unlikely traditional costumes from Sachsen and Baden-Württemberg, a bowl of fresh fruit that looked like a Dutch still-life painting, an ornate china dish in which four Niederegger marzipan chocolates were arranged around a miniature room-service menu, and a tall Rosenthal vase holding ten fresh pink long-stem roses. The elaborately painted doors of the armoire were opened to reveal a giant-screen TV complete with VCR and a selection of Hollywood films on video. Through the panelled connecting door I could see the adjoining bedroom, where soft indirect lights shone upon the silk bed cover and oriental carpet.

'Will you have dinner with me, Gloria?' I said it hurriedly as if indifferent to her answer.

She looked at me as if I was a complete stranger to her. She no doubt noticed my bruised face and hollow cheeks but she made no reference to any of that. 'How did you know I was here?'

'I heard a rumour. I was passing by, so I just called in. Will you have dinner with me?'

She spoke very slowly as if weighing every word: 'Of course I will, Bernard. I'll do anything you want. You know that.'

'Bret's not here with you?'

'Bret? No. I came instead of Bret ... He had to go to Washington again. Oh, I see. The suite? Yes, it was booked in Bret's name.'

'There are things we should talk about.'

'Are there? What?'

'It's good to see you, Gloria.'

'Is it?'

'I hoped you'd say it was good to see me,' I said.

'No, it's not good, Bernard. It tears me to pieces if you really want to know. I told you that, didn't I? That's why I wanted to take the job in Budapest.'

'How is it going? Your new job with Bret?'

'I'm on the top floor, Bernard,' she said, as if that was all I needed to know.

'Trouble-shooting for Bret. Yes, I know; sounds good to me.'

'I go and do what Bret tells me to do. He uses me to do his hatchet jobs. But people all think it's me throwing my weight around. I get a lot of flak, Bernard.'

'They know it's Bret; they know it's his doing, they know it's not your idea.'

'It suits them to think it's me. It gives them someone convenient to hate when hating Bret doesn't suit them.'

'Is that why you are in Berlin?'

'We're cutting back on the radio monitoring. I broke the news to them this morning; they were furious. They took it out on me; everyone does.'

'Does Bret know you're getting that sort of flak?'

'He says I should use my charm. He says he chose me because it's going to be a year of flowing blood.'

'Is that why they brought Bret in? To clear the decks? To do all the firing and demotions and lay-offs, and then let someone else come in and smell of roses?'

'Of course. And when Bret goes I'll be dumped.'

'But you'll have severance pay?'

'Yes. Bret was decent about giving me a contract. You were right about that.'

'Who'll get Bret's job?'

'That's the really tantalizing question isn't it?'

'You must have heard hints,' I said.

'No. The plan is that the Director-General retires next year. Whoever is appointed to replace him will have the chance to choose his own Deputy D-G.'

'I've been hearing that the D-G was going to retire next year since I was in knee-pants.'

'The D-G's not well. Half the time he's at home, wrapped in a cashmere shawl, resting and feeling sorry for himself.'

'Yes, well, the same goes for Dicky, but it doesn't mean he's likely to retire any moment.'

'The D-G will retire within a year, Bernard. An outsider will come in. The D-G will go, Bret will go, I will go and the whole top floor will change.'

'And Fiona? Would she be in the running for replacing Bret?'

'I would think that with an outsider at the top of the tree they will need an experienced Deputy.'

'And Fiona is very experienced. But why not Dicky?'

'Too much opposition from Bret. You know how it always is with these top jobs. It will have to be someone Bret approves and wants to hand over to.'

'Shall we eat in the hotel or do you want to go somewhere more cosy?' I offered.

'You want to eat here in the room, don't you?'

'Why do you say that?'

'I know you, Bernard. You don't want to take the risk of being seen with me. You want to be with me but you don't want to have any of your friends see us together.'

'There's a jazz club in Kantstrasse.'

'You're ashamed of being seen with me; and that's not easy for me to take, Bernard.'

'Or Hardtke – German food – if you're hungry. If you want to dance …'

'I don't want to dance, Bernard.'

'I'm sorry. I know I've screwed up your life, Gloria. In fact that's what I really came here to say.'

Her mood softened: 'You couldn't help it, Bernard. I was wrong the other day. I didn't mean what I said.'

'I hurt too, Gloria. All the time. I hope you know that.'

'Should that make me feel better? To know that you are suffering too?'

'Fiona is in Jamaica. She's taken the children.'

'I know, Bernard,' she said patiently. 'I see your wife all day every day. I work on the top floor with her. We exchange sweet bits of news and gossip with all the intensity that women who hate each other always do. It's ghastly. I thought that as long as I didn't keep seeing you, I would be okay. But seeing her hurts just as much.'

'No nice young men to take your mind off the past?'

It was the wrong thing to say and I should have known that. She picked up the phone, stabbed at the buttons and spoke.

238

'Room service? Send me two toasted steak sandwiches. Saignant. French mustard. Side salads and a pot of coffee with fresh cream. Two warm apple strudels to follow.' She hung up the phone and went to the minibar before giving me a chilled export Pils and a glass. For herself she selected a half bottle of German champagne.

'Okay?' she said with a big plastic smile.

'Okay, Gloria,' I said.

'So take your shoes off.' It was what I always did as soon as I arrived home.

The food arrived. We ate the sandwiches and the warm strudel arrived on time. It was only then that she remarked on my bruises and upon the fact that I looked unwell. I had slept until the effects of the medicine wore off, but when I fully awoke I watched the hands of the clock going round, and finally had to get up and go and see if Gloria really was in town. I didn't tell her that, of course. I didn't tell her that I so badly needed just to look at her, and be near her, that I had crawled out of my sick-bed. We sat around and talked the sort of lightweight chit-chat that we'd exchanged regularly when we were living together so happily. Then without warning she said: 'Bret is determined to retire Frank. You know that don't you?'

'Frank will never retire; he's another permanent fixture. He'll be here in Berlin for ever.'

'When Frank goes, you could get Berlin. This job you've got is a sort of test, to see how you handle things as second-in-command.'

'Thanks for telling me.'

'You must have seen that.'

'It crossed my mind. But thanks for spelling it out for me just the same. Is that why Frank is staying at home over Christmas?'

'He's not staying at home. Bret has sent him off to a Harley Street clinic for a complete physical examination.'

I chuckled. 'He won't get rid of Frank as easily as that. Frank is a permanent fixture. He's been to bed with half the pretty women in Berlin, and God knows where else. He's gone back to smoking that filthy pipe, he drinks nonstop and never seems to need sleep. Frank is made of titanium – silicon-coated. The Wall will fall down, Honecker will die of old age, and still Frank will be here running the Field Unit. You'll see.'

'Bret wants you promoted. It's not just that he doesn't like Frank. He's determined to make some radical changes while he's in a position to do so. You are one of them.'

There was a knock at the door and a hotel room maid came in. She had a jangling bundle of keys in one hand and some clean pressed bedsheets draped over her arm. Her Saxon-accented German was too rapid for Gloria, and I translated. 'They had a girl sick today. The bedsheets were not changed, and you need fresh towels in the bathroom. She says is it okay if they do it now? They don't need to come through here.'

'It looked all right to me,' said Gloria. 'Do we look as if we are in urgent need of a bed?' she asked me.

'Maybe,' I said, not sure whether she was being provocative or cruel. I only knew that bedding Gloria right now would be a disastrous mistake that would make all three people even more miserable than we were at present. In any case I was not going to risk being rebuffed; my ego was too fragile. 'Go ahead,' I told the maid.

In order not to disturb us the maids went into the bedroom from the corridor. Discreetly they closed the bedroom door and I could hear them as they dashed about changing the bed linen and the bath towels and whatever else room maids do.

'I guess the maids were hoping we'd go out to dinner, so they could fix things without you knowing they'd got things wrong,' I said.

240

When they had finished they went away without disturbing us again. 'Have they gone?' Gloria asked, and without waiting for a reply she went to the connecting door to listen for them talking. Failing to hear any conversation, she looked at me and shrugged.

'Finish your strudel,' I said.

'I don't want any more.'

'Finish my champagne then.'

She tried the handle of the door as if about to burst in on them, but decided against it and came back to the sofa and sipped her champagne. 'When I was with the big-wigs of the monitoring service today ... They guessed what I'd come for. They brought along boxes of signals. They wanted to show me some intercepts from the peripheral monitoring, that Bret is determined to close down. They wanted to prove it brings in some worthwhile material.'

'Yes, they would,' I said and waited for the rest of it.

'Some of the signals, dated over the last three weeks, concerned Berlin-Warsaw routine radio traffic. There is an important package going to the Stasi desk in Warsaw on the Berlin–Warsaw express train. No date as yet. Preparations are well advanced and look elaborate. Half of the signals are in codes we still can't break, but I think I know what it was all about.'

'Let's have it.'

'I think it must be the body of Tessa Kosinski. Her husband is in Poland, isn't he? Now we know what he's waiting for.'

'Why a body?'

'Because there are so many documents to be delivered with the package. Everything to be signed two or three times. Certified translations of the documents to be prepared for the Polish customs officials. It must be something very unusual. To be put into a separate reserved compartment on the train, with a lock on the door? That was a specified item: the lock on the compartment door. An officer courier? All this for a package? I ask you, Bernard ...'

'Did you point all this out to your radio wallahs?'

'Why should I? It's not normal procedure to interpret their signals. Translate them, yes.'

I helped myself to a couple of the potato chips she'd abandoned. 'Do you want anything more?' I said. 'Brandy?'

'No. And neither do you,' she said.

'How do you know what I want?'

'I know. Girls know these things.'

'The restaurant downstairs used to be famous for the *Klump*,' I said.

'But it's gone downhill lately,' she said soberly, and then laughed, unable to stare at me and keep the sober face. 'What is *Klump*?' she said, still giggling.

'Potato dumplings. They come in a cabbage stew called *Krautklump* ...'

'You're making it up.'

'No. It's true.'

'You beast. You're always trying to make a fool of me.' She laughed. 'And I always fall for it.'

'Do you?'

'I used to.' She put down her glass and got up to go to the connecting door again. This time she opened it. She went inside and from the next room I heard a little gasp and a choked-off shriek. I turned to see her backing out of the bedroom. She turned to me. Her face was white and bloodless and she seemed to have difficulty speaking. 'Bernard,' she said. 'Bernard.'

'What is it?' But by the time I was with her and holding her I could see what it was.

There was someone asleep in her big double bed: a young man as white-faced as she was. His pale lips were half-open to reveal uneven teeth. He was tall. The outline of the bedclothes

242

showed the way his feet were stretched to the very end of the bed. His bare arms were above the bedclothes, arranged like the arms of a dummy; or a corpse.

'It's one of our people,' I said, without letting go of her. 'He went over there a few days ago.'

'He's dead?'

'Yes, he's dead.' I gently broke away from her and went to look at him.

Gloria remained by the door as if nervous of being in the same room with the dead man. 'One of your Berlin people?'

'Yes.'

'Did you send him?'

'What difference does it make?'

'What shall we do now? Shall I phone London and tell Bret? I have contact numbers – his car and his mobile phone.'

'Berlin is my territory.'

'Why don't you go? Leave it to me? There's no need for you to be involved.'

I looked at her. She was as scared as hell. I never loved her more than I did that moment. 'Thanks, Gloria, I appreciate your offer,' I said. 'But it's better if I do it.'

'What can I do?'

'Pour me a drink while I use the phone.'

If this had happened while Frank was in town, he would have started off by making a few calls to his highly placed chums. Frank's influence in Berlin, his ability to get things done by everyone from top German officials to British army brass, was due more to his energetic social life than to the authority Whitehall granted to him. I didn't have even a fraction of those top-level contacts. My friends and acquaintances functioned at a much lower level. That was why I doubted my ability to take over from Frank and run Berlin in a way that Whitehall would approve. Over the years he had managed to suppress scandals, cover up disasters and smooth over all those happenings that had in the past got other Rezidents into deep trouble.

But Frank wasn't in town. I was in charge. So I did the next best thing to summoning Frank, I telephoned Lida.

'We have a "worst case" on Robin,' I told her. 'No need to look any further. Do you follow? A worst case and it is here at the Kronprinz Apartments in Wilmersdorfer Strasse. Third floor. I am in the one booked for Mr Rensselaer.'

'Ja, Herr Samson,' she said with reassuring calm.

'First we need the army. Bomb-squad technicians acquainted and equipped for anti-personnel. Have we got a reliable contact at this hotel?'

'Better if we go through the German authorities, Herr Samson.'

'Whatever you say, Lida.'

'Better the army remove everything also,' said Lida. 'The Military Police and the Medical Corps ... But we should have a Berlin police officer at the door to answer questions ...' Her voice trailed away but I knew her mind was racing on.

'Good, Lida,' I said. 'I'll wait here until you phone back or come here. Tell the Night Duty Officer that we have a "number one alert". No need to tell London yet.'

'I'll go to the office. There are things I can only do from there, Herr Samson. Then I will come immediately to you.'

'Thanks, Lida. And I think we should get Miss Kent back to London. Will you ask the RAF if they have anything tonight? Ask them to hold if necessary. Don't say it's top priority unless you need to.'

'Yes, Herr Samson.'

I hung up.

'What will they do?' Gloria asked.

'They will pretend that it's a British soldier who suffered a heart attack. Some smart-arse will spread the word that it happened in bed with a girl, and that will be the end of it.'

'Was that Frank's secretary?'

'Yes, Lida. I don't know where Frank found her but she's worth her weight in gold.'

Gloria went and looked at the kid again. I didn't stop her. If they'd put Semtex charges under the body they would be tremblers, not timed charges.

'They did it for you,' said Gloria, and when I didn't reply added: 'They brought the body up here so that you would find it.'

'The room was booked in the name of Bret Rensselaer,' I reminded her. 'The body was put there as a warning to Bret.'

'You can't fool me, Bernard. You don't want me to worry but they did it to get at you.'

'No.'

'Those people don't bring a body up the service stairs to a third-floor room without watching to see who is using the room. They must have seen me check in. They must have seen you arrive. Then they brought the body.'

'They'd have to be bloody quick. I didn't know I was coming here myself until half an hour before I arrived.'

'Didn't you really, Bernard? How you do deceive yourself. They guessed you'd show up here, don't you see that?'

'How could they have guessed?' I said, allowing my irritation to show.

'I guessed you'd come here,' said Gloria sadly. 'It wouldn't be beyond others to do the same.'

She was right. No matter about how and what they'd guessed: they'd put him there for my benefit. I'd killed one of their hoodlums by accident; a shot on a dark night in Magdeburg. It went a trifle low and took the top of his head off. And I suppose they thought the bomb under the pastor's Trabbie was my doing. Oh well, I couldn't take a full-page advert in the *Herald Tribune* to deny it.

245

I gently pulled her away from the connecting door. It was giving me the creeps to see her standing there looking at the corpse as if she still couldn't believe he was dead. Even after I'd closed the door, she leaned against it as if on the point of fainting. I raided the minibar. 'Have another drink,' I suggested.

'No, I feel sick.'

'It's better you go back to London,' I said. 'I'll get someone to drive you over to the airport. Was there anything for you still to do here?'

'Nothing that can't be done on the fax. But I'd rather stay. Why don't I move into another apartment here? I know they are only half full.'

'No, not here. They know their way around in this place. They probably have contacts and their own people working inside. Let's not take chances on them trying another little joke. Go back to London: it's what Bret would advise.'

'They thought you'd take me to bed. You see that don't you? We would have gone in there … maybe in the dark. It was a macabre little joke.'

'Maybe. Maybe not. They are not noted for their jokes: even little macabre ones.'

I poured another little drink and had hardly started on it before Lida knocked at the door. She was wearing a short fur coat and shiny high-boots. With her she had Picard the army doctor, an Engineer major with his corporal assistant, a couple of men without badges and two military policemen. They were all in uniform. So Lida was playing it like that: the high-profile way.

'I told you to stay in bed,' said Picard.

'I had a bad dream,' I said, 'and this was it.' He went towards the bedroom. 'Better let the bomb squad go first, Doc,' I said. 'This one's not going to respond to aspirin, vitamin C and glucose.'

Picard gave a grim little smile and we watched the Engineer officer and his soldier assistant flick a metal detector quickly

246

around the bed. Knowing we were watching him he turned round and said: 'You'd better go back into the drawing-room. The next bit is very technical.'

We withdrew a pace and he tied a ball of twine to the corners of the bedclothes and stood well away from the bed while pulling the covers back inch by inch, watching all the while to see if there were wires or any attachments. It was a damned dangerous way of checking for booby traps, but I suppose you become instinctive after a long time with the bomb squad: instinctive or suicidal, or dead.

'Nothing there,' said the Engineer officer and laughed. His corporal smiled dutifully.

The kid had been dead for a long time. His upper body was bare and obviously unharmed, so that only the softness of it proclaimed that life was extinct. He was still wearing his trousers but they were crumpled; the upper part of them stiff and shiny like plastic. It was dried blood – he must have lost gallons of it. But now it was completely dry, so that it had left a dusty reddish-brown powder all across the starched white sheets.

'I suppose you want a time of death?' said Dr Picard.

'I'm not the investigator,' I said. 'I'm just a passer-by.'

'Over twenty-four hours. We'll do a post-mortem first thing in the morning, and have something for your office by midday tomorrow.'

'Thanks, Doc.'

'One of your boys, was it?'

'I knew him.'

'I'm sorry,' said Picard. 'But at least the family will have him to bury. That means a lot to parents. I can tell you that from personal experience with next-of-kin.'

'I know.'

'A word in your ear,' said Picard lowering his voice. 'This one has been eviscerated.'

247

'Literally?' The bleeding of victims was an old Mafia device, done to make the disposal of bodies easier, neater and tidier. But this was a new one for our pals across the Wall.

'It would increase a cadaver's shelf-life,' said Picard. 'They could have stored him indefinitely and plonked him anywhere at any time.'

I nodded my thanks to the doctor and plucked at Lida's sleeve. 'Lida. Was there a plane tonight?'

'Yes, and London want you to go there too. Something has happened at the other end.'

'Do you know what it is?'

'They said you should take any warm winter clothing you have here with you. You are going on somewhere after the briefing. Mr Harrington is cutting short his stay and coming back here.'

'Just as we were getting to know each other, Lida.'

'Mind your back, Herr Samson. Here they come.' The kid was zipped into a body-bag and manoeuvred out into the corridor on a stretcher. No worries now about his career after fifty.

The RAF plane that took me and Gloria to England that night did not provide an opportunity for intimate chat. Travelling with us there was an RAF football team returning after winning a friendly game against a Berlin police team. They were exhilarated, a condition helped by the hour's delay they'd suffered waiting for us to arrive. The time had been spent drinking, and having exhausted their celebrations and recollections of the football match they settled down and began singing: 'Home on the Range'.

The flight crew provided a seat for Gloria up front, with a door between her and the noise. But I was seated between the football team's captain, a physical training instructor, and an elderly civilian meteorologist who was going to see his seriously sick daughter. In my pocket I found the large shiny pills that Picard said contained only glucose, vitamin and aspirin: whatever they contained I needed them. I swallowed a couple without water. They left a bitter taste in my mouth; I suppose they were cutting back on the glucose.

From under the cloth-covered freight behind my seat there came regular sniffing and scratching noises. I suspected that someone was smuggling a pet dog back to England and avoiding the quarantine laws. I wondered if this animal's proximity to me was so that I could take the blame for it if the customs men found it. 'Do you play football?' the man beside me asked, but I closed my eyes and pretended I was already sleeping. The gusty winds we met over the North Sea made the plane lurch and slew, picking off the singing footballers one by one until all were quiet.

At the other end, separate cars were waiting for us. Gloria went directly home. I helped her with her bag, and when she said goodbye she gave me a kiss. 'Stay well,' she said. If Gloria had been looking for a way of gently breaking the news to me that our love affair was finally over, then that kiss did the trick. So did the way she sank thankfully into the back seat of the car and smiled her sad goodbye. She didn't lower the window.

Stay well? As Gloria's car moved forwards the bus carrying the football team rolled past, gathering speed. They were once more joined in jovial song: 'She'll be Coming Round the Mountain'.

'Mr Samson?' It was my driver. Despite the lateness of the hour I was due at Dicky's home for a meeting with Dicky and one of our SIS people from the Warsaw embassy.

'Had a good trip?' said the driver.

'Not too bad,' I said. At least I didn't get accused of smuggling the pooch.

*

When Dicky first got planning permission to build the extra room above his garage, the girls in the office were whispering that it was because Daphne was pregnant again. They said the new room would be ready in time to make a warm little nursery, or into a self-contained unit for a live-in children's nurse.

But those who knew Dicky better were less ready to make such assumptions. Daphne wasn't pregnant – just over-weight – and the new extension became what Dicky called his 'den'. Into this room, with its commanding view of the next-door neighbour's garden shed and frostbitten vegetable patch, Dicky had brought everything he needed for comfort-able seclusion. The family's biggest TV and the newest stereo VCR, and the only hi-fi he had that could be operated by a remote control. As Dicky explained, once you get stretched out in a big recliner, you don't want to be jumping up and down adjusting the graphic-equalizer. The den's wallpaper was a pink and mauve Liberty pattern, although there wasn't much wall to be seen since Dicky had become smitten by Baron von Richthofen.

Looking back, I can see that Dicky and the Baron were made for each other. What I had mistaken for a Polish proletarian theme was a tribute to Snoopy's other half. But I still wasn't ready for the devotion and dedication that Dicky had brought to this new interest of his. On the walls he had large beautifully framed reproductions of aviation art. The detail in the paint-ings was remarkable: the fields and trees, the fluffy clouds, and even the dents in the engine cowling, all faithfully recorded. The scarlet three-winged job I recognized immediately, but here on Dicky's wall, the leather-helmeted Baron was also to be seen at the controls of three other brightly coloured planes. Apparently the Baron, while jealously keeping the triplane for his own exclusive use, felt free to borrow any of the planes belonging to subordinates assigned to his squadrons, or even visitors just passing through. In this respect he reflected something of Dicky's attitude to the Departmental motor cars.

I arrived little short of midnight, and Bret was there already. He'd just flown back from Washington and had stopped off only long enough to change into his official undress uniform. The Savile Row outfit, obligatory in the halls of power, had been exchanged for what Bret liked to think was 'leisure wear': tailored grey flannel pants, silk kerchief escaping from an open-neck white tennis shirt and a dark blue blazer. It made him look like he'd been washed ashore from some long-ago summer's Jazz Festival. On his knees he was balancing a lovingly framed section of weather-worn fabric bearing the national emblem of Imperial Germany.

'Part of the tailplane from von Richthofen's Albatross,' explained Dicky, tapping it so energetically that it almost slipped from Bret's grasp. 'Should be in a museum really.' He glanced up at me and waved a greeting.

'I can see that,' said Bret.

I dumped my coat on the chair. The house was silent – I suppose Daphne had long since gone up to bed. 'All right if I help myself to a drink?' I knew that Bret and Dicky both thought I drank too much. Had I been born with half of Dicky's natural guile, I would have spent the meeting sipping Perrier water, looking alert and dependable, and leaning forward poised to laugh at the jokes. But I could never resist reinforcing their stupid prejudices: 'I really need one.'

'What the hell happened to you?' Dicky enquired as he noticed my bruises.

'I fell downstairs.'

'Help yourself,' said Dicky, rebuffed by what he thought a flippant reply. For a moment I thought he was going to insist upon taking my temperature, a device he had more than once wielded on office staff to exercise his tiresome sense of humour.

'But hurry, Bernard. We've been waiting for you.' He was dressed in khaki gabardine pants and a forest-green British army style woollen sweater, its elbows and shoulders reinforced with leather patches.

'Yes,' I said and, malt whisky bottle in hand, raised an eyebrow at Bret.

Bret shook his head sternly and reached out to the side-table, covering his Pepsi, to indicate that he didn't want any. It was not a good omen.

So I smiled at Rupert – a malt whisky drinker if I've ever seen one – and he smiled in return. He used a finger and thumb to indicate a moderate refill and I gave him a dash of booze.

Rupert Copper, 'our man from the Warsaw embassy', was the only other person at our meeting. He was about forty, a constipated stuffed-shirt but a very able linguist. As well as Polish he had a good grasp of those Balkan languages which I'd seen defeat some of the brightest and most ambitious of our Foreign Office colleagues. He was particularly up to date on the intricate details of Greek political extremists. He wasn't a close friend: we'd chatted together at dull conferences and meetings. He'd started off with the diplomatic people and then transferred to SIS as a way of staying in Warsaw. Married with two teenage children, he was the subject of persistent rumours that his real love affair with Poland came in the shape of a middle-aged Polish countess who'd been seen in close attendance on him for at least ten years.

Rupert was elegantly perched, legs crossed, on the chair where the Cruyers' cat was usually curled up asleep. Rupert had just been taken out of his box: dark blue suit, crisp striped shirt, Wykehamist tie and polished black brogues. He had dark deep-set eyes, thin bloodless lips and a hairline moustache that looked as if it had been applied with an eyebrow pencil. Even more than other FO employees, he had the sleek and shiny look of a prosperous pimp. But it had to be said that he was competent, cautious and precise; qualifications so rarely found among employees of the Foreign Office that I was reassured by his presence.

After sampling the whisky I added an extra measure and settled down on the sofa alongside a brightly lit glass case containing model aircraft. Dicky was still explaining something about Richthofen's military funeral to Bret. Rupert caught my eye but his face was expressionless. He upended his whisky and the ice-cubes slid down and hit his nose. Hiding any surprise he might have felt, he took a monogrammed handkerchief from his cuff and dabbed his face. Then he put his glass on the sideboard as if distancing himself from further temptations.

'Well, let's get down to business,' said Bret eventually. He rested the framed section of fabric down on the carpet while Dicky went and sat in his recliner, pulling the lever tight so that he didn't slide into the horizontal position.

'You heard what happened?' Bret asked me.

'No,' I said. No is my default reply. There's nothing to be gained from saying yes to such questions.

'George Kosinski has been sighted,' said Bret. 'In Poland.'

'Oh, in Poland,' I said, and turned to look at Rupert, who nodded to confirm this entirely unsurprising item of information.

'Just when we were all quite certain he was dead,' prompted Dicky.

'He certainly keeps us on our toes,' I said, in order not to disturb the mood of heightened expectancy.

I thought I'd been summoned to London on account of the murder of the kid in Berlin. Alternatively I thought they might have unravelled the material that the monitoring service had shown to Gloria. But neither of these subjects was brought up, and my instinct for self-preservation told me I shouldn't mention either matter myself.

253

'Rupert says there is another Kosinski house,' said Dicky, motioning for Rupert to join in the conversation.

Rupert said: 'They have a güest-house out there. It's a couple of miles away from the family home; maybe more. Used to be a hunting lodge back in the old days. Nazis, such as Field Marshal Göring, liked to go there to hunt wild game when that region was part of Germany. The lodge was badly damaged by the war but they have spent a bit of money doing it up.'

'That's where they were hiding him,' said Dicky. 'The bastards had us dangling on a string.'

'They are family,' I said mildly.

'He's on some damned vendetta,' said Dicky angrily, but a warning look from Bret calmed him.

'Why is he there, Bernard?' Bret asked me.

'He's been moving heaven and earth to find out how his wife died,' I said. 'He's upset; he's not entirely rational.'

'But why are the Stasi and the Bezpieca playing along with him?'

'Are they doing that?'

'Come along, Bernard,' said Bret. 'You know how these folk operate. They are helping him. I'm asking you why.'

'They want to monitor him, I suppose. George has money, and money talks in the intelligence game. It's what makes the wheels go round. George can afford the best. He employed "Tiny" Timmermann to go over there and find out how his wife died. Tiny was a pro, a tough old-time CIA man who burrowed his way right into the Smersh compound in Magdeburg. Tiny was worth his pay. How would we feel if some joker was employing some capable rent-a-spies to come digging in our vegetable patch?'

Bret nodded. There was no need to draw a diagram for Bret, but Dicky made sure I didn't come out of the story unsullied:

'And the Stasi blew the top of Tiny's head off and left him for you to find. Except that you misidentified the corpse and played right into their hands.'

Bret ignored Dicky and said: 'If George was giving the other side a headache wouldn't they just blow him away?'

'No,' I replied. 'Not in Poland, and George knows that. George has a brother, very influential, very pally with the army regime in Warsaw. With things getting tough for commies everywhere these days, Normannenstrasse need all the help and goodwill they can get from the Poles. None of them are going to be cheering when George sends pensioned-off CIA men to probe their secrets – it sticks in our throats too, doesn't it? But they probably figure that the way to counter a crazy man like George is to cosy up to him; to help and advise him, and make George a good friend.'

'Quite a turnaround,' said Dicky. 'How would they start on that one?'

'They go to George and say don't waste your money on private investigators who just make trouble for everyone. We are just as interested in getting to the truth about Tessa Kosinski as you are. Let us prove to you that we are not bad people.'

'But the Brits and the Yanks are bad people.' Bret finished the story for me. 'Drip by drip they poison his mind against us. Yes, I'll buy that one. Patience and planning: that's always been the Moscow method, and it's the way all their stooges do it. While we run around in a constant panic, putting Band-Aids on wounds that need major surgery, our opponents are screening and recruiting university students who will be agents of influence in twenty years' time.'

I said: 'Is this an official abandoning of the theory that George ran away because the stock-market crashed?'

Dicky, who had been clinging to that theory for some time, decided that his best course of action was to throw a spanner into the works. He said: 'Bernard believes Tessa Kosinski is still alive.'

255

Bret didn't ask me if that was what I thought. He looked at me and said: 'George Kosinski has been told that a contract killer named Thurkettle killed his wife.' He finished his drink and waited for me to respond. Looking up, he said: 'No reaction, Bernard?'

'Told?' I said. 'Who told him?'

Bret responded to that question with one of his own. 'Could he be persuaded to come back?'

'George Kosinski?' I said.

'As you convincingly surmise, the Stasi and their Bezpieca buddies will be playing with him. We hear stories that they may have promised to finger Tessa's killer for George, and we wouldn't like that. I don't want anyone standing in the dock in Warsaw facing murder one, and making headlines in a trial that has a feature role for Fiona's sister. The Department couldn't handle that kind of exposure. We'd have bus-loads of Japanese TV crews sorting through our shredder bags, and airing talking heads of your Portuguese help.' A pause. 'Do you hear me, Bernard?'

I said: 'And George has been spotted?'

Rupert spoke: 'By one of our people.' Did I hear a measure of reservation?

'Someone who knows George Kosinski?' I asked him.

Dicky interposed: 'It's a positive identification. There can't be two people who look like George Kosinski.'

'Three Warsaw purchases for which George Kosinski's Visa card was used,' said Rupert, looking at me quizzically. 'Two high-priced restaurants and a man's shop.'

'Sounds like George,' I said. I was flattered that they were all regarding me as the person who had to be convinced, but then I saw that this was because I was going to be the idiot who returned there, trudging through the snow and ice, and resuming the goose chase for a man who'd already demonstrated commendable skill at hiding.

'Okay,' I said. 'I'll go to Poland, if that is what it's all about. Can I have authority to look at all the Berlin monitoring traffic?'

'Anything you want; make a list,' said Bret. 'When would you plan to be in Warsaw?'

'Right away, Bret,' I said, not without a touch of sarcasm. With Christmas only days away I felt a resentment at the way I was being steamrollered.

'Good,' he said, and got to his feet and went to rip open another can of chilled Pepsi, giving me a mangled kind of smile in passing. 'You'll have diplomatic cover, but Copper will be *de facto* case officer. Can you hold still for that, Bernard?'

'Okay.'

'Diplomatic cover,' said Bret. 'You won't be deniable; so play safe.' He held his glass, and the rum bottle, high so that he could accurately measure the amount of booze he was pouring.

'Play safe,' I said and nodded. That summed up the top floor's win-without-risk philosophy. Do the impossible but play safe.

'Copper will keep in touch with Dicky,' said Bret. 'Do as you are told and don't argue.'

'Could you top this one up too, Bret?' I said, holding out my empty glass.

Rupert gave me a lift home in his rented Ford when he heard I had no car. He was staying with his sister in Fulham. He said that Mayfair was on his way, and took me right to my door. I noticed him studying the quiet grandeur of the portals of my apartment block but he didn't comment. Like everyone else in the Department, he knew it was Fiona's legacy.

'Thanks for the ride home,' I said. I looked at my watch. It was two o'clock in the morning.

'So you lost one of your people? I'm sorry.' Rupert, suitably unemotional, was staring ahead through the windscreen at the nocturnal comings and goings in the busy street.

'How did you hear?'

'Cruyer and Rensselaer were talking about it before you arrived.' He had never abandoned that Oxbridge habit of referring to his equals by their family names.

'Oh,' I said. 'I wonder why they said nothing to me about it.'

'Cruyer's frightened of you.'

'That will be the day.'

'I was at Oxford with him. I knew him well in those days. He's always dreaded people making a fool of him.'

'Do I do that to him?'

'At times you do it to everyone.'

'Oh dear,' I said.

A taxi cab swerved and pulled to the kerb ahead of us. An elderly couple emerged. The man cut a dignified figure in evening clothes, the woman in shiny furs. I recognized them as our long-married next-door neighbours. The man dug into his pocket to pay off the cabby. The woman slammed the cab door with an intemperate display of strength. Then, as they passed us, they resumed some bitter argument, their faces contorted with anger. I found something exceptionally gloomy in this demonstration that time brought no mellowing of marital strife.

'There are photos,' said Rupert. 'They decided not to show them to you. Photos of George Kosinski. My people took them four days ago. You want to see them?'

'Yes, please.'

Rupert reached over his seat for a leather document case on the floor of the car. From it he brought three photos; colour snapshots taken in a busy street. He took a tiny flashlight from the case and shone it for me to see better.

'George Kosinski,' said Rupert. 'Here, and here.' Leaning across he stabbed a finger at a blurred head and shoulders amid a dozen or more people on a busy street. The picture had been taken on one of those cameras that imprint a date and time on the negative. It was in any case obviously made recently. The people were bundled up in fur hats and woollen hats, and most of them looked blue with the cold. I recognized shop signs and a section of the Nowy Swiat, Warsaw's main street.

'Why didn't they want me to see these?'

'Oh, I wouldn't make too much of that. You are more familiar with George Kosinski's appearance than any of us. If you had dismissed the photos as being of someone else, it would have ended the discussion, wouldn't it? Cruyer didn't want to provide you with that amount of leverage.'

'Can I keep these?'

'I'm afraid not, old chap. I have to show them to the D-G tomorrow.'

'I heard he was sick.'

Rupert looked at me as if suspecting that I'd tried to catch him out. 'I'm invited to the D-G's home,' he said very slowly.

'Take sandwiches,' I advised. 'His idea of lunch these days is tea with lemon in it and a dry biscuit.'

'I owe you a big favour, Samson,' he said, as if he'd been bottling it up and rehearsing this announcement. 'I never did say thank you.'

'A favour?'

'A long time back, when that ghastly fellow Kosciuszko was blackmailing my chief ... Everyone, that is to say everyone who worked in the office at that time, felt deeply indebted to you.'

'Oh, that,' I said, although I had only a vague recollection of the business he was talking about.

'I don't know what you did, and I don't care. He was a poisonous reptile. Someone told me you threw the little bastard into the river somewhere and left him swimming for his life through the ice-floes. My God! I would have enjoyed the sight of it. I hope your good deed didn't go entirely unrewarded.' I was tired; I didn't respond. He said awkwardly: 'And I believe the best way I can return that favour is to speak to you frankly.' It was a question. I looked at him but made no response. 'Man to man,' he added.

I appreciated the effort he was making. Rupert Copper wasn't the sort of man who readily resorted to man-to-man conversations, especially with outsiders, the sort of outsiders who tossed men into the water for fun and profit. 'Shoot,' I said.

'Tonight I watched you talking to Cruyer, and that chap Rensselaer. And quite honestly, old chap, I wonder exactly what goes on in that head of yours.'

'Not much,' I admitted.

'The whole service, from London to the other side of the world, seems concerned with nothing but rumour after rumour.'

'It's what the service does to earn its keep,' I said. 'We're in the rumour business aren't we?'

'Rumours about you, Samson,' he said with emphasis. 'Rumours about your wife. They are still asking if that business really was ... what it was later described to be. Or whether she really defected with a lot of choice material, and then was lured back. No, no ...' He raised his hand, stopping my objections while he went on: 'I hear more rumours about that girl you lived with, the one that Rensselaer now seems to have some claim upon. That was a somewhat sudden elevation to the top floor, wasn't it? There are endless rumours about who killed your sister-in-law, and why. And now, a new one going the rounds in the last few days says that she was never really dead. She's alive and living in Moscow or some bloody nonsense. Now there is all this shenanigan with your brother-in-law. And that's in my bailiwick, and not something I can ignore. Do you see?'

'I don't know what I can do to stop people telling each other ludicrous stories,' I said.

He sighed and tried again. 'You're a danger to all concerned, Samson. To Whitehall and to Normannenstrasse. What do you think would have been the reaction here in London Central, had it been you stretched out dead in the Berlin mortuary tonight, instead of that kid who worked for you?'

I didn't respond.

'A yawn,' said Copper, answering his own question. 'And have you properly considered Fiona's position?'

'In respect of what?'

'In respect of those Stasi bastards. Remember that poor little Simakaitis? The Lithuanian KGB captain who came over to us with all the wavelengths? A bright fellow who got sick of seeing the rough stuff going on over there. Eight years ago next month, if my memory serves me. We brought all his family out too. It was a textbook operation. Warsaw office handled the children.'

'I remember the case,' I said.

'Normannenstrasse was determined to destroy him. The Stasi lost their Berlin codes and ciphers and wavelengths.'

'Yes, but that was a different generation of Stasi in those days. Those gorillas were the last remnants of the Stalinists.'

'The same sort of vindictive crew are holding the reins again now. Anyone less than fanatical finds himself shunted off to a frontier job, to be replaced by a dedicated Marxist. Every day in my office I see the results of what they're doing. These people are fuelled by hatred. They see Gorbachev's concessions as a threat to their sacred creed, and they have dug their heels in.'

'Well, they didn't get Simakaitis,' I said. 'I heard that someone went over to Florida last summer to get his opinion on some new radio material.'

'They didn't get Sim because the Yanks took him into one of those elaborate witness protection programmes they designed for Mafia informants: a completely new life.'

'So what did they do?'

'The KGB let Sim live. Sim's elderly parents were killed in a shooting in a filling station hold-up in Brussels. The killers didn't stop to steal any money. His wife died six months later. She went overboard from the Flushing ferryboat, and the Scheldt estuary is very cold in January. No one saw her go over. That happened one year, to the very day, after he defected. Washed up a week later. No water in the lungs. Unconscious before she went in, the coroner said. Then Sim's sister took a big overdose one summer night when she was on holiday in Spain, and in the best of spirits. His brother died in France. That happened the same day Sim went to Washington: fell from the Paris–Lyon express. His four children were all swimming together …'

'Okay, that's enough,' I said.

'Sim is in a nursing home in Orlando. I was the person who went to see him. They did for him all right. He sits and looks at the wall all day. It's just as well he doesn't want to go anywhere or do anything, because he can't even go to the toilet on his own.'

'Fiona are you thinking about?'

'Of course I'm thinking about Fiona. Sim did nothing compared to what she did. No matter about the exact circumstances of her departure, her subsequent treachery is unforgivable in their eyes. They trusted her; she betrayed them. They did everything for her, a decent place to live, a car and driver, they even gave her a department and authority. You know what those things mean in the East. She spat in their eye.'

'You think Fiona might be targeted in that same way?'

'How can you rule it out? Perhaps the wheels are already turning. Her only sister is dead. Her brother-in-law has been forced into taking a trip to Poland, for reasons we can only puzzle about. The boy was killed, perhaps because they mistook him for you. You are on your way there, and we both know how exposed you'll be out there in the sticks.'

'It would have happened by now,' I said.

'That's what Sim thought. But they don't hurry their retributions. They like their victims to think about what's coming. You know what they are like; how can you be so blind?'

He got out his cigarettes and offered me one. It was a slim silver case with his initials engraved on it. I declined. 'I'm trying to give up,' I said.

He lit up using his slim Dunhill lighter and puffed smoke, savouring its taste. Then he wiped the condensation from the windscreen with the edge of his hand. 'Forget it,' he said suddenly. 'I spoke out of turn.'

'No,' I said, and I took up the little flashlight again and studied the photos for a final check. 'Thanks,' I said as I handed the pictures back to him.

'Is there anything wrong? Is it not him?' said Rupert.

'Difficult to say with that big fur hat he's wearing. But it looks like George.'

'They haven't told us anything,' said Rupert. It wasn't a complaint. Rupert had never been the whining kind, but he wanted me to know that he thought the Warsaw SIS office was being deliberately kept out of the George Kosinski business.

'Thanks again for the ride home,' I said. 'Thanks for everything.'

Rupert was hunched over the steering wheel, cigarette drooping from his fingers, looking closely at the pictures with the aid of his flashlight. 'You saw something else, didn't you?' he said without looking up. Rupert was quick and I was tired, otherwise he'd never have detected the surprise I'd registered when looking at the pictures. 'Is one of those people in the photo Thurkettle?'

'I've never heard of Thurkettle.'

'No? Bret thought you had. Before you arrived tonight he was telling Cruyer that, in your debriefing in California, you described how Thurkettle shot and killed Tessa Kosinski. You were there; and you said you saw it.'

'I seem to remember Dicky saying tonight that I thought Tessa was still alive.'

'Dicky always likes to look before he leaps,' said Rupert. 'He doesn't express his own thoughts, he puts them into the mouths of other people to see what happens.'

'Tessa Kosinski? Still alive?'

'I can see why they are puzzled. Bret is worried that your uncorroborated evidence, about a confused exchange of shots on a dark night, is the only thing they have to say that Tessa Kosinski is dead. Nothing else. In fact everyone else denies it.'

'What about Fiona? She was there too. What did she tell Bret at her debriefing?'

'Don't get angry with me, Bernard, I'm just putting you in the picture.'

'Can you still find your way to Fulham?' I said.

But Rupert wasn't going to stop now. 'Bret said Fiona won't talk about that night. He says that Fiona is struck dumb when Tessa's name is mentioned, that she has totally repressed any idea that her sister might be dead. By never admitting she is dead she'll keep her sister alive.'

'Yes, well Bret would say that. Bret was a psychology major at high school.'

Rupert looked at me, nodded solemnly, and said: 'No one else you recognize in the photos then?'

'I'm afraid not, Rupert.'

Still holding the pictures, he lifted his hand in a despondent gesture of farewell and said: 'See you in Warsaw, Comrade.'

He knew I was dissembling, but I certainly didn't intend to tell Rupert, or any of the other Departmental diehards, that, behind George Kosinski on that busy Warsaw pavement, I'd spotted my father-in-law. What was he doing in Warsaw, I wondered. He was supposed to be with Fiona and my kids, basking in the Jamaica sunshine.

12

Warsaw.

Now Poland was truly in the grip of winter. My plane cautiously descended through the wet grey clouds that provided snapshot views of the sunless landscape below. Only here and there did roads, tracks or trees hint at the rectangular shapes of fields. For the most part the snow had made a fearsome great grey world without end.

I had not heeded Bret's hurry-ups to leave London. I had retired to bed with whisky and hot milk, enjoyed Mozart CDs, an assortment of books that I had put aside for reading some day, and assuaged my hunger with binges of fried eggs and fried smoky bacon with Heinz beans.

As on other occasions, unlimited indulgence proved a sure-fire cure for my ills. And so I was completely restored. Euphoria – the effect of favourite nourishment, heady music and guilt – soon gave way to unendurable languor. By the morning of the third day I jumped out of bed before it was light, sang while I was shaving and then booked a ticket on the first flight to Warsaw.

From the air you see only the new snow, but in the streets you saw it in layers. Like antediluvian faults the strata were of many colours, the layers dating back through blizzards and snowstorms, freezes and sleet, to the first fluttering snowflakes that long ago proclaimed the coming of winter.

Overflowing gutters contributed a delicate frieze along the roofs. Polski-Fiats splashed into the slush and sprayed it over the slow-moving pedestrians. In the street there were oozing streams, half-frozen rivers of brown and grey. Within a moment of falling, the snow was patterned by the grey residue of the exhausts of passing cars. While rattling half-frozen from the roofs, down through the giant drainpipes, the discharge had spread everywhere underfoot a lace-like bas-relief of ice that made the pavements uneven and slippery so that every step was uncertain. How well I knew these European winters, and how I hated them. I wondered what the surfing was like in Jamaica.

'Do you hate it, Rupert?' I said. We were sheltering from the wind in a doorway on Warsaw's Vilnius Station, and the whole place was virtually deserted.

'Hate it? Hate what?' I suppose his mind had been on other matters, like not freezing to death.

'All this. The snow and the filth. Poland in winter.'

'How could I hate it? I live here.'

I nodded and pulled up my collar. Rupert was different from the other Brits with whom he worked. He really believed he belonged here. He refused to see himself the way we all really were: awkward, ugly, inconvenient aliens, suspect to the authorities and a burden to our friends. He felt at one with the landscape and the people, but he never tried to be a Pole. He had the sort of self-righteous confidence that armed nineteenth-century missionaries.

As an afterthought Rupert added: 'These dark winter days … sometimes I pray for a snatch of sunlight.'

'Yes,' I said. The sky was as dark as granite, it pressed down upon the city like a weight.

'The snow is not usually as early as this,' he said. Visible above the collar of Rupert's oversize Burberry trenchcoat there was one of those quilted Barbour linings. Worn with his checked cloth cap it was the sort of outfit that I would expect an English gentleman farmer to wear on market day. It looked out of place here in the middle of nowhere. He pulled his scarf tighter around his throat and stamped his feet.

'Are you sure he said Vilnius Station?'

'Yes, I'm sure,' said Rupert.

'And he promised he would come?'

It was hard to believe that this desolate open space was so near to the centre of Warsaw, or any large European capital city. It was even harder to believe that where we stood had once been a busy rail terminal, a place the wealthy holiday-makers, the revered scholars and the business tycoons came to board the night express – with its bars, diner and sleeping compartments – to travel to the ancient city of Vilna (or Vilno or Vilnius according to which language you spoke). All the nations coveted that medieval show-place, a centre of Jewish learning and the site of one of Europe's oldest universities. Poland wanted it, the USSR grabbed it, the German invaders razed it and massacred its large Jewish population. Now Vilnius was the capital of Lithuania. But no longer did any trains leave this station and get to Vilnius. The platforms had been levelled, the old waiting-rooms and baggage-rooms demolished. Now it was just the spot where two railway lines ended. Now and again an austere little train departed to take commuters to nearby destinations. Beyond that the track had been uprooted, the sleepers burned as fuel, and the way to get to Vilnius was to go to the Central Station and travel via Moscow. And that was the way Poland's Soviet masters preferred it to be.

'He said he would come,' said Rupert, 'but that doesn't mean he will come. You know what Poles are like.'

'No. What are they like?' I took my hands from my pockets and blew on them to restore circulation. I vowed to buy gloves: big fur gloves.

'Secretive. Clannish. Do you know about the unknown warrior?'

'What about him?'

'The tomb of Poland's unknown warrior – in Pilsudski Square – is where every foreign dignitary comes to lay a big floral wreath, and make a solemn speech about peace. The Soviets are all very keen on peace and very keen on speeches about it. And Moscow to Warsaw is the right distance. It makes a perfect weekend of banquets, sightseeing and vodka. So each and every year Moscow's leaders, generals and senior apparatchiks vie to attend this solemn ceremony, where bands play suitable music, generals wear acres of shiny medals, and the wives get a chance to show off their new outfits.'

'Oh, yes,' I said. He tended to go on a bit, I'd forgotten that.

'Very big crowds always gather at the ceremony. The Poles look on with an unusually smug satisfaction. Because it hasn't yet dawned upon the Russkies that the unknown Polish soldier's body, over which they like to pontificate about the peace-loving Red Army's advance to Berlin, was not recovered from some Second World War battlefield. It contains the body of one of Pilsudski's men, who fell in the 1920 fighting outside Warsaw when the angry Poles kicked the mighty Red Army back where it had come from.'

'I see,' I said.

'Not even the most resolute Polish communist has ever revealed that secret to the Soviet comrades. That's what the Poles are like: clannish.'

'Yes,' I said. 'Well, the impossible bloody language helps them there.'

'And the religion,' said Rupert. 'Lutheran Germans to the west of them, Protestants to the north, Orthodox to the east. The Poles are Catholic, and devout ones too. Take a look around; the churches are full and a Polish Pope sits in Rome.'

'Are you a Catholic, Rupert?'

269

'No. Well, sort of,' he said. 'I was once.' I didn't take too much notice of that denial; every dedicated Catholic I know says he's lapsed.

'So is George Kosinski,' I said. 'A very serious believer. Is this him now?'

A VW Beetle came bouncing along across the ice and snow, snorting and sliding, its rear wheels spinning so that the car was skating around perilously. But I learned that this was the way many Poles drive in winter; they like to feel the car sliding around, and they get good at controlling the skids. 'I don't think so,' said Rupert.

Two men climbed out of the car and then leaned inside to pull the seat-backs forward, so that two teenage boys could extricate themselves from the confined interior. The icy wind blew the big hat from one of them, and he had to chase it to get it back. As he ran, the skirt of his heavy coat was whirled up by an especially violent gust of wind that created a twister of dirty powdery snow. 'It's not him,' said Rupert.

When the wind died down it would snow again, at least that was what the locals were saying. The driver of the VW scowled and pulled his hat down tight upon his head before getting back into the car and driving away. The other three marched off in the direction of the Russian War Memorial without looking back. Now there was no one in sight over the wide flat expanse of the old railway station. George still had not come.

'What motivates the bugger?' said Rupert.

'Love,' I said. 'He's in love, desperately and hopelessly in love.'

'What does that mean?'

'In love with his wife. Some say it accounts for almost everything he does.'

'You're a cryptic sod, Samson.'

'I don't mean to be.'

270

'I know. That's what makes it so irritating. You still don't believe it, do you? You just can't bring yourself to believe that Tessa Kosinski is still alive, can you?'

'I never said that.'

'They don't go to all this trouble for nothing. Not those Stasi bastards.' He was getting more and more bad-tempered as the cold wind chewed into him.

'Maybe.'

'Well, you would know. But in my experience they know exactly what they are doing, and why.' He didn't pursue it. He hadn't had a great deal of experience with the day-to-day cloak-and-dagger side of the Department's work. He was a money man, getting the right sort of currency to the right people at the right time. It was a hazardous task and I didn't envy him. He had carried a lot of money over the years – sovereigns and thalers and dollar bills; diamonds and rare stamps too, when that was what they stipulated. Twice he'd been attacked and badly hurt. It wasn't easy and you had to be at the top of the reliable list. It wasn't a job where you could get a signed and dated receipt.

He said: 'We're sitting ducks out here on this railway station. A man with a sniperscope ... did you think of that?'

'It did cross my mind,' I admitted. I was surprised he'd not noticed me nervously surveying all the likely spots, and squinting at every approaching pedestrian.

'Do you ever get frightened, Samson?'

'Fast heart rate, rapid breathing, measured basal metabolic rate and galvanic skin response? Is that what you mean?'

'Stiffen the sinews, summon up the blood ... Lend the eye a terrible aspect. That sort of thing.'

'No. Only public schoolboys get frightened like Shakespeare. Kids like me shit ourselves.'

'I was only asking.' He looked around and then looked at me. 'We should have remained in the car. How much longer should we wait?'

I could understand his concern, if my face was as chilled as his appeared to be. His lips looked sore and cracked, and the frosty wind had rouged his cheeks and nose like the face of a clown. 'In the car we wouldn't have been able to spot him. Give him another five minutes,' I suggested.

'The Rozycki flea-market is just along the street. Ever been there?'

'Not for ten years or more.'

'You didn't take Cruyer along there on your last visit? To show him the lower depths of life in the big city?'

'Dicky isn't into open-air flea-markets, especially not markets like the Rozycki. He likes first-class restaurants.'

'This is not his sort of town then?'

'No.'

'Two Polish traders were badly injured in the Rozycki. They are still in hospital. Beaten up by two foreigners. The police asked if we knew of any British criminals in town. It exactly coincided with the time you and Cruyer arrived.'

'Did it? Well, I'm certainly glad I didn't go along there. That could have happened to me and Dicky.'

'I don't think so,' said Rupert.

'Ambulance approaching,' I said. 'This will be it.' I don't know why I said it but I just knew that vehicle was something to do with George.

The ambulance was not one of the shiny new Russian ones I'd seen on the streets. Or the Polish army's camouflaged trucks with red crosses on the side. This was a lovely old slab-sided 'Star' from the FSC factory in Starachowice. Two men, equally old, got out and one of them opened the door at the rear.

'We've come to collect you,' said the other man in passable English. 'Mr George sent us.' The men were not threatening; they didn't have the build to be threatening. 'Thirty minutes,' promised the man as he opened the back doors.

272

I wasn't inclined to go along with them until Rupert climbed into the back of the ambulance. It was only after we were inside, and bumping along over the corrugated ice, that I began to suspect that Rupert was so cold he would have jumped into almost anything to escape the cold wind. But at the time, I reasoned that Rupert was almost a local, and he had the diplomatic passport that would probably get both of us out of trouble with the law.

'Are you armed?' Rupert asked suddenly, as if regretting his action.

'No,' I said. He was looking around in an agitated way that suggested claustrophobia. The interior was gloomy, illuminated only by a tiny yellow bulb in the roof. The main part of the ambulance was occupied by two stretchers locked into wheeled racks. Two grey army blankets were draped over each of them. A respiratory apparatus was in a rack over a hard uncomfortable bench, upon which we were now seated, crushed tightly together. Just inside the door there was a metal wall-cabinet marked with a red cross. It was secured by a brass padlock.

'There are no windows.'

'No windows in ambulances; no pockets in shrouds. They don't want us to see where we're going,' I explained. 'It will be okay.'

'I hope so.'

A peep-hole controlled from the driver's compartment snapped back and one of the men up front said: 'We'll bring you back.' Then he closed the shutter without waiting for our reaction.

I could hear the traffic around us but the ventilator in the roof provided no chance of seeing out, not even a glimpse of the sky. I noticed we did not make an excessive number of turns and I guessed that they were going directly to our destination, so I settled back and waited. I decided it came into the category of 'calculated risk', the sort of hazard I was paid to suffer.

The ambulance journey took only twenty-five minutes. When the doors were opened at the other end we were in a parking bay outside a large ugly building standing in a dozen acres of grass most of which was now hidden under the snow. Regimented trees lined the drive and there was a sign at the gate announcing that this was the Madame Maria Sklodowska-Curie Clinic. The double Nobel Prize-winning Madame Curie was much celebrated in her home town but a large section of the sign's wooden supporting trestle was missing, suggesting that some passer-by had wanted to pursue radiation experiments of a domestic nature.

I knew more or less where we were. You can't get lost in Warsaw since the Soviets built the world's ugliest building there and made it so tall you can see it from Vladivostok. We followed the two Poles in through the main entrance of the building. As we entered the lobby they removed their hats and looked around respectfully, as if entering a cathedral. Then a grey-haired woman came striding along and engaged them in rapid Polish. She was dressed in black skirt and blouse. What not so long ago was the uniform for female office workers throughout Europe now made her inadvertently chic.

I raised an eyebrow at Rupert, who explained softly: 'We are about to meet the head administrator of the clinic.'

The long corridor along which we were taken was bare and cold. We passed doors that opened on to small wards with half a dozen beds in each. 'Here,' said the grey-haired woman. From somewhere behind one of the doors a baby began crying and another joined in.

The head administrator's room was slightly larger, warmer and marginally more comfortable than any of the wards we passed on the way to it. He was introduced as Dr Urban and, despite the white cotton coat, my suspicion that he was not a physician was soon confirmed when he told us that he had previously been managing a printing plant in Lodz. He laughed when

274

he told us this. But his spoken English was fluent, due he said to having spent a year as an exchange student in New Jersey.

'I want to be frank with you. Clear and above board. And that's why it is better that Mr Copper is here to represent your embassy. I don't want you saying that you were tricked by those crafty Poles.'

'We were expecting George Kosinski,' I said. The grey-haired lady took our overcoats, put them on hangers, hung them in a closet and then departed.

'Your brother-in-law,' said Dr Urban. 'It's better to do it without him.' He smiled conspiratorially. 'Much better.' Anyone locked into the notion that all Poles were thin, reflective and lugubrious had not met Dr Urban. He was a short restless man with a thick mass of wavy auburn hair, a chubby cheerful face and piercing blue eyes. His time in the United States had obviously had a profound effect upon him, for his informal manner and his style – loosened tie and feet resting on a pile of books – was markedly transatlantic.

'Is he all right?' I asked. Dr Urban waved at a chair and I sat down.

'He is all right. Our friend Mr George? Yes, but he becomes too anxious. We understand why; he has endured a stressful time.'

'Yes,' I said. After spiralling round like a restless dog Rupert settled into a battered armchair.

Rupert said: 'Mind if I smoke?' Such formality seemed superfluous, since Dr Urban had filled the air with acrid blue smoke and was still working at it. On the table there was an open packet of Benson and Hedges. He swivelled it round, offering the cigarettes to Rupert, but Rupert took one of his own from his monogrammed silver case. Having blown a little smoke, Rupert said: 'The body is it? The body of the wife?'

'Ah!' said Dr Urban, opening his eyes wide to look at Rupert as if he'd not expected him to do anything but sit quietly and listen. To counter this unexpected development he said: 'You'll take coffee?'

There was another delay while the coffee was brought to us and poured out. Through the window I could see the car park. There were half a dozen cars there veiled in snow, variously heavy coatings of it according to how long each had remained unused. The two Poles were standing by the ambulance talking together. I had the feeling that they expected to wait a long time.

'Where were we?' said Dr Urban after he'd put down his cigarette and settled back in his creaky swivel chair with his coffee balanced in his hands.

'Mrs Kosinski,' supplied Rupert.

'I went to Berlin last week to make the travel arrangements,' said Urban. 'The Germans can be very difficult but in this case everything has gone smoothly. She arrives at the end of the week.' Dr Urban stopped talking as he found something undesirable floating in his coffee. He bent forward, held his cup above the waste-paper basket, and expertly flipped the foreign body into it using his spoon. I had the feeling that he'd done it before. He looked up: 'An insect,' he said and then drank the coffee with relish.

'Does Mr George Kosinski know all this?' said Rupert.

'Of course,' said Dr Urban. He put down his half-empty coffee cup and rummaged around on his desk to find a United Kingdom passport which he held in the air like an author on a TV talk show. 'George Kosinski has become a Polish citizen,' he said. 'This passport is no longer valid.' Rupert stood up and reached for the passport. Urban said: 'Look at it, yes. But you can't keep it. It has to be returned through the official channels.'

'Why are you telling us this?' I asked while Rupert, a broody look on his face, examined George's passport page by page.

'Don't you want your coffee?' He stirred his own coffee zeal-ously, and then set it aside and picked up his cigarette and blew on the end to get it alight.

'It's delicious,' I said. In fact I didn't want it. The look on his face as he evicted the insect from his own cup had quenched my thirst.

'Because they tell me you are going off to Masuria to find him. He's become a Polish citizen with full rights and privileges. His parents were born here. It was a simple matter once he'd decided. But now he would need permission to leave Poland, even if you persuaded him to go with you.'

'George Kosinski is my brother-in-law,' I said.

'Yes, I know,' said Urban. 'It makes no difference. The wife is Polish too.'

'Are you saying she's alive?' I said.

'Tessa Kosinski?' He put a new cigarette in his mouth and lit it from the butt of the old one. Then he stubbed out the butt in an ashtray made from a brass shell case. Only after all that did he give a brief laugh. 'Very much alive. More alive than most of the people on the District Hospitals Management Board to which I report.'

'You spoke with her?' I said.

'I've just told you; I went to Berlin to see her and make the travel arrangements.'

'She wanted to come to Poland?' asked Rupert.

'Yes.'

'And the Germans are letting her go?'

'She wasn't a prisoner,' said Urban. 'She was just a patient in the Charité hospital in Berlin. Making her a Polish citizen simplified the paperwork for everyone: here and there too. Technically she is being repatriated.' He smiled and then explained the joke: 'She's never been to Poland before, but technically she's being repatriated.'

'In hospital?' I said.

'Don't try to make a fool of me, Mr Samson,' said the cheerful doctor, becoming a trifle less cheerful. 'You know the score. So do we all. You know why she's coming back here.'

'No, I don't,' I said.

'You're talking in riddles,' Rupert told him, closing the passport and putting it on Urban's desk amid the other clutter.

Dr Urban looked from one to the other of us, a smile trying to get out of the corners of his tightly closed mouth. 'You English,' he said in grudging admiration. 'You're the best actors in the world. Not only Shakespeare, Bacon and all the way to Pinter. And Noel Coward, Lord Olivier and the Rolling Stones and the rest of them. I love them all, but acting is a talent flowing through the veins of each and every one of you. You don't even realize you are doing it, do you?'

'Acting apart,' said Rupert patiently. 'Why is she in hospital?'

Again the smile came. 'You've come here today and you still pretend you don't know. You come to the best maternity hospital in the sub-district – in the whole of Warsaw perhaps – and you say is the mother-to-be still alive? Really, gentlemen. It is time now to wipe off the greasepaint I think.'

'Pregnant?' said Rupert.

'That is the whole point of it all. Why do you think that the Kosinskis wanted to become citizens? Why was the father so keen that his wife should be here in the homeland at this crucial time?'

'So that the child will be Polish,' said Rupert.

'We Poles are a sentimental people,' said Dr Urban proudly. 'He wants a Polish son; yes.'

'And you will control the parents through the child?' said Rupert. 'Your jurisdiction will enable you to manipulate the parents and have them say and do anything you wish.' Rupert looked at me. He was alarmed as he thought of what it all meant. And how he would explain this bizarre Polish *fait accompli* to London.

'No, no, no,' said Dr Urban, without putting his heart and soul into the denial. He got to his feet and said: 'This is a fine hospital. Let me show you around. We can do as well as the Germans in maternity care. Our only concern with the Kosinski woman was whether a mother should travel at such a late state of pregnancy. Some can, some can't, it's a matter of stamina … of constitution. That's why I took our resident obstetrician with me. I don't want an emergency on the train next week. In any case there will be a doctor and a nurse with her. There is nothing to worry about.' A quick look from one to the other of us. 'But they are Poles. If the worst came to the worst, at least I would not be facing a political dimension.'

Rupert was furious, but he kept his anger under tight control. He saw it all as solely a device to render the embassy people powerless. He said: 'You don't have to explain it in even greater detail, Doctor. We see the point of the naturalization procedure.'

'And George Kosinski goes along with all this?' I asked.

'Mr Kosinski is a deeply religious man. He has always prayed for a child; they both have.'

'And now their prayers have come true?' I said.

He looked at me with narrowed eyes: 'Not quite yet,' he said. 'But they enjoy something for which to light a candle or two.' He buttoned his shirt collar and tightened the knot of his brown tie. 'You'll see.' From behind the door he took his jacket from a hanger and put it on. I should have guessed all along I suppose. Poland was still under *de facto* martial law, no matter what soothing noises were coming from the government.

Dr Urban's jacket was khaki and complete with campaign medals and badges of rank. A major in the supply services. Every institution was under the direct control of the army, so why not the finest maternity home in the sub-district? 'We have only a few days to wait,' said Urban, looking at me. 'I would dearly like to get this absurd misunderstanding settled once and for all. So can I have your assurance that when you speak with Mrs

Kosinski, and hear her say that she prefers to be a Polish citizen, you will report in those terms to your masters in London?'

'Tell me, Major Urban,' I said politely. 'Exactly what are the full rights and privileges that come with becoming a Polish citizen?'

'You will have your little jokes, you Englishmen,' he said, and laughed as he strapped on his leather pistol belt.

It was only after we were back at Vilnius Station and in the car that Rupert had left there, that Rupert gave vent to his frustration and rage. 'The little bastard. Bezpieca! I could see that from the start.'

'Maybe,' I said.

'I can recognize a secret policeman when I see one.'

'You mean he was a secret policeman wearing a uniform as a disguise?'

'Why are you always so damned argumentative?'

'I was just asking.'

He shuddered. 'When we were in that stinking old ambulance I thought they were going to slit our throats.'

'They wouldn't want to mess up their nice clean blankets,' I said. 'They wanted to make us a little nervous.'

'Well, with me they succeeded,' said Rupert. 'Can you imagine what London are going to say when I tell them how we've been outmanoeuvred? It's not even worth your chasing after George Kosinski any more. You can see how they've twisted him round their finger.'

'Poor George.'

'And the child will be Polish. As two Polish nationals there can be no question of the baby getting a UK passport.'

'No,' I said. It was typical of Rupert and all his clan that every situation was rendered down into its relevant paperwork. These are the sort of bureaucratic pen-pushers who think a peace treaty is more important than a peace.

We sat there in the car with neither of us speaking. Vilnius Station was even bleaker now that evening was approaching. The sky was almost black and the sodium lamps on the station were orbs of orange-coloured light made fuzzy by the condensation on the car's windows.

'The Poles are not bad people,' said Rupert, as if to himself. I could see that he was trying to think of some way of presenting the bad news he would be sending to London. 'The regime is caught between the devil and the deep blue sea. Between Moscow's tanks and Wall Street.'

'Tanks and banks,' I said. 'It's a predicament.'

'You're a lot of bloody help aren't you?' he complained. 'Yes. No. I suppose so. What the hell's wrong with you?'

'You're preparing a message for tonight?'

'They'll need something more than a message,' he said. 'This development will have them climbing the walls.'

'So why not hang on for a day or so?' I suggested.

'Can't.'

'That wasn't an official meeting. Who was there? You, me and his nibs. If we forget that it happened, Dr Urban might as well have been talking to himself.'

'Probably tape-recorded.'

'I doubt it. He was too relaxed.'

'I'll have to tell London sooner or later.'

'Later.'

'It's all very well for you to say later. You won't get the rocket when suddenly they hear that Tessa Kosinski is in Warsaw and having the baby.'

'Write a memo to yourself about the meeting. Say I didn't believe a word of it, and neither did you.'

'That won't cover me, Samson, and you know it.'

'Say in the memo that you immediately sent me off to check the story.'

'Check it with George Kosinski? Is that what you mean?'

'That would be one way of doing it,' I agreed.

'You're a devious bastard, Samson.'

'It was just an idea.'

He looked at me and wet his lips nervously. He didn't like the idea of conspiring with me. I was not one of his intimates, and deceiving authority was in any case distasteful to him. 'You don't give a damn, do you. I suppose you falsify your reports whenever it suits you to do so.'

'Of course not,' I said.

'Sometimes I wish I could be like you, Samson. Life is so much easier if you bend the rules to your own convenience.'

'Are we going to sit here all night while you sing my praises? Or are you going to summon up the guts to do what you know has to be done?'

He looked at me without answering. Then he switched on the engine and said: 'Let's get you back to that flea-bitten little place you're staying. Even for workers' apartments: that's an unusually grim place. Why do you choose to stay in places like that?'

'I feel at home there.'

'Okay,' he said. 'You go and find George Kosinski. I'll take responsibility.'

When we got to where I was staying with an old pal of mine, a man who sold American electric generators on the black market, Rupert stopped me from getting out of his car.

'But before you go, Samson, tell me one more thing. Why is George Kosinski giving us all this trouble? Why doesn't he just phone the embassy and ask us what we want from him, and get it over with?'

I looked at Rupert and tried not to sigh audibly. What was wrong with me? I never made sufficient allowance for the slowness of people like Rupert, Dicky and Bret and the rest of them.

They never understood what was really happening. Even after I'd drawn them a large-scale street map and made chalk marks on the pavement, they fell into the first manhole they encountered.

'Look, Rupert,' I said slowly and pedantically. 'George went to all kinds of trouble to fake a suicide, hide himself in a disused underground bunker, and God knows what else to avoid us finding him. What reason could he have?'

'That's what I'm asking you,' said Rupert.

'Because he thinks we are trying to locate him in order to kill him,' I said.

'My God!' said Rupert. 'You can't be serious.'

'Go and lie down in a darkened room with two aspirins, Rupert,' I said. 'Your mind is too pure for this kind of work.'

'Perhaps you are right, Samson,' he said, and was visibly shaken. 'I know you're a loner. But let me know if I can help you: cash, drops, motor car or help to catch a ship to England. You know the way it works.' He flipped open his wallet and put on the seat a bundle of Polish money. Alongside it he placed a thick roll of American bills. Beside that he put a roll of plastic gummed parcel tape. And a zip-gun: two smooth steel tubes which could be screwed together to hold a single .22in round. The whole thing was not much larger than a big executive fountain-pen, and about as elegant. And about as lethal, at the range that I preferred to do business. I couldn't help thinking that the money, the sticky tape and the zip-gun represented three methods of getting George out of the country. 'I was told to bring you this,' he said regretfully. 'This' was wrapped up in ancient newspaper, and turned out to be a VZ 61, a Czechoslovak submachine-gun which, despite its tiny 7.65mm rounds, limited accuracy and low muzzle velocity, has a good rate of fire, a very light weight and, stock folded, is less than twelve inches long.

'Well, well,' I said. It was a comforting accessory, and almost as useful as the dollar bills.

'Bret said that would make your eyes light up,' said Copper. 'He said get you a Skorpion or an Uzi and I couldn't get an Uzi. He said to remind you you had diplomatic cover and to only take the gun if there was an emergency. I can keep it for you.'

'No. I'll take it with me,' I said. 'I'll think of an emergency later.' A toy like that goes into a trenchcoat pocket. Copper got an extra magazine and a cardboard box containing fifty rounds from the glove box and gave it to me. I took the money and the tape too. I gave him the zip-gun back, in case he got mugged going home with his silver cigarette case.

At last Bret and Copper seemed to be getting the idea.

'And Bret said I was to alert the Swede,' said Copper.

'That's right,' I said. 'Alert the Swede.'

13

Masuria, Poland.

'Don't do this to me, Bernard,' said George.

I hadn't done anything. We'd scarcely been through the hello-and-how-did-you-find-me routine. I suppose he knew everything I was about to say. Perhaps I should never have come. It might have been better for everyone if I had left everything the way he wanted to keep it.

'I love her. Do you know, when she's away I hear her voice every day,' said George. 'We don't have to phone or write.'

'Fi said more or less the same thing,' I said. 'I understand how you feel.'

'You *don't* understand how I feel. You're a loner; you don't need anyone. I'm different. Without Tessa my life is nothing.'

'She loved you too,' I said.

'You think so? I'm not sure. I've thought about it a lot of course, but I'm not sure. No, the way I …' He looked up and pinned me with his glaring eyes. 'So why are they saying she's safe?'

'She's dead, George. I was there. I saw it happen.'

George was wearing brightly coloured ski clothes. It was a salutary way of countering the cold, but such a fashionable figure was an anachronism in this gloomy timeworn interior. He went and sat down by the fireplace, almost disappearing into the gloom. His voice came from the darkness: 'She's coming next week, they said.'

'She's dead, George. Face it.'

'You keep saying she's dead.'

'I keep saying it because I want you to get it into your head. You've got to carry on with life, and unless you face the truth you'll not be able to think straight.'

'John O'Hara ... John O'Hara the writer, told about George Gershwin's death, said – I don't have to believe it if I don't want to.'

'Yes, well he was a writer, and they are all full of shit.'

'Stefan is a writer.'

'And he's full of shit too. Yes.'

'Perhaps I too am full of shit. I know people see me as a ridiculous little man – but Tessa never made me feel like that. Even when she was unfaithful to me I never felt really humiliated. Does that sound stupid?'

'I can't make it easier for you, George. I wish I could but I can't.'

'She thought jumping in and out of bed didn't matter. She knew I'd give her anything she wanted – cars, apartments, jewels – so why not the freedom to sleep with men she fancied?' He got to his feet and went to the window, which was patterned with fern-like patterns of frost. In that sombre region of the Great Masurian lakes, each winter day brings only a couple of hours of real daylight. Today there came news of the sun, a pale yellow egg-yolk faintly discerned behind the milky sky. 'But all that is past, now I am home. It's snowing again.' It wasn't snowing. The flurry of snowflakes fluttering past the window was loose snow dislodged from the roof by the wind. But George was distraught and tormented minds can't think straight about anything.

'It's not snowing and this is not your home, George. It's not even the real world.'

'This morning I found the tracks of wolves at the back. They come down to raid the rubbish-bins outside the kitchen door.'

'Foxes; or perhaps wild dogs.'

'No: wolves. They wake me at night howling. You hear explosions too sometimes. These forests are riddled with minefields left here from the war. Only the big wolves trigger them; the other animals are not heavy enough to detonate the pressure pads.'

'Okay, wolves. And maybe it is snowing. But you are not Polish, George. That's one thing I'm certain about. You are very very English.'

'I speak the language,' said George.

'No, George, you don't speak the language. You speak some old-fashioned heavily accented Polish gobbledegook that leaves a trail behind you that a child could follow.'

'Do I?' He seemed dismayed.

'The crazy man, speaking funny old Polish? That's what they said in the village when I asked about you. Everyone you ever speak with goes telling everyone he meets about a man from England speaking comical old Polish.'

George dismissed this with a wave of the hand. 'How can you understand? It's not just a matter of the local accent; it's in the heart. I discovered how Polish I was back in 1978, when Pope John Paul was elected.'

I knew what was coming. Just as popular legend says that everyone in the West remembers what they were doing when they first heard of the shooting of President Kennedy, so Poles can all remember where they were when Cardinal Karol Wojtyla, the Archbishop of Krakow, was elected: the first non-Italian Pope for 456 years.

'Warsaw,' said George. 'I was walking down Nowy Swiat after a long service in the Jesuit church. My legs were stiff. There were little groups of people, standing on the street corners, singing. Then down the street there came a tramcar

– and all the passengers were singing and shouting. You know Warsaw, Bernard. You know the people. Can you imagine that? A street-car with passengers leaning out shouting and singing? Not easily, eh?'

'Not easily.'

'I waved back at them, and I found myself crying with happiness and a feeling of being present at the most wonderful family celebration. It was then that I knew I was Polish. I watched the TV news that night, and the news announcer – a long-faced fellow who never smiled – was laughing and bouncing around the studio in a performance no one would have thought possible. Yes, I was truly Polish, but at first I didn't fully admit it to myself. And I knew it wasn't something I could safely go around confiding to people in England, even Tessa. The English don't hate foreigners, but they draw the line at foreigners who boast of being foreign.'

I smiled to acknowledge his quip, but he scarcely knew I was there. It was a monologue, and it was little more than displacement activity, while his mind tried to deal with the prospect of life without Tessa.

'So in the summer of 1981 I came back to Warsaw to try and sort my feelings out. I chose the date so I could attend the funeral of Cardinal Wyszynski. I was expecting a crowded church, a solemn eulogy and a respectful burial. You should have been here, Bernard! The first sign of what was going to happen was the way that all the theatres and movie houses closed their doors. Only religious music was transmitted on the radio. People flocked in from all over the country. Crowds gathered in the streets. The funeral became the biggest demonstration of religious faith I've ever seen. When Victory Square was used for communist demonstrations it was only half filled; but on that day I couldn't get within half a mile of the platform. They say a quarter of a million people were packed into that

Square for the funeral. At one end of it they'd erected a gigantic cross; well over forty feet tall. And if there was any last doubt that this was some miraculous kind of revolution, that doubt was dispelled when the President arrived. The President of a communist government had come to pay homage at the funeral of Cardinal Wyszynski, his most outspoken critic.'

'Yes, well, before we both fall down and drown in a sea of tears, let me tell you one of *my* vivid memories of big-city life. If you'd stayed in Warsaw until the December of that same year, you would have seen your jolly Polish family getting their skulls cracked open by grey-uniformed anti-riot squads, as they eliminated "trouble-makers" and dragged them off to their cosy detention camps. You could have switched on your TV and seen General Jaruzelski on the early-morning programme proclaiming not martial law but "a state of war". Solidarity was banned and even its minor rank and file were tossed into prison without trial. Strikes and demonstrations were prohibited, the night curfew was enforced, and the courts were told not to be too fussy about the nicer points of law. Telephone calls and all mail were subject to the censor. Even while the General was telling us all this, the radio and TV stations, and just about every other vital institution, were being taken over by teams of armed soldiers, and his tame "military council" took over the government.'

'That was during the time of military law,' said George.

'Are you blind, George? Ending martial law – and this phoney amnesty – were just deceptions to persuade the foreign bankers not to call in their loans. Martial law hasn't ended. Your precious "family" is in the tight grip of the generals.'

'You can't make an omelette without breaking eggs.'

'Can't you, George? I'll write that down and try and remember it. Is that your personal political philosophy, or simply a cookery hint to save for a time when eggs are not rationed?' He

289

gave me a sour smile. 'What I need to know is exactly when you decided to work for the Bezpieca. Was that before the omelette-making began, or afterwards?'

His head snapped back as if I'd slapped his face, but then he looked at me and smiled wearily to let me know he wasn't stumbling into my trap: he was marching into it. He was prepared. 'Before, Bernard. I wanted to help Poland.'

'But you didn't stop when the General took command, did you? You reported whatever you could find out about the work that Fiona and I did?'

'I told them nothing important. I never took money from them; I never gave them anything more than gossip.'

'How can you have been so stupid, George? You were moved by the way the Church confronted the communist State; but you went to work for the communist State?'

'I felt those two elements were no longer divided,' said George. 'And they got nothing important out of me.'

'Maybe they put you on hold,' I said. 'You move in influential circles, George. What you call your gossip is useful to them.'

'Perhaps. But I'm not a spy, Bernard. I couldn't take the stress of it. That's why I got out and went to Zurich. I told them I had to leave England. I thought they'd stop pestering me after that.'

'But these folk don't take no for an answer, do they? Is that why you hired Tiny Timmermann?'

'I wanted him to find out about Tessa.'

'Tiny was murdered. I found him in Magdeburg; they'd blown the top of his head off.'

'I asked him to talk to them. To act as an intermediary ... persuade them to let me off the hook. He said he knew everyone. He said he could do it.'

'I bet he did. When Tiny was strapped for money he sold short on promises.'

'I was desperate to know about her.'

290

'And when you came to Poland, what did they say about Timmermann?'

'I didn't know he'd been killed. They said that Timmermann had talked with them and that they would let me off the hook. But that first they'd show me their good faith. They would start an inquiry into Tessa's disappearance.'

'So Tessa's death became her disappearance, with all the promise that evokes. So you didn't run back here because the stock-market took a dive?'

'No, no, no. That was a coincidence. I wanted to escape, Bernard. I thought I'd managed it at one time.'

'There was a severed hand with your family crest on a signet ring.'

'I thought I was being clever. Stefan helped. He showed it to someone in the British embassy in Warsaw, to convince everyone that I was dead. We never intended that it should go to London.'

'Well, it went to London and one of their people was shot.'

'I know. Everyone here was angry. It was my fault. The local Bezpieca people did everything to retrieve it and then went to London after it. I was deeply indebted to them after that. They said I must come here, to my brother's house, and wait.'

'Wait?' I said. 'Wait for what? They sent you here to wait for Tessa? Alive? How could you have swallowed that fairy story?'

'She's alive and she's pregnant,' said George, as if this disclosure would catch me off-guard.

'She's dead,' I told him.

'No. Next week they said.'

'Because they will invent an emergency. And they will tell you she died in childbirth. Then they will foist off a look-alike body for the burial. And they'll bring you a smiling baby they will persuade you is yours. The baby will be Polish and they will have locked you up really tight. That's their plan, George.'

'You can't leave anything alone, can you, Bernard?'

'Don't tell me you never had the thought of such a deception cross your mind?'

'Next week we'll see.'

'You think you're a big-shot, George, but for the people you deal with here you are a nothing. The first stage of grief is denial. But now it's time to move on.'

He sank down into a chair. 'Our delightful father-in-law said more or less the same thing. He doesn't believe Tessa is still alive. I'm the only one who believes it. I persuaded the old pig to come out here to Warsaw. One of the Polish security men went all through the post-mortem and photos of the dissected body with him. I couldn't bear to look at any of it but they say it's clearly not Tessa; it was a Stasi lieutenant – a woman – who was there on the Autobahn that night.'

'But father-in-law still thinks his daughter is dead?'

'He's stubborn,' said George. 'He said I'd ruined his holiday in the Caribbean, and that I should refund his air fare out here. It was a joke of course; but you know his jokes, don't you?'

'He's realistic,' I said. 'I saw the same post-mortem material; they brought it to London and then killed the man who delivered it so we couldn't interrogate him. I have the same junk in a file at the office. It's phoney, George. I'm sorry to say it but it's an example of the trouble they take faking their disinformation evidence, and getting rid of anyone who knows the truth. Tessa is dead.'

George picked up my map, got up and went to the window to study it by daylight. 'So this region was part of Hitler's wartime headquarters? Where did you get this map?' He took off his glasses and peered at it closely. 'Look at the size of the place …' The map was a photocopy of a wartime German one. It showed all the wooden buildings, bunkers, roads, checkpoints, and the railway line and the sidings and the train stations and the airstrips, that comprised the *Wolfschanze*. 'They tried to put a bomb under him, didn't they? Somewhere out there in the forest there's a rotting splinter of that wooden hut ... Have you seen all that broken concrete and the half-buried steps and ventilation shafts ...? Dig out the earth from those collapsed tunnels and we'd find the maps and operations rooms and maybe the dead generals too.'

'I don't think so, George. Generals are smart: they pack up and go away long before the enemy arrives.'

'And that's what I should do? Is that what you mean?'

'There's still enough time to get you out of here. But if you stay, you'll lose British nationality and my people will do nothing for fear of creating a diplomatic brawl.'

'In London they'll put me on trial for spying.'

'Not if you come clean with them.'

'But you said they knew ... Weren't you sent after me because I'd been an agent for the Bezpieca?'

'That was just one of my hunches, George.'

'Not really an agent. I could explain to your people ... I wouldn't have endangered any of you, Bernard.'

'That's good to know, George.'

'You don't understand.'

'I understand, George. They've made a fool of you. These people – Bezpieca, Stasi, KGB – they all work hand in glove. Their latest gimmick is to tell you Tessa is still alive. Have they threatened to betray you to the British? Well they like stick and carrot; it's the way their minds work. But you have nothing to be afraid of, have you?'

'It's all my own fault.'

'Come home, George. Come and tell us all you know. You're a Londoner; you're not Polish. Forget all this crap they've been feeding you.'

'Stefan says ...'

'Stefan made his own pact with the devil. His wife is a part of the regime. But you are still free to choose.'

There was a long silence while he refolded the map with exaggerated care. 'They arrested Uncle Nico. Stefan did nothing to stop them. Nico is in a camp in the south. He took that damned biography of Bishop Stanislaus to a publisher. It was read by an army censor, and they said it was treason.'

'I thought it was about a bishop who lived in the eleventh century,' I said. Poor Uncle Nico. Even the best of the army's detention camps provided rigorous conditions for young fit men. He was unlikely to survive a harsh winter there.

'That's right; Stanislaus the Bishop of Cracow, our patron saint. He excommunicated the tyrant Boleslaw II and the brutal knights that were at his court ... Boleslaw had him executed, or did it personally if you want Uncle Nico's version. The execution of the Bishop brought a curse upon the royal line. Church versus State. You see how dangerous that could be?'

'I can see the regime wouldn't take to it as a story-line.'

'Uncle Nico let me read the typescript. It was a thinly veiled attack on the present regime. Cleverly done but too long, and too boring, I would have thought. There were sly little touches, and contemporary parallels. And the death of Father Jerzy Popieluszko in 1984, which has been blamed on the Bezpieca, was artfully worked into it. But the book needed editing and a lot of work.'

'What are you, a literary critic?' I scoffed. 'Why didn't you warn the old man what he was getting into?'

'How could I guess he'd have the nerve to take that bundle of scribble to a publisher? He'd been rewriting it for years and years. It was nowhere near fit to publish.' Again George paused, thinking about the old man, and perhaps remembering everything the old man had risked for the two boys. I didn't break into his thoughts. 'If you think you can get me out of this, Bernard, get me out of it without trouble coming to me, and I'll do what-ever you say.'

I plunged right in. 'There's an airstrip, part of the old *Wolfschanze* complex. It's just over five miles from here. There's a small plane coming from Sweden tonight. It's a tight fit but the pilot is a mercenary; and he only gets paid if he gets us out. I know him; he's been into worse landing places.'

'It sounds risky.'

'I went there yesterday. At one end the trees have all grown taller, but the other end is a lake. There will be space enough. It is sheltered from the snow and most of the vegetation is dead.'

'An airstrip? In the forest?'

'The *Wolfschanze* had several strips; this one is the best-preserved. If the Luftwaffe could land a big Junkers there, it's big enough for my man. And in this sort of cold weather he doesn't have to worry about nosing over in the mud.'

'What if the weather closes in?'

'He'll try again tomorrow, and again the next night. He'll want his money: I know these bush pilots. Cloud and mist doesn't stop them. He'll come in using braille.'

He turned away. 'And you are sure she's …'

'Dead? Yes. I was there, George. I saw it.'

'What are you looking at?' he asked, noticing me glance at the snowy scene through the window.

'Tonight when we leave they will follow us,' I told him.

'Is there someone out there now?' said George.

'Yes, they're out there somewhere, and when we leave they'll be close behind us.'

'They'll stop us.'

'No, George, they won't stop us, but they might try. You must understand that when they do try, I might have to deal roughly with them. It will be too late then for you to change your mind, because we'll be leaving behind some very hostile natives.'

'I said I'm coming with you.'

'Well, don't change your mind, George. This is a costly way to travel, and when Elizabeth Windsor is picking up the tab she doesn't like no-shows.'

We left in a Fiat as soon as it became dark, and made a detour so that I could see who was interested in us. It was a big black Volvo estate. There were four of them inside it; big men bundled up in overcoats as if they were expecting a breakdown and ready to push. They made little effort to hide the fact that they were following us.

The wild forest, preserved from forestry experts, was a magnificent jungle of beech, firs and birch. The ground was hard and frosty and the narrow forest tracks, sheltered from the snowstorms, meandered away and disappeared into the night. I was pleased to have spent a few hours of the previous day doing a tourist's run around the neighbourhood. Now, as we approached it from the northern side, I knew the airstrip was coming up, and at the very edge of the strip there was a place where the track was too narrow for them to overtake us. When I stopped the car they would have to stop behind us.

I looked at George. He was girding himself for a big effort. 'This is what I want you to do after I stop the car, George. Get out and make a fuss. Get well away from both cars and get their attention. Scream and shout. Tell them you are being kidnapped. Tell them you are hurt. Tell them anything. But get their full attention. Can you do that for me?' I was driving very slowly by that time. In the mirror I saw the Volvo with the main beam headlights flashing to tell me that the game was up. One of the men was leaning out of the window waving his hand. He was wearing gloves, I noticed. That was encouraging. Men wearing gloves are not quick on the trigger. 'Where the track widens out to the lake I will stop.'

'What are you going to be doing?' said George.

'I'm going to steal their Volvo. These are local security cops, posted to this godforsaken region because they are not smart enough to be in action where the real trouble occurs.' I looked at the lake, swamped in a malignant and mysterious haze. To the other side of us there was forest where slim black trees – their lower trunks hidden by deep snowdrifts – seemed to be suspended in midair. Between forest and water there ran a drained strip of land, its function as a wartime airstrip long since forgotten.

'But if you steal their Volvo, they'll simply steal our Fiat.'

'No they won't. And you get their car key. I don't want to be grubbing around trying to find it in the snow.' I knew in fact that they would all be carrying a car key, and in a last resort, that hot-wiring their car was only a thirty-second task, but it was better that George had something to think about.

'How can you be sure what they will do?' said George. He was nervous and he was agitated. I had to get him fully occupied or he would freeze on me. I'd seen it happen before.

'Several reasons – you'll see. But the principal reason is that while you are holding their attention I am going to kill them. Okay?' George's face went as white as a sheet. Without waiting for a reply, I gave him a hefty shove and said: 'Jump out and start screaming. This is it.'

George put everything he had into his performance. He jumped and shouted and threw his arms in the air. No one could have resisted it.

And while the boys in the wide-brimmed hats were watching his solo dance performance and jumping out of their car to grab George, I was splashing the contents of a bottle of petrol over the interior of the Fiat so that when I tossed a lighted match into it the fumes ignited with a whoomp that took my eyebrows off.

You've got to understand what it was like for those men to watch someone set light to a precious motor car. In the West, to reproduce the deep emotions my action generated, you'd have to watch some yuppie torch his Bentley-Turbo or Ferrari.

The hot engine helped, and the flames went up twenty or thirty feet, so that the whole clearing was lit by brilliant light that caught the five men as if in a flashlight photo. The picture is printed upon my mind. George had stumbled into a snowdrift and was half-turned, his hand held up to his face as if shielding his eyes. He was as surprised as anyone to see me torching the car. The security men had turned to see it. There were four of them: dressed in long overcoats and large felt hats, their faces gleaming in the light of the fire, their faces registering shock and bewilderment. While the others remained still, George moved. Now he realized what was coming. He was backing away, stumbling through the deep snow and kicking away the frozen debris as his feet encountered it. George thought I was after all five of them.

I could hear the buzz-saw engines of the plane. The sound of its piston engines was reflected from the lake to make a deafening sound as he came over us very low. The pilot with his face pressed against the glass was no doubt worried sick about what was happening. This was the moment of maximum danger.

As the plane droned out of sight I was hit by a suffocating smell of burned rubber and plastic from the blazing car. Big red sparks darted around like fireflies and then I was enveloped in a sudden billow of black oily smoke. The security men began shooting at something on the other side of the blaze. Perhaps it was the movement of the smoke that attracted their shots, or a wild animal disturbed by it.

Whatever it was that caught their attention, I was grateful for the respite. I quickly folded back the Skorpion's skeleton metal stock and pulled it tight into my shoulder. The sights were crude and virtually useless, so I fired with both eyes open. The Skorpion has a simple blowback action, but like all such lightweights it rises and rises and will end up firing straight up into the air if you don't hold it tight and point it low.

'Rrrrip.' The rate of fire was faster than I remembered it. The first burst hit the nearest of the men. He crumpled, but by that time two of the others were firing back at me. I fired again – two very short bursts – but I couldn't see if I registered hits or not. I listened: no aircraft engines, no shouts, no cries of pain.

The silence was broken by half a dozen aimed shots from them, the last coming uncomfortably close. That was always a sign to move on. They had only hand-guns. Their automatic weapons would be in a rack in the car, I could almost hear them cursing their misfortune. At this range and in this light, their single-shot fire was a risk I could afford to take provided I kept moving. It was darker now. The initial flare was over. The Fiat's choicest morsels were ash. The excited yellow flames had become orange and red, and were settling down to enjoy devouring the car slowly, like a lion with a juicy carcass.

I didn't have enough time, or the inclination, for a gun battle. Suddenly the engines of the plane sounded very loud as he roared over the tree-tops to get a last look at what was happening before turning on to finals. There was nothing for it but to finish this off. I fitted the second, and last, magazine into the Skorpion and got to my feet and ran forward. It was dark, the flames making moving shadows everywhere. There were more shots and I fired back, hose-piping the whole magazine as I went. I wasn't trying to find a way of killing them, I just wanted to make sure that all four men had a few disabling wounds to keep them from chasing us and giving me trouble.

George was struggling with the door of the security men's Volvo by the time I reached it. 'I got the key,' said George. 'I got it from the one you shot.'

'Good man. Jump in,' I said, although hearing four danger-ous opponents referred to in the singular was disconcerting. I got into the driver's seat and started up the car and went as fast as I could drive towards the other end of the strip, bumping over roots, rotten tree-trunks and who knows what.

'Jump out and stand off fifty yards, George. I'm going to torch this one now.'

'They'll see us for miles.'

'I hope so.'

The Volvo went up in flames so quickly that it scorched my hair. With a flaming car marking each end of the strip the Swede came right across the lake, descending gently for a nice soft landing. I knew what he'd be flying: a curious old BN Trislander, its long nose extending like a crane's neck, and its third engine perched up high on the tail. The Swede had lost none of his magic touch. He was the best of our contract people. There was snow and ice – more than I'd reckoned on – but I suppose a few years based in Sweden had provided him with plenty of practice.

'You didn't have to kill them, Bernard,' said George, having looked for our pursuers without spotting them. Perhaps this admonition was designed to cool my overheated blood. If so it didn't work, it simply made me want to beat sanctimonious George over the head.

'Stay where you are!' I said. 'He'll swing round and then brake. We'll go together. The door is this side. Watch out for the prop blades; he won't switch off the engines. The security stiffs? They are just scratched. Don't worry about them.'

'I'm not sure,' said George. He could be a lot like Dicky at times.

The pilot reached back and opened the door and I heaved George up into the cabin. It was a prop-driven eight-seater with extra tanks built into the cabin. The tanks divided the pilot from the seats we were in; they had to keep the weight forward to preserve the centre of gravity.

'Trouble?' shouted the Swede.

'No. Just friends seeing us off,' I said.

'Strap in. Here we go. I thought it would be you when I saw the bonfires.' He revved up and let go of the brakes and we went rushing forward, skimming the tops of the dark trees. I looked back and saw the two burning cars. From up here they looked very close together: getting into the strip wasn't quite the simple task it seemed from ground level. By now the Volvo was almost burned out, glowing deep rosy red. Our car, the Fiat, was still bright with flame – the burning fuel had poured out of it to make flaming petals flat on the ground. There were sparks coming from a third place, nowhere near the cars, but these sparks turned out to be gunfire from the spooks, a reassessment confirmed by the smacking sounds of rounds hitting the tailplane as we banked steeply before skimming low across the dark still water of the lake.

George sat back breathing deeply, and with his eyes tightly closed. 'Are you all right, George?' I said.

'Did you plan that?' he said between catching his breath.

'No. Plan what?'

'Did you let them follow us all the way so that you could have a burning car at each end of the strip. Did you kill those men and then just wait for the plane?'

'No, George. I didn't torch the car until I heard the engines of the plane. And I didn't kill them; I just fired in their direction to keep them from killing us.'

'You said this pilot would try night after night. What would you have done if he'd not turned up tonight?'

'I would have thought of something.'

The Swede was reaching back over the auxiliary internal gastanks. He didn't look back: he was watching the dark forest that was almost close enough to touch. His hand held a bottle and he waggled it to get attention. I took it from him. Johnny Walker. I uncorked it and took a swig. 'What about you, George?' I said and offered it to him. But George made a retching sound and was dramatically sick into a tin can.

'Take it easy, George,' I said.

He was trying to say something. I leaned close. 'I'll pay for it to be cleaned up,' said George. 'Tell him I'm sorry.' He was winding his rosary tightly around his wrist, and unwinding it to reveal deep indentations, as though this self-inflicted pain might preserve him from something worse.

'It's all part of the job, George,' I said. 'Cleaning up other people's mess is what people like me and him are employed to do.'

The plane was battered by the gusting wind so that we skidded and bumped through the turbulent air.

George closed his eyes and concentrated upon feeling sorry for himself. 'I wish you'd never told me, Bernard. I wish you'd let them give me the baby, and let me pretend. Wouldn't that have been kinder?'

'I don't know, George. Try and sleep. It's a long flight; these old planes are very slow. This whole coast is dotted with the Soviet navy's electronics. He'll have to fly low to get under the radar.'

'Those dead men will be on my conscience,' said George.

It was the point at which I'd had enough. I leaned across and grabbed him. 'Don't lecture me, you sanctimonious little stooge. You're nothing but a lousy traitor, so don't tell me about your rotten conscience because I don't want to know. See the man up there at the front? He's over sixty years old: he's the best man we have, and he doesn't do these trips to keep his cross-country qualification. I should have wasted those bastards back there but I didn't have the guts to do it and I'm ashamed. Do you hear that, I'm ashamed. Because the next time the old Swede drops in to some battered little wartime airstrip, to pull some poor bastard like me out of trouble, they are likely to be waiting for him. Got it, George? They'll be waiting for him with a complete description of me, and this funny old plane, and him and how he works. And that is all because of you and your stupid fantasy life.'

I had him tight by the collar and was shaking the life out of him. Now I released my grip and he slumped back in his seat inert, as if I'd scared him to death. I suppose he'd never seen me lose my temper before. It wasn't something that happened very often.

'The coast,' shouted the Swede. 'Order your duty-free.'

'We might get shot at again,' I told George. 'And he'll throw the plane around. They don't like unidentified aircraft flying low at night, and you can't get insured against flak.' George showed no reaction. I looked out of the window. The grey Baltic Sea is a daunting prospect in winter when seen from spumed wave-top height. I thought about George and about the night in London when he collected that injured man and took him off to see a doctor. George had obviously done a useful job for the regime when he became a generous supporter of Polish expatriate organizations. I wondered how the gold from the moneybelt fitted into the picture. Perhaps it was the way in which George was funded. Perhaps some enterprising expatriate had grabbed the gold for himself. I pushed it out of my mind; the interrogators would get it out of him, I was sure of that.

As we crossed the Swedish coast the sky was streaked with sunlit red clouds. 'Home sweet home,' said the Swede. It was a private airfield built alongside the extensive buildings of the Schliemann company, which once made wooden office furniture and exported its entire production to Russia. I'd never been able to fully understand why the USSR, a vast land covered in forest, imported not only wooden furniture but lumber too. But it did. Now however the Russians had little money to import anything from anywhere. Mr Schliemann's factory was boarded up and most of the machinery sold. Mr Schliemann lived in Antibes and rented his airstrip, and an outbuilding, to three middle-aged pilots who shared the costs of this funny old Trislander plane and had printed notepaper that claimed they were an 'all-Sweden air service'. They had Panamanian passports, a registered office in the Cayman Islands, took payments through a bank in Luxembourg and did any kind of work that came along.

'You've got a welcoming party,' the Swede called to me as we were taxiing back to the shed he used as an office.

'You did good, you old bastard,' I said feelingly. The Swede smiled.

There were three of them: a doctor, a man from the embassy and a woman in a smart new coat and a fur hat. She was waving furiously as I climbed out of the plane.

Gloria!

While we exchanged hellos the Swede went to examine the bullet holes in the tail. George climbed into a Saab with diplomatic licence plates. The embassy doctor got in too. There was also an embassy official who shook hands through the lowered car window. He didn't want to get out of the car because it was too cold. George would have a physical examination and then be photographed for a locally issued UK passport. George slumped back in his seat and looked at me through the frosty glass. He gave no sign of recognition. His long wavy hair, usually so carefully arranged, was in total disarray, his skin was pale, his eyes shiny, his whole expression lifeless, like an unwanted waxwork dummy headed for the storeroom. There wasn't room for me in the car but I had Gloria looking at me and grinning as if she'd caught me doing something foolish.

'Hello, Bernard,' she said.

'Hello, Gloria.'

'Mr Rensselaer sent me to meet you.' Her cheeks were glowing and her eyes soft and moist. These were of course the marks of a young woman in love, but standing on an airfield in

304

the northern wind in December could also redden the cheeks and make the eyes water.

'Did you bring money?' I said, forgetting that my pockets were bulging with Rupert's money.

'There are more important things in life than money, Bernard,' she said.

'Prove it,' I told her.

On the far side of the landing space, crouching low and ready to spring, there was a sleek and shiny twin-turbofan Learjet: the sort of thing the presidents of big international corporations buy for themselves because they think their shareholders wouldn't like them to be standing in line at airports. What a machine it was, compared with the slab-sided little British-built plane that the Swede had used to collect us. That was the difference between the Brets of the world, and the Bernard Samsons.

Gloria, having watched the others climb into the Saab and drive away, turned to me and said: 'Thank God you're safe. Bret was worried. So was I.' She looked at me. 'You are all right?'

'Yes, I'm fine.' She glanced again at the departing car, and she looked at me. I suppose she could see some kind of reservation in my face. George was the third one to go. Tessa was dead, Fiona was a hollow shell, and George was going to face a lot of hard questions. He'd never be the same man again, and I wondered if he knew that. 'It went better than I hoped,' I said.

In my pockets I still had the bundle of dollar bills and the zlotys and the roll of gummed plastic tape for gagging and binding George. I hadn't used any of it. 'Everything went according to plan,' I said.

She said: 'Perhaps we should have crowded into the car with them. They said there would be two embassy cars.'

'What are you supposed to do now?'

'Bret was certain that Kosinski was going to arrive injured. In that case he was to go back to London directly. Bret didn't want him in a hospital here. Not even a private clinic.'

'He's okay,' I said.

'He looked like hell.'

'He thought he'd found a home in Poland but he hasn't got a home anywhere. It's tough.'

'I know,' said Gloria. 'I thought I was English once, but the girls at school made sure I knew I was a foreigner. It's what we have in common.'

'You and me?'

'You've lived all your life in Germany but you are not German. Are you really English?'

'At least I know which side I'm on,' I said. 'George Kosinski never decided.'

'He came out here because of his wife, didn't he? Was that so bad?'

'Oh, he loved Tessa. Perhaps that was the only genuine thing about him.'

'Not his religion?'

'Perhaps. But I suspect that his devout churchgoing, and all that counting his rosary, was a part of his cover as an anti-communist.'

'I can't believe he was working against us,' said Gloria.

'Him and his brother. They travelled the world servicing the Polish army's intelligence networks. They are both as guilty as hell.'

'I suppose we shouldn't be surprised,' said Gloria. 'It's just what Dicky Cruyer has been saying all along, isn't it?'

'Is it?'

'Oh, Bernard, you know it is. He's been saying it over and over. You argued with him.'

'Dicky does it again,' I said, with all the joy I could muster.

'But you risked your life bringing him out. You had diplomatic cover; you could have just walked past customs and immigration.'

'I brought him out because I want that bastard sliced open and chopped into pet food. He's as guilty as anyone could be but he thinks he's going to sweet-talk his way out of it.'

'He's always so sweet … George Kosinski I mean,' she added hurriedly.

'He thought spying made him a big man. It helped him overcome the shame he felt at his wife going to bed with other men. God knows what he reported back to Warsaw or Moscow or wherever the best material was ending up.'

'They use people,' she said. 'They are clever at that.'

'There are no alleviating circumstances,' I said. 'It wasn't intellectual writer Stefan, using his power and influence to protect honest old George Kosinski, capitalist charmer and devout Christian. George was the leader; Stefan the anchor. Between them they kept their old mansion intact and the big estates in his family's private hands. They did it by spying for their communist masters, for the army and for anyone else who had to be placated. I have a nasty feeling that we'll discover that George is the tip of something very big and important. He's been provided with a cover story that will "prove" he was recruited as late as 1983 but he was spying for them for ages before that. It will all come out when they start questioning him. He hasn't got the guts to resist.'

'You sound as if you would like to interrogate him personally.'

'I'd like to hang the little bastard personally.'

'Did Tessa know what he was doing?'

'It's the big question isn't it? But his Bezpieca masters no doubt convinced George that we killed her for exactly that reason.'

'And I was feeling sorry for him,' said Gloria. She took my arm. She knew me well. I was angry and tired and talking too much.

'I should have dumped him into the Baltic Sea,' I said. 'It went through my mind to do it.'

'You'll get into trouble one day, saying things like that,' Gloria warned.

'And what will they do to me? Send me on a dangerous mission?'

'Oh, Bernard. I did worry. Bret could see how I felt. He sent me to meet you.'

'He always was a romantic sort of fellow.'

'That's the air-ambulance I came on. A Learjet. Bret rented it from an insurance company he's connected with. I've never been on a private jet before.' There was a fuel bowser alongside it, and men probing the engines.

'Is that how you're getting back to London?'

'The plane has to return today,' she said. 'Tomorrow is Christmas Eve and the crew want to be at home. Come and see it: it's beautiful.' She grinned nervously, like a little girl. 'I don't think those bloody embassy people are going to send a car for you.'

'Yes, it's Christmas Eve, I forgot. Going away?'

'I've nowhere to go. Daddy and Mummy are away. I'll just stay at home, raid the freezer for food, and watch all those awful television shows. And you?'

'I can't go home until I've had our engineers to check my apartment for bugs. There's no telling what George might have planted there when he moved out.'

'Poor, homeless Bernard. The engineers won't come out on Christmas Day.'

'I love you, Gloria,' I said. I'd been trying not to say it, but I blurted it out. She squeezed my arm without replying.

The Swede finished inspecting the bullet holes and climbed back into the cockpit of the Trislander.

I took Gloria's hand and we walked in silence towards the jet. 'My overnight bag is in the plane,' she said. 'Do you have luggage?'

'No. No luggage.'

The Learjet pilot was standing by the wing signing a clip-board for the driver of a fuel bowser. There was a strong smell of jet paraffin in the air. 'So what's the verdict?' the pilot asked Gloria. 'These Swedes want me to file a flight plan. It's always the same with these horse and buggy outfits, they always want to do everything by the book. Are you both on diplomatic passports?'

'Yes, we can leave,' said Gloria. 'No need to do any customs and immigration.'

'Great! I'll go over to the office and do the airport paper-work,' said the pilot. He looked at his watch. 'You may as well get aboard, out of the cold. There's food in the galley. I'll be back directly. Then we'll crank up and get out of here.'

The plane had its own steps and the interior was luxuriously equipped as an air-ambulance. Gloria removed her coat and hung it in the wardrobe. Directly behind the flight-deck there was a cabin for the nurse, doctor and wealthy relatives, the soft leather seating arranged around a polished table. On the cabin walls, over the tinted windows, there was a drinks cabinet, racks of magazines, and on a polished-wood panel there were instruments and gauges which relayed altitude, airspeed, cabin temperature, and the time in the financial centres throughout the world where ambulances were most needed. Part of the space was a tiny galley – no more than a closet really – with a sink, a coffee machine and a shelf packed with groceries: shrink-wrapped sliced chicken and bread and canned soup.

I opened a leather-covered door to find another larger cabin. Behind me I heard Gloria putting water into the coffee machine. I went through the door, marvelling at the deep carpeting, and at the beds with crisp sheets and pillows. 'Look at this!' I called as I went into the main cabin. 'Big soft beds!'

'Goodness,' said Gloria, looking at me and smiling demurely.

'Did you tell the embassy not to send a car for me?'

'Beds,' said Gloria. 'I never noticed that.'

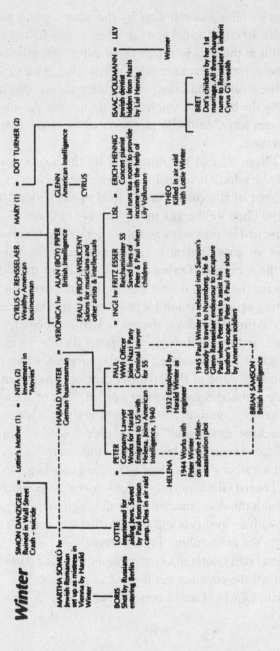

Winter

MARTHA SOMLÓ lw — SIMON DANZIGER — Lottie's Mother (1) — HARALD WINTER — NITA (2)
Jewish Romanian | Ruined in Wall Street | | German businessman | Investment in
set up as mistress in | Crash – suicide | | | "Movies"
Vienna by Harald |
Winter |

BORIS
Shot by Russians
entering Berlin

CYRUS G. RENSSELAER — MARY (1) — DOT TURNER (2)
Wealthy American
businessman

VERONICA lw

ALAN (BOY) PIPER
British Intelligence

GLENN
American intelligence

CYRUS

FRAU & PROF. WISLICENY
Salons for musicians and
other artists & intellectuals

INGE lw FRITZ ESSER
Reichsminister SS
Saved lives of
Peter & Paul when
children

LISL — ERICH HENNIG
Lisl runs tea room to provide | Concert pianist
income with the help of
Lily Volkmann

THEO
Killed in air raid
with Lottie Winter

ISAAC VOLKMANN — LILY
Jewish dentist
hidden from Nazis
by Lisl Volkmann

Werner

BRET
Dot's children by her 1st
marriage. All three change
name to Rensselaer & inherit
Cyrus G's wealth

LOTTIE
Imprisoned for
aiding Jews.
Saved by Paul
from prison
camp. Dies in air raid

PETER
Company Lawyer
Works for Harald
Emigrates to US with
Helena. Joins American
Intelligence, 1940

PAUL
WW1 Officer
Joins Nazi Party
Criminal lawyer
for SS

HELENA
1944 Works with
Peter Winter
on abortive Hitler-
assassination plot

BRIAN SAMSON
British Intelligence

1932 Employed by
Harald Winter as
engineer

1945 Paul Winter is released into Samson's
custody to travel to Nuremberg. He &
Glenn Rensselaer endeavour to recapture
Paul when Peter tries to assist his
brother's escape. Peter & Paul are shot
by American soldiers

lw = liaison with
—— = connected by family

Game

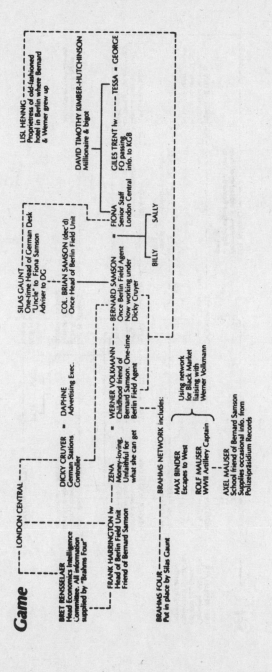

BRET RENSSELAER
Head Economics Intelligence Committee. All information supplied by "Brahms Four"

FRANK HARRINGTON hw
Head of Berlin Field Unit Friend of Bernard Samson

BRAHMS FOUR
Put in place by Silas Gaunt

LONDON CENTRAL

DICKY CRUYER = **DAPHNE**
German Stations Controller — Advertising Exec.

ZENA
Money-loving, Unfaithful for what she can get

WERNER VOLKMANN
Childhood friend of Bernard Samson. One-time Berlin Field Agent

BRAHMS NETWORK includes:

Using network for Black Market liaising with Werner Volkmann

MAX BINDER
Escapes to West

ROLF MAUSER
WWII Artillery Captain

AXEL MAUSER
School friend of Bernard Samson Supplies occasional info. from Polizeipräsidium Records

SILAS GAUNT
One-time Head of German Desk "Uncle" to Fiona Samson Adviser to DG

COL. BRIAN SAMSON (dec'd)
Once Head of Berlin Field Unit

BERNARD SAMSON
Once Berlin Field Agent Now working under Dicky Cruyer

=

FIONA
Senior Staff London Central

BILLY   **SALLY**

LISL HENNIG
Proprietress of old-fashioned hotel in Berlin where Bernard & Werner grew up

DAVID TIMOTHY KIMBER-HUTCHINSON
Millionaire & bigot

GILES TRENT hw
FO passing info. to KGB

TESSA = **GEORGE**

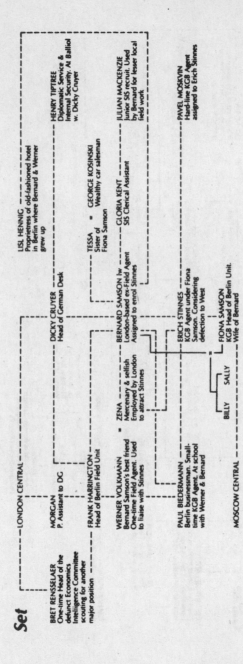

Set

LONDON CENTRAL

BRET RENSSELAER — One-time Head of the defunct Economics Intelligence Committee scouting for another major position

MORGAN — P. Assistant to DG

FRANK HARRINGTON — Head of Berlin Field Unit

WERNER VOLKMANN — Bernard Samson's best friend One-time Field Agent. Used to liaise with Stinnes
= ZENA — Mercenary & selfish Employed by London to attract Stinnes

PAUL BIEDERMANN — Berlin businessman. Small-time KGB Agent. At school with Werner & Bernard

DICKY CRUYER — Head of German Desk

BERNARD SAMSON — London-based ex-Field Agent Assigned to enrol Stinnes

ERICH STINNES — KGB Agent under Fiona Samson. Considering defection to West

FIONA SAMSON — KGB Head of Berlin Unit. Wife of Bernard

BILLY
SALLY

LISL HENNIG — Proprietress of old-fashioned hotel in Berlin where Bernard & Werner grew up

HENRY TIPTREE — Diplomatic Service & Internal Security. At Balliol w. Dicky Cruyer

TESSA — Sister of Fiona Samson
= GEORGE KOSINSKI — Wealthy car salesman

GLORIA KENT — SIS Clerical Assistant

JULIAN MACKENZIE — junior SIS recruit. Used by Bernard for lesser local field work

PAVEL MOSKVIN — Hard-line KGB Agent assigned to Erich Stinnes

MOSCOW CENTRAL

Match

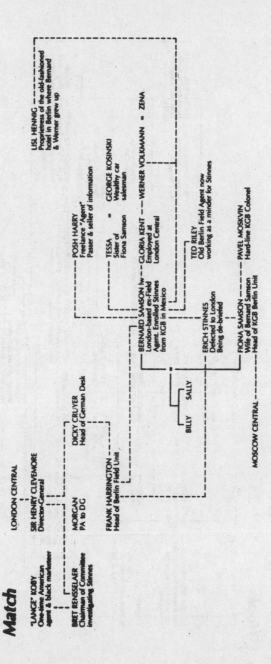

LONDON CENTRAL

'LANCE' KOBY
One-time American
agent & black marketeer

SIR HENRY CLEVEMORE
Director-General

BRET RENSSELAER
Chairman of Committee
investigating Stinnes

MORGAN
PA to DG

DICKY CRUYER
Head of German Desk

FRANK HARRINGTON
Head of Berlin Field Unit

POSH HARRY
Freelance "Agent"
Passer & seller of information

TESSA = **GEORGE KOSINSKI**
Sister of   Wealthy car
Fiona Samson   salesman

GLORIA KENT – – **WERNER VOLKMANN** = **ZENA**
Employed at
London Central

TED RILEY
Old Berlin Field Agent now
working as a minder for Stinnes

PAVEL MOSKVIN
Hard-line KGB Colonel

BERNARD SAMSON lw– – –
London-based ex-Field
Agent. Enrolled Stinnes
from KGB in Mexico

ERICH STINNES
Defected to London
Being de-briefed

FIONA SAMSON – – – – –
Wife of Bernard Samson
Head of KGB Berlin Unit

BILLY   **SALLY**

MOSCOW CENTRAL – – – – – – – – – – – –

LISL HENNIG – – – –
Proprietress of the old-fashioned
hotel in Berlin where Bernard
& Werner grew up

Hook

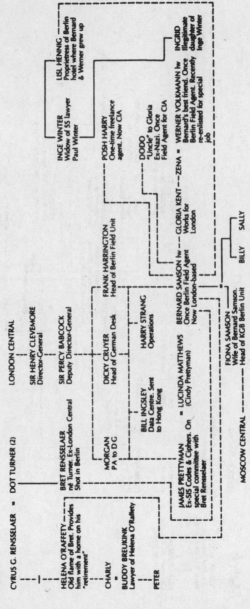

CYRUS G. RENSSELAER = DOT TURNER (2)

HELENA O'RAFFETY — Old flame of Bret. Provides him with a home on his "retirement"

CHARLY

BUDDY BREUKINK Lawyer of Helena O'Raffety

PETER

BRET RENSSELAER né Turner. Ex-London Central Shot in Berlin

LONDON CENTRAL

SIR HENRY CLEVEMORE Director-General

SIR PERCY BABCOCK Deputy Director-General

DICKY CRUYER Head of German Desk

FRANK HARRINGTON Head of Berlin Field Unit

HARRY STRANG Operations

MORGAN PA to D-G

BILL INGSLEY Data Centre. Sent to Hong Kong

JAMES PRETTYMAN Ex-SIS Codes & Ciphers. On special committee with Bret Rensselaer

= LUCINDA MATTHEWS (Cindy Prettyman)

BERNARD SAMSON lw Once Berlin Field Agent Now London-based

GLORIA KENT Works for London

FIONA SAMSON Wife of Bernard Samson. Head of KGB Berlin Unit

MOSCOW CENTRAL

INGE WINTER Widow of SS lawyer Paul Winter

LISL HENNIG Proprietress of Berlin hotel where Bernard & Werner grew up

POSH HARRY One-time freelance agent. Now CIA

DODO "Uncle" to Gloria. Once Ex-Nazi. Once Field Agent for CIA

ZENA = WERNER VOLKMANN lw Bernard's best friend. Once Berlin Field Agent. Recently re-enlisted for special job

INGRID Illegitimate daughter of Inge Winter

BILLY

SALLY

Line

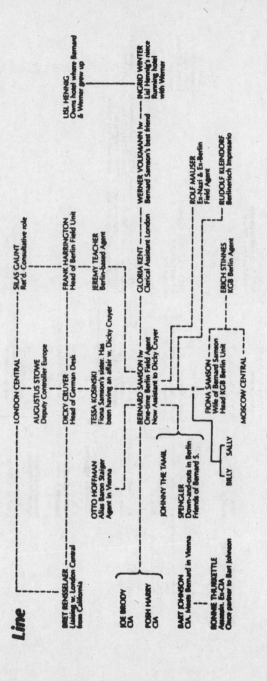

LISL HENNING
Owns hotel where Bernard & Werner grew up

INGRID WINTER
Lisl Henning's niece
Running hotel with Werner

LONDON CENTRAL

BRET RENSSELAER
Liaising w. London Central from California

SILAS GAUNT
Ret'd. Consultative role

AUGUSTUS STOWE
Deputy Controller Europe

DICKY CRUYER
Head of German Desk

FRANK HARRINGTON
Head of Berlin Field Unit

JEREMY TEACHER
Berlin-based Agent

OTTO HOFFMAN
Alias Baron Staiger
Agent in Vienna

TESSA KOSINSKI
Fiona Samson's sister. Has been having an affair w. Dicky Cruyer

GLORIA KENT
Clerical Assistant London

WERNER VOLKMANN hv
Bernard Samson's best friend

BERNARD SAMSON hv
One-time Berlin Field Agent
Now Assistant to Dicky Cruyer

ROLF MAUSER
Ex-Nazi & Ex-Berlin
Field Agent

RUDOLF KLEINDORF
Berlinerrich Impresario

JOE BRODY
CIA

POSH HARRY
CIA

JOHNNY THE TAMIL

FIONA SAMSON
Wife of Bernard Samson
Head KGB Berlin Unit

ERICH STINNES
KGB Berlin Agent

SPENGLER
Down-and-outs in Berlin
Friends of Bernard S.

MOSCOW CENTRAL

BART JOHNSON
CIA. Meets Bernard in Vienna

BILLY   SALLY

BONNIE THURKETTLE
Assassin. Ex-CIA.
Once partner to Bart Johnson

Sinker

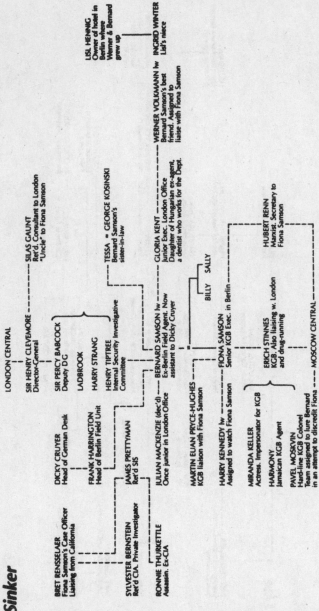

BRET RENSSELAER
Fiona Samson's Case Officer
Liaising from California

SYLVESTER BERNSTEIN
Ret'd CIA. Private Investigator

RONNIE THURKETTLE
Assassin. Ex-CIA

LONDON CENTRAL

SIR HENRY CLEVEMORE
Director-General

SILAS GAUNT
Ret'd. Consultant to London
"Uncle" to Fiona Samson

SIR PERCY BABCOCK
Deputy DG

LADBROOK

HARRY STRANG

HENRY TIPTREE
Internal Security Investigative
Committee

TESSA = GEORGE KOSINSKI
Bernard Samson's
sister-in-law

DICKY CRUYER
Head of German Desk

FRANK HARRINGTON
Head of Berlin Field Unit

JAMES PRETTYMAN
Ret'd SIS

JULIAN MACKENZIE (dec'd)
Once junior in London Office

MARTIN EUAN PRYCE-HUGHES
KGB liaison with Fiona Samson

HARRY KENNEDY lw
Assigned to watch Fiona Samson

MIRANDA KELLER
Actress. Impersonator for KGB

HARMONY
Jamaican KGB Agent

PAVEL MOSKVIN
Hard-line KGB Colonel
Team assigned to lure Bernard
in an attempt to discredit Fiona

BERNARD SAMSON
Ex-Berlin Field Agent. Now
assistant to Dicky Cruyer

FIONA SAMSON
Senior KGB Exec. in Berlin

ERICH STINNES
KGB. Also liaising w. London
and drug-running

BILLY   SALLY

GLORIA KENT
Junior Exec. London Office
Daughter of Hungarian ex-agent,
a dentist who works for the Dept.

HUBERT RENN
Marxist. Secretary to
Fiona Samson

LISL HENNIG
Owner of hotel in
Berlin where
Werner & Bernard
grew up

WERNER VOLKMANN lw
Bernard Samson's
best friend. Assigned to
liaise with Fiona Samson

INGRID WINTER
Lisl's niece

--- MOSCOW CENTRAL ---

Faith

LONDON CENTRAL

SIR HENRY CLEVEMORE
Director-General

SILAS GAUNT
Ret'd. Consultant to London
"Uncle" to Fiona Samson

LISL HENNIG
Owner of hotel in
Berlin where
Werner & Bernard
grew up

DAVID KIMBER-HUTCHINSON
Manipulative, wealthy businessman

DICKY CRUYER = DAPHNE
Controller German Stations
Acting Head of Operations

WERNER VOLKMANN
Bernard Samson's best friend
Employed by London to liaise
with "VERDI"

FRANK HARRINGTON
Head Berlin Field Unit

FIONA SAMSON
Lately under cover in Berlin
KGB office

TESSA = GEORGE KOSINSKI

BRET RENSSELAER
Case Officer while Fiona Samson
under cover. Acting Deputy DG

GLORIA KENT
New PA to Bret Rensselaer
Bernard Samson's mistress
while Fiona was away

BERNARD SAMSON
Ex-Berlin Field Unit Assistant
to Dicky Cruyer

BILLY

SALLY

VALERY FEDOSOV
Red Capt. Red Army HQ Berlin
Supplied information to Bernard
Samson's father post-war

ANDREY FEDOSOV
"VERDI": KGB officer
considering defection

MOSCOW CENTRAL